Forever Under Blue Skies
Valerie Massey Goree

Disclaimer
Dear Readers: I have taken liberties with the location of towns and sheep or cattle stations that I have located west of Cunnamulla, Queensland. Those named exist only in my imagination.

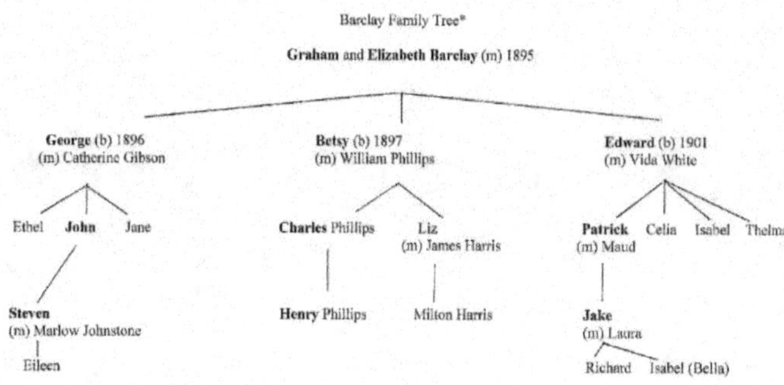

*Only names pertinent to the story are listed.

"Love does not delight in evil but rejoices in the truth."
I Corinthians 13:6 (NIV)

Chapter 1

Queensland, Australia,
November, 1983

Driving nearly eight hundred kilometers from Brisbane to Cunnamulla in Queensland's interior might not qualify as the most foolhardy action of her life, but it came close.

Marlow Barclay adjusted her sunglasses and stared at the narrow, tarred road shimmering ahead that sliced through the paprika-colored earth like an arrow aimed toward a target on the horizon. The beauty of the Australian heartland had long ago morphed into monotony. No houses. No people. Just scrubby trees, clumps of blond spinifex grass, and acre upon acre of flat land, if possible, flatter than west Texas. Despite aching shoulders, nothing could suppress the excitement bubbling inside her which energized her every more. Another day in this fascinating country, another adventure. And she was eight hundred kilometers closer to her destiny.

She glanced at the odometer. Eight hundred and one.

A gold star for knowing the kilometer-to-mile conversion rate by heart. Five hundred miles. To fulfill Steven's dying wish, she'd drive five hundred more.

Before the accident, Marlow and Steven had made plans to visit Australia to celebrate their fifteenth anniversary and to honor Great-grandfather Graham Barclay's wishes. In sorting through family papers, Steven had discovered a letter from Graham. The cryptic missive asked, no, demanded that his oldest great-grandchild reunite with cousins in Australia after his or her fortieth birthday.

And now almost two years after Steven's passing, Marlow was *en route* to meet the last cousin on the list.

"You have ranches in Texas, but here we call 'em sheep stations." Marlow mimicked Cousin Milton's Australian accent. His lighthearted reprimand made during her visit with his family in Melbourne two weeks ago brought a smile to her lips. And besides, talking to herself helped pass the time on the longest road trip she'd ever made alone.

"Well, I'm tired of driving, Milton. How much further is Jake Barclay's station? Almost there you say? It's about time." She patted the plush koala named after Milton and set it upright on the passenger seat. How was chatting to the stuffed toy any different than talking to a volleyball named Wilson? Doing so kept her sane.

Spotting a mob of kangaroos thundering through the barren land along the road to her right, she eased up on the accelerator. Unusual. Her research indicated they usually traveled in the early morning or late at night, and here it was midafternoon. She glanced at her camera on the passenger seat and—

A sickening thud.

The SUV lurched. Marlow slammed on the brakes, tires screeched as she steered onto the graveled shoulder. She shifted into park. Eyes squeezed tight, she covered her ears, but the memories invaded her mind, and the sounds and sensations overpowered her heart's pounding. Metal scraping metal. Glass shattering. Truck horn blaring. Screams. Warm blood dripping down her forehead. Her darling daughter dead, and Steven severely injured.

Breathe. That was in the past. You're in Australia.

Marlow opened her eyes, her chest heaving with each breath. What had she hit? Queasy, she peered into the rearview mirror. A kangaroo lay in the middle of the road, its legs flailing.

"Please get up." She chewed her bottom lip, silently begging it to obey her.

The animal batted its short front legs in the air, reared up, then bounded toward the distant cloud of dust.

Drawing in deep breaths to slow the adrenaline sill coursing through her blood, Marlow rested her forehead against the steering wheel. A trickle of perspiration slithered between her shoulder blades. She massaged her tight neck muscles. So far, she'd collected two of the three puzzle pieces. If Jake didn't have the last section, she was going home. She'd have done all she could to solve the Barclay family mystery, and Steven wouldn't know she quit. Marlow thumped the dashboard. But she would.

She slammed the gearshift into drive then floored the accelerator, as much to get to her destination as to keep her thoughts from languishing in the mire of the past.

Several kilometers and two kangaroo crossing signs later, Cunnamulla's welcome sign flashed by. Marlow followed Milton's directions to the Grand Skyview Hotel where Jake stayed when in town. The size of the community, the green lawns, and bougainvillea vine-covered trees down the medians all surprised her. She was embarrassed to admit she didn't expect such a pleasant oasis in the Queensland desert.

Marlow parked close to the hotel—a single-story, pale yellow building with caramel brown trim. She shoved her camera into her large purse then climbed out of the SUV into the broiling heat, but stood beside her closed door as if glued to the ground.

She'd traveled to Australia to fulfill two goals. Marlow had never given her ancestry much thought, but when Steven unearthed Graham's mysterious letter and decided to arrange the reunion in Australia, she'd harbored the desire to locate her mother's family. That mission ended in failure and disappointment. While in Melbourne, she'd visited the Genealogical Society, but found no record of Marie Kate Johnstone born in 1926, her mother who passed away when Marlow was eighteen.

Now faced with the opportunity to fulfill her second goal, a flock of butterflies churned in her stomach as she followed the sidewalk leading to the hotel's entrance. She trailed her fingers along the railing's intricate wrought iron scrollwork. Shaded by a corrugated metal, bullnose roof, the *L*-shaped verandah anchored the hotel to its corner lot.

Several Barclay cousins had portrayed Jake as straitlaced, standoffish. Marlow didn't care, as long as he treated her cordially and allowed her to visit his sheep station to locate his piece of the puzzle.

"The *last* piece," she muttered. Once she had fulfilled her promise to her husband, she would focus on what she wanted to do with her life instead of on want Steven dictated.

Chin up, shoulders back, Marlow entered the lobby which

provided little relief from the heat. A floor fan circulated the odor of stale tobacco.

A heavyset man seated behind the reception desk glanced up from his newspaper. His gaze traveled from her boots, over her jeans and shirt, all the way to the top of her head.

Did he just wiggle his eyebrows at her?

"G'day."

She removed her sunglasses and approached him, but words stuck in her throat.

The man stood, dusted cigarette ash off the counter and scrounged among a pile of tattered magazines to unearth the guest register. "You're not local because I know every pretty sheila in town. Are you checking in?" Pen in hand, he waited to write down her details.

Marlow grinned. It wasn't the first time she'd been called a sheila. "Hi. I don't need a room yet, thanks. I'm looking for someone."

"American. I knew it." He straightened and sucked in his belly. "I'm Lion Williams, the proprietor. Maybe I can help."

She leaned on the counter. "I hope Jake Barclay is here this weekend. I'd rather not drive to his isolated sheep station by myself."

"Too right. The road to Long Gully is terrible, but no worries, luv." Lion jutted his whiskered chin toward the door. "You're in luck." All business now, he stubbed out his cigarette, his eyes squinting through the last curl of smoke. "The area's most eligible bachelor just walked through the door." He motioned. "Jake, you have a visitor."

Footsteps pounded on the concrete floor behind Marlow.

"A visitor? Righto."

She spun around at the sound of a deep, gravelly voice. The silhouette of a tall, muscular man filled her vision. Bright light from a large window behind him prevented her from seeing his face, but she continued to stare at the dark shadow under his hat, trying to distinguish a recognizable feature.

"The lady's been asking about you."

"Has she?" Jake stepped closer to the counter, and his face emerged from the shadows.

Marlow drew in a sharp breath. This was not a stranger's face.

Jake could be her husband's brother. Same square jaw and dimpled chin. Same blue eyes—although, at the moment, Jake's eyes were tinged with iciness. He was also beefy, a tad over six foot and even had a little gap between his two front teeth.

"Hi. I'm Marlow Barclay." She extended her hand. "You are, um, were, related to Steven, my late husband. Your grandfathers were brothers, and you're second cousins, or first cousins twice removed. Something like that. I can never remember lineages and relationships and…" Marlow clamped her lips together to give him no more reason to think she was a blabbering idiot. Five-hundred miles alone with nothing but a toy named after a cousin to talk to could do that to a person.

Jake stared in silence for a second or two, then his rough hand engulfed hers in a firm grip. "My Aunt Celia has mentioned the family branch in America." He placed his stained and worn stockman's hat on the counter then tucked his thumbs into his belt loops. His movements failed to conceal his keen visual inspection of her.

The second man in Cunnamulla to give her the once-over.

Heat crept up her neck. "I've traveled through Australia getting acquainted with Steven's relatives, and you're the last one."

"You've come a long way to meet me. You thirsty? I have time for a quick drink at Annie's Place."

What a perfect opportunity to show him the family tree and ask about the missing piece of the puzzle. Before she could respond, Jake had already grabbed his hat and propelled her toward the door with a firm hand on her lower back. He opened the screen door and waited for her to exit.

Jake shoved on his hat, and joined her as they crossed the wide, sunbaked street. He pointed to the sunglasses she held. "Those won't do any good unless you put them on."

She glared sideways at him but couldn't hide the unbidden smile as she donned her shades. He was definitely related to Steven— same commanding personality. Fine with her for now, as long as he didn't criticize her every thought and action like her husband had.

At the next intersection Jake turned left onto a eucalyptus-lined street. The trees' sharp fragrance swirled around her. She never tired of the invigorating smell.

"How did you know I'd be here this weekend?" he asked.

"Cousin Milton said you usually come to Cunnamulla the second weekend of the month. I planned my trip accordingly."

"Milton?" Jake's eyebrows shot up. "You met him and survived?" His cynical tone spoke volumes yet contrasted with her opinion of his cousin.

After she'd acquired Cousin Henry's piece of the puzzle, Milton had entertained her, provided tips to survive the outback, and gave her a cute, stuffed animal for a companion. "Not sure what you mean by that, but I don't want to discuss him right now."

"Suits me." Jake slowed when they approached the corner.

"What brings you to town once a month?"

"I shop for supplies, and the trip allows Isabel, my daughter, to socialize with her school chums. Several of the families from surrounding stations bring their children to town the second weekend. The kids know each other from their School of the Air program."

"What about your son?"

"Rick works on a cattle station about seventy kilometers from us. Sometimes I purchase supplies for him, too, and then he travels down to our place to get them."

"He must be a lot older than Isabel."

"We call her Bella, and yes, she turned twelve last month." Jake opened the door to Annie's Place. "He'll be twenty-two next birthday."

The temperature dropped the moment they entered. Marlow spied Annie's secret weapon against the incessant heat—an arsenal of whirring fans placed in strategic locations. Lace curtains fluttered at the windows, tables sported small vases of artificial flowers, and painted scenes of a lush countryside graced the walls. Refreshing.

Marlow chose a two-person table against the wall, sat, and set her purse on the floor.

A dainty woman bustled out from behind an embroidered screen. She tugged on her frilly apron and beamed at Jake. "What brings you back so soon, luv? Can't get enough of my scones, I'll wager. Who's your friend?"

Jake removed his hat and balanced it on his knee. "Annie, this is Marlow Barclay from America, my cousin Steven's widow. Marlow, Annie Rushton. Tea and a plate of scones, please."

"Welcome to our little town. I'll have your order ready in a tick."

Marlow returned a nodded greeting from the patrons at the only other occupied table. Jake, though, seemed more interested in her. She was tempted to remove the clip that held her hair up in a knot but settled on brushing strands out of her eyes. "I like this cozy little haven."

Before he could respond, Annie delivered the tea along with a plate of scones topped with strawberry jam and whipped cream. A delicate hint of lavender accompanied her. "Enjoy, luv." She patted Marlow's shoulder, gave Jake another wide smile, and headed to the door to greet three women who entered.

Jake looked at the teapot then at Marlow.

"Is there a problem?" she asked.

"You being American…"

She waited for him to explain more. When he didn't, she leaned forward and whispered, "What does my being American have to do with tea?"

"Sorry, I didn't think to ask if you drank hot tea."

"I do."

"Good. Aunt Celia says when a lady is present, she should have the privilege of pouring." He hesitated, reached for the teapot. Hesitated again, and finally grabbed the handle.

Marlow stopped him from lifting the pot. "I would be honored to serve us tea." When his hand didn't move from under hers, she added, "My mother taught me the correct way."

His brows rose.

"With milk."

He moved his hand. "In that case…"

With confidence from the familiar action, she poured the milk then the steamy brew. "Mom used to say, 'Tea is not tea without milk'. She loved a cup any time of day, no matter the weather." Marlow set down the teapot. "I am much like her."

"Is that a warning or a boast?"

Marlow chuckled. "You decide." Dainty china cup to her lips, she studied Jake over the rim as she sipped her tea. His dark brown hair was graying at the temples, which added to his rugged good looks. The tiny strip of white skin around his ears and hairline indicated a recent haircut. According to the family tree, he was widowed, in his mid-forties, and his bronzed skin confirmed he spent a lot of time outdoors. Ah, those Barclay blue eyes, so much like her husband's had been. Jake's eyes had lost some of their iciness, but even now, a hint of frost lurked at the edges.

He bit into a scone and licked the cream off his upper lip.

Marlow lowered her gaze and cleared her throat. *Locate the last puzzle piece. Return to Texas. No time for frivolous thoughts.*

As she refilled his cup, she reflected on why his relatives curtailed their association with him. Milton's remarks led her to believe Jake might be a churchgoer. Maybe that's why he chose Annie's Place rather than the hotel pub. Anyway, Jake Barclay seemed to be a decent guy, but she'd thought the same when she'd met and married Steven.

"What brought you out here to meet me?" Jake asked, cutting off her thoughts. "I have several business transactions to complete before sunset, and I can't spend much more time yacking over a cuppa." His smile negated the hint of criticism.

Marlow placed her empty cup in the saucer then searched through the plastic-covered papers in the accordion file in her purse. She removed the family tree document from its protective cover and spread it on the table. The paper was yellowed with age and creased from the numerous times it had been folded, but the beautifully written names were clear enough to decipher.

"Here is the Barclay family tree created by George who was my husband's grandfather and the eldest child of Graham and Elizabeth. He began the document in 1919, soon after moving to Texas. Over the years, he corresponded with his nephew, Charles Phillips, who provided additional details of births and deaths. I stayed with his son, Henry, in Melbourne, and met the other family members."

"Henry and I are the same age. I often spent school holidays with his family. How did you locate them?"

"Would you believe one of the letters Charles sent to George was included in his papers which were handed down to Steven. We took a chance and wrote to the address and received a reply. Charles and his wife still live there."

"I remember their large home. How is Henry? I've only seen him once since his stroke."

"Although he has to take it easy, he gets around well in his wheelchair, and, according to his wife, he hasn't lost his sense of humor."

"I must write to him more often." Jake rubbed his chin then

pointed to the diagram. "The information of my branch is all correct, including the names of my deceased twin siblings. I don't remember much about them. They died when I was seven."

"That must have been hard on your parents."

"It was, especially on Mum. I do recall she spent a lot of time in her room crying. Gran helped take care of me. My dad handled the loss by spending time away from the station." Jake paused and shot Marlow a cold stare. "You didn't have to drive to the middle of Queensland just to prove the family connection and to serve me tea."

She folded her arms and swallowed. Jake's condescending tone touched a nerve. Maybe he would thwart her quest of locating the final puzzle piece.

Chapter 2

Seconds passed without Marlow answering. Jake tapped the table. "I don't have all day. Why did you really come?"

A flush covered her cheeks as she withdrew another plastic sheath from her bag. "This correspondence was written by your great-grandfather, Graham Barclay. As the eldest descendent of the eldest child, my husband had it in his possession since his father died."

Jake picked up the document. The fancy calligraphy made the words difficult to decipher.

Dear great-grandchild:

 I wrote an important message in code, divided it, and gave one piece to each of my children, George, Betsy, and Edward, along with the instructions from this letter. They, in turn, must give the message to their eldest child when he or she is forty years of age. The paper must be passed on to the eldest child in each branch, for two generations, until my great-grandchildren have the messages. When the descendent of George who has the paper reaches age forty, he or she must arrange a reunion to gather the other two pieces, choose a cousin to help decipher my message then follow through with the instructions. I regret to add, there may be legal or financial implications.

Sincerely,
Graham Barclay,
Bendigo, 1924

"Is this some kind of joke?" Jake handed the page back to her.

"No. I have Steven's section, and after a long search, Henry located the part originally given to Betsy. Once you find your piece handed down from Edward, then we can solve the mystery."

Jake checked his watch. He had no time to waste on her frivolous venture. "I can't help you. I have no idea where my 'coded message' is."

"Would your Aunt Celia know?"

"Celia?"

"Milton told me she lives with you."

"Of course, he did." Jake huffed out a breath. Aunt Celia *might* know. She had enough family albums and letters to entertain Marlow for days, weeks even. For that to happen, he'd have to take his newly found cousin-in-law to Long Gully. He could not issue that invitation.

"When I get home, I'll ask Celia to look for this…this letter."

"And then what?"

His business could be delayed a few minutes longer. "Can I see the coded messages?"

She withdrew another plastic cover from her bag. "I removed the contents from the original envelopes. The instructions at the top of each message are the same. The puzzle parts seem to be a word or words with the letters all jumbled up. Here are Steven's and Henry's sections."

Jake studied the two sets listed on the pages, which meant nothing. "Have you tried to crack the code?"

"Yes, but it stands to reason we need the third piece."

"Naturally." Shaking his head, he slid the papers toward her. "No wonder Graham used the word *code*."

Jake picked up his hat and ran his fingers along the brim. He studied Marlow as she returned the documents to the file in her fancy handbag. Attractive, confident, and way too fascinating for his peace of mind.

She turned a bright smile upon him. "Well?"

"Well what?"

"May I come home with you?"

There'd been no hint of flirtation in her tone, yet Jake's neck warmed. This American woman with smoky gray eyes—whom he had known for an hour at most—had come into his world like a flash of lightning and was going to bring refreshing showers or destructive storms. Maybe both.

"No."

Her eyes widened. "Why not?"

"This quest of yours can be resolved through the post." He began to stand, then sat again. "How long were you in Melbourne?"

"Two weeks."

"Why didn't you write and ask me to locate Graham's letter? Milton obviously told you a lot about me and has my address."

She cleared her throat. "He, uh, said you weren't interested in genealogy and suggested I arrive unannounced. That way you'd be more likely to hear me out."

"Well, dear old Milton got that wrong." He glanced at his watch again. "It's been…interesting, but I have to complete my business before dark. Leave your contact details with Lion." Jake placed cash on the table and called a farewell to Annie.

Marlow hurried outside after him. "We're not done."

"Yes, we are." He started to shake her hand but decided against another reminder of her soft skin. Muttering, "G-day," he turned on his heel. His destination was a block down from the hotel, but common sense told him to take the long way. Alone.

****

After Jake crossed the street and disappeared from view, Marlow retraced their path back to the hotel, her shoulders drooping. She had not expected such a negative reaction to her mission. Waiting in Cunnamulla for Jake to locate his letter was an option, but collecting the three pieces only fulfilled the first part of Graham's instructions. As Steven's proxy, Marlow had to solve the mystery, and naively, she'd expected to do that at Jake's station.

A plan formed as Marlow removed her suitcase from the SUV. "Well, Jake. We are *not* done." She grinned and walked to the hotel entrance. "Chances are we'll meet again before the sun sets."

The screen door squealed as she opened it.

"Welcome back." Lion set aside his soda bottle.

Slinging her purse strap over her shoulder, Marlow stopped at the counter. "I'm not sure how long I'll be staying."

"No worries. We're only booked solid for the Melbourne Cup which was last week. Most race fans have gone home already. Fill in this form, please."

"Sure." She completed the information. "What about meals?"

"We serve a large variety of items in the pub. Our restaurant hours are posted on the dining room door." He pointed behind her. "Evening meal is served from six to nine."

"Thanks. Do I need to make a reservation?"

Jake laughed, his belly jiggling. "No, luv. We're not that kind of place." He handed her a key attached to a small wooden slat adorned with the hotel's name and a picture of a star-studded sky. "Your room is in the south wing. Straight down the corridor to your right, fifth door. Bathrooms and toilets are at the end."

Marlow walked through the lounge area and headed down the hall, the heels of her boots clicking atop the concrete floor. Communal bathrooms. No problem as long as the facilities were clean.

A delicate citrusy scent met her when she unlocked her door. Blue-and-yellow-striped spreads covered the two single beds. Rolled-up white towels lay near the pillows. No longer surprised at the twin beds, Marlow set her suitcase on one and opened it.

Polyester-blend items may be wrinkle free, but after her first day in Sydney, she'd realized they were stifling in the Australian summer. Cotton sundress, sandals, toiletries bag, and towel in hand, she ventured to the bathrooms. No other guests were showering this late in the afternoon, but she hurried anyway. She'd have to commend Lion on the selection of liquid soaps provided. Aussie Dream suited her mood. Naturally, eucalyptus featured as a key scent.

The white dress and sandals were a welcome relief from blue jeans and mid-calf length boots, attire Milton advised in case she was stranded in the outback. She used the towel one last time to squeeze water from her hair, then ran a comb through her locks, confident the bone-dry air would give them just enough wave to be attractive.

Marlow gathered her belongings and hurried back to her room. The restaurant would open in ten minutes and she wanted to catch Jake unawares. She locked her door, slipped the key into her pocket, and returned to the lounge. A stack of newspapers on a side table drew her attention. She sorted through them and was surprised to find a week-old edition of the *New York Times*. During her Australian stay, she hadn't kept up with news from home. She sat in the padded armchair and scanned the headlines. One intrigued her. President Reagan had signed a bill establishing the third Monday of

January as Martin Luther King Day.

Halfway through the article, Marlow looked up as a young girl entered, flopped onto the sofa, and drew her legs underneath her. Navy blue shorts and a white T-shirt hung on her petite frame.

She smiled at Marlow. "Are you waiting for someone? I always have to wait for Dad. My Aunty Celia says he was even late for his wedding." The pre-teen picked up a magazine. "Is it six o'clock yet?"

The family resemblance was obvious. Brown hair, high cheek bones, the deep dimple in the middle of her chin. But one conspicuous trait was different. Bella did not have the Barclay blue eyes—hers were an intense hazel.

Meeting Jake's daughter before the meal was not part of Marlow's plan, but what a break. "It's five minutes before six."

"Ooh, you're American." She set her feet on the floor. "Where do you live? Have you ever met any film stars? Why are you in Cunnamulla?"

Marlow chuckled at Bella's barrage of questions but a sharp intake of breath behind her halted her reply. She looked up. Oh, my. Jake had showered and changed into charcoal slacks and a crisp, gray shirt. Whiffs of eucalyptus accompanied his movements. He must have used the same soap she'd chosen. His damp hair, which he'd combed straight back, appeared almost black. A few dry strands curled on his forehead.

"What are you doing here?"

Marlow opened her mouth, but Bella spoke first.

"This is where I always meet you." She huffed out a breath.

"I don't mean you, Bella." His stared at Marlow. "Well?"

"I'm waiting for the dining room to open."

"You know each other?" Bella's gaze flew from her father to Marlow.

"No, we don't."

"Yes, we do," Marlow countered and stood. "I'm your father's cousin. I was hoping to visit your station and meet Aunt Celia."

Bella rose and grabbed Jake's arm. "We have an American cousin?"

"Cousin-in-law." He grimaced. "Bella, meet Marlow Barclay. She's my cousin Steven's widow."

Bella stepped toward Marlow.

The twelve-year-old barely reached Marlow's shoulder. A prick of sadness hit her soul. When Eileen exceeded Marlow's height of five foot four, she'd whooped and hollered for days.

Eyes sparkling, Bella shook Marlow's hand. "It's nice to meet you. Oh, I'm sorry. Widow. That means your husband is—"

"Not now, Bella."

"Okay." Her brow furrowed, then she brightened. "Are you going to eat with us?"

"I'd be honored." Marlow ignored whatever Jake muttered. "I came all the way from Texas to meet y'all."

"Texas. Wow."

Jake took Bella's hand. "Let's find a table."

Marlow followed, suppressing a grin. Score a point in her favor.

They joined the other guests entering the dining room. Red tablecloths were adorned with intricately folded white napkins. Photographs of race hoses covered the lemon-yellow walls, and exotic, spicy aromas wafted from the kitchen.

Marlow ordered the curried lamb with all the trimmings.

Bella chatted non-stop about her afternoon at the swimming pool with two friends, switching subjects without taking a breath. "Trish is going with Beryl and her family on holiday to Cairns. Are we going anywhere? It's been a long time since we—"

"Not this year."

Bella dropped her fork onto her plate. "But, Dad, you promised."

Jake lowered his chin and eyed her. "I said I'd think about going."

"It's not fair." Her lips drooped into a pout. "Beryl and Trish always go on holiday."

"Bella," Marlow interjected, "please pass the butter. I really shouldn't have another roll, but they're so good." Bread in hand, she waited.

Bella set the dish in front of Marlow. Her pout disappeared as quickly as it had formed. "If you like these rolls, you should taste Aunty Celia's bread. Her cakes and biscuits are also the best."

"Bella, luv. Enough of the ear bashing."

Unfazed by Jake's interruption, Marlow said, "I would love to visit your station, but I don't think that's possible." She eyed him through her eyelashes.

"She has to return to America." Jake focused on his action of scraping butter on a crusty roll.

"Not necessarily. I have a six-month visitor's visa." It took all of Marlow's self-control not to laugh at the incredulous expression that crossed Jake's face.

"Dad, that means Marlow can come. I think Aunty Celia would want you to invite her." Bella folded her arms and tilted her head at her father.

Game. Set. Maybe not match. Yet.

Jake's scowl aimed at Marlow didn't soften even when Lion approached their table.

"Anyone for sweets?"

"Not me," Bella said.

Marlow rolled her eyes and patted her stomach. "Me, neither."

"That makes three of us. Thanks for a good meal, Lion." Jake's scowl changed into a genuine smile so quickly Marlow thought someone had waved a wand. He cleared his throat. "Is the room available?"

"Yeah, it's ready anytime you want."

"Marlow, would you like to help us set up chairs?" Bella bounced in her seat as if sitting on a spring.

"What chairs?"

Jake sighed. "Bella, get started. I'll come in a jiffy." Once she was out of the room, he set his elbows on the table and cast a sheepish look at Marlow. "I apologize for the way I've spoken to you. That was not the real me, but your visit and request caught me off-guard. I have not acted as a Christian should."

Talk about being caught off-guard? Marlow reared back in her chair. "You are a believer."

He shrugged. "Yes, but not proud of my recent actions."

The conversation hit too close to home for Marlow. She reverted to her original question. "The chairs?"

"Right. A group of Christians meet here in Lion's all-purpose room. Several local families attend, and a good number of people like us, who live out on the stations, come when in town. Billy McIntosh preaches. He's a local store owner. The rest of the service is conducted by whomever is willing and able."

Marlow twisted her hands in her napkin.

"Would you like to join us tomorrow?" His blue eyes seemed to penetrate her confusion.

She immediately shifted her gaze from Jake's face to her empty plate. The discussion to attend a church or not had waged war in her soul too many times to count over the past two years. To avoid any uncomfortable conversation, she said, "I'll be there." A sudden headache could always be her excuse to renege later.

"Would you like to help us set up chairs for the service?"

She nodded, scooted from the table and followed Jake. She'd never had to arrange chairs for a worship service before. Maybe the chore would also help her rearrange her spiritual priorities.

Chapter 3

Catching up on the wool industry news was always a highlight for Jake when he visited Cunnamulla. He spent a couple of hours with fellow graziers playing darts at the far end of the verandah and discussing the state of the industry. And relaxing, which none of them had time for at home.

Bella and a few school chums surrounded Trish's dad while he played his guitar. The kids danced and sang along, making enough noise to keep the neighborhood awake.

At the end of his round, Jake handed the set of darts to Ezra, his teammate.

Ignoring him, Ezra pointed toward the other end of the verandah and whistled. "Who's that sheila?"

Jake turned and gulped. Marlow stood on the steps, hands clasped in front. Her white dress and the ambient light gave her an ethereal appearance. He shook his head to lose the image, but guilt stabbed his conscience. She reminded him of a lost lamb, and he felt obligated to talk to her. He thumped Ezra's shoulder. "Sorry, chaps. I have to go."

He hadn't seen Marlow since she helped set up chairs, but her appearance brought her quest back into focus. Stay at Long Gully while they search for a letter that might not exist? Not going to happen. It wasn't that he was averse to visitors. He and Celia had hosted stranded strangers when necessary, but he was unsure of Marlow's real motive and remained adamant she not visit. After all, she had manipulated Bella to get to eat with them earlier.

"Evening. Would you like something to drink?" Jake approached Marlow determined to be polite but firm.

"Hi, Jake." She smiled. "A soda, please."

He stepped to a small table close to the railing. "Have a seat."

He pulled out the chair for her then entered the pub and placed his order, all the while questions accumulated in his mind. Setting the glasses on the table, he sat opposite Marlow and gave her no time for small talk.

"I want to know more about Henry and his part in this charade." Jake had not intended to come on so strong, but the words were out, and he wouldn't take them back.

Marlow frowned, took a sip of her drink then responded in a flat tone. "I suppose I can see this from your point of view. A perfect stranger asks to stay at your home and search for a document, but I assure you I'm not playing a role. I'm on a genuine quest for answers."

The irony of her words was not lost on him. "How did you convince Henry to participate?"

"I told you in the café this afternoon that I wrote to Charles and explained the situation. He remembered the letter he received from his mother and confirmed he'd passed it on to his eldest child." She ran her finger along the rim of her glass, the vein in her temple pulsing.

"I don't understand. If Henry had his letter all this time, why didn't he open it or tell me to look for mine?"

"Your great-grandfather stated on the envelope that it should only be opened when he was contacted by George's oldest grandchild. That would have been my husband."

Jake snickered. "I can see Henry obeying the words on a piece of paper. He always followed the rules."

"And you don't?"

Jake hiked a shoulder. She won that argument, but he wasn't done. "Steven is gone, so why are you pursuing this journey? Are you obligated to, or are you interested in the financial situation Graham mentioned? Remember, you're not a blood relative."

Lips pressed tight, Marlow narrowed her eyes.

Jake leaned back to get away from her intense stare.

When she spoke, her words were measured and stilted. "If you recall Graham's actual script, he said, 'I *regret* there may be financial implications'. Henry and I discussed the matter and concluded that we, that is, the Barclays might be dishing *out* money and not profiting from the venture."

Her argument made sense, but she hadn't answered all his

questions. "And what part did Steven play?"

Marlow turned away and blinked. She swallowed and slumped into the chair.

Could you be more insensitive, Jake? "Sorry, but I'd like to know what happened to him."

She laced her fingers and set her hands on the table. "Two years ago, we were involved in a terrible car accident. Our thirteen-year-old daughter, Eileen, died instantly, and Steven received severe injuries. He passed away three months later." Running a finger along her hairline, she added, "I only suffered cuts and bruises."

Jake began to speak, but she held up her hand. "Let me finish. Steven had already opened his letter from Graham although he was supposed to wait until he turned forty. He never followed the rules." A wry smile touched her mouth for a second. "In lucid moments in the hospital, we discussed the Australian vacation we'd planned for our fifteenth anniversary and his fortieth birthday." Exhaling a deep breath, she looked at Jake. "So, yes, I promised my dying husband I would make the trip and solve the family mystery, however trite you might think my endeavor."

For once, Jake had no ready comeback. He drained his glass and swiped his mouth with the back of his hand. He could see himself fulfilling a promise to his dying wife. If he'd ever made one to Laura.

Marlow scooted back her chair. "It's been a long day. I'm going to bed."

"Wait. Please. I have a few more things to discuss."

She tilted her head. "More questions about my integrity?"

His face warmed. He deserved that jibe. "No. About your situation. I still think it best you stay here or travel to other parts of Australia, even return to America, and I'll post my part of the code if I find it. Or, give me Henry's and Steven's pieces and let me solve the mystery."

She shook her head vigorously, her hair swishing back and forth. "You're forgetting the second part of Graham's instructions. George's descendant must arrange a reunion to gather the other two pieces and choose another cousin to help decipher the message. Since Steven passed away before he could fulfill his mission, I took on the task. I have an affidavit he signed, making me his proxy." Marlow tapped the table. "I'm not going anywhere, and I'll hold on to the pieces I have."

To avoid Marlow's hard expression, Jake turned. A row of vehicles lined the curb, including her SUV. She could drive to Long Gully and he couldn't stop her, but maybe she hadn't thought of that. And he'd stay far away from the suggestion.

"Thanks for the drink." Marlow stood and sidled between the occupied tables.

Jake rose and set his hands on his hips. He survived the confrontation relatively unscathed, but then Bella's little group broke up and she spied Marlow.

"Marlow. Did you hear us singing? I want to learn to play the guitar. Are you coming to our church service tomorrow?"

Marlow smiled at Bella, but then, eyebrows raised, glanced at Jake. "I'm not sure. Good night." She turned and entered the hotel.

Talk about pricking his conscience! A chunk broke off, and he hung his head. He had no need to be so callous.

Chapter 4

Disappointment or anger—she wasn't sure which—spurred Marlow's hurried retreat to her room. She unlocked her door and collapsed onto the bed. Koala Milton lay on her pillow. She picked up the soft toy and gave it a squeeze. "Grrr. You didn't tell me your cousin could be so pigheaded."

Sitting with Jake at dinner had been awkward enough. At least Bella's presence had tempered Jake's hostility, but his recent conversation on the verandah swarmed through her mind. Questioning her motives, her loyalty to a dead spouse, her right to even be involved. She tossed the toy aside, reached for her purse and dumped out the contents of the accordion file. One document caught her attention—the rental car agreement. Aha. She could drive to Long Gully anytime.

"What would you say to that, Mr. Jake Barclay?" She paced to the door and back, but sank onto the bed again.

Although she could accomplish her goal of searching for Jake's letter at the station, she was not welcome, and even with the strong motive of fulfilling Steven's dying wish, she could not take advantage of Jake and Celia. "Why not just tell me why you're so adamant I not visit Long Gully?"

If she knew his reason, she might accept his refusal. She could wait in Cunnamulla for Jake to mail his piece of the puzzle, but how would she occupy her time?

Marlow picked up the affidavit Steven had signed three weeks before he passed away. He had cast so many doubts about her ability to make the trip without him, yet demanded she do so. Although only a Barclay by marriage, she was curious about Graham's mysterious message and wanted to solve the puzzle, not just because she'd promised Steven, but because she hoped it would bring closure to a part of her life. She held the document in its protective covering to her chest and fought back tears. Closure on her married life with Steven. But not on Eileen. Never on Eileen. Looking back, she knew Steven became more overbearing the longer they were married, but in spite of his faults, he was a loving father. Eileen adored him, and Marlow had done her best to keep her disappointment and hurt hidden from her daughter. Family was of prime importance to her, and she'd wanted Eileen to grow up with both parents. Not like Marlow who never knew her father.

Setting aside the letter, Marlow pulled a royal blue dress from her suitcase on the off chance she'd attend the service the next day. Whenever she'd thought about it, her stomach roiled. It had taken her a long time after Steven's death to accept the reason why. He'd been the king of hypocrites. He treated other woman as a Christian man should, and she'd found it harder and harder to accompany him to services, donning a happy face when she was miserable.

Marlow released a deep sigh. Solving Graham's mystery would allow her to begin the next phase of her life.

Exhausted from the trip and the confrontation with Jake, Marlow readied for bed. Under the sheet, she stared at the fan shadows swishing across the high ceiling. The hypnotic rhythm lulled her to sleep.

A cat screeched outside her window. Marlow bolted upright and blinked at the sunlight pouring through the thin curtains. She checked her watch. Seven fifteen. She had nothing to lose by attending, and everything to gain if she could get through the service.

By the time Marlow entered the all-purpose room, people were milling about and choosing seats. She spied Jake and Bella in the group. He wore khaki jeans and a pale blue shirt. Bella's straight strawberry pink dress with flounces along the hemline added to her elfin quality. A white ribbon held her ponytail in place which swung back and forth as she walked.

Jake looked up. "Good morning. You look nice. I didn't see you at breakfast."

His deeply tanned face intensified the blue of his eyes. Clean-cut features, except for the cleft in his chin, added to the aura of strength that encircled him. A flush crept up Marlow's neck and heated her cheeks. It was good to be noticed, missed, and paid attention to. She was widowed, not dead. "I took toast and coffee to my room."

He sent a brief smile her way, then turned as if embarrassed.

Bella waved and ploughed through the group. "Come join us, Marlow." The young girl grabbed her hand. "Daddy, let's sit here." She indicated the fourth row and sat before Jake replied.

Thankful Bella was between her and Jake, Marlow held the thin hymnal close, ready to bolt if the experience overwhelmed her. But she needn't have worried. The simple yet authentic service opened a crevice in her soul. The strains of "Just As I Am" nourished her parched spirit.

After three more familiar old hymns, Jake led a prayer. The sincerity of his words testified to his strong convictions and deep faith. But Steven had also prayed with conviction.

Who was the hypocrite now? Worship was supposed to glorify God, and all she could do was dwell on the past and how Steven had soured her experiences.

Jaw clenched, Marlow offered her own silent prayer, the first in almost two years. *Thank you, Lord, for my safe travels. Help me to be open to Your spirit, to be receptive to the message, and please guide me on the next phase of my journey.*

Billy McIntosh based his message on the story of Lazarus, using John 11:1–44 as his text.

No matter how many sermons Marlow had heard on Jesus's friend, a new nugget of truth always found its way to her heart.

To conclude the lesson, Billy asked, "Would you agree Lazarus's resurrection was a miracle?" He scanned the audience as if waiting for someone to refute his statement. "Of course, it was. He listened to his Master's voice and exited the tomb. Immediately, mates. No hesitation. And something else you need to know about this deed. Lazarus was one of the few people recorded in the Bible who received his miracle without being touched by Jesus." Billy closed his Bible. "If you need to respond to the Master's voice, don't wait."

Marlow bowed her head. Her soul was entombed. *Help me listen to Your voice, Lord.*

After the lesson, a man introduced as Charlie, made the announcements.

As he shuffled through his papers, Jake reached across the back of Bella's chair, touched Marlow's arm and whispered, "That's Lion's son. His wife, Rosie, is in charge of the meal. He persuaded his dad to let us use this room for worship services." Jake straightened and folded his arms across his broad chest, eyes straight ahead as he listened to the conclusion of the announcements.

Marlow forced herself to look away and concentrated on Charlie's instructions concerning the fellowship lunch to follow.

"Give the ladies time to set up. And I have it on good authority Dolly brought plenty of chook for everyone. Tomorrow is Billy's birthday, so he can be first in line."

At the conclusion of the service, people rearranged the tables and chairs, and soon the room was back to its former state. Jake completed his share of work and then stood near the door conversing with a tall brunette. A bright yellow dress showcased her curves and accentuated her olive-toned skin. Jake stood close and dipped his head to either hear what she said or to whisper in her ear.

Marlow sought out Bella. "Who is your dad talking to?"

She rolled her yes. "That's Bridgette O'Bryan. She lives on Maroola Downs, a neighboring cattle station."

Not a fan, according to Bella's disdainful expression. Although a dozen more questions about the woman sizzled in Marlow's mind, she changed the subject. "Does Lion provide some of the food?"

"Yes. Local families bring dishes and out-of-towners, like us, give Lion money to cover the cost of the food he cooks." Bella waved to a young girl across the room.

"Is she one of your buddies?"

"That's Trish. I'm so happy her burns have healed, and she can swim with us again."

"Burns?"

"There was a fire at their station." Bella's lips quivered.

"I'm glad she's improving. Go, have fun with Trish. I'll be fine."

Bella hurried away, but almost as if drawn by a magnet, Marlow's gaze landed on Jake and the brunette. She leaned in and cocked her head while talking. He appeared to listen, shrugged. Nothing too intimate, but then he brushed a curl of hair off her cheek. Marlow's stomach knotted, and she blinked.

Lost in her confusing thought, she was startled by a shrill whistle.

Rosie set two fingers against her lips and whistled again,

motioning everyone to gather close. "We're ready. Charlie's going to say grace. Remember, Billy goes first. Leave some for the rest of us, preacher man."

A host of chuckles followed her words.

Bella skipped toward Marlow with Jake in tow. She held their hands as Charlie offered a blessing for the food.

Acutely aware of Bridgette's glare from across the room, Marlow pursed her lips. Could the brunette be the reason Jake didn't want female company at Long Gully?

Chapter 5

At least half the congregation left after consuming the variety of cakes, biscuits, and puddings. Those who remained mingled and chatted allowing Jake to catch up with friends and neighbors. Rosie kept her audience amused with the antics of her young twin daughters and how they responded to their older twin brothers. Later, Marlow entertained the group with snippets of her life in America, and her impression of the Australia she'd seen thus far. Bridgette, who sat uncharacteristically silent during the exchange, sent Jake a seductive smile. He quickly turned away. Why couldn't she accept that he wasn't interested?

He straightened in the chair as a plan fought for attention. When Bridgette eyed Marlow, the expression on her face was nothing short of jealousy. He could use that to his advantage and invite Marlow to Long Gully. Stone the crows. What a great idea. Solve the Barclay mystery and curtail Bridgette's pursuit. Besides, he'd had time to evaluate Charles's and Henry's acceptance of Marlow. If they cooperated with her, then he could, too.

Now, to get her on her own, but that proved difficult.

After the last of the families departed, Bella tugged on Jake's arm. "Daddy, may I go swimming with Trish and Beryl again? Beryl's mom is coming."

"Have you completed all your schoolwork?"

"Yeah. I finished it yesterday."

"Be back before dark." He gave her ponytail a gentle tug.

Jake turned to Marlow who straightened chairs around a table. "Will you join me for a soft drink on the side verandah?"

"Sounds good."

He filled two glasses with orange squash and carried them outside where he and Marlow sat at a table facing the western horizon.

"Although you never told me your religious preference, I'm glad you came today. What do you think of our church community?" Jake stretched his legs and took a swig of his drink.

Folding her arms, she glanced at the floor.

"Forgive me. It's none of my business."

She hiked a shoulder. "I haven't been to church since the accident, but I must admit the service jarred loose a couple of the nails holding my soul captive."

"I understand how tragedy affects people in different ways." He'd had no intention of telling her about Laura, but the words spilled out. "Rheumatic fever weakened my Laura's heart as a kid, and four years ago, she died of a heart attack. I neglected worship for several months, but Bella reminded me Laura would not have approved."

Marlow stepped to the waist-high verandah railing and perched on it, balancing with one foot touching the ground. He followed her gaze to the distant horizon where sunset tinted the sky with peach and rose.

"Reminders are good." She swung her leg back and forth. "Bella mentioned Trish was recovering from burns. What happened?"

Good on ya. A deft change of subject, even if it was also tragic. "Six, seven months ago, one of the sheds on their station burned down. Trish went inside to rescue her kittens and suffered burns to her back and thighs. She insists the scars are worth saving three lives."

"Oh, my. What a brave kid."

"Too right." He recalled how distressed Bella had been. His young daughter had a tender heart.

Silence hovered between Jake and Marlow for a minute or more. Although he had a reason for issuing an invitation, he couldn't bring himself to introduce the subject without sounding like he flip-flopped.

Then Marlow hugged her arms close to her body and said, "I noticed the nights are much cooler than I expected."

Easy topic to address. "Many visitors to the outback say that. Because of low humidity and little or no cloud over, the heat radiates up and away." He chuckled. "We have a large fireplace in our living room at home because winter nights can get frosty."

"A little frost would have been welcome on my drive yesterday."

"And tomorrow." A perfect opening. "I've been thinking about your visit—"

"You changed your mind?" She hopped off the railing and tripped over his outstretched legs.

He grabbed her around the waist in time, and she righted herself. His fingers tingled as he let go. He opened his mouth but words from his well-thought out speech melded together when she sat and stared at him, eyes sparkling.

"I can visit Long Gully?" She set her elbows on the table, rested her chin on her folded hands and blinked.

Careful, Jake. "I…I have a couple of ideas." Using Marlow to ward off Bridgette's attentions seemed like a good idea earlier, but now he cringed at his motive. "Follow us in your car then you can leave whenever we find the letter."

"Wonderful, but I'd rather stay with you to solve the puzzle instead of travelling all the way back to Melbourne."

"What do you mean?"

"Remember Graham stated George's descendant had to choose a cousin to help unravel the mystery." She tilted her head. "Why can't you and I complete Graham's instructions?"

"Don't push your luck." He finished his drink while giving himself a mental kick in the rear. Civil one moment, rude the next. "I…I'm sorry. Celia can work with you because I'm too busy to entertain anyone."

She released a long sigh. "Thank you. I won't take advantage of your offer. Maybe Graham's demands can be handled quickly."

Her graciousness jabbed at his heart. He could ease up on his animosity. "Henry trusted you, so I will, too." His initial reason for not inviting her when she first asked loomed large in his mind. "I need to address an area of concern." Balancing the chair on two legs, he rocked while deciding how much to tell her. Might as well relate the whole story.

"After Laura died, I poured my energy into raising my kids and maintaining the station's profitability. I had no time for personal plans until Gail Carson waltzed into my life about eighteen months ago. Although Bella and her mother were very close and she took Laura's death hard, she grew to love Gail. We were only engaged a few weeks when the woman's true nature surfaced."

Scowling, he shook his head. "I tell you, a real fairytale, as in the wicked stepmom kind. Gail made plans to send my daughter off to boarding school without consulting me. She said Bella was immature for her age and needed to mix with other kids. I know Bella will have to attend a regular high school, but the one Gail chose was in Brisbane. Brisbane!" He swiped his hand across his face. "As if that wasn't enough, she also filled my little girl's head with lies about Laura. Gail and Laura had been school chums. Bella can't keep a secret and told me everything."

The scowl on his face intensified. "I thank the Lord every day that I discovered Gail's cunning and manipulative ways before we married. But Bella is still all over the map emotionally. Upbeat one day and withdrawn the next." The front legs of the chair thumped to the ground. "Please keep that in mind when you talk with her. She's never met a stranger, and I don't want her hurt again."

During his tale, Marlow's expression had morphed from excitement to sympathy.

She reached out to touch his hand, but withdrew. "I'm sorry you and Bella endured such emotional turmoil. Believe me, I don't want to hurt anyone."

The sincerity in her tone and demeanor convinced him she was serious.

"Remember, I had a young, impressionable daughter."

"I haven't forgotten." He tugged at his shirt collar. "I had to explain why I'm so protective of Bella and don't want anyone to take advantage of her naiveté."

"I understand." Marlow leaned back. "Let me explain a couple of things, too. I won't encourage Bella to get attached, but it's natural for me to engage with children because I'm a teacher. I also have a degree in counseling. I know how to keep personal and professional issues separate while interacting with kids, and I never take advantage of their vulnerability."

"Thank you for your explanation." A children's counselor. Depending on what happened at the station, he might ask her to address some of his concerns about Bella's behavior. He glanced away from Marlow's intense gaze. *Make up your mind, Barclay. Don't give her a reason to stay longer.*

"Speaking of my daughter," he tapped his watch, "she should be back soon, but I have one more question before she arrives. What arrangements did you make with the car hire company?"

Some of the spark returned to her eyes. "I have an open-ended drop-off date, and I also paid extra to leave the SUV in Cunnamulla in the event you let me ride with you. After complying with Graham's request, I thought I'd take the bus back to Brisbane."

He nodded. "Good plans. In fact, I've changed my mind—"

"No!" She straightened and frowned.

"Whoa. Not what you think. You can ride with us." He should never have suggested she drive by herself. Even Laura hadn't made the trip alone. "The road is atrocious." That's all he needed to say. "I'll arrange for a station hand to bring you back after we conclude our business."

"Thank you." She covered her cheeks with her hands. "Whew. What a relief."

Although he smiled, another piece of his conscience suffered a jab. "I know the bloke who has contracts with car hire companies. I'll get the paperwork and take your SUV to Frank this evening."

"Great."

He mentally compared her SUV to his travel-worn vehicle and cleared his throat. "By the way, my cruiser has made this trip too many times to count. It has heavy duty shocks so it rides rough, and no matter how well I clean it, there's a layer of red dust over everything. The trip will be no picnic."

"I'm tough. If Bella can handle it, so can I. Steven and I worked on a cattle ranch in Texas for several years." She sipped her drink. "Were you able to purchase everything you needed?"

Jake nodded. "I loaded most of our supplies onto the trailer already. In the morning we'll pack our personal items and the perishable food."

"What time will we leave?"

"We must be on the road by seven and will eat breakfast along the way."

He recalled her sandaled foot swinging back and forth. "Sandals and dresses are fine for town, but I suggest you wear long trousers, you know, jeans, and boots for the trip. In the unlikely event we're stranded out there."

"Yup. Milton gave me the same instructions."

That name again.

"Hey, Daddy and Marlow. Are we going to eat soon?"

Bella skipped along the verandah and draped her arm over his shoulder. He welcomed her interruption and gave her damp hair a tussle. "Yeah."

She hurried toward the door.

Standing, he gestured to Marlow. "Will you join us?"

"I'd love to." Marlow gathered the empty glasses and followed Bella. "Did you enjoy your swim?"

"Sort of. Beryl and I had a fight. She says I always want to be the boss, so she stayed in the shallow end. But the water was super, and Trish and I swam five hundred laps." Giggling, Bella twirled as she entered the hotel. "At least it seemed like hundreds. Anyway, I'm hungry."

Hands in his pockets, Jake trailed behind the two. "I wonder what Lion has on the menu tonight."

Although he'd eaten his fill at lunch, he wolfed down a steak. Bella and Marlow chose fish and chips. With Bella present to keep conversation general, the evening passed without incident, until Jake said, "By the way, luv, Marlow will ride with us to Long Gully."

Squealing, Bella sprang out of her chair and hugged Marlow. "I'm so glad. I want to learn about America and Texas and—"

"Calm down, young lady." Jake lowered his head and eyed her.

"Sorry, Dad." She returned to her chair, but bounced so much she almost upset her glass of orange squash.

"I'll only be there a few days, a week at most. But I'll share everything I can about my country." Marlow shot a glance at Jake before bestowing a sweet smile on Bella.

"Having you there will be so much fun. I miss talking to people who aren't as old as Aunty Celia. I love her, but it's not the same. I mean, Nellie and Mary are all so busy they don't have time to chat. Same as you, Dad." Although her tone had mellowed, she couldn't have talked any faster if she'd been paid to. "How old are you, Marlow?"

"Isabel! That's—"

"I don't mind telling. Thirty-seven. And I'll talk to you any time you want." Marlow looked at Jake with what she hoped was a bland expression. "That is, if it's all right with your dad."

He said nothing, only nodded. Probably dwelling on his daughter's sentiment of missing a woman, a mother-figure, to talk to.

At the conclusion of the meal, they retired early in anticipation of the long drive the next day. Jake escorted Marlow to her room where he collected the keys and papers for her hired vehicle.

Bella stepped between the adults and stared into Marlow's face. "I'm so glad you're staying with us. Night-night." She stood on tiptoe and kissed Marlow's cheek before skipping down the hall to their room.

Jake stared after Bella then shook his head. "What did I tell you?"

"I promise to keep your concerns in mind when chatting with her."

He acknowledged her words with a brief smile then pivoted, strode back to the lobby and phoned Frank to explain the situation with Marlow's car.

"No worries, mate. But don't bring the vehicle here. Leave the keys with Lion and I'll collect it in the morning."

"Thanks. See ya next month." Jake returned to his room and quietly prepared for bed as Bella was already asleep.

Intrusive thoughts of Marlow plagued him most of the night. One minute he regretted inviting her, the next he admitted his growing interest in Graham's mysterious request. And in Marlow. Turning on his side, he stared at the sleeping form of his daughter in the other bed. He'd brought a somber, withdrawn little girl with him on Friday. Her mood had started to change when her school pals arrived, but she'd blossomed after meeting Marlow. Was Marlow using her expert skills, or was this how she'd interact with any young girl? He'd soon find out. Although, it didn't matter as long as Bella wasn't hurt in the process.

The strident blast of the alarm penetrated his hazy dream. Jake sat upright and bashed the clock, silencing the squawk. "All right, I heard you." He blinked at Bella as she rubbed her eyes.

"Daddy, it can't be half past six already."

"Sorry, luv. You can kip on the way home. I'll meet you at the cruiser." He gathered his kit and duffle bag and hurried down the hall to the bathroom.

As arranged, boxes of produce and perishable foods packed in ice sat beside his vehicle, along with the basket from Lion with a thermos of tea, mugs, and bacon sandwiches for breakfast, and an ice chest containing their lunch. Jake stashed everything except the basket in the back of the cruiser. He rested one booted foot on the bumper and surveyed the dawn-touched golden heavens. Time to go. He should have rapped on Marlow's door as he passed.

Bella dashed out of the hotel, whistling. "Here are my things."

"I'm proud of you, luv. You're ready early today."

"That's because I can't wait to start our trip home. It's going to be so much fun showing Marlow the sights. She's really interested in Australia, isn't she? Have you seen her this morning?"

Jake deposited Bella's small suitcase in the rear. "Not yet." Now would be a good time to remind her. "Don't get too excited. Remember, she's only staying a few days."

"I know. Do you want me to see if she's ready?"

"Yeah. It's going to be a stinker today, and we must be on our way."

After Bella entered the hotel, Jake rubbed his smooth chin. Truth be told, he was excited too, but as much as he wanted his Bella Bear and Marlow to be friends, he had to be vigilant.

Chapter 6

Awake at six o'clock, Marlow had showered and packed her suitcase in record time. No way did she want to keep Jake waiting. At the last moment, she decided against wearing hoop earrings and opened her cloth jewelry bag to return them. The old, silver pendant necklace, a high school graduation gift from her mother, had slipped out of the side pouch as if begging for her attention. She fingered the large stone and sighed. No trace of her mother in the birth records, and since her father's name was not listed on her birth certificate, locating any family members seemed hopeless. For the umpteenth time, Marlow regretted not pressing Mom for details. Being a single mother had never seemed to bother her, but it always nagged at Marlow.

She attempted to tie the cloth bag closed, but in her haste, several small earrings spilled out. On hands and knees, she gathered them together.

A knock on her door, and Bella poked her head in. "Are you ready?"

"I will be as soon as I find my earrings."

Bella joined the search and located several under the bedside table.

"Thank you. Oh, great. My studs. The only diamonds I possess." Marlow placed the bag in her suitcase and zipped it up. "I'm ready."

"I'll carry your small bag."

Keenly aware of Jake's warning, Marlow tried to curtail her excitement as she followed Bella down the hall and out of the hotel.

"Sorry to keep you waiting, Jake." Marlow draped her purse strap over her shoulder as she hurried to the vehicle. "I dropped my jewelry bag and Bella helped me pick up the pieces."

"I'm good at finding things." Bella smiled and climbed into the backseat, humming a familiar pop tune.

Marlow passed her suitcase to Jake. "Bella's in fine form this morning."

"She's as keen as mustard about your visit to the station." He wedged the case between two boxes of supplies in the back then stowed a basket next to Bella. "Our breakfast is in here."

Bella chose that moment to cease humming and, instead, sang along with the song playing through the headphones of her little tape recorder. Jake and Marlow chuckled, almost in unison.

Although he appeared relaxed, Marlow sensed a wariness beneath his casual remarks. She would do all in her power to assure him she was no threat to Bella. Climbing into the cruiser, her knees bumped against radio equipment mounted on the dashboard. She slid the bucket seat back as far as it would go. Red dust did linger on every surface. She draped her camera strap around her neck then stuffed her purse beside her on the seat.

With everyone buckled in, Jake eased out of the parking lot and drove past the gas station on the corner.

Curiosity piqued, Marlow asked, "Is gas, um, petrol, available along the way?"

"There's one service station about mid-way, but their supplies are inconsistent. I've already filled the regular and reserve tanks. Never take chances with fuel. Or water. I have a large container of fresh water and individual canteens. Let Bella know when you need yours."

"Thanks." Marlow adjusted her seatbelt more comfortably across her lap, preparing for the long haul. Pleasant, cool air rushed in the open windows. The sky brightened behind them as they headed west out of town on Adventure Way and crossed the Warrego River.

Surprised at the width, Marlow said, "I was not expecting that much water."

"This river is typical of many in the outback. Most are seasonal, but prone to flooding if heavy rains fall up north."

She fingered her camera.

"I will stop for you to take photos."

"Thanks, but I don't want to prolong the trip."

Bella sang a few bars of a song, and Marlow stole a side-ways glance at Jake. The corners of his mouth twitched. The trip in close quarters might not be as awkward as she'd envisioned.

Determined to learn all she could about the Australian outback, Marlow asked, "This road is fine. When does it get atrocious, the word you used?"

"The road's fairly good as far as Malindela about two hundred kilometers away. Then we veer north onto a dirt track." Jake nudged Marlow's forearm resting on her knee. "What you've driven on so far during your travels has been cushy compared to what's ahead."

He swerved to avoid a dead kangaroo on the road.

"That's another hazard we have to contend with—dead animals." He laughed. "And live ones. Did you notice the 'roo bar on the front of the cruiser? Without one, I'd have wrecked several vehicles by now."

"My hired vehicle had a bar. Good thing, too." She related her experience with the kangaroo she'd hit.

"You're fortunate you'd already slowed down. The large male roos are the worst. They can weigh as much as, uh, two hundred pounds, if my conversion is correct."

"When I left Brisbane, I was prepared to drive to your station if you weren't in Cunnamulla. But I'm very thankful I'm not making the journey by myself." Marlow stared at the flat, desolate land whizzing past.

He shot a quick glance her way. "I'm glad you're riding with us."

"Me too." Bella leaned her arms along the back of the Jake's and Marlow's seats. "Can we eat now? I'm hungry."

"Yeah. Be careful when you pour the tea. Don't fill the mugs all the way to the top."

"Do you need any help?" Marlow twisted in the seat.

"I can manage, thanks." Bella handed her two sandwiches wrapped in wax paper. "Give a sanger to Dad, please."

Marlow had heard the term before and opened a sandwich partway before passing it to Jake.

"Ta." He chomped and smacked his lips. "Good on ya, Lion."

Next, Bella passed over two mugs of milky tea. "Lion never adds sugar. I hope you don't mind, Marlow."

"This is fine, thanks." She placed one mug in the holder and sipped from the other. Perfect. She'd never eaten a bacon and butter sandwich before, but she consumed the rich, filling treat in a hurry, washing it down with the tea. "Excellent breakfast."

Emptying his mug, Jake handed it to Marlow. "Next time you see Lion, give him your compliments. He always provides breakfast and lunch for our trips."

Bella collected the mugs and wrappings, then returned to her music, pausing often to point out to Marlow something of interest in the countryside. Her interjections became less frequent as the miles marched by.

With the increasing heat, and the mesmerizing rhythm of the tires on the tarmac, the occupants of the vehicle all seemed to withdraw, and conversation ceased. Marlow noticed low mounds in the scrub and the color of the earth change to tan, gray, back to red, but she had little energy to inquire. An hour later, Bella handed Marlow two stainless steel canteens. "For you and Dad. Mine's almost empty already."

"Thanks. You read my mind." Marlow passed one to Jake, then took a swig of her cool water. It had a slight mineral taste which was unusual but not unpleasant. At least it was refreshing. "I have a question for you, Bella. Why is the sky so blue? Cobalt, I believe is the right description."

"Rick says the sky's color is enhanced by the red earth. What do you think, Dad?"

"Something like that, and the dust in the atmosphere."

"Whatever the scientific explanation, I've never seen anything like it before." Australia's beauty was fast gaining a foothold in her soul.

With the windows open, Marlow's hair kept flying around her face. Tired of plucking strands out of her mouth, she searched in her purse for a rubber band and formed a thick ponytail.

"You look like a kid now," Bella said.

"That's what Eileen used to tell me."

Bella leaned forward and tapped Marlow's shoulder. "Daddy told me about your husband and your daughter. I'm…sorry."

The emotion in the last two words touched Marlow's heart. "Thank you, sweet child."

"Bella?" Jake glared at her over the seat.

"I remember what you said, Dad, but can't I ask about her daughter?"

He elbowed Marlow. "You don't have to answer."

I can talk about Eileen for hours. Marlow swallowed. "I'm all right. What do you want to know, Bella?"

"Dad said she was thirteen. We would be cousins, sort of, right?"

"Yes." Marlow dug in her purse for her wallet and withdrew the last school picture she had of Eileen. Eighth grade. Long dark hair, sparkling blue eyes, a smile to warm a mother's soul. "Here." She passed the photo to Bella.

"Oh, she is so pretty. I wish I had blue eyes. Like Dad and Rick. And her hair is wavy. Not like mine which is so straight and plain brown." Bella returned the photo, fingered one of her braids then retreated to her corner of the backseat.

Marlow peeked at the child who stared out the window, chin in hand. She had her own brand of beauty and would probably drive boys crazy in a few years. But right now, her self-worth depended on her fragile view of her world. Beloved mother, gone. Gail, a woman she also loved, out of her life. Marlow chewed her bottom lip. She'd have to be extra careful that she didn't become a third casualty for Bella.

So focused on her own thoughts, Marlow didn't realize Bella had leaned on the seats again. "I hope I didn't make you sad. Can I still ask you questions?"

"Certainly. Ask away." She turned slightly so she could see Bella and Jake without getting a crick in her neck.

"What kind of job do you have?"

"I work for the Dallas Public School system. I was a Special Education teacher for many years. Now, I supervise other teachers who work with children with special needs."

"Special, like…oh, I know. Beryl has a little brother whose arms and legs are all twisted. She says he's paralyzed."

"Probably cerebral palsy. There are many reasons why children need extra help."

"I bet that's hard work. You must be very smart."

"Just about average, but—"

"Oh, goody-goody-gumdrops. There's the sign for Malindela." Bella tapped Marlow's shoulder. "We always stop in town to use the toilet."

"This is our last civilized rest stop." Jake slowed the vehicle. "You can also get something to drink if you like. But we'll drive a few miles out of town to have lunch."

"I'm fine, thanks."

Bella bounced on the seat. "Hurry, please, Daddy."

"We'll be there in two shakes." Jake turned into a lot beside a small store, parked, then pointed out the window. "Look, Marlow. What did I tell you?"

The gas station on the corner displayed a large sign by the pump. *Sorry, no petrol. Delivery expected tomorrow.*

"Glad I filled up in Cunnamulla. Let's go. Don't take take too long, Bella."

"I won't. Come with me, Marlow. The toilets are this way." The child skipped ahead, twirled, then beckoned Marlow.

She grinned. Never a dull moment.

Ten minutes later, Jake pulled out of the lot and headed northwest a few miles then veered right onto a dirt track, clouds of red dust billowing behind them. "We'll be traveling at a snail's pace the rest of the journey. Usually on dirt roads we can only do about fifty Ks an hour. Thirty miles, and sometimes less."

Marlow thought they had been driving slowly already. She figured the heavily-loaded trailer and vehicle accounted for their lack of speed. The one noticeable change of course was the stifling presence of dust.

Bella rested her chin on her arms draped across the back of the front seats, her head bouncing up and down, a puzzled expression on her face. "What about your job? Won't the Dallas schools miss you?"

"I'm taking a year off with the assurance of a position when I return."

"I'm glad you're a teacher. Maybe you can help me with my schoolwork."

"No, Bella." Jake's tone held a note of finality. "Marlow will leave as soon as she finds a special document from your grandfather."

Whatever easing of tension had occurred over the last few hours vanished. Marlow glanced at Jake. Jaw clenched, hands gripping the steering wheel. She needed no further reminder she was on borrowed time.

Chapter 7

Bella's squeal shattered the silence in their vehicle. "Here it comes, Daddy. Quick, Marlow, roll up your window."

Marlow flinched and cranked the handle, searching for a swarm of bees or something equally lethal. A large dust cloud mushroomed in the distance. "What is it?"

"A road train." Jake slowed and moved as far left as he could. "The trucks can pull two, three, or sometimes four cattle trailers. They are dangerous—either to pass or be passed by. We usually encounter one on our trip to or from Cunnamulla. It's always…"

He coughed as the roaring leviathan rumbled passed, churning up clouds of suffocating dust which infiltrated the invisible pores in the metal.

"…an interesting experience."

Bella and Marlow succumbed to the dust-drenched air invading the vehicle. They coughed in unison. Jake continued to drive slowly, but before the russet cloud subsided enough to see the track clearly, a large, feathered creature loomed through the thick air. Jake veered left to avoid the animal.

Catastrophe averted, the bird disappeared, and Marlow sighed.

Thud! Her seat belt cut into her shoulder.

The vehicle lurched to the side. Jake slammed on the brakes.

"What was that?" Her quivering voice was barely audible.

"The first was an emu and the second may be a rock." Jake turned to Bella. "You okay back there?"

"I'm fine, Dad."

He opened the door and stepped out.

Most of the dust had settled. Marlow pulled her folded hat from her purse and shoved it on her head. She opened the door, but a large boulder blocked her way, creating a narrow opening through which she squeezed. The cruiser had ploughed into a pile of rocks.

"Well, I'll be gob smacked." Jake stood at the front of the car and pointed to the left tire.

Bella joined her father. "Can you fix it?"

"I'll give it a go, but first I need to contact the station." He returned to the vehicle where he used the two-way radio.

Standing in front of the cruiser, Marlow heard the word 'over' a dozen or more times. She arched her back in an effort to release the fabric that stuck to her moist skin. Perspiration tickled her upper lip and beads formed at her hairline. The heat she'd experienced in Cunnamulla was nothing compared to this. The temperature must be over one hundred. *But it's a dry heat. Yeah, right.*

Hat in hand, Bella sat on a boulder near Marlow. "Daddy's calling a neighboring station. Probably the Davidsons. They'll pass on a message to Aunty Celia. That's how we do it out here. We relay messages for each other." She placed one of her braids along her upper lip, then let it fall.

Marlow grinned. "Something else for me to add to my list of differences."

"You have a list? I'd like to know what you've written."

"I'll share it with you later." She glanced around. "Where's the emu?"

"Probably ran off. They're hardy birds, and we were going slowly. But like Dad said, if you hit a kangaroo…"

Jake shut the door and examined the front of the vehicle. "The Davidsons will let Celia know what happened. I told them we don't need any help. Yet." He moved a few of the smaller rocks.

Now the damage was more evident. The 'roo bar had protected the winch system and most of the grill, but the left front fender had been smashed onto the tire.

He knelt to examine it. "The tire doesn't seem to be punctured. If I can twist the metal back, we should be all right. But I have two spares if it's damaged." He stood and wiped his hands on his jeans. "I'm going to need help. Marlow, are you game?"

"Just tell me what to do."

"Can I help?" Bella put on her hat and jumped off the rock.

Jake nodded. "Get my tools, please, luv."

"Righto."

While Bella unearthed the toolbox from the back of the cruiser,

Jake pulled two crowbars from under the driver's seat and examined the mangled metal again. He took out an array of tools, then directed Marlow to hold a crowbar first this way, then another. Bella passed him tools when requested. After using the other crowbar, a mallet, pliers, and his fingers, he pried the last piece of metal away from the tire.

"That's it. Now let me see if I can reverse out of here."

Jake tossed aside the tools. He knelt again and peered under the cruiser and trailer. "There aren't any rocks underneath big enough to be a problem. Wait here, ladies."

He dusted himself off and climbed into the vehicle. The cruiser hesitated, then backed up, pushing the trailer.

Marlow held her breath.

When Jake stopped close to the track, Bella cheered, "You did it."

He wiped his sleeve across his face. "Put away my tools, luv, and get us all a drink while I let the Davidsons know we're okay. I'm sure your canteens are empty by now."

Marlow helped Bella gather the tools then fill their canteens from the large container. She closed the rear doors and gulped her water. It wasn't ice cold, but the liquid slid down her parched throat like quicksilver. Bella delivered a canteen to Jake before sliding into the vehicle and downing her drink.

"Thanks." Jake took several gulps. "The Davidsons will let Celia know we're on our way. And that you are staying a few days." He fastened his seat belt and adjusted the rearview mirror.

Settling into her seat, Marlow said, "That's short notice. Are you sure Celia will be all right with my sudden appearance?"

"Definitely. One thing you'll learn about families out here, we're always ready for visitors. Sometimes travelers get lost, or run out of fuel. We watch out for each other."

The incident with the truck and the emu played over in Marlow's mind. A knot formed in her stomach. What if she'd been on this road alone in her SUV, encountered a road train, and swerved into a pile of rocks? Unless someone came along to help her, she'd have been stranded. And Steven would have been proven right. He'd demanded she take a traveling companion, but she'd refused. Tears gathered in her eyes. She blinked and rubbed her middle. As much as she wanted to be free of his overbearing and demeaning views of her, they still had the power to cripple her, to make her feel weak and unsure of herself. To shroud her in uncertainty.

Please, dear God, help me free myself from the shadow he cast over me.

Closing her eyes, she drew in deep breaths. She'd asked God for help and had immediately felt a sense of peace as if she were not alone in this new environment. New, exciting, so different to anything she'd experienced. And she was open to all possibilities.

Marlow opened her eyes and studied the landscape creeping by. They had left behind most of the trees and all she could see were clumps of yellowed spinifex grass, some scrubby bushes, and miles and miles of red, interspersed with patches of gray. "Where are the wires and poles? There are none along this stretch of road."

A mirth-filled chuckle. "I forgot to mention that we don't have local electricity. It's way too expensive for the lines to extend to these outlying stations. But no worries—we don't rely on candles too often. We have a diesel-powered generator, solar power for hot water, and a gas stove and fridge."

"I never gave it any thought before."

"We might not have all the modern conveniences, but we live a good life." He wiped a grimy hand on his dark jeans. "We'll stop for lunch soon and we can wash up then."

"Marlow, can you share your list with me now?" Bella resumed her place, arms draped along the back of the seats.

"Sure. The list is in my suitcase, but I tell you what I remember. First of all, you guys drive on the left side of the road."

"I know you drive on the right from watching American films. Was it hard to make the change?"

"Not really. If there were other cars on the road, I could follow them. Turning corners was confusing at first and learning to use my left hand to change gears was a chore."

"My brother learned to drive when he was thirteen, but Dad says I have to wait until I'm older."

"And taller, Bella." Jake eyed her in the rearview mirror. "Right now, you can't see over the steering wheel."

"I know, but it's not fair. What else is on your list?"

"The light switches are opposite. In America up is on and down is off."

Bella whistled. "That's so silly. I wonder why."

"And the electrical outlets and plugs are different. Yours are much larger. And of course, all the words and expressions."

"Ooh, I have an idea. When we get home, we can make a list of the words, and maybe my teacher will let me turn it into a school project." Bella retreated to her corner and hummed a tune she'd sung earlier.

An interesting child, for sure. Marlow had made several mental notes concerning Bella's behavior. Obviously, she needed more time with the child, but she'd come to one conclusion that agreed with Gail's assessment. Bella was immature for her age. She tended to hog conversations, her feelings were easily hurt, and she seemed desperate for attention. The child skipped and twirled as Eileen had done at a much younger age. Maybe her emotional growth had been stunted by her mother's death four years ago. Before Marlow returned to Texas, she wanted to share her assessment with Jake since he'd mentioned his concern.

A grove of trees shimmered several miles in the distance. Marlow squinted. It had to be a mirage, but the image increased in size, and Jake slowed down. He parked under one of the eucalyptus trees, not the towering giants Marlow had seen in Brisbane, but rather over-grown bushes with swollen trunks and gnarled, twisted limbs. Fortunately, despite their short stature, they provided shade.

Marlow climbed out of the vehicle and stretched.

Grunting, Jake exited, too, and yawned.

The only one with any semblance of energy was Bella who bounded down a narrow path and yelled, "Come sit by the water, Marlow. Daddy and I will get our lunch."

Through the blue-green leaves, Marlow spied a small pool, surrounded by grasses and shrubs that looked alien in the expanse of withered spinifex. She nabbed her camera case off the passenger seat. "Am I dreaming? How can this beautiful blue pond exist out here?"

Chapter 8

One surprise after another. No amount of research could have prepared Marlow for the reality of the outback. She draped the strap around her neck, readied her camera, and took two shots.

Jake opened the back doors of the cruiser. "Bella can explain the presence of the water while I get the food ready."

"Good idea." Bella cleared her throat, assumed a serious expression and began her instruction. "In this part of Queensland, there is a huge artesian basin. Do you know what that is?"

"Yes." Marlow kept a straight face by plucking a leaf off a branch. She crushed it and held it to her nose. The unmistakably scent of eucalyptus permeated the air.

"Sometimes the water comes to the surface naturally, like this, and forms a billabong—pool, that is. In other places people drill bores or wells, and then they can use the water as they need it on their farms or stations. We have lots of bores at Long Gully."

She paused, hands on her hips. "That was fun. I was teaching the teacher."

Still struggling to control her amusement, Marlow patted Bella's shoulder. "Well done. I understand perfectly now, thank you. When I first arrived, I bought a book that described Australian flora with beautiful pictures, but it never mentioned pools in the outback."

During Bella's explanation, squeaks and squawks in the branches above had punctuated her words. Marlow scanned the foliage. White plumage rustled, restless, erratic. Suddenly, as if on cue, hundreds of white birds exploded from the trees and took to the sky.

"Wow. How gorgeous." Each bird had bright pink feathers under its wings and belly, streaking the late morning sky with rose.

"Galahs. They're all over. Beautiful but noisy and messy." Jake set the cooler near a downed log. "One thing Bella didn't mention. In some places the artesian water comes out piping hot."

"What about the bores you have?"

"None of ours are hot." He picked up a heavy stick and beat on three large logs, set end to end in a semicircle. "To chase away any snakes. Come sit and eat."

"Uh, all right." Marlow shuddered as she chose the middle log beside Bella.

"Bella, would you like to say grace?"

"Righto. Let's hold hands."

Relieved Bella sat between her and Jake, Marlow bowed her head.

"Dear Lord, thanks for a safe trip so far, and for our food. Also, I'm so glad Marlow is with us, even if only for a short time. In Jesus's name." She released their hands. "How was that, Dad?"

Glancing over his daughter's head, Jake looked at Marlow. "Perfect, Bella."

"Good. I'm starving."

Marlow checked her watch. Nearly eleven thirty. Early for lunch, but they had been on the road almost five hours.

He opened the cooler and removed bottled drinks and a large plastic container. "The ice has melted so we use the little bit of water to wash. You go first, Marlow."

The cool water on her hands and face removed the grime, but also dropped her body temperature a degree or two. "Oh, that feels so good." She dried her face and hands on a couple of tissues she found in her pocket.

After Jake and Bella had washed, she handed out the drinks, all grape soda, and he opened the plastic container. As soon as he did, a hoard of bush flies descended as if they heard the swish of the opening lid. The annoying insects had appeared as soon as they exited the vehicle, but this lot meant business.

Marlow swatted them away, to no avail.

"You've learned the Aussie salute." Jake chuckled.

"The what?" Hand flapping in front of her face, she sighed. "Aha. Guess I have."

"Lion packed meat pies. His are the best. I'm sure you've had them somewhere in your travels. Here's one to start, but he supplied extras." He passed pies to Bella and Marlow along with bags of potato chips. Crisps, to the locals.

Savoring a bite, Marlow nodded. "Delicious." They looked nothing like American potpies, but rather, were similar in shape to empanadas, and could be eaten without utensils. "I had my first pie in Melbourne with Cousin Henry."

"Not Milton?"

She licked a blob of gravy off her lip. "Considering the fancy restaurants he took me to, I doubt he's had a meat pie in years."

Jake grunted. "I believe it."

They completed their meal in silence. Even Bella had nothing to say.

Pies and crisps devoured, Jake removed his hat and scooped a handful of water over his hair. Droplets lingered, glistening in the sunlight. "Time to go. We're more than halfway home. Should get there about half past one or two o'clock, in time for one of Aunt Celia's cuppas."

"We never leave any rubbish behind." Bella poured out the soiled water from the cooler and placed the trash and empty bottles inside.

Removing temptation did not deter the flies that kept buzzing and annoying everyone.

"Dad, should I fill our canteens again when we get back in the car?"

"Yeah." Jake picked up the cooler and headed down the path. "This last section of road is the worst."

Marlow groaned. "I don't know if my bones can hold together if we face more ruts and carcasses, but I'm ready to leave these flies behind."

"Wherever you stop in the bush, you'll find another hoard waiting for you. Mozzies too, if there's stagnant water about."

"Mosquitoes we have in Texas, but these flies, now they're something else."

Last in line, Marlow stopped and glanced back to the seating area and patted her jeans pocket. As she suspected, the damp tissues had fallen out. She returned to the log, looked behind it. "Aha." Grabbing the piece of trash, she muttered, "Leave nothing but footprints."

As she straightened, a long brown object slithered across her boot. The black-headed snake struck at her leg, and she squealed,

"Jake, snake! I think it bit me." Although she didn't feel the sting of fangs or heat of venom entering her system, she wasn't going to take any chances. She'd had enough experience with rattlers in Texas to be cautious. She should have remembered that before reaching behind the log.

"Don't move, Marlow. Bella, get the first aid kit." Jake scooped up Marlow and carried her to the cruiser. "Describe the snake." He set her on the hood. "Where?"

"Left shin." She set her hands on the hood to keep from sliding off. "It had a black head and brown body."

"Gwardar. Very poisonous." Jake untied her boot and ripped it off, followed by her sock. Next, he pushed up her jeans and exposed her bare leg. "I don't see any fang marks." He raised her foot and examined her calf.

Was it vain to be thankful she'd shaved her legs this morning? "I know it struck me." Marlow huffed in and out. "Maybe the the fangs hit my boot, or…or the bite didn't go through my jeans."

"Possibly. They have short fangs." Jake lowered her leg and wiped a hand across his face. "Whew, that was close."

Speechless, Marlow nodded, and drew her knee to her chest. She rubbed her calf and shin just to be certain. No broken skin. Not only was her heart thumping, blood pounded in her head. She blinked against the dizziness that threatened to topple her off the vehicle.

Bella, holding the first aid kit, picked up Marlow's discarded boot and sock. "Here." Tears glistened in her hazel eyes. "I'm going to lie down in the backseat."

"Thanks." Marlow slipped on her sock with hands that shook like leaves on a quaking aspen tree. She struggled with the boot until Jake assisted. He tied the lace and yanked down the leg of her jeans.

Without asking, he lifted her off the hood and set her beside the passenger door. "We need to get going."

The vehicle crawled slowly away from the oasis onto the sunbaked strip of red track that stretched through the yellowed spears of spinifex grass. Senses still heightened, Marlow gazed at the change in the scenery. Sporadic mulga tress and clumps of Mitchell grass began to make an appearance. Stifling dust swirled through the vehicle, adding another coat of red to everything.

A heavy silence hung over the occupants as the miles snailed by.

She twisted her hands in her purse strap. How could she have been so foolish? She should apologize.

"I'm sorry—"

"You were—"

Marlow shot a look at Jake. "Let me go first. I'm sorry I caused so much anxiety. I know better. It was all my fault."

"And I should have cautioned you when we first sat down. We have many venomous snakes and other reptiles whose bites are lethal. I take the blame."

A voice from the backseat hushed their conversation. "You're both at fault. Don't scare me like that again. I don't want another funeral." Bella set her headphones in place and rested her head against the seat, eyes closed.

Thoroughly chastised, Marlow faced forward. She had nothing to add, and by Jake's stoic expression, neither did he. No one could accuse Bella of being irrational. With them traveling hours away from medical treatment, if Marlow had been bitten, she would be dead by now. A shiver scurried across her shoulders.

The vehicle devoured more miles, and still no one spoke. Muscles tight, Marlow rubbed her neck. Maybe if she concentrated on pleasant topics her tension would ease.

Since the snake incident, Jake had become unapproachable, aloof, as if he had barricaded himself in a fortress. A good time for observation. Marlow turned a tad so she could focus on him without appearing to stare.

Light blue shirt sleeves rolled up to the elbows exposed tanned, muscled forearms. That had carried her. His right arm rested on the open window frame, both hands on the wheel. The hat pulled low over his forehead lent his profile a gallant air. Steven had worn a hat well, too. *Stop. Stop.*

She stared out the window, then continued her visual examination. Dark glasses shielded Jake's eyes, which Marlow suspected were flecked with ice chips. Scattered silver hairs shone in the dark stubble on his chin and cheeks. Muscles twitched in his set jaw. What emotion was he holding in check?

He glanced at her, and she averted her eyes. Her heated cheeks tingled. Why did she feel as if she were a high school teen caught ogling the popular quarterback?

54

Chapter 9

A large, grayish mass lay near the middle of the track. Jake slowed and veered around the kangaroo carcass, the third one today. Aware of Marlow's scrutiny, he kept his eyes forward. He didn't need her tale of hitting a kangaroo to remind him how hazardous traveling out here could be. Not for the first time, he silently thanked the Lord that she'd found him in Cunnamulla. In spite of what he'd said earlier, no way would he want her to travel these treacherous roads by herself.

Faint strains of a song drifted over the seat. Bella's headphones must have detached from her tape player. He bit his lip. Her words to them after the snake bite ordeal seared his soul. No more funerals. Too right. How could he have been so careless? Harming Bella or Marlow was the last thing he wanted, but he'd almost done both.

Movement next to him caught his attention.

Marlow undid her seatbelt, reached to the back, and returned with Bella's tape recorder, bumping Jake's shoulder. "Sorry." She turned off the machine then snapped her seatbelt in place.

Good thing he had to keep his full attention on the road, otherwise he might have blurted out his thoughts.

After Laura died, he hadn't gone looking for romance, but he did worry about Bella. As much as he loved and appreciated Aunt Celia, he'd often wondered if his daughter needed a mother figure. And then Gail returned to the station she'd grown up on north of Cunnamulla, met them when in town, and, well, the rest was history.

Glancing at his bare ring finger, he imagined the gold band Laura had given him. It lay buried in his sock drawer. Praise God he came to his senses and didn't enter into that second marriage. But the fiasco with Gail was never far from his mind. The relationship with her had been impulsive. He'd never prayed about the decision to marry Gail, and who suffered the most? Bella Bear. She adored the woman, and he'd never do anything to hurt her again.

How was Marlow holding up? He snuck a peek. She rested against the seat facing him.

Since Gail's departure, Jake prayed frequently for guidance in the personal relationship aspect of his life. He and Laura had been happily married. To be honest, he wanted a close, loving connection again.

What if Marlow was the answer? No way.

A still, small voice whispered to his soul, "Wait upon the Lord."

He broke out in a sweat, not unusual considering the temperature. After removing his hat, he drew a handkerchief from his shirt pocket and wiped his brow. The wind rifled through his damp hair. Ah, that felt good.

He smiled and glanced at Marlow. "What's on your mind? You've been staring at me for ages."

"No, I haven't." She blushed. "Okay, I might have been, but I have a couple of questions and was waiting for you to, um—"

"To stop being uptight and unapproachable?"

"Something like that."

"Sorry. I have a lot on my mind." He shoved on his hat. "I'm all ears, now."

She adjusted her ponytail. "Why did your family move from the Melbourne area, and how did they become involved with sheep?"

"That story could take hours." He grinned. "But we have the time."

"I'm ready."

If he didn't provide the information, Celia probably would. "Edward, my grandfather, worked in the gold mines as did many people in Bendigo, north of Melbourne, in the early 1900s. He was an exceptional man. While other people were facing financial crises, he made sound investments, spent wisely, and had revenue from shares in an opal mine in New South Wales. He had great plans for his family who all preferred the outdoor life. So, when he explored the country and wrote home describing the sheep station in Queensland, he had no opposition to the move."

"That must've been a drastic change, from civilization to the outback."

"It was, but he had the finances to make life as cushy as possible for his wife and kids. Don't forget, when they moved in 1925, life was hard for many people, even in the cities."

"Your grandmother must have been a hardy soul."

"Granny Vida was formidable." He drummed his thumbs on the steering wheel. "Not only did she design the layout of the new homestead, but she helped with the construction. Over the years, they added more rooms, and we've made a few changes, but it's basically the same house. Edward's nickname was Lucky Ned. True to the name, he succeeded in his sheep endeavors. Two of their daughters married and moved away."

"And Celia? Why does she live with you?"

"Ah, yes, that's a long story. She won't mind me telling you, but she doesn't like to discuss her past."

"I'll keep that in mind."

"She became a nurse and worked in Brisbane. After twenty-plus years of dedicated service, she was falsely accused of causing patients' deaths. That, combined with a failed romance, soured her on city life, and she moved back to Long Gully. It was just after Laura's third miscarriage, so we were glad to have her home."

Sharing intimate details with Marlow brought back memories, but also acted as a balm. He didn't often speak of such private matters.

"Third miscarriage? How heartbreaking."

"Yeah." Jake swallowed hard and squinted at shredded black strips along the track. Some poor bloke lost a tire.

"I can't imagine the sorrow." She cleared her throat. "What about your parents?"

"Dad was wounded in the last days of World War II, had to have a leg amputated, and died in 1950. I was only twelve, but he had already instilled his love of the land in my heart."

"His death must have been hard on you."

"Yeah, but my grandparents were still living on the station. Mum went to pieces, so Lucky Ned and Vida held the family together and continued running the place. Eventually, Mum recovered and did her share of work in the day-to-day operations of such a large spread."

"I need to record all those dates and details for the family tree."

"Aunt Celia will inundate you with all the facts and figures your notebook can hold."

"Good." Marlow shifted in the seat.

"By the time I was through with school and old enough to take on more of the responsibilities, Lucky Ned had developed a serious lung condition and was advised by his doctor to move closer to a medical facility. One of my aunts lived in Sydney, so Ned and Vida moved there in the early 1960s. He didn't live long. We're not sure if it was the lung problem that killed him or his being far from his beloved Long Gully. Vida died a few years later."

"You were running the place by then?"

"Yeah. Laura and I married in '60. Mum continued to help on the station and was present for the birth of Richard the following year, and ten years later for Bella's arrival. She died in 1974."

He slowed to negotiate around a deep rut. "How did George end up in America?"

"According to Steven, he had a major disagreement with his siblings, and sailed for America in 1918 soon after the war ended. The family eventually settled in Texas."

No wonder his grandfather never mentioned his brother.

"How about your parents? What do they think about your travels?"

Folding and unfolding her arms, she sighed. "My mother died when I was eighteen, and I never knew my dad."

"Sorry. That must have been tough. Did you have grandparents or other family close by?"

"No, but friends helped out."

Talk about life being hard. Parents gone. Husband and daughter, too. "I'm—"

"You know about my quest to solve Graham's mystery, but that's not the only reason I came to Australia."

Here it comes, her true motive. Teeth clenched, he gripped the steering wheel. He'd allowed her sweet talk to soften his resolve. "What is that?"

"My mother was born in Australia. She never shared any details of her family, so I tried to locate her birth certificate while in Melbourne, but I wasn't successful. I just thought you needed to know."

He'd certainly misjudging her. Jake relaxed his jaw and hands. "I'm so sorry." He had ancestor names galore on his family tree, and she had one. Words failed him.

Marlow sent him a little smile. "Don't feel sorry for me. After we complete this task, I want to do something different with my life. Not sure what yet, but the world is full of opportunities." She looked over her shoulder. "I think Bella's waking up."

Bella yawned loudly, effectively ending their discussion. She resumed her perch with her arms folded on the back of the front seats. "We're almost there, Marlow. See those trees to the left? They're close to our home. Aunt Celia is putting on the kettle right now."

"How does she know?"

Jake lowered his sunglasses and peered at her over the rims. He wiggled his eyebrows and stuck his top teeth over his bottom lip. "Ve have our vays."

Chapter 10

Heart full to the brim after revealing her family dynamics, Marlow still managed to smile at Jake's silly accent. She turned to Bella. "I think your dad's brain has been broiled. Will you please tell me how Celia knows?"

"She can see our dust trail."

"Of course." Marlow clutched her purse.

They approached another fence, but instead of a gate, a metal archway spanned the opening. The name *Long Gully* in fancy letters hung from the frame.

The absence of a gate was remarkable. In their travels today, they must have opened and closed at least a dozen. Jake had been firm in his tutelage of gate etiquette—always leave a gate as you find it—if open, leave it open, if closed, close it.

Crossing the cattle guard jarred Marlow into activity. She consulted her watch. It couldn't be one thirty already. But her aching bones attested to the fact she'd spent many hours on the worst road she could have ever imagined.

Aunt Celia waited their arrival. Marlow adjusted her ponytail and patted her cheeks. A thin layer of dust covered her face, and her hair was as straight as the spinifex grass through which they'd traveled, every wave ironed out by the dry wind. She raised her shoulders. Her clothes stuck like a second skin.

Her only consolation—Jake and Bella were in the same boat. Marlow released her anxiety with a long exhale and focused on their destination. A sprawling, single-storied house on sturdy stilts spread before her, the inviting screened-in verandah surrounded it on at least three sides. A wide, flared staircase with a low wall on each side led to the driveway where flowering shrubs added a tropical flare. A door banged. A tall, lanky woman in a bright floral dress waved a welcome as she glided down the stairs.

This was certainly not what Marlow imagined the homestead would look like. Vida and Lucky Ned chose well.

Aching in places that had never ached before, Marlow climbed out of the cruiser as did Jake and Bella, each stretching and moaning.

"Give me a kiss, Bella." Celia held out her arms and embraced the young girl. "And you must be Marlow. Come, you get a kiss too." She released Bella, and then pecked Marlow on the cheek and wrapped her arms around her. A hint of lavender wafted past. Must be a popular perfume.

"Hi, Celia. Sorry to barge in."

"Don't concern yourself. Family is family and I know we're going to have a good time together. Jake, dearie, a big hug for you. I'm so glad you were able to fix the mud guard." Nearly as tall as her nephew, she snuggled against his chest as he placed his arm around her shoulders. "Now, inside, the lot of you."

Bella bounded up the stairs with Celia on her heels.

Jake removed his hat and slapped it against his thigh. A cloud of dust billowed. "After you." He gestured for Marlow to precede him.

She tramped up the well-worn concrete steps then onto the verandah via the screen door Bella held open.

By now Celia had entered the house and called from the long, dark hall. "Let's have tea first and you can give me all the news."

The temperature dropped considerably once inside. A breeze floated through each door leading off the hall. A steady tick-tock from the grandfather clock in the corner lent an air of old-worldliness to the home. Marlow followed Celia who turned left into another hallway which led into a large, bright kitchen. White cabinets edged in red lined two walls. A rectangular, wooden table covered with a red-checkered cloth was centered on the black and white tiled floor. A six-burner stove stood to the left of the counter, and the sink and a pale green refrigerator occupied spots on either side of the back door. Marlow removed her hat and set it on the counter along with her purse and camera.

"Just this once, I'll let everyone wash at the sink." Celia nabbed a towel from a rack and gave it to Marlow. "Usually the men have to clean up outside before entering my kitchen."

Probably a wise rule.

Once they'd all washed their hands, Celia took the towel and tossed it into a basket near the door. "Washing day tomorrow."

"Have a seat here, Marlow." Jake pulled out a chair, and then sank into the one opposite. "Is Paddy back yet?"

Standing at the counter facing a window, Celia answered, "Yep. Here he is now."

Footsteps trod up to the door. "Welcome home." The screen door opened, and a young man wiped his boots on the mat then took one step inside. He immediately removed his hat as he glanced at Marlow. "Sorry. I didn't know you had a guest."

"No worries, lad. This is Marlow, a distant cousin." Celia set mugs on the table.

The 'lad' dipped his head. "G'day." His gaze strayed to Bella, then shifted quickly to Jake. An unmistakable blush heightened his tan. "Want me to start unloading, boss?"

"Yeah, Paddy. I'll be out soon."

The young man with the Barclay blue eyes slipped out of the kitchen. With peach fuzz covering his jaw, he couldn't be older than sixteen. Was he a relative?

Chapter 11

Neither Jake nor Celia seemed the least bit interested in explaining Paddy's place in the family, Marlow set aside her curiosity for a more convenient time.

"I don't want tea, Aunty Celia. I'm going to bath." Bella set a cloth bag on the table. "Here's the post." She whistled as she skipped down the hall.

"Did you buy the tatting needle and cotton I wanted?"

"Yeah." Jake rocked the chair back on two legs. "Your supplies and magazines are in my duffle bag."

"Ta. I can't wait to get started on a new piece." Celia poured milk into three mugs. "Hope you don't mind, luv, but we use powdered milk most of the time. We'll have fresh for a few days once Jake unloads the supplies."

"That will be fine." Another detail of living so far from town that never crossed Marlow's mind.

Celia added, "And I keep my good china for fancy tea parties."

"No problem." Marlow accepted the mug from Celia. "A mug holds more, anyway." From the first sip, she knew she'd have to purchase pounds of the brand of tea to take home. "This is so good."

"The tea is specially blended to be brewed over a fire. The station hands use it all the time out in the paddocks." Jake drained his mug, smacked his lips, and stood. "I'm going to unload the supplies. See youse later."

"That gives us time to have a good chinwag." Celia sat and blew on her mug of tea. "Unless you want to bath after Bella?"

"I would like to clean up."

"Of course. We'll have plenty of time to talk about family later. Bella won't be long. We have to conserve water, so we take quick showers." She chuckled. "We always say 'bath', but never do."

"I prefer a shower, anyway."

Celia set down her mug. "More tea? I would like to ask a few questions before you go."

"Yes, thanks." The third degree, or general queries? Marlow couldn't tell by Celia's demeanor whether she was glad Marlow was here or not.

After refilling both mugs, Celia cleared her throat. "The radio message I received only relayed that Jake was bringing an American relative home for a few days. Now, don't get me wrong." She patted Marlow's arm. "You're welcome to stay. That's not the problem, but I need to know why you've come." Her green eyes narrowed. "I love Jake and Bella as if they were my own kids, and I won't see them hurt again."

Straight to the point. Marlow liked that, and she could understand Celia's concerns. She cradled her cup, looked the older woman in the eyes, and briefly explained the reason for her visit.

"That is the strangest thing I've heard in a long time. We have boxes of papers and ledgers passed down from Lucky Ned and my brother who was Jake's dad. I think most of them are in the attic. The letter you seek might be with that lot."

"Good. Then maybe you can help me solve the puzzle." Marlow covered a yawn. "I assure you I plan to return home as soon as I can."

"Sorry if I came across as a sergeant major, but my Jake has women falling at his feet. He is the wealthiest grazier in the area, not to mention good-looking, and, well, decent. He's a nice chap. Did he tell you about Gail?"

Marlow nodded.

"She was one of many, but the only gold digger who succeeded in setting a wedding date. She had big plans for his money. You should have seen the remodeling ideas she had for this house. Good thing Jake hasn't lost his head like that again."

"Enough said. When I show you the letter from your grandfather, you'll understand why my late husband asked me to arrange this reunion trip. I have no intention of staying." Marlow scooted away from the table and gathered her hat, purse, and camera.

Celia stood and fiddled with the clip holding her wispy red hair in a knot. "I speak my mind, luv. Hope I didn't hurt your feelings."

"I appreciate your straightforwardness." Marlow held out her hand which Celia grasped. "Family takes care of family."

"Too right." Celia towered over Marlow, her smile softening the lines of her remarkably smooth face. "I hear Bella's out of the shower. Come, I'll show you where the towels are. You probably could do with a lie down after."

A lie down? Oh, a nap.

They traversed the long hall then Celia pointed to the left. "Here's the bathroom, and the loo is next door. Towels are in the cupboard by the sink." She turned right. "Down this way are the bedrooms. Jake's with an ensuite, then Bella's, and here is yours at the end. Mine is across the hall from yours, and all rooms open onto the verandah as well. We usually keep the doors and the windows open during the day to create cross-ventilation. I think Jake has already put your suitcase in your room. Let me know if you need anything else."

"Thank you, Celia. I appreciate your hospitality. And your frankness." She slipped into her room.

The cream-colored walls and pale aqua bedding and drapes evoked gentle ocean waves and soft sand, not an old homestead in the middle of the outback. Marlow sighed and plopped onto the bed. Her mind buzzed with remnants of Celia's conversation, but her need to bathe and change clothes pushed the incident out of focus. She unearthed her robe and toiletries bag from her suitcase which had been placed on a chair by the window and hurried to the bathroom.

The cool, rushing water erased the stains of travel and refreshed her soul. She couldn't identify why she felt as if she had returned to something familiar when she'd never been in a more alien environment before. Especially after Celia's comments, although not unwelcoming, but she certainly let Marlow know she was keeping watch.

Maybe it was just that Celia was related to Steven and therefore, in a way, to her, and she longed for an extended family. The older she grew, the more important it became. Steven's parents had been aloof, and his cousins, which she'd never met, lived on the California coast.

Marlow donned her robe and towel dried her hair before scurrying to her room where she collapsed onto the soft bed. She'd closed the door to the hall, but the one leading to the verandah was open, as were the windows on the east and south walls. The breeze teased the lace curtains, coaxing them back and forth, their passage hindered by the screens, but it seemed they wanted to escape.

Crossing her arms behind her head, she smiled as she watched their dance. She was tired beyond belief, and her head spun as if she had jet lag. The fluttering curtains mesmerized her. To some extent, she identified with them, all serene and chic on the outside, but with an inner desire to run, to escape. What exactly? Her life in Texas, her former life with Steven? Although she'd loved him, she realized after he passed away that he'd browbeaten her into submission, but during the last two years, she'd proven time and again she could handle anything. Even traveling eight and a half thousand miles, and now look at her—visiting a sheep station in the middle of back of beyond, as the locals called the outback.

Chapter 12

With Paddy's help, Jake off-loaded and stowed the supplies in thirty minutes. The kid's eagerness surprised him. When first hired, he had to be reprimanded for shirking his duties a couple of times, but his work habits soon improved. At eighteen, he had a lot to learn.

On Jake's way through the kitchen, Celia waylaid him.

"Marlow's gone for a lie down." She punched the wad of dough on her board. "I'm interested in hearing about the family news."

The way Celia handled the dough led him to believe she might have been too frank with their guest. "Aunty Celia, what did you say to Marlow?"

Another punch. "We had a nice chat."

"About?"

"I told her…um, I asked why…" She cut the dough into four sections, shaped each piece then dropped them into loaf pans.

Jake waited for her to complete her task before sliding his arm around her shoulders. "I know you're watching out for me. And I love you for how you take care of us. But I'm a big bloke. I learned my lesson with Gail."

"Harrumph. Move out of my way, please, I need to baste the roast." She grabbed two potholders and opened the oven.

Jake blew her a kiss then tromped down the passage to his office, closed the door, and lowered himself into his easy chair. Once he removed his boots, he wiggled his cramped toes and stretched his legs over the footstool. He rubbed his hand over his face and sighed. Paddy had shared unsettling news. More fences had been cut during Jake's absence. Who was intentionally setting out to disrupt life on the station and possibly destroy hundreds of animals by cutting the fences? Time and again. Surely not one of his station hands.

Everyone on a sheep station knew the importance of maintaining the fences. Not only to keep sheep in or out of paddocks, but to protect them from predators. Dingoes posed the greatest threat, but Jake had seen his share of livestock destroyed by feral pigs and packs of wild dogs. Kangaroos and wallabies, who vied with sheep for the sparse vegetation, were harder to control. Adults roos could destroy a fence but had no need to use wire cutters.

A worn leather-bound Bible lay on the small table beside his chair. He opened it to Psalm 121, his favorite, and recited the first verse. "I lift up my eyes to the hills—where does my help come from?"

Since there were no majestic hills anywhere near Long Gully, he'd often been asked why the psalm meant so much to him. Maybe it was the idea that the psalmist emphasized the act of lifting up one's eyes away from the mundane and trivial that consumed everyday time and energy.

Jake scanned the other verses. 'My help comes from the Lord. He will not let your foot slip. The Lord will keep you from all harm. He will watch over your life.' He closed the Bible and leaned back in the chair.

Why did he feel the need to read his psalm today? His gaze drifted to his desk. The photograph of Laura cuddling baby Isabel held his attention. Her sweet smile always elicited a smile from him. When he made the decision to ask Gail to marry him—or as he now referred to the event as when he accepted her proposal—he'd had a chat with Laura. He'd assured her that he would never forget her. She seemed to say via her hazel eyes that he was free to seek happiness again.

Shoving aside the footstool, he set his elbows on his knees and groaned. *Well Barclay, that didn't exactly work out, did it?*

His conversation with Celia niggled his conscience. Yeah, he was aware of women in the area who sought his company, Bridgette in particular, but he'd vowed to never be a victim again. Marlow's presence on the station was different. She had a legitimate reason for her visit. The family connection, and the mystery set in motion by Graham Barclay. Her actions while at Long Gully would confirm her reason or reveal her true motive. And in the meantime, he would focus on his job and remind Bella that their visitor would return to Texas.

He knelt by his chair and bowed his head. "Father God, thank You for a safe trip home. Open my heart to Your guidance in my relationships. I'm content to serve You alone, if that's Your will. And please help us find the person cutting our fences. He must be in need of Your grace. In Jesus's name. Amen."

Blowing out a breath, he picked up his boots and rose. Time to shower.

****

"Mmm. That's good." Celia took a second taste of the gravy and grinned. Jake always praised her cooking. Would Marlow?

"Do we need spoons on the table?" Bella asked, leaning on the arched entryway to the dining room.

"No thanks, luv, there's no sweets tonight. Please see if Marlow's ready."

"Yes, yes, yes." She skipped down the passage.

"What happened to Bella in Cunnamulla?" Celia patted Jake's shoulder as he sat at the table reading the newspaper.

"She's excited about Marlow's visit. You know how she loves an audience." The flimsy paper rustled when he flipped to the next page.

Celia tore lettuce into a bowl. Yup, Marlow's presence would probably impact the whole family. Even the veiled warning issued to her earlier hadn't caused her to flinch. Good for her. Showed she had a backbone. Although their chat had been brief, Celia sensed honesty and integrity in her responses and attitude.

Roast potatoes arranged around the beef to her satisfaction, Celia stole a glance at Jake. Oh, he was a good-looking chap, even if she said so herself. There was a boyish aura about him right now. Damp hair combed straight back, the characteristic curl flopping over his forehead, clean shaven—which was unusual for this time of day— knee shorts, T-shirt, barefoot. And he looked ten years younger. Was the change due to a shower and clean clothes? Or because of their guest?

Celia almost dropped the platter as she thought about the planned trip to Maroola Downs in two weeks. What would Bridgette have to say about Marlow's visit?

72

Chapter 13

Meow! Meow!

Marlow stirred and blinked against light filtering through the lace curtains. Another pleading yowl, and she set her feet on the floor. A dream? No, there was a black cat pawing at her verandah door. "Not going to let you in, kitty." It seemed like a lifetime ago when cats interrupted her sleep at the Cunnamulla hotel.

Rolling her stiff shoulders, she moaned. *You need more exercise, girl, especially if you want to find out what life on a sheep station entails.*

After a quick rummage through her suitcase, she unearthed the least wrinkled item, a pastel striped sundress. She hung up the rest of her clothes then brushed her hair. The door shook with a pounding knock.

"Come in."

Bella opened the door, a wide grin emphasizing her high cheek bones. "Oh, you're up. Dinner's ready"

"A cat demanded to be let in, but I didn't oblige."

"Oh, that's Toffee." Bella stepped to the door. "She gets out by pushing open the screen door, but she can't get back in. I'll let her in my room."

"She's not caramel-colored."

The young girl chuckled. "No. She's all black with a white star on her chest. I got her when I was six and named her Toffee because she's so sweet. See you in the dining room." Bella exited to the verandah and called for the cat.

Marlow buckled her white sandals and then followed a savory aroma to the kitchen where Jake sat alone at the table, bare feet propped on a chair. Overcome by a sudden wave of shyness, she hesitated at the door.

He gazed into the distance chewing on a chunk of bread, but jumped up when he noticed her. "You look, um, rested." The rest of the bread disappeared into his mouth.

"I am, thanks." Because of his visual inspection, heat rose to her face. Thankful Celia chose that moment to enter the kitchen, she asked, "Can I help?"

"Please. Take the salad, and the bread before Jake eats it all." Celia poked her nephew's chest. "Don't you dare sit at my dining table barefoot. Get your shoes, please."

"I've been caught. Excuse me." He executed a bow and hurried down the hall.

Carrying the salad bowl and basket of sliced bread, Marlow followed the woman through the archway. Celia set down the food on the large rectangular oak table that occupied the center of the pale blue room, and Marlow added her load to the placemats. There were eight chairs around the table, but it could seat at least twelve people. An oak buffet along the wall to the left was tastefully cluttered with silver serving dishes displayed on intricately crocheted doilies. Or were they tatted? Marlow had no idea how to tell the difference.

A wisp of air stirred Marlow's hair. She skirted the table and pressed her face against the screen of the open French doors, peering into the gathering dusk. Beyond the verandah, she spied the driveway they'd used earlier, but the cruiser was gone. In the distance, ghostly shadows swayed above the barely visible out-buildings. Peach and gold hues dusted the sky. At some point in her travels, she'd developed an insatiable hunger for this land.

Footsteps and voices announced Jake and Bella. Marlow sighed and turned.

A frown creased his brow, and he squinted at her. What had she done now?

"You can sit by me, Marlow." Bella indicated a chair in the middle of the table. Before she sat, she turned on the overhead light.

When everyone was seated, Jake said, "Bow with me, please." All signs of disapproval had vanished. "Thank You, Lord, for our countless blessings. May we use them for Your glory. Thank You for Celia's love and care for us. Keep us safe in Your hands. In Jesus's name. Amen."

"I missed your prayers while you were gone, Jake." Celia passed the platter of meat to him. "By the way, Marlow, the roast beef and

Yorkshire pudding are special treats. Usually we eat lamb or chicken. And, of course, we can only have fresh salad after Jake brings supplies, or in cooler weather when we can grow our own."

Vegetable garden in the outback? What next? "It looks delicious." Marlow spooned gravy over her meat and potatoes. "I haven't had homemade bread in ages."

The adults had a hard time wedging conversation in between Bella's excited renditions of her exploits in Cunnamulla. Celia laughed and commented when possible, and Jake cocked his eyebrows at Marlow more than once.

The child was in top form, wriggling in her chair, hands gesturing with every word. Her elevated pitch added to her exuberance. She was bound to crash sooner or later.

Jake's intervention was well-timed. "Isabel Joan, you need to do more eating and less talking."

The use of her full name arrested her chatter. "Sorry." She calmed down and forked a slice of potato into her mouth.

"Celia, can we review the family documents tomorrow?" Marlow wiped her mouth on the linen napkin.

"Yes. Which reminds me, Jake, please fetch your grandad's boxes from the attic. I'm sure the letter will be in one of them."

"First thing in the morning." He placed his knife and fork on his empty plate. "Bella, your turn to do the dishes."

Once the table had been cleared, Jake ushered Marlow through a door to the dark sitting room, and then to French doors that opened onto the verandah. Patio chairs lined the wall. He set three in a semi-circle. "Have a seat. Celia will join us soon."

Marlow sat and absorbed the atmosphere. Thick darkness permeated the verandah. No light pollution from cities, and the trickle of rays that emanated from the house did little to penetrate the night.

"What's your impression of our home?"

Direct and to the point. She rubbed her bare arms. "I didn't think you lived in a shack, but this house is way beyond what I imagined. I'm awed by the opportunity to learn more about your family and life on a sheep station. Thanks for agreeing to my visit."

"You can learn a lot in a couple of days." He sprang up. "Here comes Celia with the tea." He opened the screen door, took the tray from her and set it down on a small table. The tray included an oil lamp.

"A nice cuppa before we go to bed. This time I used the fresh milk Jake brought." Celia poured tea into three mugs. "The generator is on a timer and will turn off soon, Marlow, but you have a lamp in your room."

She accepted the mug from Celia. "Thanks. Yes, I noticed it, and I brought a flashlight."

"Good. Lamps are essential, but a torch is safer." Smacking his lips, Jake set his mug on the tray. "Bella only has a torch. It's not that I don't trust her, but her cat is mischievous."

The feeble light that had shone from the house was extinguished, and Bella banged through the screen door. "Dad, can I watch a film?"

"Yes, luv, but don't stay up too late."

She spun on her heel and reentered the house.

"We don't receive TV service, but we have a VCR and rent films in town."

A soundtrack indicated Bella had loaded her video.

Minutes later, Celia sighed and stood. "I've had a long day. I'm going to my room to write some letters. Welcome again, Marlow."

Jake and Marlow bade her goodnight, and she entered her room through the door off the verandah.

Marlow placed her empty mug on the tray and rubbed her arms again.

Picking up the tray, Jake said, "I'll be back in a jiffy."

Well, at least he wasn't going to leave her alone on the verandah.

He returned seconds later with a light jacket which he placed around her shoulders.

"Thank you. I forgot how cool the evenings can be." She lowered her head and took a deep breath. The musky, masculine smell of his jacket tickled her nose, in a pleasant way. A shiver crossed her shoulders, and it was not from the chilly air.

"Why did you decide to visit during our summer?"

No dancing around the issue with Jake. Marlow bit her lip. Resentment toward Steven and the degree of control he had over their finances still ate at her. "I had to complete the school year, which ended in June. Then, um…" Might as well spill the messy details. "Steven handled our finances. After he passed away, there was a lot of paperwork and red tape involved before I had access to our accounts and investments. I had to wait for CDs to mature, and well, that's why I couldn't leave until October."

During her explanation, Jake's expression morphed from interest to something akin to dismay.

Embarrassed about sharing a part of her married life she'd rather forget, Marlow stared into the ebon night and expected Jake to respond. But he didn't.

Barking in the distance broke the silence.

"Where are the dogs?" she asked.

Jake straightened and cleared his throat. "Some are in a corral near the stables, others live with the stockmen. We use well-trained kelpies to work the sheep. Bella would love a pet dog, but Celia can't tolerate them in our home. She has allowed Bella to have a cat."

"I met Toffee this evening."

The screen door squeaked open, and Bella flopped into the empty chair. "I didn't like that film. Besides, I'm tired."

"Me, too." Marlow stood and let Jake's jacket slide off her shoulders. "See y'all in the morning." She hesitated. Which door led to her room?

"I'm going in, too. I'll show you the way, Marlow. Night-night, Dad."

As she stooped to kiss him, he wrapped his arms around her.

After a few seconds, she pulled away. "What was that for?"

"Can't a father give his favorite daughter a hug?"

She didn't answer, but giggled and backed away.

"Goodnight, Bella Bear. I love you."

Bella clasped Marlow's hand and drew her down the verandah and around the corner to the first screen door.

They entered, and Bella flipped on the light. "If you need anything during the night, remember my room is right next door." Tears glistened in the young girl's eyes.

Chapter 14

No way could Marlow let the child leave. She held out her arms, and Bella fell into her embrace. "What's the matter?"

Bella clung to her, shoulders heaving.

When the sobbing eased, Marlow said, "Let's sit." She turned and settled on the bed, and Bella sank beside her.

Marlow yanked out a handful of tissues from the box on her side table and passed them to Bella. "What's bothering you?"

After wiping her eyes and blowing her nose, the young girl shrugged. "I don't understand what's going on with my dad. He hasn't called me Bella Bear in a long time. I thought he stopped because it was a baby name. So why did he use it tonight? And why did he hug me and tell me he loved me?" She twisted the tissues into shreds. "Is he dying?"

Those words cut Marlow to the quick. She wrapped her arm around Bella. "No, no." At least she had no knowledge of any illness. "He does love you, and he's concerned about you." That much Marlow did know.

"Why?"

Now was not the time to delve into deep therapy, but what could she say to address the immediate question? "He—"

"Because I'm happy and upbeat one minute, then sad the next?"

Marlow couldn't have said it better. "Exactly. Do you know why?"

"No, but when I'm excited, I talk too much. My friends always tell me so. I can't help it if I have lots to say, or when I'm with people who are too quiet. My mum used to give me the *look*. You know, the one she only used on me."

"Yes, I think all mothers have that *look*."

"That was her way of telling me to stop talking. Sometimes she used my full name, like Daddy did tonight."

Aha. So Bella's tendency to talk a lot didn't start after her mother's death. An important fact to keep in mind. "You've raised a few good points. What makes you subdued like you were toward the end of the meal tonight?"

She hung her head. "Well, Dad reminded me, and I think he's learned to use a *look* of his own." Her giggle eased some of the tension. "That's funny. I never thought about it until now."

"Quite possible. My husband used to scowl and purse his lips. Then Eileen knew he meant business." And so did Marlow.

"I wonder if Dad knows he has his own *look*? He used to tease Mum about hers all the time. I'm going to ask him." She began to stand, but the room turned dark. "I'm sorry I stayed so long. I'll light the lamp for you."

"Thanks, but don't bother. Let's use my flashlight." Marlow fished it out from the drawer she'd placed it in earlier. She turned it on and patted Bella's leg. "Don't leave yet. I have one more question."

"Okay."

"When you came into my room tonight, you seemed sad. Why did you get upset because your dad called you Bella Bear and hugged you?"

"That's a long story. I'm going to need more tissues." She reached across Marlow and nabbed the box.

"I have plenty of time."

"Mum's nickname for me was Bella Boo. And you know Daddy's. He's not a hugging kind of person, and he doesn't often say 'I love you'. So, that's why I thought something was wrong with him." She sniffed into a tissue. "I still do. Not the dying part, but he changed after Mum died."

"In what way?"

"Right after. We were all so close, but then Rick left to work on a neighbor's cattle station, and Dad, well, he sort of left too. I don't know how to explain it. He was here, but he wasn't. Do you know what I mean?"

"Sure. He was present in body, but his mind was elsewhere."

"Yeah. He worked all the time, and when he was home, he hardly talked at all. He never spoke about Mum. I'm so glad Aunty

Celia was here. She's always the same and lets me jabber on and on."

The behaviors Bella described were all too familiar. "Your daddy was, maybe still is, grieving. People handle the passing of a loved one in different ways. Some show their true emotions, and are better for it, because they express what's on their hearts. Others try to hide behind normal, everyday activities and are afraid to show any emotion at all. They give the impression they're all right, when in reality they're hurting very much."

"Do you think that's what Daddy did?"

"What do you think?"

"Probably." The young girl swiped away a tear. "He kept his hurt to himself. Maybe he didn't want to bother me, but he never talked about Mum's illness. I had to ask Aunty Celia why she died."

"It's hard to discuss events that cause us pain. What about you? I know Celia has been here for you, but how did you handle your hurt?"

She hiked a shoulder. "I didn't do anything special. Like I said, I talked to Aunty Celia, and I drew lots of pictures. Mum liked my artwork. What still hurts me is that I wasn't allowed to go to her funeral."

Big red flag. "That's too bad. You didn't get the opportunity to say goodbye." Marlow sucked in a deep breath. "When Eileen passed away, there were so many people at her service. Lots of neighbors and school friends. They shared stories about my child, and I appreciated their love and support." She cherished those memories to this day. "Why couldn't you attend the funeral?"

After sniffing into another tissue, Bella shook her head. "I was sick. Something contagious, I don't remember. I wasn't even allowed to see the people who came here."

"That would have been hard for anyone to handle."

"I know Mum died four years ago, but I still miss her. Is that natural? Do you miss your husband and daughter?"

Marlow set the flashlight on the bed, then slipped her arm around Bella's waist and pondered a reply. "Yes, it's natural to miss a loved one who passes away, no matter how long ago. It would be a problem if you couldn't move on, if you were sad all the time." She blew out a breath. "And, yes, I miss my family." More than that she wasn't prepared to share with a vulnerable young girl.

"I'm not sad, exactly, but I miss the fun times we had, and…" Bella lay her head on Marlow's shoulder.

"I understand. Mothers and daughters share a special bond." Oh, Eileen, my sweet. "There are—"

Raising her head suddenly, Bella clasped Marlow's arm. "Was I wrong to want Daddy to marry Gail? You know about her, right? At first, she was everything."

"She filled the emptiness left by your mum."

"That's what I was trying to say."

"You weren't wrong about wanting your dad to remarry. Consider this. Did he love your mum? Of course. Did he love Gail? I suspect so since he asked her to marry him, but that doesn't mean he stopped loving Laura. The same applies to you."

"Yeah." Bella set the box of tissues back on the table. "But no one can ever take Mum's place." Her heavy sigh escaped into the silence.

A few seconds later, Marlow asked, "Did our chat help?"

"Yes, thanks."

"If you are still worried about your dad, maybe you should talk to him. That might spur him into sharing his feelings with you, which would be good for you both."

"I suppose." Bella stood and turned when she reached the door. "I'm glad you came to visit."

"Me, too. I hope there'll be time for you to show me around."

"I'd love to. Tomorrow. We can get started right after brekky."

"I'd like that. Goodnight."

"Night-night." Her steps plodded down the hall to the next room.

Swamped by all Bella had shared, Marlow rubbed her forehead. The child had a good handle on her problems. She just needed Marlow's professional guidance and support from Jake.

Marlow picked up the flashlight, located her toiletries bag, and headed to the bathroom, but was waylaid by Celia holding an oil lamp.

"I heard you and Bella talking. Would you mind coming to the kitchen with me?"

"Okay." Was she in for another lecture?

Once in the kitchen, Celia set the lamp on the table and sat. "I hope you don't mind, but I'm curious about your chat."

Marlow settled opposite Celia and related the gist of their

discussion.

"My little Bella is worried about Jake. That's just like her. She has such a sweet, gentle soul."

"In my opinion, she processed Laura's passing surprisingly well for an eight-year-old." Marlow tilted her head. "However, I think it still rankles that she wasn't allowed to attend the funeral."

Sighing, Celia traced lines of color on the checkered tablecloth. "She had the mumps, poor kid."

A good enough reason to keep her isolated.

"I've been so concerned about Jake and Bella, especially after that Gail women entered their lives. Praise the Lord, he came to his senses before they married, but that set Bella back."

"Did Jake tell you I have experience in counseling children?"

She nodded.

"I'll help Bella as much as I can while I'm here."

Celia reached over and took Marlow's hand. "Thank you, luv."

They sat hand in hand for a few seconds.

No longer intimidated by the older woman, Marlow squeezed her fingers. "I'm going to turn in." She stood, and then a tangible way to help Bella budded in her mind. "Where is Laura buried?"

"There's a cemetery out beyond the far storage shed. Huge gum trees stand guard by the stone wall." She paused. "All our family is buried there. My parents, Ned and Vida. My brother Patrick and his wife Maud, who are Jake's parents, and their twins. And, of course, Laura."

Marlow headed down the darkening hall, the light from Celia's lamp waning with each step. A family cemetery close to the homestead. Another aspect of bush life Marlow never anticipated.

Chapter 15

A harsh light infused the room. Squinting at the lace curtains fluttering like captured butterflies, Marlow eased out of bed. The sensation of calm and peace she'd originally experienced when first entering the room remained. She checked her watch. Just after six. The sun had been up for almost an hour. Surely, Jake and Celia were awake. She slipped into her robe and tiptoed to the bathroom for a quick wash. Back in her room, she donned an aqua skirt and white blouse, buckled her sandals, and brushed her hair. She made her bed and set Koala Milton between the pillows, then changed her mind. He was cute and all and would always serve as a reminder of her time in Melbourne, but for now, he could reside in the top drawer of her dresser.

Eager to explore, Marlow opened the door to the verandah. A rooster crowed in the distance. The cool night air that required her use of a thin blanket had already turned traitor. She approached the stairs that led to the garden and glanced at the other bedroom doors. No one else in sight. Good. The screen door was latched and squeaked when she opened it. A spring attachment closed it automatically behind her.

Facing east, the sun hit her full in the face as she descended the stairs. Should have brought her sunglasses—and camera, but she had plenty of time to take pictures. On the last step, she shaded her eyes with her hand and absorbed the scene. A fenced area about the size of a tennis court contained an in-ground pool, a tank more likely as the water was not crystal clear, lawn, flowers, and gum trees. Jake hadn't said much about the house, but Marlow never imagined such beauty could exist in the arid expanse they'd traveled through yesterday. But then she recalled Bella's lesson on their use of artesian water.

Marlow followed a stone path lined with thick honey-myrtle bushes. Their sweet scent mixed with the tang of the eucalyptus. The walkway led to a long metal bench on the far side of the pool. Shrubs surrounded the area, sheltering her from the sun behind and the house in front. Toffee sauntered over the grass and jumped onto her lap. She stroked the soft, purring body and glanced toward the homestead. Bella's room was next to hers, and Jake had the last room.

As if summoned by her thoughts, he appeared on the verandah. He opened the screen door, waited for it to close, then propped one foot on the low wall, and rested his elbow on his knee. He shaded his eyes and surveyed the area. Because of Marlow's position, he couldn't see her, but she had a clear view of him. In brown jeans, boots, an unbuttoned beige shirt, and his hair in a disordered mess, he looked like a young boy.

Heat rose to Marlow's cheeks, and she forced her gaze to the shimmering water. Her pulse raced, and her palms were moist. What was wrong with her? She looked at Jake again. Granted, he was probably one of the most attractive men she'd met, but why her adolescent reaction? Aha. His vulnerability tugged at her heart. She wanted to climb the stairs, smooth his hair, ease the frown from his tanned forehead.

No. You're going back to Texas.

Jake buttoned his shirt then turned to open the door, but paused and glanced into the garden. Marlow held her breath, leaning back as far as she could. Relieved to hear the bang of the door, she pushed Toffee off her lap, scurried through the garden and up the stairs to her room. The accordion file containing all her documents lay on the bed, a timely reminder as to her reason for being at Long Gully. She snagged her hair into a ponytail and headed to the kitchen.

No one was in the room, but place settings and covered serving dishes filled the table. She searched the counter tops for the coffee maker. The nutty aroma mingled with the smell of bacon, but there was no sign of the pot. Of course. On the stove. They wouldn't use appliances when electricity was limited. She filled a mug, added milk, then spied an ajar door on the far wall. Sipping the coffee, she peeked around the door into a pantry the size of a small bedroom, lined with shelves groaning under the weight of jars, cans, boxes, containers of all sizes. Enough food to feed an army. She took one last look then stepped to the screen door.

Jake's cruiser was parked under the carport. Large trees provided shade, but there was no lush lawn or flowers. A packed earth path led to another fenced area. Exploring would have to wait because she'd asked Bella to be her guide and didn't want to disappoint her. Marlow turned as footsteps and voices approached from the hall.

"There you are." Bella gave Marlow a one-armed hug. "I'm starving."

"Morning. Did you sleep well?" Jake asked as he sat.

"Yes, thanks." She set her mug on the table. "Need any help, Celia?"

"No thanks, luv. Everything's ready. Let's eat."

The platters filled with bacon, plump sausages, scrambled eggs, and grilled tomatoes soon emptied. Even Jake joined in the upbeat conversation until the door opened and a squat, fiftyish woman entered.

The raven-haired visitor said, "Hey, you're making so much noise I thought you had a dozen guests." She set her hands on her amply hips and cocked her head.

"Sorry, Nellie. This is our American cousin, Marlow. She's staying a few days." Jake gestured toward Marlow. "Nellie's son, Ernie, works for me. He's my deputy manager. Nellie and Mary, her daughter-in-law, help with the housework."

Nellie placed fresh eggs on the counter and shook Marlow's hand. "Welcome. I saw you arrive yesterday. If you have any washing, put it in the basket in the bathroom." She tweaked Bella's cheek. "And you, little lady, get your clothes out before I start the machine. Not like last week when I had to hunt for them." Humming, she sauntered down the hall, her denim skirt swaying with each step

"I will, Nellie. I promise." Bella carried a stack of dishes to the sink. "Dad, I'm going to show Marlow around. How far can we go?"

"Only to the outbuildings."

"But Dad—"

"That's all you'll have time for this morning." Jake stood and snatched his hat from the rack by the back door. "Marlow, you should change out of those sandals. Closed shoes are best for the outdoors where spiders and scorpions abound. They come inside at times."

"I've noticed."

"Bella, concentrate on your schoolwork."

The girl rolled her eyes as she tucked her yellow shirt into her khaki shorts. "Daaaad."

He smiled, bopped her on the head with his hat, and opened the door. His retreating steps crunched on the gravel driveway.

After her visit with Bella the previous evening, Marlow desperately wanted to chat with Jake. She'd have to wait until evening. "I'm curious about the School of the Air program." Marlow carried the last of the dishes to the sink.

"Aunty Celia, I have a super idea. Can Marlow supervise me while I work today? She is a teacher, after all." Bella's eager expression bounced from her aunt to Marlow.

Celia glanced at Marlow. "Yeah. That will give me time to look through the boxes of old papers. See if I can find the letter."

"That reminds me. I need to show you what the envelope looks like and change my shoes." Heading down the hall, Marlow remembered Nellie's admonition, and she called over her shoulder, "Don't forget your clothes, Bella." Back in her room, she slipped on a pair of socks and sneakers, stuffed her sunglasses into her pocket, and located all the necessary documents. Next, she gathered her dirty clothes and carried them to the bathroom where Nellie had three piles already sorted.

"Thank you, Nellie. I appreciate your help."

"No worries, luv. The machine does most of the work."

Papers in hand, she returned to the kitchen, passing Bella along the way.

"This is the letter from Graham. After you read it, you'll understand why I made the trip. I have the family tree, the original envelopes addressed to George's and Betsy's descendants, and the instructions with the coded word or words." Marlow set the items on the table.

Celia viewed the yellowed envelopes. "At least now I know what to look for. I'll get started as soon as I clean up."

"When the school session is over, I can help with the search."

A frown marred Celia's forehead for a moment.

Marlow fingered her sunglasses. "Cousin Henry was hesitant, too. He seemed to enjoy going through his old records."

"I want to do it by myself. After all, the papers belonged to my father and my brother."

"I Understand."

"Bella's a good student, so you shouldn't have any problems." Celia turned on the faucet over the sink. "She's in Year six. Her teacher works with about thirty-five students, divided into smaller classes. The kids are scattered over several hundred miles, and time is of the essence. No dilly-dallying. Let me know if you need a break in the school room, which, by the way, is part of Jake's office. The two-way transmitter is battery operated. Oh, and any emergency messages will take precedence over the lesson."

An outback 911 service. "I've read about the school program, but I'm excited to see it in operation."

"It's been part of our lives for so long."

"Bella missed last Friday and Monday sessions. Are those absences counted against her?"

"No, no. Of course, the ideal would be for children to participate every weekday, but kids in the outback are given some leeway. A certain number of sets in each subject have to be completed before the final exams. We make sure Bella keeps up with her classmates by doing the work she misses during the week." Celia sloshed soapy water over the dishes. "I worked her extra hard last Thursday."

"I remember Jake asked her about schoolwork yesterday. What a great accommodation."

On entering the kitchen, Bella pointed to the wall clock. "Marlow, I have to sign in before nine. We have about thirty minutes to explore. Are you ready?"

"Yes. Where do we start?"

"This way." Bella opened the screen door, and Marlow followed her down the concrete steps to the driveway. "One thing to remember about the rooms in the house is that they all open onto the verandah. Even the kitchen. Obviously not this door, but the one by the stove which we don't use much. That's why we have a rolling storage cart there. And there's a ping-pong table on the other side. Rick and Dad used to play all the time. I don't play much."

Marlow noticed a faucet over an old sink against the wall, several pairs of well-worn boots lined up under it, and a few small towels stacked on the side. "That's the place to wash up."

"Yeah. Aunty Celia is very strict, especially about muddy

boots." Bella giggled and kept walking. "But we don't have mud very often."

Marlow had to lengthen her stride to keep up. They reached the gum trees and fenced area she'd spied earlier. The vegetable garden measured at least thirty by thirty feet and contained rows of raised beds. A tarp provided shade to a section at the back.

"Here's our veggie patch. You can see we have tomatoes, cabbages, spinach, and those purple things. I can never remember the name. Abergrins. I don't know."

"Aubergines. We call them eggplant in America."

"That's funny. But they do look like big, fat eggs. Do you want to go in? The gate's by the washing room." Bella pointed to the rear of the house where Nellie and a younger woman entered carrying baskets of clothes.

"Another time."

"On the other side of the garden are the clothes' lines."

Who needed a tumble dryer when the sun did the work for free? Marlow tilted her head. "What's making that humming sound?"

"That's our generator. Diesel powdered."

Marlow spied a rectangular, metal contraption close to the washroom.

"Dad says if the fuel wasn't so expensive we could have electricity all the time. The generator is on a timer. We have power from nine o'clock in the morning until one, then from six in the evening until ten. There's another generator by the shearing shed, and the workers have one, too."

"Interesting. Let's keep going."

Glowing with gusto, Bella walked backward along the path like a professional tour guide. "You should see the garden in the cooler months. We have beans, cauliflower, spinach, broccoli, tomatoes, and lettuce." She turned and skipped, her braids bobbing on her shoulders. "And that is one of our water tanks."

The circular concrete tower stood close to the house. "I saw one by the pool, but it was metal."

"This one catches rainwater. We use it for drinking, and the concrete helps to keep it cool. The water we use in the bath, the pool, and for the washing comes from the artesian well. It's drinkable, but doesn't always taste nice. Dad says it's something about the high mineral content. Whatever that means. And you'll notice another tank by the shearing shed. Since the building is so long, it's a good place to catch rainwater."

Marlow wiped sweat from her upper lip. Only eight-thirty and already her blouse stuck to her skin. She'd read that this area of the outback received about fifteen inches of rain a year. She could do with a shower about now. "What's next?"

"Come this way." Bella strode away from the house, then shielded her eyes as she turned and pointed to the roof. "Solar panels heat our water. We have a metal roof. Do you know why?"

"No."

"The same reason we have stone and not wooden walls. Well, another reason we have stone walls is because termites would eat the wood."

"Slow down, Bella." Marlow used a low tone. The child's enthusiasm level was reaching boiling point. "How about we continue tomorrow?"

Bella took in a deep breath and checked Marlow's watch. "We have time. Just a few more things to show you since Dad won't let me go past the sheds." She latched onto Marlow's arm. "Fires. Grassfires. That's why we have stone walls and a metal roof. And see those large letters on the roof? They spell Long Gully so pilots know which station is which."

"I suppose from the air, one homestead looks much like another."

"Yeah. Let's go to the sheds." They headed west along the forked driveway. Bella pointed to the left. "That's the way we drove in yesterday, so we'll go this way."

Weathered stone and corrugated iron buildings hunkered down among the tall gum trees. The branches swayed in the breeze, stirring up the ever-present tang of eucalyptus.

"I'll tell you what all the building are used for, and then we can go inside some of them." Bella picked up the pace. "Here is our chook house. Sometimes I collect the eggs, but ol' Flash, the largest rooster, doesn't like me."

"There are lots of chickens." Of course, not only for eggs, but for consuming.

"Yeah. Next are the stables."

Four horses ate from a trough and several more stood at the far end vying for the shade from the nearby trees. Tails swished non-stop. Unseen dogs barked a greeting.

"I don't see Dad's horse in the corral, that means he rode Sullivan this morning."

Jake on horseback. Marlow's toes curled in her sneakers. "What kind of horse does he ride?"

"A bay. Beautiful red-brown coat and black tail and mane."

The unmistaken aroma of the stables and corral followed them. Marlow covered her nose. "Do you ride?" Flies buzzed incessantly. No wonder screens protected every door and window of the homestead.

Bella shrugged. "Not much. Come on, we need to keep going."

Two pickups and another SUV shared space with a trio of motorbikes parked beside the closest building, all vehicles coated in red dust. "Who rides the bikes?"

"Dad and the stockmen. Sometimes they take the horses, but mostly they use the bikes." Bella tilted her head. "Have you ever ridden a bike? Dad could teach you—"

"I have, but we need to move on."

"Righto." Bella pointed ahead. "The shearing shed and woolshed are by the West Two paddock."

In the distance, Marlow could see fencing marching off into the distance.

"Long Gully is divided into six paddocks. Daddy got the smart idea to name them. We have West One and Two, Central One and Two, and East One and Two."

"On such a large place, it's probably helpful to identify them. What's that circular fenced area used for?"

"That's for when we muster the sheep for shearing. Each paddock has a fence parallel to the main one, like a special lane. Sheep are driven into them, then they come out here, and wait for the shearing. Daddy can explain more."

"I'll be sure to ask him." If he gave her the chance.

"Why didn't you bring your camera?"

"I was in a hurry. Besides, I like to take my time and plan my shots." At the pace Bella set, Marlow would have wasted film.

"Here are the barn and the machinery shed where Dad stores lots of things. And, of course, you see the silo for feed storage. Behind these building are cottages for the married station hands. The single men share living quarters which are way down the drive." She stopped so suddenly, Marlow almost bumped into her. Her mood transformed as perceptibly as if it changed color. Shoulders slumped, a frown creased her brow, and the corners of her mouth turned down.

"What's wrong, Bella?"

The girl set her hands on her non-existent hips and stared into the distance.

Marlow glanced at the child and then at a clump of trees shimmering in the heat-haze about a quarter mile away. "Bella?"

She offered Marlow a ghost of a smile. "Let's go in the shearing shed."

"It's almost nine o'clock." Not only was it time for school, but Marlow wanted to be present when Celia found the letter.

Bella pivoted and marched toward the house, yelling over her shoulder, "You can see the rest by yourself." She broke into a run.

Dismayed by Bella's swift mood change, Marlow glanced at the distant grove of trees again and then at the figure of the young girl disappearing around the house. Since Celia insisted on searching for the letter, Marlow would have more time to address Bella's behavioral issues, if Jake agreed.

Chapter 16

When Marlow entered the office a couple of minutes before nine o'clock, Bella had already signed in with Miss York. The young girl's tone toward her teacher gave no hint of her earlier behavior, and Marlow let the incident slide. For the moment.

The School of the Air program was organized to the max. Bella gave Marlow a large envelope containing the lesson plans and indicated she sit in her father's armchair near his desk. The comfortable, brown plaid chair had a matching footstool. Marlow propped up her feet, and followed the explicit instructions provided for the helper. According to Celia, kids in the outback were provided with the same work as their classmates in regular schools.

The thirty-minute arithmetic lesson concluded, followed by instructions for a history project due next week, and for the English grammar and composition assignments which needed to be completed before class the following day.

"That's all for today, Year sixes." Miss York's voice echoed in the office. "Time for my next group. Work hard, boys and girls. Cheerio. Over and out."

Whistling, Bella operated a couple of dials. The transmitter squawked. "Another school day to mark off my calendar."

Marlow's mind reeled. The back and forth conversation over the airwaves was hard to follow at first. Not only did Bella and Miss York talk, but other students did, too, punctuated by static and the word *over* every two seconds, it seemed.

"That was interesting, Bella. Thank you for letting me sit with you."

"It was easy today, but I don't like arithmetic. Sometimes Aunty Celia has to help me." The transmitter sat to the left of a long table against the wall. Bella gathered her materials and rolled her chair to the other end of the table. "Um…" She hung her head. "I'm sorry I shouted at you. Are we still friends?"

Not what Marlow expected. Any words of censure she might have used disappeared in a heartbeat. "Of course." She rose and stood over Bella, hand on her shoulder. "It sounded like you were angry. Is there anything you want to talk about?"

Bella shook her head and sniffled. "Not now. I have lots of work to do. Please get my grammar workbook from the basket on the middle shelf."

The bookcase behind Marlow contained a number of baskets and containers filled with various school-related materials. She handed the workbook to Bella and stepped back.

"Ta. I think I understand my assignment, but can you check it when I'm done?"

"Certainly. What else will you do this morning?"

"I have to complete my composition. I'm almost halfway done. We have to write a story about someone we admire. I chose Aunty Celia, but please don't tell her. If I'd met you last week, I could have written about you. Maybe I still can. I have time to start over."

The child was on a roll. Marlow held up her hands. "Thanks for the compliment, but your original idea is perfect. Celia will appreciate your story. Now, open your workbook."

Bella blushed. "Yes, Mrs. Barclay. Certainly, Mrs. Barclay." She grinned and opened the book. "Oh, and I want to begin my history project."

"Good. It never pays to procrastinate."

"I know that word. Pro—"

"Bella."

She turned, looked at Marlow, and pressed her lips together.

They both chuckled, then Bella bent over the workbook and began to read.

Before Marlow could return to her chair, Celia entered the office carrying a tray with teapot, two mugs, a couple of napkins, and a plate of Empire biscuits—delicious shortbread-type cookies sandwiched together with red jam, and covered with a thin glaze. Milton's mother in Melbourne had introduced them to Marlow.

"Thank you. We're ready for a break." Marlow took the tray and set it on the corner of Jake's desk.

Instead of leaving, Celia hovered by the door, a deep frown

creasing her brow. She twisted her fingers together, obviously troubled.

Aha. Marlow's stomach flip-flopped. "You found the letter."

"No. It wasn't in those boxes. I'll have to ask Jake where other important papers are kept. He might know his dad better than I did." She spun on her heel and left the room.

"I'm thirsty."

Bella's statement jostled Marlow's worrisome thoughts about Celia. "Me, too." She poured the tea and set two cookies on each napkin.

"I'm not allowed to eat or drink where I'm working. I'm messy sometimes." Bella propelled her chair to the other corner of Jake's desk. "Thanks."

They sipped and nibbled and chatted about Bella's history project on former British Colonies.

"I've been thinking, Marlow." Bella set down her mug, drew her legs into the oversized chair, and hugged her knees. "America was a British colony a long time ago, right?"

"Yes."

"Maybe I can incorporate your list of differences into my project. If you agree, I'll give you credit for the details."

"That's a grand idea."

"Ooh." Bella squeezed her legs. "I bet no other kid will include anything about America."

"I'm glad you remembered my list." Marlow took the last bite of her biscuit. "Do any of the workers' children ever join your school sessions?"

"There have been a few. All were older and are now in boarding school or working. Some of those in high school will come home for the holidays." Bella glanced at the clock above the transmitter. "Enough time off. You don't have to stay with me, but you can if you like. Dad has lots of books on the shelves behind his desk." Seated in her chair, she scooted herself back to her work area.

"I'll stay." Marlow was curious as to what troubled Celia, but decided it best to let her broach the subject.

From the comfort of the swiveling chair, Marlow surveyed the office. Except for Bella's school setup to the left, the room was definitely a man's domain. Large, oversized furniture devoid of lacey doilies. Items on the mahogany desk which faced the door were arranged efficiently. No unnecessary clutter or fancy pencil holders or cute calendars.

Marlow picked up a small picture frame that she must have nudged sideways earlier. She sighed. This must be Laura, holding a baby. She had the same intense hazel eyes and chestnut hair as her daughter. A soft smile graced her beautiful face.

Loss. Reminders could be both painful and therapeutic.

Marlow replaced the photo and glanced at Bella. Muscles in her stomach knotted. The child was so young when her mother passed away. Bella hummed a pop tune and wiggled in her seat as she wrote in her workbook. Although only twelve years old, she exhibited her share of resilience.

Blinking back a tear, Marlow continued her surveillance. Rays from the open skylight reflected on photographs of sheep in various stages of life displayed on the opposite wall. Underneath them, an aerial shot of the station begged further inspection. But next to the armchair, Marlow spied a small oval table which held a well-worn Bible. She closed her eyes and imagined Jake sitting there reading from his favorite verses.

Rustling papers, and Marlow's eyes flew open. She shot a glance at the photo of Laura. She seemed to be staring right at her. But instead of feeling intimidated or uncomfortable, Marlow had the impression Laura welcomed her.

Whoa. Marlow shook her head. *Focus, girl.* She studied the wall above Bella's worktable. A map of Australia, a world map, and a chart of measurements covered the area. She supposed a similar setup existed in many homesteads across the outback. What a contrast to the numerous classrooms where she'd spent a lifetime.

"I'm done." Bella whistled and approached the desk, a stack of papers in hand.

Marlow sat up.

"Please look in Daddy's bottom right-hand drawer. Take out an envelope and put my work in it."

"Certainly." She did as Bella requested. This was the second time she had asked Marlow to do something. The child seemed to enjoy giving orders, but since the requests were worded politely, Marlow didn't mind.

"The mail plane comes on Fridays to pick up our out-going post."

"Does the mailman do door-to-door delivery?" Marlow suppressed a smile.

"No, silly. Oh, you're teasing me."

"Trying to. But seriously, how do you get your, um, post?"

"When anyone from the station goes to Cunnamulla they take our post and bring back whatever's in our box. But the mail plane comes every Friday, usually in the afternoon. Paddy—you met him your first day here—is responsible for collecting the out-going post which is always placed in here." Bella unearthed a large canvas bag from a cabinet under her table and gave it to Marlow. The name *Long Gully* was stamped on the side.

"When I'm finished with my school assignments, Aunty Celia takes the bag to the kitchen and everyone can put in their post. Then, when the pilot radios us or when Paddy hears the plane, he takes everything on a motorbike to the airstrip, and comes back with our stuff."

"Very interesting. Which reminds me. I need to write to my friends back home again." She took the papers from Bella. "What all do you have here?"

"My grammar pages, my arithmetic assignment, and my completed composition. Miss York's going to like my story."

"Do you want me to check anything?"

"No, thanks. I understood the assignments, and I think I got everything correct this time."

"All of this will be mailed to your teacher?" Marlow slid the pages into the envelope and placed it in the bag.

"Uh-huh. Our work must be sent in each week to be graded." She paused and a frown marred her forehead. "The final exams will be mailed to us soon because the term is almost over."

"So, a plane comes by once a week. Why can't it deliver fresh food and other supplies?"

Setting her hands on her hips, Bella planted herself in front of Marlow. "Well, because it's a small plane, and it wouldn't be able to carry everything we and the other stations out here need. And besides we aren't—" She clicked her tongue. "I don't know all the reasons. Ask Daddy."

"I will."

"Whew. I'm tired. And hungry."

Marlow checked her watch. It was close to twelve thirty.

"I'll work on my history project this afternoon. Come, let's see if Aunty Celia needs help with lunch."

Bella picked up the tray, and Marlow followed her slowly down the hall. She really needed to talk with Jake about the child. From a counselor's perspective, she had one set of questions, but from a grieving mother's point of view, she had many others.

Light from one of the opened doors fell onto the pale yellow wall, revealing a large landscape depicting an Australian outback scene Marlow had not noticed previously. She stopped and traced the red hills in the distance to the line of gum trees and down to the blue-gray billabong. Acrylic. No artist's signature. Hmm. The feel of the paint made her fingers itch to dabble with acrylics as she had in college and the early days of her marriage. But then Steven's critical comments regarding her creations rammed into her mind. Covering her ears, she marched to the kitchen. She would not allow Steven's negativity to cloud her adventure, and she forced a smile as she sat opposite Bella.

Celia had roast beef sandwiches and salad on the table. She poured boiling water into the teapot then covered it with the tea cozy. Her silence and ram-rod straight back reminded Marlow of Celia's odd behavior earlier.

But Bella set the tone for their discourse. "My favorite. I love leftover beef on your bread, Aunty Celia. Wait until you try the sangers, Marlow. They're the best. Do you cook extra so you have leftovers?"

"Shush, child." Celia sat without looking at her grandniece. "Marlow, will you say grace, please?"

Caught off guard, she answered, "Yes." Then had to corral her memories to a time when she gave thanks regularly. But the words wouldn't come. She resorted to phrases she'd heard repeated all her life. "Dear Father, thank you for this food, and bless the hands that prepared it. In Jesus's name. Amen."

If Steven had heard her prayer, he would have… *Stop*. Neither Bella nor Celia reacted negatively and that's what mattered. Heated cheeks were the only reminder of her embarrassment Marlow needed. Would spending time away from the hustle and bustle of general life enable her to loosen more of the nails holding her soul captive? She shook her head, and bit into the thick sandwich.

Celia had used an unusual spread on the bread. Horseradish,

maybe. Marlow was hooked by the first bite. "You're right, Bella. These are delicious."

"I told you."

"Does Jake come home for lunch?"

Covering her mouth with her hand, Bella said, "Not often. Most days he eats with the stockmen."

Celia cocked her head. "How many times have I told you not to talk with food in your mouth?" She glared at Bella, then added, "If the men are going to be out all day, they might cook over a fire, or take ready-to-eat tucker. Besides helping with the housework, Mary and Nellie take turns cooking an evening meal for the single blokes. I used to, but I'm getting too old for that responsibility."

The tone of Celia's words indicated she was still miffed. Marlow finished her salad without looking at the older woman.

"Can I have another sanger, please, Aunty Celia?"

"Finish your salad first." Celia poured tea into mugs and passed one to Bella. "Why did you come running in from your tour?"

Nothing escaped her. Marlow was interested in the child's answer, too.

Chomping on a piece of cucumber, Bella glared at her aunt.

"Don't look at me in that tone of voice."

Bella swallowed and blinked. "How'd you know? Oh, never mind. You always know everything." Salad finished, she carried her dishes to the sink. "I don't want another sanger now."

"Watch your attitude, lass. Answer my question, please."

Bella hung her head. "Sorry. I ran because…it was time for school." She kissed Celia's cheek. "Thanks for lunch. I'm going to my room to work on my history project."

Marlow was surprised by the answer, and by Celia's raised eyebrows, it was not what she anticipated, either. Bella had rushed back to the house way before sign in time.

"That child. I hope you can help her sort out her moods because I'm running out of patience."

"I will try. One moment she was describing in minute detail, what each shed was used for. The next, she bolted like a frightened kangaroo. By the time I entered the school room, she was talking to Miss York and acted as if nothing had happened."

"Her rapid mood swings are what I don't understand. She can turn as quickly as a windmill in a storm." Celia added milk and more tea to their mugs. "Was the school session anything like you expected?"

"Much more. I was fascinated by the students' rates of participation, and how they all interacted with each other. Everything is so well-organized. Bravo to School of the Air."

"We're proud of them all right." Celia drained her mug but cradled it in her hands.

Marlow studied her face. Something definitely troubled her. "Celia, when you brought the tea tray to the school room—"

"Not now." She scooted back her chair and scowled. "I need time to digest what I discovered. And please, don't tell Jake."

That serious?

Chapter 17

Shade from the lone ghost gum tree barely covered Jake and his horse. He swiped a hand across his sweaty brow. When he set out this morning, he had no idea he'd need to visit W-1 paddock to check on fence repairs. Although he preferred to do most jobs on horseback, today his motorbike would have been more suitable. His two-way radio crackled on his belt, but he wouldn't use it as Ernie had requested a face-to-face report.

A dust trail heralded the stockman's approach. Jake swigged the last of the water from his canteen as the whine of the bike grew louder.

Ernie performed a half donut move and came to a stop. He grinned and removed his goggles. "Hey, boss, we finished the repair. Greg thinks the damage is recent. The wire is shiny, and it hasn't snagged any wool or grass yet."

"In the last day or two?"

"Yeah. Whoever did it, left no trace. Just like the other incidents."

"Do you have any idea who's doing this?"

"Sorry, boss. I know all the blokes who work here, well, except for young Paddy."

Jake dismounted and rubbed Sully's head. The bay snorted. "It can't be Paddy. He wasn't here when the cutting began."

"Too right."

"I can't hire more chaps just to patrol the fences. That means extra work for all of us." Jake dug in the dirt with the heel of his boot. "I've been thinking about one of the ringers I hired for the mustering this year."

"Frank, the bloke who never smiled? Who had a chip on his shoulder so big it made him walk lopsided?"

"Yeah, I'd forgotten his name. Could he be the culprit? I know he wasn't satisfied with his money, but I paid him what we'd agreed on."

"I don't think so. Heard he'd been arrested in Brisbane and is still in the clink."

"Well, all we can do is be vigilant and make repairs as soon as possible."

"I trust Greg like he was my brother. We'll keep closer watch on the others. But I sure hope it's an outsider." Ernie used his shirttail to wipe a layer of dust off the lenses of his goggles. "Um, were you home this morning when Mary and Nellie came to do the washing?"

"Yeah."

"I'm worried about Mary."

"Why? She didn't come in the house, but I heard her in the washroom."

"This is why I didn't want to give my report over the radio. I'd rather not speculate, but can Miss Celia check her over?"

"Something medical then?"

Ernie dipped his head. "Yeah."

"Of course. No need to ask. You know Celia likes to keep her nursing skills honed."

"Good. I'll tell Mary. Better get going." Ernie revved the motor.

"Wait. Is the waterhole in the C-2 paddock full?"

"Yeah. Why?"

"I'm going home that way and Sully needs a drink. I'll tell Celia to expect a visit from Mary. Hope it's nothing serious. Ta, Ernie, see you tomorrow." Jake set his hat on his head and climbed into the saddle. He urged Sully forward as Ernie sped away.

The journey home via the C-2 paddock would take a little longer, but Jake needed time alone. He'd spent the whole day with Greg, his manager, catching up on station business. Wool sales, the increased cost of fuel for vehicles and running the homestead, controlling the infestation of noogoora burr. And the fence cutting.

"All in all, Sully, we're doing all right."

The horse's ears twitched. Probably used to Jake's monologues by now, the animal seldom reacted. He'd been ridden hard today and deserved a slow walk home.

"If the price of wool holds, we'll be in the black. Now we need to keep all these wooly rocks safe. You're a smart old thing, Sully.

You wouldn't eat noogoora seedlings, would you? How can sheep be attracted to something so toxic?"

They made steady progress toward the waterhole which shimmered in the distance like a mirage, except Jake knew it was real. He'd help dig out the hollow when he was a teen. Sheep weren't in this paddock right now, and the vegetation had already recovered. With the wet season on the horizon, the red earth would soon be covered in green. A welcome sight.

Sully increased his speed. Even Jake could sense a difference in the smell of the air. Water. A couple of kangaroos fled the scene as the horse whinnied. Jake dismounted and allowed Sully to drink his fill.

Swishing away flies, Jake surveyed the area. All seemed in good working order. Water at the optimum level, ready for the return of a mob the next day. The solar panel controlling the pump operating as designed. Banks intact, but low enough for the sheep to get in and out of the water. He checked his watch. Half past four. It'd take him an hour to get home.

"Let's go, old man."

Sully lowered his head, but stood still for Jake to mount. He steered the horse around the reservoir and headed south. Lulled by the gentle gait, Jake's thoughts meandered away from station business toward personal affairs.

Had Celia located the mysterious letter? If so, what would the puzzle reveal? Did Bella have a successful school session? Overall, she was a good student, but some days Celia reported the child clammed up and consequently, her work suffered.

And Marlow, did she enjoy her tour of the homestead? Bella would have been a superb guide as she loved to be in charge. One day at Long Gully was not long enough for Marlow to experience the harshness of the day-to-day realities of living on a remote sheep station, but he wondered what she thought about their way of life.

Jake shifted in the saddle. "Do I care what Marlow thinks, Sully?" He chewed the inside of his cheek. Although Jake kept telling himself he was not looking for romance, his heart had other ideas. Recalling how much fun they'd had at breakfast and how easily Marlow contributed to the chitchat, made him long for a soul mate. Someone whose eyes would crinkle at the corners when she smiled at him. Who would listen so intently to him it would seem as if no one else was in the room.

Sully snorted and picked up the pace.

Returned to reality with a jolt, Jake nudged the horse's flank.

Keep ya shirt on, Barclay. You still don't know for sure if she has a devious reason for visiting Long Gully.

Chapter 18

Close to five o'clock, Marlow eased out of her chair on the side verandah. She and Celia had spent a couple of hours there, enjoying the view of the garden and pool, writing letters, and chatting about family and life on the station. The more Marlow heard about the stark realities of living on a remote homestead the more she felt she'd come home to a place she'd always known. For the life of her, she couldn't fathom why. Although eager to find Graham's letter, she understood why Celia set aside the search after lunch. The secret had remained dormant for decades. A few more days wouldn't matter. Besides, Marlow was enjoying the laidback lifestyle.

She yawned. At some point, they'd both dozed off, and Celia still snored softly. Intrigued why Bella hadn't joined them and not wanting to wake Celia, Marlow entered the house through her own bedroom, then knocked on Bella's door. No answer. "Bella, how's your history project coming along?"

Sill no answer. Marlow tried the knob, and the door opened. Materials lay strewn across the bed, and an open textbook and a stack of handwritten papers covered the desk. No sign of the child.

Marlow headed down the hall and checked in the spare bedrooms, even poked her head in Jake's room. No sign of the child. She wasn't in the bathroom or the kitchen either. Standing on the back steps, Marlow called. No response. Dread slithered up her spine. Bella seemed to be a homebody, and Marlow was pretty certain the family didn't allow her to wander far.

Hurrying back to the verandah, Marlow gently woke Celia. "Celia, I can't find Bella. Does she have a special place away from the house?"

The woman rubbed her eyes. "Oh, I slept longer than I intended.

Did you say you can't find Bella?" She rose and glanced toward the garden, concern etched on her face. "It is strange. Bella swims every afternoon. It's not like her to skip, especially on such a hot day." She barged into Bella's bedroom.

"Hmm. She left a mess, and that's not like her, either. I suppose you looked through the house?"

"Yes." Marlow followed Celia to the kitchen. "Has Bella done this before?"

"No. She never strays far. The garden or maybe the mechanic shed. She loves watching Mitch work on the machinery."

"I'll check."

"All right. Oh, wait. There's Paddy. I'll ask him." Celia opened the screen door and stepped onto the threshold. "Coo-eee, Paddy, come here, please."

Marlow peered out the door, too.

The young lad sprinted to the house. "What can I do for you, Miss Celia?"

"Have you seen Bella?" she asked.

A blush instantly rose from his neck to his face, and he shifted his weight from foot to foot. "Yeah, uh, I saw her about an hour ago." He pointed over his shoulder. "She was way down the driveway. Looked like she was running after her cat."

"Are you sure?"

"Yeah, Miss Celia. Bella was…sorry, should I have called you?" He blinked and stroked his smooth chin.

"No. Ta, paddy. I'm sure she'll be back soon. Toffee likes to be indoors too much to be gone for long."

Celia closed the door and turned to Marlow. "I have to get dinner started. Would you mind going outside and calling that silly girl."

"Of course. I'll get my sunglasses and hat." Marlow returned to her room, picked up the items she needed, and stepped onto the verandah.

Although Celia seemed to accept what Paddy told her, Marlow had her doubts. His stammering, his body language. He could just be nervous around women, or he lied. All the more reason to find Bella.

Following the curved driveway, Marlow scanned the area. There were few places a person could hide, but she called Bella's name repeatedly. After she walked about fifty yards from the house, she turned and surveyed the homestead. She hadn't been out here since she arrived yesterday. The driveway led up a slight rise, providing an overall view of the house, the surrounding greenery—which looked like a lush oasis in a red desert—and the outbuildings Bella had shown her this morning.

Way off to the north, where Bella had indicated the main paddocks were, she imagined Jake on his bay, surveying his domain, counting his sheep. How many did he have? She had a slew of questions.

But where was Bella? She called again, and seeing no sign of the kid, retraced her steps. In the distance, a dust trail indicated an approaching person. Jake on his way home as it was nearly five thirty. She veered at the fork in the driveway and hurried to the machinery shop.

Banging and grinding sounds and odors of old grease emanated, and she poked her head around the door. A stocky man wearing a welder's helmet, visor up, hammered a large metal frame.

Marlow waited until he stopped, then stepped closer. "Hi, I'm Marlow Barclay, staying with the family. We're looking for Bella. Have you seen her?"

"Afternoon, Miss. I'm Mitch Evans. No. Bella hasn't been in here today. But don't worry. She never wanders far. Better step back." He donned a huge glove and slid the visor down. Sparks flew as he used the torch against the frame.

Marlow retreated and called Bella again. By the time she returned to the kitchen, Celia had pots on the stove and vegetables peeled, ready to cook. The pungent aroma of onions and garlic permeated the kitchen. "No sign of her. I even went to the machinery shed. Mitch hasn't seen her."

"I'm getting worried now. While you were gone, I checked the garden by the pool. She does have a favorite spot behind the honey-myrtle bushes and the bench. It's sort of hidden from the house. But no sign she's been out recently."

Marlow recalled hiding there from Jake this morning. She rubbed her heated cheeks. "What should we do? Set up a search party?"

"Yeah." Celia turned off the burners. "Come with me." She marched outside toward the sheds.

Forced to jog, Marlow struggled to keep up with the long-legged woman. Once they reached the shearing shed, Celia picked up a stout iron rod and banged it against a metal triangle hanging from a beam. An old-fashioned dinner bell. The sound reverberated through the buildings.

"We use this at shearing time to call the blokes for meals." Celia hung the rod on a hook. "It won't take long to bring out the stockmen. Most are in the paddocks, but some will be home. And if Bella hears it, she'll come running."

Minutes later, three men, including Mitch, and a woman appeared around the building.

"Why'd you ring the gong, Miss Celia?" a dark-skinned man asked.

The woman slipped her arm through his and cocked her head.

Marlow had not realized Aboriginal folks worked on the station, but it stood to reason.

"Jarra, is this everyone?"

The man nodded.

"Thanks for coming." Celia set her hands on her hips. "Little Bella is missing. We've searched the house and can't find her."

The Aboriginal woman gasped. "We'll help look for her."

"Good on ya, Darri. We need everyone." She scanned the group. "I see Paddy's not here, but he saw her an hour ago, apparently chasing her cat."

"I searched all the way up to the hill where he said he'd seen her." Marlow pointed toward the driveway.

"Oh, this is Marlow, a relative. She's spending a few days with us."

The clip-clop of a horse's hooves interrupted Celia. "Jake's home." She sighed and waved him over.

"What's wrong?" He dismounted and tipped his hat off his forehead.

"Bella's missing."

Although stubble covered his chin, and rust-colored dirt mixed with sweat streaked down his face, no man was allowed to be that attractive. Marlow swallowed against the raw emotion surging through her and bit her bottom lip.

Jake removed his sunglasses and squinted at Celia and Marlow. Flecks of ice infused his eyes. "Missing? When was she last seen?"

Celia told him about Paddy and described the measures they'd taken thus far.

"Well, everyone, search all the buildings." Jake slid his sunglasses into his pocket. "I know she won't go far, but she may be injured. She—"

"Wait. I hear a cat." Marlow turned and stepped to a patch of dried grass. A black tail wove through the stalks, and then Toffee appeared and meowed. He rubbed against her leg, and she bent to pet him. "Bella?" Marlow called for good measure. She needed to share her opinion of Paddy's behavior with Jake.

He eyed her, then tied Sully to the corral railing and pointed to a young station hand. "Eugene, help with the search, then take care of my horse. Spread out. I'll try the far building. Shout if you find anything."

The group complied, and Marlow ran to catch up with Jake. "Hey, I need to tell you something."

He slowed, but continued walking. "What?"

"I don't know your workers, but I'm suspicious of Paddy. When Celia talked to him earlier, he hesitated, and, well, I just got the impression he was lying. He sure blushes a lot. And here's her cat. If Bella was chasing her, where is she?"

Jaw clenched, Jake strode ahead. "Bella," he yelled. His deep voice probably reached twice as far as hers had. "Paddy might be young and impulsive at times, but I don't think he's a liar."

Marlow trudged beside him. Okay, so she may have misinterpreted the lad's reaction. But the knot in her chest told her otherwise. "Perhaps he wasn't telling the whole truth."

Jake ignored her words and called again and again. When they reached the last building, he entered while she remained outside.

This was as far as Bella had taken her on their tour. Marlow did a slow three-sixty. The shed, the drive, the paddock, and the—

She froze. The grove of trees trembled in the late afternoon heat. This was the spot where Bella's mood had made an abrupt change. The trees, or something in their vicinity, upset the child.

"Jake, I'm going further west." Marlow hoped he'd heard her. She had to follow her gut instinct and didn't wait for him to respond. Good thing she still wore her sneakers as there was no perceptible path through the stones, twigs, and clumpy grasses. She forged ahead, increasing her pace until she was at a full out run.

Trees surrounded a low wall. The late night conversation with

Celia echoed through Marlow's mind. Must be the family cemetery. Although panting, and a sharp pain stabbed her side, she put forth an extra burst of energy. The gum trees took on individual shapes, some tall and scraggy, others squat and leafy. A gate in the stone wall. Fifty more yards.

Pounding footsteps behind her. Jake called out, "Marlow, why are you running? Did you see Bella?"

She had no breath with which to answer. Arms pumping, she raced toward the wall.

Jake caught up with her. "Do you think she's at the cemetery?"

Focused on remaining upright, she ignored him, and slowed for the last few yards. Close to collapsing, she leaned against the wall. Wiping sweat off her face, she glanced around the square plot, dotted with headstones and shrubs. An out-of-place bundle of clothes lay near the far wall.

Jake opened the gate. "Bella." He approached the child curled up in a fetal position.

"Is…she…all right?" Marlow could barely puff out the words.

Bella stirred, sat up, and blinked at her father. "Daddy, why…what…? Oh, I remember." She smiled at Marlow as she stood, brushing grass and dirt off her blouse and shorts.

Marlow clapped a hand over her chest to quieten her heart. Bella was fine.

"We've been looking all over for you, Bella Bear. Even the station hands are out." A mixture of concern and anger coated Jake's words. "What are you doing here? You know—"

"Dad, don't get mad at me. I'm sorry I worried everyone, but I didn't mean to fall asleep."

"We're glad you're safe." Still panting, Marlow sat on the wall, removed her hat and fanned her face.

Jake kicked at the dirt, fists low on his hips.

Sufficiently revived, Marlow motioned to the child. "Let's go and tell everyone you're safe."

Bella nibbled a fingernail and eyed her dad before taking a step forward.

"Wait, young lady. You had us worried sick. You know you're not supposed to come out this far by yourself. Why did you?"

"It was Marlow's idea."

Taken aback, Marlow almost fell off the wall. "I never—"

"What?" Jake rounded on her.

The force of his glare nailed her to the spot. She couldn't have moved even if a gwardar slithered up her leg. "I did not suggest you come out here."

"But, Marlow, you said last night that maybe I was acting all moody and…and odd because I didn't get to say goodbye to Mum."

Her words of encouragement were coming back to bite her. "You're right, but at that time I didn't even know about the family cemetery. I certainly wouldn't…" She shrank as Jake edged closer and closer. "Um…" Mouth closed, she gulped.

"That has to be one of the stupidest suggestions I've ever heard." He loomed over her. His piercing, icy stare cut right through her.

For a moment, Jake resembled Steven enough for Marlow to cringe.

"And you're supposed to be a professional." Jake shook his head and strode out the gate, then turned and extended his hand. "Come, Bella. We're going home."

She clasped his hand, hung her head, and walked away.

In spite of the heat, Marlow shivered as if Jake had tossed a pitcher of cold water over her. Anger seared through her heart at his misjudgment. But he was not Steven, and she was not in a relationship with him.

Marlow slid off the wall, straightened her shoulders, and tramped toward the house. As much as she was enthralled with life at Long Gully, she couldn't wait to leave this arrogant man. Once they solved the mystery, he'd be history.

Chapter 19

An unpleasant atmosphere loitered over the dining room table that evening, and no one seemed interested in conversing. Marlow gave up trying and cut a piece off her grilled pork chop. In spite of dousing it in homemade applesauce, the meat tasted like cheap jerky.

Even Bella held her tongue. Cutlery chinking against china was the only sound in the room.

After ten minutes or more Marlow had had enough of the silent treatment. She set her knife and fork together on her plate and pushed it aside. "Jake, I'm sorry I suggested Bella—"

"Stop right there." He held up his hand. "I'm the one who needs to apologize. I had no right to blame you without knowing the full story, and I'm ashamed I raised my voice to you." Glancing at his daughter, he cleared his throat. "Actually, I'm embarrassed by my behavior, and have been trying to broach the subject all evening. Thank you for breaking the ice."

"Dad," Bella cocked her head, "can I tell Marlow something?"

He nodded.

The child slid off her chair and stood beside Marlow, hands behind her back. "I'm sorry, too. I didn't mean to make Daddy angry at you. When we were on our tour this morning, I saw the walled cemetery and thought about Mum. That made me miserable. Then this afternoon, I decided to visit her grave. I've never done it before. And—"

"That's completely my fault." Jake's voice cracked. "I didn't think you'd want to, Bella Bear. I thought it would make you too sad."

She hurried to her dad, and he drew her into a hug.

Eyes moist, Marlow smiled. During the first year after their deaths, she'd often visited Eileen's and Steven's side-by-side burial plots. But over time, she preferred to page through photo albums and recall fun times instead. An ache still lodged in her heart, though.

Jake looked at Marlow over his daughter's head. "Please accept our apologies, and I for one, promise I won't ever treat you that way again. As God is my witness."

Words of regret had never passed Steven's lips. Marlow studied Jake's face. The sincerity in his voice and expression were enough to soften her heart. "Thank you." She couldn't say more because her throat clogged with emotion.

"I tell you what, child." Brushing the hair out of Bella's face, Jake added, "Whenever you want to visit Mum, let me know and we'll go together. All right?"

She lifted her head from his chest. "I'd like that. And you can tell me about the other people buried there. I read their names and want to know about them, too."

Brows raised, he turned to his aunt. "Celia, would you mind coming with us? You know so much more about the family."

Throughout the exchange, Celia had been mute. Now she squinted at Jake as if she disagreed with him. She chewed a chunk of bread slowly, then shook her head. "I'll go, but before we do, you and I need to have a long chat." Stacking plates, she pursed her lips.

"You found something in the boxes." He scooted back his chair. "Tell me. What is it? The letter?"

Anyone hearing the excitement in his voice would have thought he'd hit the mother lode.

Celia rose slowly, picked up the plates, and sauntered through the archway to the kitchen. Jake followed, carrying two serving platters.

Before Bella could join them, Marlow caught her by the hand. Celia's odd behavior gave her the impression she wanted a private conversation with Jake. "Let them be for now. They'll include us when the time is right. Okay?"

Bella shrugged. "I suppose. But when you do find the puzzle thing, can I help solve it?"

"Certainly. I have the feeling we'll need all our eyes and brains working together. What we have so far is a bunch of jumbled letters that make no sense."

"I'm good at word games."

"I'll keep that in mind."

Jake's raised voice carried from the kitchen. Marlow glanced at the table. There were still a few items to clear, but she decided to avoid what sounded like a heated discussion between Jake and Celia. "Let's sit on the verandah, Bella."

"Good idea. I don't like it when Daddy gets loud."

Marlow silently concurred and followed Bella through the living room and onto the verandah. Moving a chair close to the wall, Marlow sat. Muted light spilling from the house provide enough illumination to see Bella. "Did you finish your history project?

"No, but it's not due for a few days." She hummed and pranced around the verandah before flopping into a chair where she swung her legs, her feet inches off the floor. "Are they talking about me?" If her legs moved any faster, she'd take off.

"I don't think so." But Bella's question gave Marlow another insight into her psyche. Constantly in adult company, the child probably had been the center of day-to-day activities and may have been allowed to participate in conversations whenever she felt like it. Not that Marlow believed the old adage that children should be seen and not heard, but one of the points she wanted to discuss with Jake involved Bella's propensity to dominate a situation.

"I'm sorry Daddy was angry with you, but I'm glad I went to see Mum's grave." Legs pumped as if she were on a swing. "I feel much better. Do you think I'll be able to control my moods now?"

If only a salve for grief was that easy to attain. "Everyone handles these situations differently. Identifying part of the problem is a big step, and your dad is aware of your need, so, yes, I think you will have more control because you know the source. However—"

"I don't like it when grownups say that word." Bella's legs stilled. "Something bad always comes next."

Interesting observation. Marlow weighed her next sentence carefully. "However," she smiled, hoping Bella would notice, "something as complicated as moods, or emotional temperament, can't be fixed in one simple act. As we grow up and mature, we have to learn how to control our actions and reactions."

"I get it. Like little kids who throw tantrums when they don't get their way. When we're older, we can't do that."

"Precisely." Marlow patted Bella's knee. "Sometimes I still feel like yelling and screaming when something doesn't go my way, but

I don't."

Bella giggled. "I can imagine Daddy in Annie's Place, on his back, legs kicking, and yelling, 'My tea is cold. I don't like cold tea.' Or, how about Dad out in the paddocks, lying on the ground pounding his fists and screaming, 'I don't want to work with sheep today.'" She set her feet on the seat and hugged her knees, and laughed so hard, Marlow had to join in.

She imagined more silly scenarios involving Jake and fanned her face with her hand. Whew. Good thing Bella couldn't see her flushed cheeks. Must be a sign she had forgiven him.

When they both settled down, Marlow said, "Bella, you're a fast learner. Adapting to our environment, and the people in it, is a sign of maturity. Another helpful hint is to tell people what you're feeling, or to explain what's bothering you before you act. We—"

Jake's voice bellowed from the living room. Bella jumped up and headed to her bedroom door.

Marlow hurried after her and entered the room with her. The child breathed hard as if she'd suffered a fright. Marlow slid her arm around her and waited until her panting subsided. She switched on the light and focused on Bella. Myriad emotions scrolled across her face. Marlow could almost hear the cogs turning.

Sighing, Bella dropped to her bed. "Sit with me, please, Marlow."

"Sure, kid."

Toffee, who'd been curled up at the foot of the bed, strolled across their laps. Bella stroked him, then looked at Marlow. "I see what you mean. Just now, instead of running inside, I should have reminded you that I don't like it when Daddy raises his voice."

"Exactly what I meant. Does he often yell at you?" What a hard question to ask, and Marlow held her breath, waiting on the answer.

"No. Never *at* me. And it's not yelling exactly. His voice gets deep and loud sometimes."

Marlow could attest to that.

Bella scooped up Toffee and cradled him. "When that happens, it brings back bad memories."

For Marlow to help untangle the family drama, she'd need more than a few days.

Chapter 20

"What do you mean, Dad had an affair?" Jake shut his office door and glared at Celia.

"Here are the letters I found in one of the boxes you took from the attic. The last envelope contains a photograph." Celia handed him a small, metal container. With a groan, she sat in the armchair.

Jake slumped into his desk chair. His aunt had to be mistaken. He read the first letter and eyed her over the sheet of paper. "Are they all like this?"

"Yeah. Only, the sentiment gets syrupier, if there's such a word." She wrinkled her nose. "And you'll notice Alice, his paramour, calls him Pat. *Dearest* Pat. He insisted everyone in the family call him Patrick."

It didn't take Jake long to read the remaining letters. His stomach roiled and acid inched up his throat as he studied the photo. *Dad, how could you?* "You think this is her?"

"Sure. She wouldn't send a photo of someone else. And why would Patrick hide the letters and include a random picture? It's Alice."

The chair rocked in time to Jake's agitated foot tapping. Five envelopes addressed to Patrick Barclay at Long Gully Station, all postmarked during the early months of 1945. The last letter was dated the last day of May. He would have been seven years old. "When did Dad return to Long Gully after his recuperation?"

Celia crossed her legs and tugged her skirt down to cover her knees. Trying to delay the answer, no doubt.

"Don't spare me. There's not a whole lot we can do about the situation now, but I, we, deserve to know the truth."

"He was wounded in June of '44, sent to the Rocky Creek Military Hospital—"

"Where's that?"

"Northern Queensland, west of Cairns. The hospital is closed now. Patrick had several injuries, and although they tried, the docs couldn't save his leg."

"How long did he stay at Rocky Creek?" Jake had never thought to ask his father about his war experiences.

"Six weeks, I think. The military hospital was overcrowded, and as soon as patients were well enough, they were transferred to other facilities. Patrick still needed medical care, so he stayed with his, our, sister Thelma, in Brisbane for several months."

Jake gnawed the inside of his cheek. "He could have met Alice then."

"I suppose. The first letter seems to indicate they'd already been acquainted for some time."

Shoving his chair back, he stood and stomped to the closed door. A futile effort since he had nowhere to go. He turned. "Acquainted is a nice way of saying it. Alice's words hint at a lot more." He leaned against the door. "There was nothing else concerning this woman in the large boxes? No mention of a child?"

"No, but…" Celia fussed with her skirt again.

"Out with it." He frowned at his aunt. "You knew your brother in a way I, as his son, never could. Did you sense anything suspicious when he came home? Did Mum act differently around him, or vice versa?"

Celia stared at him. "I have several ideas, but please sit. You're hovering and I don't like it."

Seated in his chair again, he folded his arms. "Tell me. Please."

She cleared her throat. "First of all, Patrick came home in October, 1944. The letters are dated the following year, indicating they saw each other after he was discharged from the army."

"Dad visited her away from Long Gully. Several times."

"Yes. Looking back, I think I can flesh out the events. The twins were born in July the following year and died two months later. Your mum was devastated. Patrick handled his grief by going off alone."

"Traveling to Brisbane often would have been costly and time consuming."

"Maybe he met Alice in Cunnamulla or another town further east."

Jake fisted his hands until the knuckles objected then he flexed his fingers. Why would his father have treated Mum that way? He gazed at the photo of Laura. Her miscarriages had brought them closer. However, he had not experienced the horrors of war, nor a life-threatening injury. He shook his head. "I don't understand any of this. But we're assuming they had an affair. Unless we track down this Alice woman, we can't prove it."

"I don't think there's any need to locate her because I believe Patrick did have a relationship, and they had a child."

This time Jake jumped out of the chair and pounded his fists on the desk. "What?"

"Calm down."

Breathing through his clenched teeth, Jake sat and waited.

"What do you know about Paddy?" Celia asked.

"What does he have to do with this situation?" Jake rocked in his chair. The image of the young lad flashed across his mind. "The eyes." His jaw gaped. "Paddy has the Barclay blue eyes."

Chapter 21

Jake and Celia remained in the office for more than half an hour. Marlow had returned to the verandah when Bella took a shower. The child was complicated, no doubt about it, and showed no sign of wanting to elaborate on her comment about bad memories. In fact, she seemed to regret sharing that information with Marlow. Once the words were out of her mouth, she shoved Toffee aside, unearthed her pajamas from under her pillow, and dashed to the bathroom.

Toffee had followed Marlow outside and curled up in her lap. Loud purring helped soothe Marlow's agitation. She stroked the cat and mulled over the conversation with Bella. The need to discuss his young daughter with Jake increased in importance.

Ready to retreat indoors and fix a glass of lemonade, Marlow nudged the cat off her lap and stood, however her progress halted when Jake pushed the screen door wide.

"There you are." The door slammed, and he leaned against the wall. "Sorry to abandon you, but Celia and I had serious family matters to discuss."

"Anything you want to share?"

He crossed his arms.

Although Marlow couldn't see his face, she sensed his hesitation. "That's all right. You—"

"I'll tell you." Exhaling a deep sigh, he leaned close. "Where's Bella? I don't want her to eavesdrop."

"In her room." Marlow pointed over her shoulder. "She showered, and I think is reading in bed now."

"Celia has gone to her room, too." He scratched his chin. "Let's go for a walk. That is, if you want to be in my company."

She had no reason to decline. "Sure."

"I'll fetch a torch in case the generator shuts off while we're gone. Come with me to my room."

"We can use mine." She pointed to her door.

"I have a heavy-duty model."

Marlow traipsed behind Jake along the verandah. He slipped inside his room and soon returned with a large flashlight. They used the stairs that led to the pool area, then Jake opened the gate and ushered her through.

He stopped and Marlow almost collided with him.

"I have to reiterate I sincerely regret accusing you, demeaning you, and…and yelling. I have no excuse and beg your forgiveness."

Time for Marlow to be honest. To a point. She may never be ready to share all aspects of Steven's behavior toward her. "I was rattled by your tone and words, but could tell you were concerned with Bella's safety." She took a step forward. "And I accept your apology." There was one major difference between Jake and Steven. Jake's body language and personality supported his contrite apology, whereas Steven seldom apologized.

"Let's put the episode behind us and shake on it." She extended her hand.

"I'll do that and more." He took her hand and bowed his head. "Father, please forgive my temper outburst and help Marlow understand that I mean her no harm. Amen."

Whew. What was she supposed to do after that? Befuddled, she withdrew her hand and turned, unable to utter a sound.

Jake cleared his throat. "There's a clump of rocks about thirty meters east of the house. I sometimes sit there and study the heavens."

They walked side by side, the flashlight guiding their steps.

"You're a star gazer?"

"Not exactly. I can name many constellations, but I like to absorb the beauty of God's creation in the silence of the night."

Marlow admired the ease with which Jake spoke of God. With time, maybe she'd be able to. Sneakers provided the stability she needed to tramp beside Jake along the uneven ground. The muted light from the house had long since dissipated, but the almost full moon shed a faint glow over the land.

"Here we are." He shone the flashlight over the rocks, most of which reached to her waist or higher. "No unwanted guests. Choose your seat."

Marlow hitched her hip onto the lowest one. She wriggled back on the rounded stone and drew in a breath. With no hint of horses or sheep, the air only carried the smell of baked earth.

Jake switched off the light, and they sat in silence for a few minutes.

"I can see why you like to come out here. I can imagine that when there's no moon, it must be as dark as pitch."

"Too right. But we're never without the light from the stars. Look up, Marlow."

She complied and gasped. Ever since she'd been in Australia, she'd marveled at sights of the Milky Way, but it had always been with city lights in the background. Out here, the gazillion stars had no competition. The swirling galaxy looked like a gash cut through the sky which revealed another layer of compact heavenly bodies, dusty white, studded with bands of colors—cream, pale blue, salmon. The stars were so close together they appeared to merge in one radiant blur. The panorama surpassed a van Gogh masterpiece. "The sight is breathtaking."

Another silence, then Jake kicked against the rock, his boots thudding on the granite. "Celia and I discovered a bit of disconcerting news about my dad."

Aware of his hesitation, Marlow refrained from interrupting.

"She found a stack of love letters written by a woman named Alice. Apparently, she and my dad had an affair when I was kid."

"That must have shocked you both."

"It did, but there's more."

Curiosity gnawed, but she waited.

Jake thumped his thigh. "Might as well say it. Paddy could be my nephew."

"Really?" Marlow recalled the first time she met the lad. The color of his eyes were distinctive. "What do you know of his background?"

"Not much. Like I told Celia, I hired him based on a recommendation from a fellow grazier. There are a limited number of blokes who want to work on stations this far from town. I rely on gut instinct most of the time, and, well, Paddy might be green, but he's done everything required of a jackaroo."

"I did notice his eyes."

"Yeah, now I see the resemblance. I'll call him in tomorrow and inquire about his family."

"If he is related, would he have a claim on the land?"

"At this point we don't even know if the affair resulted in a child. Too many unanswered questions." A noise to the right. Jake shone the flashlight, and a small, furry animal scurried into the darkness. "Ready to go back to the homestead?"

"Not yet." With Jake as a captive audience, now was the perfect time to discuss Bella. "Although you didn't ask me *per se* to evaluate Bella, you did voice your concerns. I'd like to share my observations on her behavior. Do you mind staying a while?"

He lowered his head and huffed out a sigh.

Knowing how crucial emotional stability was, Marlow waited for Jake to react. She did not expect immediate approval.

"What's your diagnosis?"

"Well, not a diagnosis as such. I'd need to observe her more and conduct an indepth interview. However, I do have some ideas and treatment options."

"Fire away."

Marlow gathered her thoughts wishing she had a written list of pertinent points. "First of all, what I'm about to say is tentative, preliminary, based on my limited time in her company. She is a darling girl, thoughtful, intelligent, and I don't want to hint that there is anything wrong with her. I have surmised a few things based on the little I do know. So bear with me."

"I understand. But I've seen her with you, and she responds differently to you. She's attentive. Doesn't argue."

"Maybe because I'm a new member of her audience, and she wants to impress me."

"That, and a lot more. She really likes you."

"Thank you, I think, Anyway, let's begin." Marlow licked her lips, ready to face the nitty-gritty. "Bella is naturally talkative—"

"She learned to talk at a young age and hasn't stopped since."

"And there's no problem with that. I assume she's been around adults most of her life, and although she has contact with kids her age, she hasn't learned restraint. And I don't mean that she needs to be made to hush, but she's been indulged."

"You mean spoiled? I can see that."

"I'd rather not use that term. To me it has a negative connotation, and I don't see that in Bella. She's been in adult company a lot and probably has been allowed to participate in most conversations, even when not appropriate."

"I agree. After she was born, Laura and I put few restrictions on her behavior." He tsked. "We were so happy to have another child that we pandered to her, gave her much more freedom than we did Rick. I see now we should have been firmer."

"Don't blame yourself. I understand how parents would do that. Believe me, I had to remind myself of good parenting skills all the time when Eileen was young."

"Yeah. By the time Bella was born, Celia had been with us a year. We all gave into our little girl's every wish. So, I think we spoiled her."

"In a nice way, with love. She's not a brat. She needs to learn to read social cues and think before she speaks."

Jake harrumphed. "We all need that skill."

"Agree. I believe from what she told me that she is aware of her inclination to take over a conversation, to be in control. On a positive note, that trait could develop into leadership qualities. But she also has to listen, and to be aware of the feelings of other people in her company."

"You got that right. Rick always says Bella's a bossy little ankle biter. Some of her school chums have also remarked about her take-charge attitude."

"Again, not all negative as long as she is aware of how her behavior might affect her friends." Marlow brushed a strand of hair out of her eyes. A playful breeze stirred up dried leaves at the base of the rocks.

"How do we, I mean how do I, get her to change?"

"As I said, Bella is smart, and conscious—to some degree—of her problem, for lack of a better term, and I'm sure will want to adjust her actions so she doesn't hurt her friends' feelings. I'll devise a plan, and we can help her together in the short time I'm here."

He shifted on his rock and glanced at Marlow. "Thanks for your insight. I always thought Bella would change as she grew older."

"Maybe so, but if she doesn't, she might alienate friends and family."

"True. You've addressed one area of concern, but how about her mood swings?"

A much more complex topic to discuss. Marlow stared at the swash of stars. *Help me Father, God. Give me the right words.* Whoa. Before another prayer escaped her lips, she blurted out, "Based on my limited knowledge and Bella's actions this afternoon, I believe she is still dealing with the grieving process for her mother." Marlow's words lay heavy in the night air. She stole a quick glance at Jake.

He gazed at the heavens. "I should have been more sensitive to her needs."

A deep breath. "I do lay that oversight at your feet. Talking to her about your grief will help her process hers, and, by the way, will help you too."

He didn't respond for a few moments. "I can see that I've held onto my grief, but I didn't think it showed. I was wrong."

"I'll tell you what I told Bella. We all deal with grief in our own way. There is no right or wrong method. You can read about the stages of grief, but we don't slide through them as if we're on a greased runway. We go forward, get stuck, retreat backward, and just when we think we've made it, something will happen. A memory or a song will catapult us back to the day, and we're in the past, reliving the event all over again. Recovery is not a one-and-done deal. We cycle back and forth, and hopefully, the pain eases as time passes."

"I should probably also talk with Rick. Although he seems to have handled his mum's loss very maturely."

"No harm in checking. In fact, all three of you should have a heart-to-heart."

"Good idea. Sunday after next, we're going to Maroola Downs for our church service. Rick will be there."

The name Maroola plucked on a memory chord, but Marlow couldn't recall the details. She shook her head to dispel the nuisance. "Bella needs to learn to tell people what she's feeling, to name her emotions instead of running away or avoiding a situation. For instance, she can use words like lonely, frustrated, scared."

"Scared? What's she frightened of?"

The discussion was beginning to affect Marlow's conscience. Naming other people's emotions always seemed hypocritical when she had a hard time handling her own. She swallowed. "Something happened this evening that concerns me." Marlow described Bella's initial reaction to Jake's raised voice.

"My loud voice scares her? I know I can get boisterous at times, but I've never raised my voice to her or Rick."

"She was quick to reassure me of that." Now would be a good time to remind Jake of how his voice affected her at the cemetery. No, they'd buried that hatchet. "Something in Bella's past makes her recall a bad memory. Do you know what it could be?"

Looking up again, he exhaled another deep sigh. "Oh, dear God, forgive me. I know exactly what she's referring to. Laura went for a long walk the night before she passed away and without telling anyone. I searched the house and the grounds for her, calling her name. I'm sure as loudly as I could. I was frantic. Eight-year-old Bella was already in bed, but obviously not asleep. I suppose the tone of my voice sounded angry to a little girl." He hugged the flashlight to his chest as if holding something precious. "Laura returned to the house ten minutes later, and we went to bed. She died in the early hours of the morning. When I awoke at five, she was gone."

Bella's bad memory associated her daddy's loud voice with her mother's passing. And she'd never been encouraged to share these innermost thoughts about the connection with anyone.

Marlow hopped off her rock and touched Jake's hand. He slipped to the ground and squeezed her hand in return.

Chapter 22

By the time Marlow entered the kitchen the next morning, Jake had already left for his station duties. Celia busied herself making toast and acknowledged Marlow's presence with a nod.

"Good morning. Can I help with anything?" Marlow poured a mug of coffee and added milk. The aroma of the strong brew permeated the room.

"Ta, but no. Jake took his tucker with him, so I'm not making a big spread just for us."

"Toast and coffee will suit me fine." And with Jake out of the picture, she wouldn't be reminded of the intimate moment shared by the rocks last night. But heat rose up her neck anyway.

Celia pulled a baking sheet from the oven and slid the golden-brown slices onto a plate. "He told me you chatted about Bella. I can see that we've treated her more like an adult than a child. We share the blame."

"No blame, merely my observations. At least she has a sweet spirit."

"Too true." After placing two jars of homemade jams on the table, Celia fiddled with a bobby pin in her hair. "So Jake told you about my brother's possible affair. And Paddy."

"Yes. Is he going to question the lad today?"

"That's on his agenda. By the way, this morning he found three old boxes in the back of a wardrobe in one of the spare bedrooms. He remembered something was stored in there from his childhood days of playing hide 'n seek. He left them in his office."

"Let's hope you find the envelope." Marlow's shoulders sagged under the burden of fulfilling Steven's dying wish for so long. "I'm anxious to combine the notes and solve the Barclay mystery."

Celia poured herself a mug of coffee and thumped the pot back on the stove. "Yeah, but there better be no more surprises." She sat and eyed Marlow while she sipped her drink.

Who would be happy to discover her brother had had an affair? Understandably, Celia still fumed. To ease the tense atmosphere, Marlow asked, "Can I help Bella again today?"

The child hurried into the kitchen and gave her aunt a kiss on the cheek. "Can she, please Aunty Celia?"

"Of course. Only toast this morning, luv."

"No worries." Bella grabbed two slices, spread a liberal amount of butter on each, then added large blobs of red jam.

Marlow read the handwritten jar labels, guava, plum. She chose guava. "This is good. Did you make it, Celia?"

"No. I buy all our jam from a lady in Cunnamulla. Even if I was so inclined, we don't grow any kind of fruit out here."

"What about canning vegetables?"

"My mum and Maud, Jake's mum, used to preserve all kinds of veggies. If we have a glut of tomatoes, I'll keep some, but these days the shops have a good selection of tinned fruits and vegetables. And we have the deep freeze, but space is limited."

"Do you have a separate freezer?" Marlow spread guava jam on her second slice of toast.

"A small one in the storeroom for our meat."

Bella dawdled over her meal, and Celia seemed disinclined to converse further.

To break the silence, Marlow asked, "The mail plane comes Friday, right? My letters are ready to mail to friends back in Texas, but I have one more to write."

"Yeah, and I must complete my history project." Bella drained her glass of milk. "Thanks for brekky, Aunty Celia. I'm going to work now so I can swim this afternoon. Excuse me from the table, please."

"You're excused, lass." Celia watched Bella as she placed her dishes in the sink and walked out of the kitchen. "She seems to have matured overnight. Did you or Jake have a talk with her already?"

"I didn't. Since Jake and I came back inside late last night, and Bella's room was in darkness, I don't think he did, either."

"Might be my imagination." Huffing out a breath, Celia stood. "Off with you, Marlow. I'll clean up and get started on Patrick's boxes. We're having stew for dinner, so I'll have plenty of time to search the contents."

"Good." She traipsed to her room and gathered her writing materials before heading to the office where Bella sat at her table scribbling away on her history project. Encyclopedias and textbooks covered the area.

Celia appeared in the doorway, carrying several photo albums. "Thought you might like to see the Barclay clan's pictorial history." She set the books on Jake's desk, then stacked two of the three worn cardboard boxes and headed toward the door. "I'll leave the other one for now. We're getting down to the wire."

When not assisting Bella with her school program, Marlow examined the photos. Many included a description, so she was able to identify Jake's parents, Celia's two sisters, and even a photo of Graham and Elizabeth. The pictures of Jake as a youngster captured his thick mop of dark hair, chubby cheeks, and an attitude of conquering the world.

She closed the album and cleared her throat. Enough for one day. Time to write to Milton. She'd told him she would keep in touch. As she described her travels since leaving Melbourne, the critical comments Jake made concerning his cousin intruded. The two men could not be more different.

Setting aside the writing pad, Marlow glanced at Bella and asked, "I'm ready for some tea. How about you?"

"Yup." Bella handed her a sheaf of papers. "Here're my arithmetic and English assignments."

Marlow stuffed the pages into the large envelope she'd used the previous day. "I'll prepare the tea. How are you coming along on your project?"

"I finished the rough draft. Now I have to rewrite it and draw the maps. Whew, it was hard work. Lots of research, which I don't like. I think you'll approve of how I used your list of differences."

"I'm excited to read your report." With the image of five-year-old Jake in her mind, Marlow hummed as she walked slowly to the kitchen where she found Celia examining a stack of papers. "I'll make tea for us. Any luck?"

Celia checked her watch. "Oh, my. Sorry I didn't realize it was so late. These documents are fascinating. I'm learning a lot about the history of Long Gully and Patrick's business dealings. Still no letter from Graham, but I'm only halfway through."

Celia, please search for the letter instead of stopping to read every scrap of paper. Marlow took a deep breath and set the kettle on the stove. She opened the canister and sniffed the billy tea. The earthy aroma reminded her of the first cup of tea she'd had at Long Gully, two days ago. Two days and still no letter. But, it had taken Henry three days to locate his envelope.

"Oh, by the way." Celia stretched and shoved a stack of papers to the side. "There's not much fresh milk. I made up a pitcher of powdered milk already. And there are a few Empire biscuits left."

"I suppose you ruled out having dairy cows at some point."

"Oh, yes. Many years ago, while I lived in Brisbane, Patrick bought three dairy cows. The venture was not successful. Not sure if it was the heat, insufficient feed, or the sheer amount of labor involved. Maud decided powdered milk or diluted condensed milk was less trouble."

"Aunty Celia, please come to the office." Bella hollered. "There's a radio message for you and Daddy."

"Excuse me." Celia dashed down the hall.

Marlow poured boiling water into the teapot and covered it with the cozy before heading to the office.

Turning the corner, she bumped into smiling Celia.

Celia drew in a deep breath. "We never know if a message will be good or bad news. No worries, luv. That was Kevin O'Bryan from Maroola Downs. They want to change the church service to this Sunday instead of next. I told him that's okay by us."

The name was familiar. Ah, yes. He must be the father of the brunette Jake spoke to at the lunch in Cunnamulla. The image of him standing close to the beauty flitted across her mind. All of a sudden, she had no appetite for tea or Celia's tasty biscuits.

Chapter 23

With Paddy Archerfield's application tucked in his shirt pocket, Jake sped toward the E-1 paddock where the young jackaroo was scheduled to work on the windmill. The motorbike bounced over the rough track, but Jake steered with precision, determined to reach his destination before Paddy completed the job. A lone raptor soared across the sky, riding the thermals, a sight Jake never tired of.

In the distance, the metal framework surrounded by a few trees and the water tank broke the monotony of the flat, red earth. The outline of Paddy's black and yellow motorbike stood stark beside a tree trunk, and movement on the small platform near the blades indicated the chap hard at work.

An assembly of emus and kangaroos scattered as Jake approached the almost dried-up waterhole, then he slowed to a stop. He removed his goggles, swung his leg over the bike, and set the kickstand. After using a handkerchief to wipe sweat off his face, he donned his sunnies and surveyed the area as the dust settled.

"Hey, boss. I'm almost done."

An anxious tone coated the lad's words, but he'd insisted he be sent to repair the windmill. Jake craned his neck and looked at Paddy. He'd question the kid about his request. "Good. I need to check on the fence and thought I'd see how you're doing while I'm out here. What was wrong with the windmill?" He didn't want to scare off the kid before he elicited some straight answers.

"I lubricated the gearbox and cleaned out a cartful of dirt. I'll be done in a tick."

Jake waited in the shade of a scraggly mulga tree and reread Paddy's application. Nothing jumped out at him as bogus. But then, he hadn't verified all the details, either. Previous address, next of kin. Two references. Jake leaned against the trunk. He'd only checked with one of those references, Nate Davidson, the grazier who'd relayed the radio message to Celia on Monday. He'd given Paddy a thumb's up, which was all Jake needed. Then.

Shoving the application into his pocket, he sauntered to the edge of the depression. He eyed the motionless vanes on the windmill, then kicked at the layer of cracked earth that marked the previous water level. Copious liters lay thousands of meters beneath his feet, but at this spot, the water needed to be pumped up. Not like the other reservoirs where natural pressure brought water to the surface.

Jake retreated to the shade and followed Paddy's movements. Banging, clanging, grunting. Ten minutes later the blades began to turn in the breeze.

"Good job, kid."

With a holler, Paddy hurried down and jumped off the framework. "What a thrill. Up so high I could see forever." He slipped off the tool belt and thrust his fist into the air. "Whew."

Water dribbled into the tank. Plink. Plink. Jake climbed the ladder attached to the side and held his hand under the pipe. The warm liquid trickled between his fingers. Several minutes passed before the flow of water increased. It would take a while for the level to reach the outflow pipe which led to the reservoir. "Did you clear out the line?"

"Yeah. Both ends were clogged. There should be no problem with the flow. I'll hang around to make sure."

Jake climbed down. "No worries. I'll stay." He pointed to his bike. "I have a flask of tea. Want some?" He wasn't sure how to question Paddy without him becoming suspicious, but he could learn a lot over a cuppa. Even on a hot afternoon in the outback. That's why he'd brought an extra plastic mug.

"Yeah." Paddy joined Jake in the shade and squatted close to his bike.

Jake unscrewed the top off the flask, filled it, and handed it to the kid. He then poured tea into the extra cup and sat near Paddy.

"Not as good as fresh brewed over a fire, but it hits the spot." Jake smacked his lips.

Paddy drank in silence, a frown creasing his brow. The poor lad was probably scared to death to be forced to sit with the boss.

To put him out of his misery, Jake said, "You have a lot of skills for someone so young. During our interview last year, you said you never worked for Nate Davidson, so where did you acquire your knowledge?"

"Um, yeah, I grew up on a sheep station. My mum was the cook."

"Where?"

Paddy drained his mug. "Near Broken Hill in New South Wales."

Just enough information to answer each question. But, no warning bells. "How do you know the Davidsons? He gave you a glowing reference."

Scribbling in the dirt with a stick, Paddy lowered his head. He hadn't once made eye contact with Jake. Was this a sign of hesitation?

"My grandfather knew his father."

Now the dots were lining up. "What was your grandfather's name? My dad was also mates with Nick's dad."

Paddy continued to draw in the sand. "People called him Slim. He died before I was born."

Slim, not Patrick? But the kid could be lying. "How about your parents? What are their names?"

With the ease of youth, Paddy stood in one smooth movement. "Boss, why all the questions? I have more work back at the homestead."

"Sorry for delaying you. I'm curious, is all. I don't know much about you." He held Paddy's gaze. "I'll let Greg know why you're late."

"Righto. Opal and Carl. My dad left us when I was little. I don't know much about him."

"That must have been hard on you and your mum."

"It was, but she's tough. And I take after her."

"I can see that." Jake grinned. "One last question. Greg said you volunteered to fix the windmill. Any reason why?"

Paddy stepped toward his motorbike. "I know a lot about them, and I like climbing up high. I feel like the king of the world up there." Up until now he'd shown little emotion, then he grinned. "It that all boss?"

"Yeah, Paddy."

"Thanks for the tea." With a roar of the engine, he took off toward the south.

Jake mulled over the kid's answers while he set the flask and cup in his saddle bag. Barclay blue eyes notwithstanding, either Paddy was not Patrick's grandson and therefore not Jake's nephew, or the kid lied about everything. A radio call to Nate Davidson was in order. He would confirm Paddy's answers and put Jake's mind at ease, once and for all. At least, he hoped so.

A blob of mud followed by a stream of water fell from the pipe into the waterhole. Jake remained in the shade and watched the liquid gush in spurts. In thirty minutes or so, he'd climb back up the ladder to make sure the fill valve was working. Situated about three quarters of the way up the tank, the gadget monitored the level and automatically shut off the motor in the windmill shaft when the water reached the designated point. That way the tank never overflowed, and the reservoir only filled to a predetermined depth. When the level dropped, the valve allowed the pump to work. All very efficient.

Heat swirled around him. He had a hard time keeping his eyes open because he hadn't slept well. In fact, he lay awake for hours, reliving his discussion with Marlow. Yes, Bella was exactly as described, and he took responsibility for not helping her deal with Laura's passing.

A strong sulphury odor hit his nose, indicating the water gushing into the reservoir came from deep underground. And it would be cool. Jake groaned as he stood. *Getting too old to sit on the ground, mate.* He removed his sunnies, held his hat under the pipe, then poured the contents over his head. "Ahh. So good." The top part of his shirt was soaked. A zany idea popped into his head. He walked into the water and plopped down. "Bonza." No Worries. His clothes would be bone-dry by the time he arrived home.

Floating on his back in the shallow water, eyes closed, he allowed his mind to drift. If Celia found the letter, that would mean they could solve the puzzle. If not, he did have one other place he could search for old documents, an old trunk of Patrick's that supposedly only contained mementoes from his army service. But if Marlow accomplished her goal, she'd leave Long Gully.

He lowered his legs and sat on the muddy reservoir bottom. Three days ago, he'd refused her request to visit. Now he wanted her to extend her stay.

Yeah, she had a life in Texas. But she also had a six-month visa.

Chapter 24

That evening after everyone had eaten their fill, Marlow stacked the plates and said, "Another delicious meal, Celia. I'll do the dishes tonight."

"Thanks, but I want to talk to you and Jake." She patted her niece's shoulder. "Bella, luv, do the dishes now and I'll give you a pass for the rest of the week."

"Super-duper." Bella gathered the used napkins. "After I'm done, I'll watch a film until you tell me I can join you."

Jake cocked an eyebrow. "Good girl." He turned toward the door and waited for Marlow and Celia to proceed him onto the verandah. "What's on your mind?"

Once seated, Celia folded her hands in her lap. "Nothing serious, but I thought this conversation might not be suitable for Bella." She gave Marlow a nod. "Mary came to see me today. You haven't met her yet, Marlow. She's Nellie's daughter-in-law and helps around the homestead."

"Ernie told me she had a medical concern. Is she all right?" Jake stretched his legs.

Marlow lowered her head, recalling how she'd tripped over those legs, and Jake had prevented her fall. *Focus on Celia, girl.*

"She might be pregnant."

"Good old Ernie. Another kid to join their teenagers." Jake paused. "But there's more, right?"

"Yeah. She's concerned about her age. Forty-four next birthday."

"So, she'll be older than usual to have a baby. What's the problem?"

Marlow figured Celia had invited her so she could add her perspective and knowledge. She cleared her throat. "There is a higher probability of a woman giving birth to a baby with disabilities after age forty. Especially Down Syndrome.”

“That’s right. I always share my magazines with Mary and Nellie. There was a long article in one last month that featured older mothers who’d given birth to babies with Down Syndrome. Now Mary is obsessed with the possibility.”

“I see.” Jake seemed to be at a loss for a couple of seconds. “What, uh, does she want you to do about it? And why include Marlow in the discussion?” He jutted his chin toward her. “No insult intended. It’s just you’re not—”

“I understand your skepticism, but I’ve spent my career working with children who need specialized care.” Marlow leaned forward. “Celia, if you think it will help, I’d be glad to talk with Mary and remind her that the possibility of bearing a child with Downs after age forty is something like one in a hundred.”

“I was hoping you’d agree to that. Now, as to my part. I performed a physical examination on Mary, but I’m not sure if she’s pregnant. Either way, she needs to see a doctor immediately and share her concerns with him and discuss her symptoms.”

Jake tapped the armrest. “I’ll tell Ernie to make the arrangements. He can have off as many days as he needs.”

“And Darrie can pick up Mary’s household duties.” Celli sighed. “I did tell Mary that I couldn’t have anything to do with her, uh, ending the pregnancy.” Her voice broke on a sob.

Scooting closer, he put his arm around his aunt. “Did she ask you to?”

Celia shook her head. “Not in so many words, but she was distraught and worried.”

“The doctor will be able to reassure her by conducting an amniocentesis test.” Marlow stared at Celia. The woman sniffed and tears glistened in her eyes.

“I doubt they can do that in Cunnamulla. Brisbane maybe.” Celia leaned into Jake and issued a shuddering sigh.

“What’s wrong, Aunty?”

She swiped at her tears. “I don’t know how anyone can think of ending a life.” More sniffles as she rubbed her belly. “Years ago, in Brisbane, Wesley and I had planned to have a bunch of children. He was my former fiancé, Marlow. I longed to be a mother, but our relationship proved to be toxic. The man not only shredded my heart, but he broke my spirit." She took a breath and straightened. "It took years to regain my sense of self, to recover to a point where I could function as a productive member of any family." Smiling at Jake, she reached for his hand. "That's when I moved back home, and now I'm mother to everyone at Long Gully."

"Wesley was a fool, but we're blessed you are part of our family."

Night insects serenaded them for a while.

Marlow placed a hand on her abdomen, too. If she and Steven had had another child, would he or she have survived the accident?

"I've been wondering, Marlow. Did you only want the one child?"

Celia's words acted like a branding iron on her soul. She gulped and glanced into the night. Anyone else asking that question would have received a withering look and Marlow would have run away. But because Celia had just shared an intimate part of her life, Marlow forgave her. "I wanted more, but Steven was satisfied with Eileen." His reason—he wanted Marlow to keep her figure as long as possible. Those had been his exact words.

Neither Celia nor Jake responded, which was fine by Marlow. She didn't want to engage in any more gut-wrenching dialogue at the moment.

Bella hollered from the living room. "Can I come out now?"

First Jake sniggered, then Celia giggled, and finally Marlow joined in. What a great icebreaker.

"Come on, Bella Bear." Jake drew another chair into the circle.

After she sat with her legs crisscrossed, she looked at each adult in turn. "What's so funny?"

"Nothing. Luv. I'm glad we're all together."

Marlow savored Jake's answer. She was more than happy to be included, and after both women had delved deep into past hurts, no one could claim Marlow was not part of the family now.

And no one mentioned the letter, Graham's puzzle, or her departure for the rest of the evening.

Chapter 25

During Bella's school session the next day, Marlow finished her letter to Milton, ready for the mail run on Friday. Keeping in mind Jake's comments about his cousin, she reported only positive experiences and observations. She had no desire to stir the animosity that seemed to simmer between the men.

Just after noon, Celia called from the kitchen, "Lunch is ready."

Bella closed her workbook and stood. "I need a break. Arithmetic is hard."

"Do you want me to review the formulas again?" Marlow sealed her letter and slipped the envelop into the designated basket.

"Please. I wonder what we're having for lunch today? I'm starving." Bella tucked her hand into the crook of Marlow's arm and led her out of the office.

A thundering noise outside caught Marlow's attention. She stopped. "What's that?"

"Let's go see." Bella pulled her to the front door, and they stepped onto the verandah.

A dust trail announced the arrival of a large vehicle. Surely not a cattle train.

"It's our fuel delivery." Bella returned to the door. "Either petrol or diesel. There are underground storage tanks near the far shed." Skipping down the passage, she said, "Come on, we'll be late."

The light from an open door shone on the landscape Marlow had noticed previously. "Bella, who painted this beautiful picture?"

The child slid to a halt and lowered her head. "My mum."

"It is a scene from around Long Gully?"

"I think so, but talking about the painting always makes me sad."

"I'm sorry. Because your mum painted it?"

"Yeah." Bella shoved her hands into the pockets of her shorts.

"She was teaching me how to use acricks…some kind of paint."

"Acrylics."

"I started one picture, but then she died."

Marlow reached out to offer comfort, but Bella hurried to the kitchen. *Dear child, come back. You're grieving the loss of your mother, and I have a daughter-sized hole in my heart.* She inhaled, straightened her shoulders, and entered the kitchen.

During the meal, an idea bubbled in Marlow's mind. Art therapy. Could that be a way to reach Bella and help the child process her grief?

****

Miss York had assigned a science experiment which Bella completed outside. Then a lengthy arithmetic workbook chapter kept her busy in her room most of the afternoon. Marlow had reviewed the math principles with the child, but remained in her own bedroom to be close to Bella, sensing their chat about her mum and the painting had upset her. While she read a magazine, Toffee sauntered in and curled up beside her.

Sometime later, a knock sounded on Marlow's door. She blinked awake and slid her legs off her bed. "Come in."

"I've finished. Can you check my work, please?" An aura of melancholy still surrounded Bella.

"Of course." When had she stretched out and fallen asleep?

Plopping on the bed beside Marlow, Bella handed her the assignment. "Thanks for explaining the methods again. You really helped me understand the process. I think I got them all correct." Her leg bounced up and down, making the bed shake. "You're a good teacher."

"I appreciate the compliment." Marlow took time to peruse the page. "All correct. Good job." She had a lot more she wanted to say, but waited to gauge Bella's mood.

The child took Marlow's breath away by laying her head on her shoulder. "I've been thinking."

A great opening. "About?"

She cleared her throat. "When you noticed Mum's painting, the old sadness almost swallowed me. At least, that's how I felt. But I concentrated on my schoolwork and finished it all. Then, a few minutes ago, I went down the passage and looked at the painting. Instead of letting the usual gloomy thoughts take over, I imagined

Mum in her smock when she worked on the verandah. I could hear her explain what she was doing, how to mix the colors on the palette, what brush to use. See her smile. Even smell her perfume."

Amazed at Bella's mature outlook, Marlow slipped her arm around the child. "And how did that make you feel?"

"Still sad, but it didn't hurt as much."

Little girl, now you are healing! Marlow squeezed Bella's shoulder. "That's how we move on with life after a loved one passes. We don't forget them, but we treasure the memories."

Time seemed to cycle in slow motion. Neither Marlow nor Bella moved or uttered a word. Then booted feet thumped down the hall and a door shut.

"Daddy's home." Bella lifted her head but made no motion to get up.

Obviously, she wasn't done. Marlow broached a tender subject. "Do you want to paint again? Finish the picture you started? I used to paint, too. I could help."

Bella shook her head vigorously. "Not yet. Maybe later."

Another mature response. Marlow took her cue from the child and remained seated. "Is there anything else you'd like to talk about?"

A deep sigh. "Yes." Bella walked to the screen door and peered out. "Remember when you helped me with my schoolwork the first day you were here?"

Only three days ago. "Sure."

"I told you the term was almost over."

"And you mentioned final exams."

Bella turned, her eyes downcast. "The last day of school is December 9. Our tests will be mailed to us the week before, one for each subject."

"What type of tests?"

"Mostly we have to choose from several questions and then write out our answers."

"Essay exams. Usually American students don't have many of those before high school."

Pacing, Bella tugged at one of her braids. "That's what I want to talk about." She stilled and stared at Marlow.

The kid looked scared to death. Marlow held out her arms. "Come here, Bella. What's wrong?" She embraced her, and then brushed strands of hair from her face. "You did such a good job explaining yourself moments ago. You can do this."

"I don't want to go to boarding school."

"I can understand that. Being far away from family—"

Bella jumped up and covered her ears. "No, I want to stay here. I won't go."

What little progress Marlow attributed to Bella's improved social skills was erased in a second. But that was usually the case. People didn't change overnight. Marlow stood and drew Bella back to the bed. "Slow your breathing, relax your shoulders, and let's talk about your reaction."

Bella's eyes misted, and her bottom lip quivered. "Sorry. I should have listened and let you finish."

"I didn't have much else to add. Hasn't your dad talked to you about next year?"

"Yes. Most of my classmates will go to boarding school, and Dad thinks I want to go. He's never asked me, though."

Marlow pursed her lips. "You should tell him how you feel."

"I will, but I want you to help me."

"We can discuss it together. But first, what's the alternative if you don't go to boarding school?"

"Correspondence courses."

Which Celia would have to oversee. Maybe she should be included in the discussion. "Let's talk to him later this evening."

"Okay." Bella sprang off the bed. "It's late. I'll see if Aunty Celia needs help with dinner."

And then Marlow was alone in the room. She drew in a breath. Navigating through Bella's myriad issues was exhausting. But she was growing to love the child.

Preparations for the meal were well underway by the time Marlow entered the kitchen. Her mind abuzz with topics to share and discuss with Jake, she set the table while Bella brought in serving bowls laden with foods that exuded savory aromas. No doubt about it, Celia was a good cook, especially considering the limitations to her larder and access to fresh produce.

A shadow darkened the archway leading from the sitting room. Marlow glanced up as Jake entered. He wore a short-sleeved blue shirt, denim shorts, and no shoes.

"Shh. Don't tell Celia." He winked at her and sat down at the head of the table.

Without thinking, she winked back, then turned quickly to hide the blush she felt creeping into her cheeks. Blue shirt, blue eyes, tanned face, engaging smile—all too much to handle on such short notice. She scooted into the kitchen and didn't return until Celia carried in the fresh bread and sat down.

After Jake said grace, he rehashed his meeting with Paddy without giving away family secrets, no doubt for Bella's benefit. "The lad's led an interesting life. By the way, Celia, his mother's name is Opal, not Alice."

Celia's eyes grew wide. "I see. So he's not…" She bit into a piece of bread.

The names Jake mentioned spun through Marlow's mind. Right. The possible affair Patrick had with Alice. So Paddy wasn't a Barclay. No wonder Celia looked relieved.

"A few minutes ago, I contacted Nate Davidson, but he's not home. He'll be gone a week or more. I can't verify Paddy's details yet, but I think he told the truth." Jake cut into his grilled chicken and swirled the meat in the creamy gravy. "While I was in my office, Rick radioed. He'll join us for the Sunday service at Maroola Downs, then he'll come back here to collect his supplies. He's looking forward to meeting you, Marlow."

"Ricky's coming home. Ricky's—" Bella bounced in her chair, then stopped and glanced at everyone. A sheepish grin spread ear to ear, and she added in sweet, calm voice, "I'm excited."

Jake stared at his daughter then at Marlow.

Marlow raised her eyebrows. The girl monitored her overreaction and made an adjustment. Progress indeed.

Chapter 26

After breakfast, Bella headed to the office and Marlow helped clear the table. Jake had left the house early that morning, and since he and Bella watched a movie last night, Marlow had no opportunity to discuss his daughter and boarding school. At some point soon, she'd have to waylay him.

Voices from the back yard drew her attention.

Celia opened the door. Nellie and the Aboriginal women Marlow had seen the day Bella went missing entered the kitchen.

"Come in, ladies." Celia removed her apron. "Marlow, this is Nellie, remember you met her your first day here, and Darri Clague. She's helping with the house cleaning today since Mary's under the weather."

Marlow greeted the women, then excused herself and joined Bella in the office. She had signed in already and had materials lined up on her table. Miss York introduced a new topic in the language workbook—making inferences and drawing conclusions based on a text. By the scowl on Bella's face, Marlow figured she'd be helping more than usual. Which proved to be the case.

Close to eleven o'clock, Marlow left the office to prepare their tea. As soon as she entered the hall, a fresh, orangey smell surrounded her. She peeked in the dining room where Darri rubbed a corner of the large table. "Oh, that smells divine."

"Yeah. It's very strong. Wooden furniture in this dry climate can crack or split if it's not protected. Celia says this polish must be used twice a month. Especially for the antique pieces."

Marlow ran her fingers along the carved edge of the buffet. Had Vida brought these items with her from Bendigo when they moved?

Celia sat at the kitchen table, reading old documents.

"I guess no letter?" Marlow had a hard time hiding the

disappointment in her voice.

"No. But I found correspondence from my parents to each other. They are so sweet. I didn't know my daddy was such an old softie. He certainly had a romantic side."

Marlow set the filled kettle on the stove. "Did Jake tell you my mother was born in Australia and I never knew my father."

"He did. I'm so sorry, luv." Celia paused then clasped her hands beneath her chin. "He also said you were unsuccessful in locating any family."

"Right, so I must complete my other goal of solving Graham's code."

"I understand. You might not have found blood relatives, but you are a Barclay."

The kettle boiled. Marlow made the tea and readied the mugs. To divert the conversation away from a painful topic, Marlow said, "I noticed the polish Darri used on the furniture. Did Vida bring the antiques with her from Bendigo?"

"She did. Most survived the move." Celia pulled another folder from the box. "There are Anzac biscuits in the green tin." She jutted her head toward the counter.

"Thanks." Marlow selected several cookies that she added to the tray, and then carried it to the office.

Bella slouched in her chair. "I'm tired. I only have one more assignment to complete for today, and then we can take the post bag to the kitchen."

"I must get the letters I wrote to my friends in Texas." Marlow hurried to her room. When she returned, Bella had poured the tea and nibbled on a biscuit. Marlow slid her air letters into the bag.

"I haven't seen that kind of envelop before." Bella popped the rest of the small biscuit into her mouth.

Marlow removed a letter and handed it to the child. "They are specifically for overseas mail. You write on the sheet, then fold and seal it. Ta-da. A letter with the correct postage and envelope all in one."

"What a great idea. When you go back to Texas, I'll use them to write to you."

"I'd like that. Your dad can buy air letters at the post office."

Return to Texas? Marlow hadn't thought about her future much in the last couple of days. Finding Graham's letter and solving the puzzle was still important, but the reminder from Bella weighed her down. Exploring life in the outback had become equally important.

****

Late in the afternoon, while Marlow sat at the shaded table near the pool, Bella swam to the edge of the tank and yelled, "I see the plane. He'll fly around once to check that the airstrip is clear before he lands."

A small, while object circled the homestead, droning like a giant bumblebee in the cloudless sky, and landed out of sight. "This is exciting. Almost like expecting a present on your birthday. What will the plane bring me?" Marlow stood as Bella climbed out of the pool and dried off.

"I always get stuff—my graded schoolwork and next week's packet." She wrapped the towel around her middle. "Are you expecting any post?" She picked up Toffee who had been sleeping on the table.

"No. I was being silly. My Texas friends don't have this address yet."

"Of course. I'll get dressed now."

They entered the house together. Bella stopped in her room, and Marlow continued to the kitchen. "The mail plane's arrived."

Celia looked up from a long document she held. "Thanks. I heard it. Paddy picked up our outgoing post a while ago and should be back with our bag in a few minutes."

"Still looking?"

"Yeah. I keep getting sidetracked."

A motorbike engine whined into the yard, and then Paddy entered the kitchen and delivered the canvas bag. He doffed his hat before leaving the kitchen.

"Ta, Paddy." Celia dropped the paper to the table and shook her head. "I can't wait for Jake to come home. He needs to read about his grandfather's life in Bendigo." She sighed and opened the bag.

It contained a dozen or more envelopes of various sizes. She sorted through them, making a stack for Jake, one for Bella, and one for herself. "Marlow, here's a letter for you."

She frowned. "Who knows I'm here?" She took the envelope and studied the handwriting.

Setting aside her mail, Celia returned to the box of old documents.

Jake barged in the door. "I heard the plane." He grabbed his pile of mail. "Finally, the letter from the Wool Growers Association arrived."

Damp hair wrapped in a towel, Bella skipped into the kitchen and stopped beside Marlow's chair. "You did get a letter, Marlow. Who's it from?"

Marlow turned it over and whistled when she saw the return address.

"What's wrong?" Jake sank into the chair next to her.

"Nothing. At least, I don't think so. The letter's from Milton."

"Milton? Why did he write to you?" Jake's tone sounded churlish.

"We did agree to keep in touch. In fact, I sent him a letter today."

"Why would you want to?"

"Why not?" Marlow frowned at Jake. "Do I need your permission?" His reaction touched on pure high school jealousy. Inwardly, her heart sang.

A flush crept up his neck. "No. Sorry. I overreacted. Just didn't think he was your type."

"Her type of what?" Bella asked.

Jake stared at Marlow, and they both chuckled.

"Don't—"

"I found it!" Celia scooted back her chair and it toppled to the floor. "The letter from Graham. Here it is." She held out a yellowed envelope, the same as the ones Marlow had seen before.

"Let me have it, please." Jake held it gingerly as if it might disintegrate any second. "It's addressed to 'The Eldest Grandchild of Edward Barclay'." He patted his chest. "That's me." His eyes widened and a strange smile lit up his face. "Whew. I'm holding something my great-grandfather wrote. I feel…honored."

"Open it." Bella crowded her father.

"Wait, luv. Graham also wrote, 'Only open when contacted by George's eldest grandchild.'" Jake looked at Marlow and clutched the envelope. "I want to shower first."

Marlow watched him march down the hall. "Celia, is it my imagination, or does it seem he's reluctant to open it?"

Chapter 27

Water stains blurred the last character on Jake's piece of the puzzle. His page with the letters *N U Y W R A A W D M* visible lay on the dining room table, along with those from his cousins Steven and Henry. Jake took a swig of his coffee. He couldn't delay the moment any longer. He'd eaten breakfast as slowly as possible without raising suspicion, but the time had come. "Any suggestions on how to begin?"

A knot formed in his chest. Once they solved the mystery, Marlow would have no reason to stay. And she'd received a letter from Milton. Jake had no idea why she'd want to communicate with that man.

Pointing to the pieces of paper, Marlow said, "I tried to make words out of the letters on each page, but nothing made sense. Obviously, we have to combine all the letters."

Celia nodded. "Yeah. We can write them down to see if we—"

"I have a better idea." Bella bounced in her chair then stilled. "Sorry for interrupting."

Jake smiled at her to acknowledge her apology. "What do you suggest, luv?"

"We can use my word game tiles. That way we can switch them around easily, you know, to spell words."

"Splendid idea. Go get your game. Oh, and feed your cat. She's been circling my feet, meowing like her ribs are sticking out." Jake leaned back. "I studied the stained section of my page, but can't make out one letter."

"I think it might be *E* or *F*." Marlow's eyes shone as she sat next to him. If only he could be that excited.

Bella returned with a box, her grin almost as broad as the table. "I'll divvy up the letters. I told Marlow I'm good at word games.

Aren't I, Daddy?"

"You used to win all the time." When had they stopped playing family games? Oh, yeah. When Gail nixed the tradition. He handed Bella the three pieces of the puzzle.

She studied the lists. "There won't be enough letters to make four piles."

"No worries, Bella. Marlow and I will share." He cocked his head at her. "All right with you?"

"Sure."

Her cheeks flushed, and he grinned. Marlow might have stated categorically that she was only here to solve the mystery, but during her short time at the station, he'd sensed her growing interest in their way of life. And maybe in him.

Bella rounded up a group of letters for herself, pushed a set in front of Celia, then gave Jake and Marlow their pile. She sat down, her brow furrowed in concentration.

"Graham Barclay, you must have had a devious streak." Jake turned over a few tiles. "Where should we start?"

"First of all, Bella, if you have enough letters, give us each another *E* and an *F*, and then we can see which one could fit." Marlow accepted the extra letters. "Let's think like he might have. What was going on in his world when he penned the instructions in 1924? He wrote Bendigo under his name. Is that where he lived? Where did he work? The gold mines?" Marlow turned over the last tile so all letters were face up. "We need to begin with what we know about him."

"I read a lot of documents from that time period." Celia shuffled her tiles.

"Good. They might prove useful. Here goes." Jake lined up all their tiles. *L G L L Y S R N I E E O G L A E W D D N R R N U Y W R A A W D M E.* What a mess. The only word that jumped out at him was Gail. He scrambled the tiles and sighed. Crossword puzzles and the like were not high on his list of favorite activities.

A soft snicker beside him. Marlow glanced up then separated the vowels and consonants. "That might make it easier."

Meanwhile, on the other side of the table, Bella attacked her pile with the enthusiasm of an Olympic runner about to cross the finish line. This combination, that combination, and then she jumped up. "I've got something. Look." She pointed to a string of letters—

LONG GULLY.

"Now, that makes sense." Jake beamed.

Celia held up her hand in a stop motion. "My father didn't move to the station until 1925. How would Graham know his son was going to call the homestead Long Gully?"

"Crumbs." What seemed like a great start fizzled right before Jake's eyes. "So why did my great-grandfather use the name?"

"All good points, but this is too much of a coincidence not to be considered." Marlow removed the appropriate letters from their set. "I suggest we keep Long Gully. What else do you know about that name?"

"Wait a minute." Celia slumped in her chair. "Silly me. My mind is full of information I've gathered from the tons of documents you gave me, Jake. There was something… Hold on, let me get the box."

While Celia searched for the papers, Jake contemplated asking Marlow about Milton's correspondence, but then abandoned the idea. However, she introduced the subject.

"In the letter I received from Milton yesterday, he asked if we'd solved the mystery, and wants to know if he can…visit Long Gully."

"Why would he want to? He's never shown any interest before." Jake mentally slapped his forehead. He knew the answer.

"Milton said he's always liked the outdoor life."

Jake almost splattered his mouthful of coffee. "There's out*door*, then there's the out*back*." Picturing city-bred Milton riding on a motorbike covered in red dust and surrounded by the wholesome aroma of hundreds of sheep pleased him no end. "Tell him he's welcome any time."

Footsteps announced Celia's return. "Here's a property deed. Graham and Elizabeth lived in a suburb of Bendigo called Long Gully."

"Bonza. And I suppose that's where Lucky Ned got the name for the station. Long Gully stays." Jake eyed Bella. "Miss Smarty Pants, what other words can you find?"

Jake watched his three collaborators maneuver the tiles. Why even try when he knew his limitations? Give him a column of numbers to add any day.

They identified several words which made no sense in conjunction with Long Gully—

DREAM, WANDER, WINDOW, LADY, YARD. Jake threw

up his hands. "This could take all day."

"Not necessarily." Marlow, who'd been staring at the three pieces of paper, suddenly drew them toward her. She lined them up. "I have Steven's message on top, because he is, was, the oldest grandchild of Graham's oldest son. Then here is Henry's piece in the middle, as the oldest in Betsy's line, and last is Edward's, your piece, Jake, as a descendant of the youngest child." She moved the papers closer to him.

Groups of letters. Might as well be in a foreign alphabet. His eyes crossed. "I don't see how this helps us."

She pointed to the first letter on each list. "*L O N.* Then the second letter. *G G U,* and the third, *L L Y.* Don't you get it? Graham wrote the words out in order, one letter for each child until he completed his message. After Long Gully, he wrote *L A W Y E R.*" She glanced at Celia and Bella, then at Jake. "Does that make sense?"

He shrugged, then straightened. "Yes. Graham said we needed to solve the mystery because there could be legal or financial implications. Let's remove those letters from our piles."

Marlow continued, "What's left should be *S W A R D.* No. Take the *S* from sward and add it to lawyer, making it plural, which leaves *W A R D.* The next word is *A N D.* Finally, *W I N D E R M E R.* The blurred letter has to be an *E* to spell Windermere. *F* wouldn't work."

Bella arranged her letters, then giggled. "Too right. Windermerf can't be anyone's name."

Marlow's and Celia' s nervous laughter added to the excitement.

"Windermerf. Good one, Bella Bear."

She glowed at his compliment. He cringed. So many of her social issues could be laid at his feet. *Please, dear God. Help me make up for lost time.*

Jake felt the eyes of the group on him, and he cleared his throat. "Lawyers Ward and Windermere in Long Gully, a suburb of Bendigo." He patted Marlow's shoulder. "Good work. Ladies, you all contributed to solving the puzzle." He folded his arms. "But we're not finished, are we? This firm of lawyers probably has important information for us."

"Makes sense to me." Celia scooted back her chair. "I'll make tea while you lot determine the next step."

"Lawyers in films always look mean." Bella gathered the tiles.

"Are we done, Dad?"

"Yes, luv. You can put away your game."

Marlow beamed and slid her pile of letters toward Bella. "The lawyers are the key. Problem is, are they still in business?"

Bella added the tiles to the box, closed the lid, and skipped down the passage.

"This is getting complicated." Jake thumped the table. "I don't have time to fly down south and hunt for lawyers—"

"Hold it right there." Marlow turned toward him. "Don't forget what else Graham stipulated. George's eldest grandchild must collect the pieces. That would be Steven, and I've done the job for him. Stands to reason I should be the person to contact the lawyers."

"How?"

A flush crept into her cheeks as she lowered her head. Her blonde-streaked hair fell forward, hiding her mouth. Jake wanted to brush the strands from her face, but then her words sobered him. "We could ask Milton to help. He often travels to Bendigo on business." She looked at Jake through her lashes.

He clenched his fist under the table hoping Marlow didn't see his agitation. "There has to be another way. I don't want to bother him."

"I think he'll be willing to help. What we discover might affect all Graham's relatives."

Put that way…but still he balked. "How about Henry? After all, he is older than Milton and therefore the oldest of Betsy's grandchildren."

Marlow shook her head. "He doesn't get out much. I think it would be an imposition to ask him."

"I forgot." Jake set his elbows on the table and rested his chin in his hands. "Looks like I'll have to ask Milton." He eyed Marlow as she sat calm and serene while his insides churned. "Do you think he'll mind?"

"No. He was excited by the whole mystery code." Tilting her head, she added, "He wanted to travel here with me, but I declined his offer."

The nerve of the chap. The image of Milton with Marlow together burned his brain. "How long did you spend in Melbourne?"

"Two weeks. I told you I stayed with Milton's parents, but he often joined us for meals, and took me sightseeing. We had a lot of fun."

Two weeks. Surely that wasn't long enough for either of them to have formed a relationship that was anything but cousinly? But then, Marlow had only come into his life a week ago. *Whoa, Jake. Slow down. Are you jealous?* "All right. Milton knows about the puzzle, yes?"

"As I said, I told all the cousins. They're eager to learn the results, too."

Jake nodded. "Here's my plan. I'll use the radio relay system and get a message to Lion at the hotel in Cunnamulla. He can telephone Milton. Wait. I don't have his number."

"I do."

Of course, she'd have it. "Thanks." His flat tone almost betrayed him. "I'll ask Milton to visit Bendigo to see if Ward and Windermere are—"

"Or, to look for their names in a telephone book."

"Right." He didn't think of that because a heavy fog clouded his brain. "Then he could ring them, explain what we found, and ask what we need to do next."

Marlow stood and stretched. "Great idea. Where's that tea? I'm ready for a break. How about you?" She walked to the window and pulled her hair into a ponytail then let it drop. Turning, she raised her eyebrows. "What are you looking at?"

You, dear Marlow. You. The fog intensified for a second, then an idea fought its way to the forefront. "Something else I remember Graham wrote." Jake eased out of his chair and poked his thumbs into his belt loops. "He said the designated person which, as you said, would have been Steven, must take a cousin of his or her choosing to follow the instructions of the message." He approached Marlow. "I want to be that cousin."

A shadow crossed her face. She side-stepped away from him and said over her shoulder as she left the room, "But what if you are not my choice?"

Jake's mouth gaped, and he crumpled against the wall. Marlow must have sensed his resentment toward Milton. He grabbed the shirt over his chest to ease the pain in his heart. lived with the problem for too long. It was time to heal the breach with his cousin.

Another idea hit him like a sledgehammer. Since Marlow had accomplished her goal of solving the puzzle, she might decide to stay in Melbourne. *Your fault, Barclay. You insisted she limit her stay on the station.* He ran a hand through his hair. The only way he could explore what he hoped was a budding relationship with her was to encourage her to return with him to Long Gully.

Chapter 28

The elation of solving the puzzle dissipated almost as quickly as it had appeared. Marlow avoided Jake for much of Saturday, which wasn't difficult, considering he closed himself in his office most of the afternoon. She'd heard him on the radio and figured he'd relayed the message to Lion. During the evening meal, they'd all speculated about information the lawyers might possess, from a British title to buried treasure. Criminal activity or secret family members. They laughed at their creativity, but left the table with another troubling question. Why would Graham Barclay want the information concealed from the family for so long?

The next morning, Marlow opened her closet to select something to wear to the church service at Maroola Downs. Although staring at her clothes, she couldn't shake the dilemma camping out in her mind. Why were Jake and Milton at odds? Milton's objection to Jake seemed to be that he was a church goer. Jake's reaction to him was much stronger. If she understood Jake's objections to his cousin, she might understand his attitude toward her writing to Milton.

Marlow removed a pair of jeans and floral T-shirt. Milton would undoubtedly obtain the lawyers' address. Without a phone and only weekly mail delivery, the information might take over a week to reach them.

Milton. The name was like waving a red cape at a bull. Maybe Milton sending her a letter at Jake's station was a deliberate provocation. Yes, and Jake's reaction one of pure jealousy. "Men. Grrr." She shut the closet door so aggressively it popped open.

Rolling her eyes, she leaned against the door to close it. Upon reflection, she was sorry she had told Jake she might not choose him to accompany her.

Then she was hit by a jarring image of Bridgette, the statuesque brunette, in a clinging yellow dress. Marlow yanked open the door and shoved the row of hangers across the rod. Another reason for her disconcertion was her growing attraction to Jake. Romance, or even a hint of Cupid, was not included in her game plan of returning to Texas. Maybe that was why she'd spurned Jake's suggestion.

Huffing out a breath, Marlow chose a slim, baby blue skirt and matching blouse she knew emphasized her highlighted hair and trimmed-down figure.

After dressing, she grimaced at her reflection. *What are you playing at, girl?* Drawn to Jake one minute, remember her promise to return home the next. She opened her jewelry bag and removed her diamond earrings and the pendant from her mother, baubles to boost her self-confidence. The teardrop studs always generated a wave of memories. Steven had given them to Marlow when Eileen was born. A time when he'd valued her as a partner.

She shook off the sadness, straightened her shoulders, secured the studs then slid the silver chain over her head. That brought a smile to her face. The dark blue, oval stone had tiny flecks of green, yellow, and orange throughout, which contrasted with the pale blue lacy folds of her blouse. As a child, she'd loved to play dress-up, and Mom had let her wear her jewelry. The necklace had been one of Marlow's favorites, and now it belonged to her. She fingered the smooth, two-inch-long stone as she did whenever she wore it and traced the swirl of silver etched into the face of the pendant. The embellishment almost looked like a fancy *F*. But that meant nothing to her. Not for the first time, Marlow wondered how her mother had acquired the elegant piece.

Celia had mentioned they would leave Long Gully at eight o'clock. Marlow checked her watch. Six thirty. Plenty of time to help Celia with her contribution to the lunch. She fastened her sandals and headed toward the kitchen, but Celia was nowhere to be seen. Marlow prepared a mug of coffee and helped herself to half an egg and bacon sandwich. Biting into the crusty bread, she almost choked when Jake tapped her on the shoulder.

"Good morning."

She pivoted and swallowed. "Morning."

"Um, I'd like to have a chat. Please come with me to the office."

Time to iron out their differences. "Okay."

He poured his coffee and stacked a couple of sandwiches onto a plate. "We can eat while we talk." His cheeks reddened.

She followed him down the hall, and he closed the door behind them. He sat at his desk, and she settled into his armchair. His musky scent permeated the room, and Marlow had to lower her gaze and focus on her mug, sure her cheeks pinked, too.

"For the second time since you've been here, I have to apologize. I can't believe I acted like a cad yesterday. Of course, Milton should be the one to help us in Bendigo." He took a swig of coffee. "I sent a radio message to Lion. He'll ring Milton, and maybe my cousin will send the lawyers' contact information."

"I'm sure he will. I was surprised at your behavior, but—"

"No excuses." Jake leaned back. "I stayed up half the night planning what to say to you, and now I can't put two thoughts together."

"You obviously have strong feelings about your cousin, but you don't have to explain them to me. However, I'd be honored if you'd share your burden." In her career, Marlow had often found that family members could cause the deepest rifts in a person's heart. She nibbled her sandwich and watched waves of emotion sweep over Jake's face.

"I know Milton divorced several years ago, but I never realized how deeply I distrust him until you entered the picture. When we met in Cunnamulla and you mentioned you'd spent time with him in Melbourne, a jab of apprehension burned through me. And the only reason I can figure is that I pictured you as vulnerable, open to be manipulated by the ladies' man I know him to be."

"That's not how he acted toward me."

"Probably not. He's good at hiding behind the nice-guy image." Jake drained his mug. "When we were lads at uni in Brisbane, Milton went out with a good friend of mine. She and I were pals, not romantically involved. I was more like her big brother. Milton broke her heart and then gloated about his conquest."

"His actions hurt you, but were they enough to make you enemies?"

"There's more." Jake rocked in his chair. "When I started going out with Laura, I split my time between Long Gully and Brisbane, a long-distance relationship if ever there was one. Milton was offered a job in Brisbane. I can't prove it, but I think he deliberately accepted it so he could pay attention to Laura. He convinced her I was seeing other women, which was a lie, but she broke off our engagement anyway."

"Now that's something to hold a grudge over." Marlow set her empty mug on Jake's desk.

"Not a grudge. He broke the bond of trust we had. It took me a long time to reassure Laura that I was not the guy Milton made me out to be, but he was behind the pain we both suffered."

Marlow witnessed Jake's eyes glaze over as if he drifted back in time. She whispered, "I can see how that affected your relationship with him."

The creak-creak of Jake's chair was the only sound in the room until he nodded and said, "Milton never acknowledged his lies. I have forgiven him, but can you see why I doubt his motives whenever a woman is involved. Especially one I…know. Not that you would be taken in by his deception, but I just don't want you to get hurt."

"Thanks for the warning, however, I can take care of myself. I did see the playboy side of him, nevertheless, I enjoyed his company."

"He can be charming." Jake stopped rocking and began to stand.

"Please wait." She felt another flush creep up her neck as he sat and cocked his head at her. "I also need to apologize. About not wanting you to accompany me to Bendigo." She might as well explain her reaction and, by so doing, spill more details of her life. "I spent too many years in Steven's company where he ordered me about and never let me make decisions. And after your attitude toward Milton ticked me off, I just wanted to put you in your place, so to speak."

Elbows on the desk and fingers tented, Jake nodded. "I understand and am sufficiently chastised. I promise I will never order you to do anything." His blue eyes took on a warm hue as he spoke. "But I will look out for you and keep you safe. Whether from deadly gwardar snakes or from predatory men, cousins or not."

Marlow didn't know how to handle the sincerity in his voice and the soft expression on his face. She stood, hesitated, then picked up her mug.

"By the way, you look very nice today. That color suits you. Complements your hair and the tan you've acquired." His smile almost made her knees buckle.

She couldn't take any more pleasant words from him and hurried out the door.

****

Two vehicles set off for Maroola Downs, the family in one and several workers in the other. Celia had loaded her contribution of fresh bread, cakes, and biscuits. The aroma filled the cruiser, making Marlow wish she'd eaten more than half a sandwich for breakfast.

"Who's in the other car?" Seated in the front, she felt obligated to talk to Jake.

"Mitch our mechanic, Greg Jennings my manager, and his wife, Yvonne. I'll introduce them when we get there."

"How far is the station?"

"About forty kilometers northeast. Should take us an hour." He stared straight ahead. "The O'Bryans have lived there for three generations. Our families have been friends for a long time."

Including Bridgette? Marlow bit her lip.

Celia tapped Marlow's shoulder from the back seat. "You met Kevin and Gracie, and their daughter, Bridgette, last Sunday in Cunnamulla."

"I remember. Does Bridgette live there, too?"

"For now. She returned home from Sydney after her divorce." Jake slowed as two emus crossed the dirt track. "And reverted to her maiden name."

The miles inched by as the sun heated the air and dust wafted through the vehicle. Marlow regretted wearing a pale color, but then she remembered Jake's compliment and smiled. Such few words, yet they lingered and warmed her heart.

Little conversation ensued for the rest of the short trip and soon Bella hopped out of the cruiser to open and then close the gate to Maroola Downs. The O'Bryan's homestead was larger than Long Gully with gardens extending down to the circular driveway. Several vehicles were already parked close to the hedge, and people milled about on the shaded lawn and verandah.

Marlow gulped down the lump in her throat. A knot of apprehension burned in her stomach. She'd see Bridgette again.

Speaking of… Bridgette was not hard to find. She ran down the stairs to the cruiser, a vision in a white sheath dress. Luscious brunette curls flowing over her shoulders, a radiant, welcoming smile for all, but her words were for one person only.

"Jake. It's so good to see you."

Unease teased Marlow's insides. She'd mentally accused Jake of being jealous of Milton, and here she experienced a similar reaction.

As soon as he extracted himself from behind the wheel, Bridgette threw her arms aground his neck.

"Bridgette!" He pulled her arms away and stepped backward. "How ya going?"

"Bonza, now." She barely acknowledged anyone else.

Jake drew Marlow forward. "You remember my cousin-in-law, Marlow Barclay."

"Yes." Bridgette turned, and the smile slipped off her face. "Welcome to Maroola Downs." She waved at Celia and Bella. "So glad you came today. Can I help carry anything?"

"We can manage, thanks," Marlow replied.

Celia smirked and nodded.

Dragging Jake by the arm, Bridgette traipsed to the group of people on the lawn.

"Well, well, well." Celia handed a basket to Bella, one to Marlow, and picked up the large cake tin. "Very interesting indeed. Marlow, we need to chat later."

Marlow followed Celia up the stairs and into the house.

Gracie O'Bryan, average height, slightly overweight, and hair-salon blonde, met them near the large kitchen. "Celia, dear, I can tell by the delicious aroma coming from your baskets that you baked your special bread." She hugged Celia then turned. "Marlow, welcome to our home." She extended her hand, but abruptly stopped and stared at Marlow's pendant. Her dark eyes misted and she reached out tentative fingers. "That looks like a Finlay necklace. I haven't seen one for so long. Where did you get it?"

Blown away by Gracie's reaction, Marlow latched onto a kitchen chair to steady her jellylike legs. "It belonged to my mother." Her words barely made it through her tightening throat.

"May I look at it?" Gracie asked.

Marlow nodded, her heart thumping in her chest.

Gracie picked up the stone with a shaky hand and almost caressed it. "Where's your mother?"

"She…she passed away many years ago."

"Sorry to hear that. Was she a Finlay?"

Chapter 29

The floor tilted, and the pale green kitchen walls swirled. Marlow sank into the chair and blinked to regain normal vision. Gracie waned in and out of focus.

"Are you all right, luv?" Celia asked as she leaned over Marlow and patted her hand.

"I'll be fine." Marlow attempted a smile, and then bedlam broke loose in the kitchen.

"Rick's here." Beaming, Jake entered with a young man.

Bella squealed and leaped at her brother.

Celia straightened and gave him a kiss on the cheek.

"Mum, come quickly." Bridgette beckoned from the doorway. "Dad needs you outside. He says there's a problem with the steak."

Her head swimming and her heart constricting, Marlow crept out of the kitchen away from the chaos. The early morning heat wrapped around her but for once she didn't object. Ice crystals clogged her veins, and she shivered. Marlow leaned against a gum tree and clasped her pendant. The *F* stood for Finlay. The name meant nothing to her, but Gracie's reaction to the necklace screamed its significance and not because it was old or valuable. How did her mother acquire the jewel?

Voices from the kitchen caught her attention, but she didn't want to face anyone and skirted around the tree. However, Jake ran down the stairs with Rick in tow.

"Marlow, there you are."

She attempted an attentive attitude.

Beaming like a proud father, Jake completed the introductions.

Rick was a taller, slenderer version of his dad with the same smile, and of course the Barclay blue eyes. Marlow corralled her confusion in preparation to chat with Rick, but Bella skipped around the corner and latched onto his hand.

"Come, I want you to meet my new friend. Her dad has just been hired on the station." Brother and sister marched off together.

"Why are you out here?" Jake removed his hat and ran a hand through his hair. "Whew. Can't believe it's so hot already."

"The kitchen was, uh, stuffy. I needed some air."

"The service is about to start. Good thing the O'Bryans have a big, shady yard." He held out his hand. "Let's go to the front."

She pretended not to see his hand and walked ahead of him, unsure if her legs would hold her upright. About twenty people were seated on the verandah steps or in chairs lined up close by. Marlow chose a chair next to Celia who handed her a small cardboard fan.

"Good for stirring the air and keeping the flies away."

Meanwhile, Jake settled on the bottom step beside Rick and Bella. Bridgette squeezed next to him and slipped her hand through his arm.

A famous TV evangelist could have led the service, and Marlow would not have been able to remember a single thing he said. Words, hymns, prayers all mixed together in a cacophony of sounds breaking in on her thoughts. She was ashamed to be so distracted, but her mind refused to let go of her immediate concerns. Gracie's comment identifying the *F* on the necklace as Finlay overshadowed everything. Graham's puzzle solved and they were in the process of contacting the lawyers to fulfill Steven's dying wish. But now, she had a glimmer of hope in regard to discovering her mother's origins. She never realized until this moment how important her quest was. *I hope Gracie can provide some answers.*

Out of the corner of her eye, she spied Bridgette fawning over Jake. Well, any concern Marlow had about them would have to take a back seat.

When the final amen sounded, Marlow stood scanning the crowd for their hostess, but Jake appeared at her side with Bridgette on his arm. A twinge of jealousy surfaced then vanished amidst Marlow's anxiety. She didn't care who Jake flirted with. Where was Gracie?

"Bridgette has a proposition for you, Marlow." Jake's eyebrows rose as he looked at her.

"Really?" Marlow eyed the woman. Her curls were still beauty-shop perfect and her makeup unaffected by the heat. Any other time Marlow would have been curious as to Bridgette's beauty regime.

Bridgette opened her mouth, but Kevin called, and she traipsed off to help her dad without saying a word.

The unmistakable aroma of charred wood and grilling meat drifted through the air. In spite of the knots in her stomach, Marlow's mouth watered. She set aside her search for Gracie and focused on Jake. "What does Bridgette have in mind?"

"She wants to take you riding. Would you be interested?"

Not really. She frowned. Why the antagonism toward a person she hardly knew? "Sure. But right now, I need to talk to Gracie. Have you seen her?"

"She won't surface until all her guests have eaten their fill. I'd wait until after she serves tea."

"Thanks." Marlow hesitated. Should she tell Jake about the necklace? Not yet. Not until she knew more.

He leaned close and waited for her to look at him. "What's wrong? You seem distracted or worried. Can I help?"

Jake. Why do you have to be such a gentleman? Marlow placed her hand on his arm. "I'm fine. A little homesick, maybe." She lowered her head. Homesick. Heart sick. Tears formed in her eyes. She turned away but not before he noticed.

"What a lout. I haven't once asked if you missed your home and friends. I assumed you were content here completing your mission." He led her to a chair and sat next to her. "So sorry, Marlow. Is there anything I can do? Would you like a cold drink?"

Words stuck in her throat, and she nodded.

Jake hurried away and returned a minute later with a glass of soda which he handed to her then sat beside her again and slid his arm across the back of her chair.

Marlow tasted the icy liquid and feeling absurdly safe with his arm around her shoulders, a semblance of calm descended over her.

****

Most of the guests had left by two o'clock, and Marlow finally had a chance to speak with Gracie. They sat by themselves on the side verandah, sipping tea and nibbling Celia's Empire biscuits.

Marlow cleared her throat. She wanted answers, but was almost afraid of what she'd learn. "Please tell me about the Finlay necklace. My mother never gave me any information about it."

"How did she come by it?"

Shrugging, Marlow set down her cup, afraid she'd spill the

contents. "I don't know. I think it might be valuable because Mom told me to always keep it in a safe place."

"Do you mind if I hold it?"

"Of course not." Marlow slipped the chain over her head and passed the pendant to Gracie.

She studied the front then turned it over. The flecks of color in the dark stone shimmered. "Yes, it is a Finlay." Gracie leaned back and sighed. "I'll tell you the story. Before I married, I worked in a large, upscale woman's clothing shop in Melbourne called Finlay's Fashions. They had branches in all the major cities. Arthur and Ida Marie Finlay were the proprietors, but they sold the business when they retired, about ten years ago, and moved to Perth. They were great bosses, and Ida Marie and I became close friends."

"Ida Marie. Interesting." Marlow's ears tingled. Her mother was Marie Kate.

"Yes, and you'd better use her full name or she'd get annoyed." Gracie chuckled. "The biggest upset we ever had was when I asked why she had to use both." She handed the necklace back to Marlow. "Ida Marie never said, but I always used both names after that."

"What about the pendant?"

"Sorry, I'm getting sidetracked. Arthur had three of those necklaces made, one for Ida Marie, one for their daughter, and one for his mother."

Heart thumping a loud tattoo, Marlow gasped in air. One for their daughter. "Who is their…daughter?"

"A sad tale. Katie was their only child. She got involved with a nasty crowd of youngsters and moved to Sydney. I think she went overseas in 1946. At least, that's what Ida Marie believed."

"Overseas, as in America? Do you know if Katie took her necklace with her?"

"Yes, luv. You're wearing it." Gracie grasped Marlow's hand. "When I first saw you last Sunday in Cunnamulla, I thought you looked familiar. Now I know why—you remind me of Katie. She knew how valuable that necklace is and wouldn't have given it to just anyone. It's a Lighting Ridge black opal. Unique and worth a bundle."

"I don't care about the value of a stone. Katie Marie Finlay might be my mother's real name."

"I agree."

"Do…are Arthur and Ida Marie still alive?"

"Yes. I have their address. Wait here, and I'll get it for you."

Alone on the verandah, Marlow almost floated off the chair. The Finlays could be her grandparents. The evidence stacked up. The necklace. A wayward daughter who moved to America. Gracie's recognition. Katie Marie grew up in Melbourne. Is that where she enjoyed her beach vacations as a kid? The only time her mother spoke of her life in Australia was when she reminisced about playing in the waves, building sandcastles. Eating fresh pineapple sandwiches.

Marlow's mouth watered at the thought. Her mother used to make the treat whenever they visited Galveston.

First thing she'd do when she returned to Long Gully would be to write to Arthur and Ida Marie. Joy bubbled up within her, and she stood, suppressing a giggle. Where was Jake? She had to tell someone her good news. Marlow swung around and almost knocked Bridgette over. "Oops. Sorry."

"No worries. Mum asked me to give this to you." She handed Marlow a slip of paper.

"Thanks. I hope—"

"I'm glad we have a moment to talk by ourselves." Bridgette patted the seat Marlow had just vacated. "Please join me. I won't keep you long."

The smirk on Bridgette's face tempered Marlow's feeling of euphoria. She folded the piece of paper and slipped it into her pocket. What did the fashion plate want?

"Jake told me so much about you. He says you'll be going back to America soon."

Considering what she'd just discovered, that might not be the case. But to humor the woman, Marlow answered, "Probably. Why?"

"That's a pity because you'll miss the wedding."

"Who's getting married?"

"I am."

A weight lifted off Marlow's heart, and she brightened. "Congratulations. Who's the lucky groom?"

Bridgette slowly sipped her glass of lemonade and eyed Marlow over the rim. "Jake."

A cold mantle settled on Marlow's shoulders, as if Bridgette's ice-cold words drizzled over her. The blood drained from her head and she clutched the arms of the chair. "Jake…Barclay?"

"Uh-huh." Bridgette fluttered her false lashes. "But don't mention the wedding to anyone. We're keeping our engagement a secret." With that, she pranced down the verandah and entered the house.

Marlow stumbled blindly down the steps and through the garden. She hadn't thought to ask why they were keeping the engagement secret, nor had she tried to gauge whether or not Bridgette was manipulating her. All she could dwell on was Jake and the closeness that seemed to be developing between them, and not just on her part. No. He couldn't be as sensitive as he was this morning yet be deceptive at the same time. There must be a logical explanation, but she was too numb to consider other possibilities.

While Jake and Celia packed up the cruiser and everyone said their goodbyes, Marlow struggled to process the fact she might have found her grandparents along with discovering Jake was getting married. She figuratively curled up in a fetal position in the front seat.

Once on the road, Jake asked, "Marlow, what's the matter?"

"I have a headache. Must be the heat." She closed her eyes and longed for the jolting, sickening ride to be over. Whatever interest she might have had in Jake flew out the window to mingle with the dust. Although she'd been given a possible lead on her family, what if the Finlays were not related?

Milton better respond quickly. Marlow was hurt and confused. She couldn't wait to leave Long Gully.

Chapter 30

Dawn painted the sky in golden hues. Jake stood outside his bedroom taking in the glorious sight. In a few minutes, he would accompany Rick and Bella to the cemetery. Thank the Lord Marlow had made the suggestion. Marlow. Since their return from Maroola the previous day, she'd been, well, standoffish. After dinner, the family had gathered on the verandah, and although Marlow had participated in the conversations, she volunteered little, and went to bed early.

He'd noticed her fancy necklace as she exited the cruiser in the afternoon, but what with helping Rick load his supplies and catching up on his son's exploits, he'd not broached the subject with her. He did wonder how Marlow came into possession of a Lightning Ridge black opal. The stones weren't rare, but one of that size certainly was. Oh, well. He'd ask her later in the day.

Tucking his shirt into his jeans, he entered his room then made his way to the kitchen.

Rick sipped from a mug of coffee. "Morning, Dad."

"Ricky boy."

The lad grinned. "Don't call me that. Anyone would think I'm five years old."

"You'll always be my kid. Sleep well?"

"Yep. After a great day, good food, and yacking with family, I slept like a, um, five-year-old."

Footsteps pattered down the passage. "Morning, Dad, Rick." Bella hugged her brother as if she'd never let go.

It was good to see his children together, and happy. "Let's go." Jake opened the kitchen door. "Come on, slow pokes."

Bella walked between Jake and Rick and insisted on holding their hands. Not a bad idea, as the action seemed to solemnize their venture. "I should have done this long ago, and I apologize for not thinking about how you two were coping with Mum's passing."

No reaction from Rick, but Bella squeezed Jake's hand. "That's all right, Dad."

Her voice was remarkably steady. Jake had stuffed tissues into his pocket in case anyone needed them.

Jake and the kids made the rest of the trek without talking. Diamond doves in the gums serenaded their approach as he opened the small gate in the stone wall. "Have you been here since the funeral, Rick?"

He cleared his throat. "A couple of times, but not recently."

"I didn't know." Jake knelt and pulled up scraggly weeds from around Laura's headstone. "I stopped coming because I'd rather remember her by looking at photos. Or when I catch Bella smiling at certain moments. The same smile as Mum. Same eyes, hair."

Bella knelt beside him. "Do I look that much like her?"

"Yes, Bella Bear. More so as you get older. You have the same subtle beauty she had."

"Yeah, sis. I agree." Rick joined them on the ground.

"I'm glad." Bella rested her head on Jake's shoulder.

A calm silence surrounded them which Jake didn't want to interrupt. How he regretted not doing this sooner. Tears formed, and he swiped at his eyes. He wasn't supposed to cry.

Rick elbowed him. "You're going to make me sob now."

"Me too." Bella sniffed. "But I'm allowed because I'm still a child."

Jake handed out tissues and used one himself. "Adults can cry, too, young lady." Joints objecting, Jake eased up and moaned. "Do either of you want to say anything?"

"No," Rick responded without hesitation. "Her soul is not here. Sometimes when I'm out on the station, I talk to her. Tell her what I've been doing. Or if I have a problem or a decision to make, I'll use her sort of as a sounding board." He stood and brushed dirt off his jeans. "Funny, because she probably already knows about my problems, but I draw comfort from our chats, and they help me come to conclusions."

Wise word from his twenty-two-year-old son. Jake patted Rick's shoulder. "Well said, son. Very mature outlook."

"I thought if I talked to Mum, people would think I'm loony."

Shoving her used tissue in her pocket, Bella rose and squinted at Jake.

"I see your point, luv. Come, let's sit." Jake stepped to the wall and perched on it, and his kids followed. "Sometimes when I'm at my desk, I look at the photo of you and Mum, and I'll tell her what we've been doing. Like last week, I told her Marlow was visiting from America. Now, the loony bit would be if I expected Mum to answer."

"Righto. I don't talk to Mum all the time, and never when other people are around. I keep my conversation private." Rick kicked the wall. "It's a little connection to her that I hold dear."

"I couldn't have said it better myself. Understand Bella Bear?"

She nodded. "I might try, but I prefer to talk to a living per…person." She sniffled then sobs wracked her small body.

Jake took her in his arms while Rick hovered. "My dear child. Don't hold back. Cry all you want to. All you need to."

Her weeping lasted several minutes, and Jake kept a tight hold of her.

After a while, Rick placed his arms around Jake and Bella. "Father, God. Please bless us today as we remember Laura. She was a wonderful wife and mother, and servant of Yours. Help us to move on and live happy, fulfilling lives, as she would want for us. Thank You for Marlow's influence, and be with her as I sense she's carrying a heavy burden. In Jesus's name. Amen."

Stunned at his son's powerful words, all Jake could say was, "Amen." When had Rick's faith developed so deeply, and how did he come by such insight? Jake smoothed the hair from Bella's damp face and shook his head. He didn't deserve such great kids.

The unmistakable fast chirp-chirp chattering of the mulga parrot sounded in the branches above. Jake looked up. Sure enough, there were several of the blue-green birds splaying their dark blue tail feathers. He smiled. "Your mum's favorite bird. Now, who says she's not watching out for us?"

Rick and Bella stared at the birds, too. Seconds later, the small flock flew away.

"I think that's our cue to go home." Jake extended his hand to Bella. "Are you all right, luv?"

She blew out a sigh. "Yes, Dad. Thanks for bringing us. Can I come back again?"

"Of course. But tell someone where you're going first and let me know if you want me to come too."

"I will." She closed the gate and hesitated. "Bye, Mum." She pivoted and walked beside Jake.

He placed an arm around each child. "Your mum would be so proud of you two. Just as I am. I love you." His throat tightened.

The kids kept pace and slipped their arms around him.

But true to form, Bella interrupted the calm scene. "I'm hungry. See you later." She dashed away without a backward glance. Toffee jumped out of the brown grass and ran after her, a streak of black.

Jake didn't need to be a professional to realize Bella had a breakthrough experience. So had he, to be honest. And he'd learned much about his son during the short visit to the cemetery.

"I'm going to say it again. I'm proud of you, Richard Edward Barclay. When did you get to be so…so deep?"

"From watching you and Mum. You always put God first." Rick shoved his hand into his pockets. "These are the kinds of things I chat to her about."

"I'm glad you have that connection. Um, tell me why you think Marlow is carrying a burden? Did you talk with her?"

"No. I just observed. Something happened at Maroola. She seemed distracted, almost sad. And then after we came back to Long Gully, sure, she was here in body, but her mind was far away. Do you know why?"

"Not really. Hang on. She did say she was homesick that morning. I sat with her a bit, but Kevin and Greg had station business to discuss, and I, well, I forgot about Marlow's situation." He gave himself a mental thump. What an oaf. Too concerned about himself. "Marlow is dealing with grief, too. Her husband and daughter died after a car accident two years ago."

"Bella mentioned the puzzle you solved yesterday—the reason Marlow is here. It must be hard on her without her husband, the Barclay cousin."

"Yeah. Again, I haven't taken her circumstances into account. She is fulfilling her husband's dying wish, and I've acted like a selfish brute."

"I'm sure you haven't, Dad."

"I've been too wrapped up in my own life to notice. You have shown me up again, son. I can learn a lot from you."

They slowed as they neared the house. The enticing smell of bacon wafted out the window.

"All I do is observe, read body language. Something my little sis needs to do."

"We're working on it. Marlow has helped already."

"How long will she stay?"

"I invited her for a few days, but then we didn't know the details of the puzzle. Now we have to wait to hear from the lawyers. I guess the length of her visit will be determined by what they tell us. She has a six-month visa, so she can stay longer."

"Righto."

Jake halted and frowned. "What do you think of her?"

"I like her. Solid, assured. A good match."

"What do you mean?"

"Good match for you." He grinned. "I'm hungry too. Can't wait for Aunty Celia's big brekky. Then I have to hurry back to my job. Don't want my boss to think he can run Dongara Station without me." He ran up the stairs.

Jake followed Rick. A good match? He shrugged. Well, the lad *was* smart.

****

His heart bursting with pride, Jake waved goodbye to Rick and ushered sniffling Bella back into the kitchen. "We'll see him in a couple of weeks. He'll be in Cunnamulla next time we visit."

"I miss him."

"Me too, Bella Bear. By the way, I want Aunty Celia to work with you today. Marlow and I have business to discuss."

"Daaad, why?" She pouted and plopped into a chair, arms folded as if ready to defy the world.

He cocked his head and eyed her. They'd just shared a special time at the cemetery, and he didn't want to reprimand her.

"Sorry, Dad." She smiled and stood. "I acted inappropriately. I'm twelve years old and need to behave accordingly."

Mouth gaping, Jake stared at her. Had Marlow been tutoring her on social graces and giving her vocabulary lessons?

"Don't look so surprised. I've done heaps of thinking about my behavior, specially after sharing stuff with Marlow. She has a special way of telling me things, probably because she's a teacher, but I get what she says because she puts it in terms I can understand.

She never said I was acting childish, but I know I have been." Bella licked her lips. "There was a new girl at the service yesterday. Her name's Lynn, and she's very nice. Her dad works for Mr. O'Bryan. Anyway, she's thirteen. We stayed together the whole day. I watched her and she, well, she didn't behave like me or Trish and Beryl. She's a little different, but she acts so…grown-up."

"I saw you with her. I'm glad you have someone your age close by."

"Maybe we'll see each another again." Bella tilted her head. "There is one thing…no, I'll wait. It's time for me to check in with Miss York. See you later." She gave him a brief hug and walked calmly out of the room.

Still stunned, Jake sat and leaned back in the chair, balancing it on two legs. "Who was that young girl?"

Chapter 31

The shaded bench in the pool enclosure served as the perfect spot for Jake to share a private moment with Marlow. She seemed unhappy, depressed, he wasn't sure which. He pulled a few leaves off the honey-myrtles and inhaled the sweet scent while he waited. Rick's comment about Marlow being a good match for him kept intruding. He'd been thinking along the same lines, but hadn't had the courage to speak his mind. And after the coldshoulder treatment she'd dished out, maybe now was not the right time, either. Toffee circled his feet and rubbed against his leg, but he ignored the cat.

Light footsteps sounded on the path. Jake stood and watched Marlow approach. Her yellow dress flowed around her knees as she walked. He swallowed. Not matter what she wore, she always looked gorgeous. Warm inside and out, he wiped his forehead.

"I'm here as requested." Marlow settled on the far end of the bench and crossed her legs.

Not a positive sign. Jake sat and set his elbows on his knees. He'd already prayed for the right words, and now found his lips dry and his throat tight. He coughed. "Thanks for coming. I have so much to say and don't know where to begin. First, I'm sorry I neglected you yesterday. There were so many people..." He straightened. "No, I won't make excuses."

The color drained from Marlow's face, but she said nothing.

He continued, "Interrupt me any time."

She nodded and reached down to pet the cat.

"You were homesick, and I should have spent more time with you. I—"

A groan escaped, and Marlow covered her mouth.

He moved beside her in a second and hesitated to slip his arm around her, but she leaned into him. She felt so…so right in his arms. Marlow didn't cry, but clung to him as if she were afraid of falling. "What's wrong?"

A minute ticked by, and as much as he wanted her to open up, he hoped the moment would last for hours.

But she lifted her head and looked at him. Dark circles under her gray eyes intensified a depth of pain he'd not seen before. "What is it, Marlow? Are you ill?"

"No, yes. Homesick, but not for Texas. For family, roots, close ties."

Again, she fell against him, and he cradled her. "I don't understand. Please explain. Take all the time you need." *There's nowhere else I'd rather be.*

"Two things happened yesterday that…that shook my world." She seemed to be struggling to form the words. "I…I don't know where to begin."

"Does it have anything to do with Gracie? You were adamant about talking to her."

Marlow shifted out of his embrace and turned to face the pool. "Yes." She brushed hair out of her eyes. "Did you notice the necklace I wore?"

"Yeah. A Lightning Ridge black opal."

"You identified it? Of course, you know opals. Well, Gracie recognized the setting. She called it a Finlay. Apparently, Gracie worked for Finlay's Fashions—"

"I remember that shop. Mum liked their clothes."

"Well, Arthur Finlay had three of those necklaces made. One for his mother, one for Ida Marie, his wife, and one for their daughter, Katie Marie."

Seconds slipped by while Jake processed the information that had profoundly affected

Marlow. "I remember you said your mother was born in Australia and died when you were eighteen."

Marlow lifted her face to the sky. "I've always believed her name to be Marie Kate Johnstone. She moved to America the same time Gracie said the Finlays' daughter left Australia."

Standing, Jake shoved his hands on his hips. "So this Katie Marie could be your mother."

"Yes. And Gracie gave me Ida's address. I wrote to her

yesterday."

"Isn't that exciting?" Jake squatted in front of Marlow and grabbed her shoulders. "The Finlays could be your grandparents. Where do they live?"

"In Perth." A smile hovered at the corners of Marlow's lips.

Jake studied her face as the smile slipped. "Why the sadness?"

"What if we're wrong? What if my mother stole the necklace? Obviously, she used a false name. That's why I couldn't find her birth record in Melbourne."

"But what if it's all true?"

Marlow removed Jake's hands. "I can't let myself believe in the Finlay connection yet. I've longed for family ties for so long, but I'd rather not be disappointed."

Jake straightened and paced. "I understand. And it explains why you were so apathetic yesterday. Again, I apologize for not inquiring. Rick noticed and even prayed for you at the cemetery this morning."

"Now it's my turn to apologize. How was your time together?"

"Fine, if that's the right word. I'm grateful you suggested the visit. We opened up to each other, and I learned a lot about my kids. Thank you."

She peeked at him. "What did Rick say in his prayer?"

"You seemed to be carrying a heavy burden. Finding out you might know the whereabouts of your grandparents qualifies." Sensing she had more to say, he sat beside her.

Head lowered, she sighed. "Remember, I said two things happened."

"Uh-huh. What else set you off kilter?"

Turning toward him, she looked straight into his eyes. The glow he'd noticed moments ago had vanished.

"I had a conversation with Bridgette."

Not what he expected. "About riding with her?"

She shook her head vigorously, her hair swinging back and forth. He could almost see the cogs working overtime as she mulled over her choice of words.

"Do you have anything to tell me?" Her gaze bore into his soul. "I mean, you embraced me just now, but was that because we're sort of related?"

"I don't understand. We are sort of related, but believe me, I don't hug my cousins that way."

"What game are you playing? I *will not* be hurt again."

Frowning, he stared at her. "I have no intention of hurting you, but I still don't know what you mean."

"When's the wedding?"

He shrugged. "Who's getting married?"

Marlow swallowed and stood, gazing across the pool. "Bridgette said you two are secretly engaged."

He opened his mouth to respond, but she stood and held a hand out in a stop gesture. "I admit I'm emotionally distraught at the moment, but I have to say this. You are under no obligation to share your personal life with me. But in future, don't act as if you might consider me anyone other than a cousin-in-law trying to solve a family mystery." Huffing out a deep breath, Marlow strode away.

Jake sank onto the bench. Bridgette causing more problems was not the surprise. Marlow's reaction to Bridgett's absurd claim knocked him for a six. Was it possible she shared his romantic notions?

Chapter 32

By the time Marlow calmed down enough to face anyone and entered the office, the School of the Air session was over.

"There you are, luv." Celia rose and smoothed her skirt. "Another tough lesson today. I hate to impose on you, but while searching for Graham's letter this past week, I let some of my responsibilities slide. Would you mind supervising Bella again?"

"It will be my pleasure." Marlow acknowledge Bella's grin with a smile of her own. Anything to take her mind off Jake, the Finlays, and Bridgette.

At the door, Celia said, "Call when you're ready for tea."

"Thanks." Marlow settled in Jake's armchair, trying to wipe their recent encounter from her mind.

Reviewing the concepts of Bella's assignment kept Marlow busy. When Celia opened the door, Marlow was surprised to see her carrying the tea tray. No thoughts of Jake for over an hour.

"Great. We both need sustenance." Marlow cleared a spot on his desk.

"Mary just popped in. She and Ernie are off to Cunnamulla for a couple of days. Do you have any post for her to take? She'll come back in a few minutes to collect any items we have." Celia turned to leave. "I'll be in the kitchen."

"I do have a letter." Marlow hurried to her room. What an opportunity to get her missive in the mail before Friday. She stared at the address. Perth, on the other side of the continent. She cradled the envelope to her chest. Would Ida Marie reply? The Finlays could be her grandparents, but what if they ignored her?

Marlow traipsed down the hall toward the kitchen. So much emotion had gone into the letter. She'd written four drafts before she was satisfied with her words. If only she could enclose a photograph of the necklace to convince the Finlays.

Seated at the table, Celia sipped her tea. "I'll be interested to hear what Mary's doctor says."

"Me too." Marlow spared barely a moment of concern for Mary before she handed her envelope to Celia. "This is all I have. I had thought I'd give Mary my film to be developed, but I changed my mind. Since I…I'll be leaving shortly, I'll wait until I'm home." She pivoted and almost fell over in her haste to exit. Home. Where was home? If she found family in Perth, could she make a home there? Would being a Finlay qualify her for Australian citizenship?

Marlow shook her head and joined Bella in the office. Enough what ifs and questions for one day. Back to Year six academics.

****

Marlow and Celia lazed in the shade by the pool while Bella swam. The women had developed a comfortable routine and didn't feel the need to talk all the time, but Marlow's actions in the garden that morning intruded. She had no claim on Jake, so why mention his engagement but not stay around long enough to hear his side? Embarrassment heated her cheeks. He hadn't denied an engagement *per se*, but his shocked expression verified Marlow's opinion that Bridgette had lied.

She shrank into the lawn chair reliving her accusations. She cared too much. And that was a problem because, as she told Jake, she would not risk getting hurt again. She had loved Steven, but his domineering ways had killed her passion for him.

New rules. Be pleasant, but keep saying to yourself, 'You're leaving soon.' Texas or Perth? It didn't matter.

Bella climbed out of the pool and dried herself off. "Time to go in."

Marlow followed Celia and Bella inside. "Can I help with dinner?"

"Certainly. I never refuse an offer." Celia donned her apron. "Please peel the potatoes."

Meal prep kept Marlow busy until Jake blustered into the kitchen, scowling.

"Now, now, Mr. Barclay." Celia wiped her hands and set them on her hips. "This is not the woolshed. Please enter with decorum."

He eyed her then burst out laughing. "Have you and Bella been studying the dictionary?"

"I'm an educated woman. I can use fancy words if I so choose. What has Bella been saying?"

Sinking into a chair, he rolled up his shirt sleeves. "I don't recall her exact words, but this morning she apologized for pouting and said something like she'd been childish and was no longer going to act that way. She sounded like a young lady, not a kid." He glanced at Marlow. "You've accomplished so much with her in such a short time. I can't believe how mature my Bella Bear is these days."

"Thanks, but I think it's because we focused on the reasons for her behavior. Together. We all played a part. And don't forget to give Bella credit, too. As you said, she is aware of her childish actions and recognizes the need to change."

"Yeah, but her choosing to change wouldn't have happened if you hadn't intervened. Thanks again."

"I'm glad I was able to help."

"I agree with your assessments of Bella. But why did you blow in here like a whirlwind?" Celia asked.

"Greg found more downed fences. This time we lost two dozen or so sheep. Wild dogs, maybe, and who knows how many sheep escaped through the gaping hole." He wiped a hand across his face. "I'm as mad as a cut snake. Why can't we find out who's doing this?"

"Sorry to hear about the sheep and the fence. It's bad enough you have to deal with fluctuating wool prices and inadequate feed." Celia removed a pot from the stove. "But dinner will be ready soon. Off you go to shower."

He grunted and stood. "Marlow, after we eat, can we continue our discussion from this morning? Please."

The pleading expression on his face convinced her to agree. She didn't trust her voice and just nodded, ignoring the question in Celia's eyes.

Bella chose to watch a film after the meal, and Celia departed to her bedroom. Marlow had to face Jake alone. But she'd repeated her new mantra over and over. 'You're leaving soon'. And she added a second verse. 'Steel your heart against his charms'.

In the muted light on the verandah, she couldn't see Jake's expression as he sat in the chair next to her. Good, because that meant he couldn't see hers, either. She crossed her legs and folded her arms, waiting for him to initiate conversation.

"I've thought a lot about what you said this morning. Did you give Mary and Ernie your letter to the Finlays?"

"Yes. Now the waiting. What, about two weeks? If Ida replies, surely the letter won't be in this Friday's delivery."

"Right. Two weeks. That's a long time."

"When do you think we'll hear from Milton about the lawyer in Bendigo?"

"If he followed through right away, we could get a letter this Friday." Jake leaned forward, closing the distance between them. "But let's focus on our morning chat, please. Bridgette and I are *not* engaged. Never will be. We're old friends. She went through a rough divorce and sometimes needs a shoulder. We did talk a lot on Sunday, and she might harbor romantic thoughts about me, but I assure you they are not reciprocated."

The dull light from the living room now fell on his face. Lips parted, eyes wide. Marlow had no doubt he was telling the truth. Was he trying to tell her something else? For a brief moment, her heart clenched. But when he reached out for her hand, she drew back. *No, not going there.*

"Jake, I overreacted this morning." She couldn't bring herself to admit the reason. "I'm sorry. Don't forget that after we follow Graham's last instructions, and I find out whether or not I'm a Finlay, I'll be leaving Long Gully."

Head tilted, brow furrowed, he opened his mouth, but the transmitter squawked from the office, and he rose. "Sorry. That might be an emergency."

He hurried inside, and Marlow let out a deep breath. A reprieve. Now all she had to do was keep her mantra in mind whenever in Jake's company. Or whenever she thought about him.

Five minutes later, he returned and plopped down, sighing. "Not good news. That was Nate Davidson. I asked him about Paddy. Turns out the lad lied. He didn't work in Broken Hill like he told me. He grew up on Gail Carson's family station just north of Cunnamulla. Yes, my former fiancée's family." Jake slouched in the chair. "Which means I'll have to chat with him again to find out why he lied. I might have to fire him. Drat. It's so hard to get reliable station hands."

Feeling safe now the conversation was no longer about her and Jake, Marlow said, "I know the isolation of Long Gully is a problem.

Do you hire single guys as opposed to married couples?"

"We have four couples and a dozen or more stockmen. Married couples with children are always concerned about schooling."

"I don't understand. Isn't School of the Air available to all kids out here?"

"Yeah, but some people don't want to send their older children to boarding school."

What an opportunity! "Speaking of high school. Bella and I had an interesting discussion the other day."

"About school?"

"Yes. She wants to stay here and do correspondence courses."

"Phfft. No way. Next year she's going to high school in Cunnamulla and will stay with friends."

"You've talked with her about the plan?"

"Yes, well, no, not exactly. But she knows what's in store. All her friends are in the same boat. Come Year seven, it's boarding school." Jake straightened. "I...wait. You know something I don't. What did Bella say?"

"She's adamant about not going." It was Marlow's turn to lean forward. "Bella said you assumed she wants to go, but never asked her. I think her aversion to leaving home is more than not being consulted on the decision. You should talk with her."

"I'll do it now." He raised his voice, "Bella, luv. Turn off the movie, please, and come outside."

The soundtrack stopped, and Bella pushed open the screen door. "What's wrong, Dad?"

"Nothing, but we must chat about next year."

"1984. What about it?"

"Come sit, luv."

Bella dragged over a chair and parked it close to Marlow.

"High school in Cunnamulla. Marlow said you don't want to go."

The kid threw Marlow a wide-eyed stare. "You told him?"

"Yes. You two need to discuss the situation. I'll act as referee, if necessary."

"All right." Bella reached for Marlow's hand.

"I'm listening." Jake's tone softened. "What are your reasons for not wanting to go?"

"It's far away, and I won't see you and Aunty Celia." Bella hung her head. "I'll get homesick."

Marlow squeezed the child's hand. There had to be more to her objection than homesickness. "Tell him everything, sweetheart. Now's not the time to hold back."

"Yes, luv. I won't bite off your head. I promise."

Drawing up her legs, Bella hugged her knees and pursed her lips. "It's not easy, Dad."

"Take your time."

"I'm worried about what Gail said."

Jake scooted forward as if ready to jump up. "How is she involved?"

Marlow placed her hand on his thigh, a subtle reminder to stay calm. "What did Gail say?"

"She told me stories about how mean kids are at boarding school. She also said… Dad, I promised her I wouldn't tell." Her voice cracked.

"Bella Bear, my dear child. Come here." She clambered out of the chair and knelt on the floor at his side. He embraced her. "Gail's not worthy of your promise. What did she say?"

Choking back a sob, she looked at him and then at Marlow. "I told her I didn't want to go to boarding school, but she said I had to. If I kicked up a fuss, she threatened to…to send me to a school far away. And if I caused trouble, she'd convince you to not let me come home for the holidays. I sometimes have nightmares about it." Bella swiped at her wet cheeks. "Please, Dad, don't make me go. Let me stay home at least one more year."

"Oh, my sweet little girl. I won't let anything bad happen to you." Jake stroked her head. "I did know Gail wanted to send you to posh school in Brisbane, but I didn't know she threatened you, luv."

A lump formed in Marlow's throat. What nerve Gail had to threaten a vulnerable child. An idea brewed in her mind. She almost said, "I'd love to stay and teach Bella and the workers' children." But she caught herself in time and instead, stood, and said, "I'm going to bed. Good night." She hurried to her room and collapsed onto the bed.

Marlow, erase that notion from your head.

Chapter 33

Life on the station marched along with no drama. No discussions about high school, no mention of destroyed fences, and not a peep about Bridgette. Marlow sat with Bella during her school sessions, helped Celia in the kitchen when necessary, and felt more comfortable with her decision to leave Long Gully. She had no business fantasizing about a romance. After all, he'd spent a night in the paddocks, and she'd hardly missed him. *Sure, Marlow.*

She flipped a page of her magazine while half-heartedly listening to Bella's and her teacher's exchange, until she heard the words *American guest.*

"Yes, our guest, Marlow Barclay from Texas is here with me. Over."

"Ask her what is special about tomorrow. I'll get back to you in a bit. Over."

Bella switched a knob and faced Marlow. "What is Miss York talking about?"

"I don't know. Let me see. It will be November 24. Thursday. Oh, it's Thanksgiving Day. A special holiday in America." She'd been so preoccupied she hadn't realized the significance of the date.

"I've heard about it." Bella fiddled with the dials again. "Miss York, tomorrow is the American holiday of Thanksgiving. Over."

Static accompanied the back and forth conversation.

"Good on ya, Bella. I want you to interview your guest and present a Thanksgiving report to the class on Tuesday next week. Over."

"That will be super. Over." She grinned and gave Marlow a thumbs-up.

Miss York signed off a minute later.

Tomorrow would be the second Thanksgiving without her

husband and daughter. Marlow manufactured a smile for Bella, but turned away before the child noticed her tears. Thanksgiving was a time for family, and she still grieved her losses. Probably the expectation of meeting her grandparents played a role, as did the conversations about Bella's secondary schooling. Marlow would never have been able to send Eileen away at age twelve or thirteen, even if boarding school was the standard and expected way of handling high school for children in the outback.

"When can I interview you?" Bella rolled her chair to the desk. "I don't know where to start. Marlow—"

She held up her hand. "Slow down, young lady. First of all, devise a set of questions. Later today or tomorrow, we'll set aside some time. You'll need to write down my answers and comments, and then compile them into a concise, organized report. I'll help, but this will be good practice for you."

"Ooh, I can't wait. I'll finish my assignments first." She scooted back to her table and opened a workbook, humming and bopping to the beat of her rock and roll tune.

Half an hour later, Celia delivered the tea tray. "I have good news. Our Mary is pregnant. She and Ernie just returned from Cunnamulla. They brought the post, but there was nothing for you, Marlow."

She hadn't expected anything, but disappointed draped over her. Maybe Milton's reply would be delivered by the mail plane on Friday. "Did the doctor allay Mary's apprehension?"

"Yeah, to some degree." Celia motioned for Marlow to join her in the hall. "Ernie and Mary decided not to travel to Brisbane for an amniocentesis test. Although still concerned, they're going to count the child a blessing no matter what."

"I've worked with so many children who have Down syndrome. They were all precious, loving souls."

Celia nodded and walked down the hall, and Marlow returned to the office.

True to her word, Bella completed her schoolwork before preparing her interview questions. Much to Marlow's satisfaction, she even consulted an encyclopedia.

Unable to wait until the next day, Bella convinced Marlow to conduct the interview late that afternoon. Still occupied with the project at six o'clock, they had to be called to the dinner table.

The aroma of Celia's baked pastry permeated the kitchen, and the meat pies were mouth- watering, but Jake's somber mood was hard to ignore.

"What's eating you?" Celia asked.

He dropped his fork, and it clattered on the plate. "I confronted Paddy about his lies. He said he didn't want to admit he grew up on the Carson station because he knew about my failed engagement to Gail and thought I'd hold it against him." Jake leaned back and sighed. "The lad's a good worker, but he lied on his application and to my face."

"Give him a second chance, Dad. His reason for making up a story makes sense. At least to me."

Jake eyed his daughter, then looked at Marlow. "I agree with you, luv. I'll keep him on. Now, tell me, what have you been doing all day? Aunty Celia says she's seen neither hide nor hair of you for hours."

****

With the Thanksgiving report and all school assignments complete, Bella spent Friday afternoon practicing various strokes in the pool. Marlow had taken plenty of photos of the homestead and garden, but shot a few more. Then, settled back at the shaded table, she studied Celia, crochet needle and cotton in hand. A devoted aunt, competent housekeeper, former nurse, but she never discussed her past. "Do you miss your work at the hospital?"

Without looking up from her tatting, Celia said, "I did at first, but I'm so used to running this place, I wouldn't want to return to a career. I enjoy the wide-open spaces, the freedom of being my own boss." She chuckled. "Don't tell Jake I said that. He thinks he sets the agenda."

"Thank you for preparing my Thanksgiving dressing recipe to serve with your roast chicken last night. Bella must have shared it with you, and it was a treat."

"The least I could do. Too bad I didn't have ingredients for a pecan pie."

That would have been too much. Eileen loved Marlow's pie and wouldn't eat any other. She blew out a breath. No family left in Texas, but she was fast bonding with those on the station. "Celia, I have to tell you, I'm impressed with how dedicated you are to Jake and Bella."

193

Celia glanced at Marlow, a faraway look in her eyes. "After my fiancé absconded with my life savings, Jake offered me a home here at Long Gully. I owe him…so much." Her voice faltered. "Um, I hear the drone of a plane."

Marlow sat up straight. Would there be a letter from Milton? "I'll go in and wait for Paddy to deliver the mail bag."

"Ta. I'll be in soon."

Marlow hurried inside, sure a couple of hamsters rode exercise wheels in her stomach. She grabbed her abdomen and took in calming breaths. Come on, Paddy, where are you?

The high-pitched whine of the lad's motorbike sent Marlow to the kitchen door.

Paddy parked the bike by the shed and ran to the door. "Afternoon, miss. One full canvas bag today." He doffed his hat and backed out. Seconds later, he buzzed away.

Marlow's hands shook as she opened the bag and dumped out the contents. Dozens of envelopes. She began sorting them as Celia had done, but the process took too long. She rifled through the remaining pile, and there, at the bottom, was an envelope address to her. From Milton.

Sinking into a chair, she wiped a hand over her sweat-beaded brow. Her round-the-world-trek was about to be rewarded, and her promise to Steven fulfilled. With trembling fingers, she opened the envelope and withdrew two sheets of pale blue paper. Milton filled the first page with news of the family and asked myriad questions. *Come on. Get to the meat.*

The second page detailed the information she craved. Ward and Windermere law offices moved to Bendigo twenty years ago. Floyd Windermere agreed to meet her as Steven's widow and proxy. Appointment Wednesday next week. Milton's mate, Quin, will pick her up by plane from Long Gully Tuesday, about ten o'clock. Quin had been on a fishing trip in Queensland. No problem for him to stop by the station. He'll fly her to Melbourne. Milton will drive her to Bendigo for the appointment. Henry says he doesn't want to be included. If necessary, Quin will fly her back to Long Gully.

As jumpy as if she'd consumed a gallon of coffee, Marlow perched on the edge of the chair. If the lawyer agreed to the appointment, it must mean he had information from Graham Barclay. A chill tightened her chest, and she had a strong desire to flee. The communication was what they hoped, so why dread the meeting?

She stared at the ceiling and again drew in air. *Take it easy, girl.* Marlow continued to read. Lawyer requires proof of identity. Birth certificates, her marriage certificate, Steven's death certificate. At the last minute, she had packed all those documents. *Thank You, God.*

Stunned at her prayer, she blinked, then wilted against the chair. God had been with her all the way. Had never left her. She's the one who had distanced herself. Marlow bowed her head. "Thank You, Father, for Your constant watch over me. Please help me on this last leg of my journey to Bendigo and maybe to Perth."

Celia's and Bella's voices sounded in the hall, and Jake whistled as he approached the kitchen from outside.

Roused from her moment of quiet, Marlow glanced at Milton's letter. He never indicated that he expected Jake to accompany Marlow. She chewed her bottom lip. Did she want Jake with her?

Chapter 34

Two days since Milton's letter arrived and Marlow still hadn't asked Jake to accompany her to Melbourne. He had several reasons why he wanted to go. To spend more time with her, to be present when she spoke with the lawyer, but most important, to shield Marlow from Milton's advances. He had no doubt his cousin would set his cap at her. He paced the verandah outside his bedroom. Should he ask her, or assume she wanted him to go? No. Marlow didn't seem the kind of person who took kindly to assumptions. He'd have to be cautious. Since their trip to Maroola Downs last weekend, she'd been distant, cool. Even after he denied Bridgette's claim.

A door squeaked open. He tiptoed to the corner and peered around. Marlow stood at the verandah screen, staring out into the ebony night.

He cleared his throat. "Can't sleep?"

"Right. I'm hot." She paused. "And anxious about our visit to Bendigo."

Our visit? Jake sank into a chair. "Care to join me?"

She shook her head. "I'd rather go to the rocks where we sat before."

"Great idea. I'll put on my boots and get a torch." He hurried to his room and returned within seconds. The star-splashed sky could only enhance his cause.

They walked slowly to the rocky outcrop. He shone the light to ensure there were no unwanted creatures about, then waited for Marlow to hitch up on a rock before he perched on another.

"So." He hesitated. "Do you want me to go with you on Tuesday?"

Silence, except the chirping of night insects. Not a positive sign, but he dared not ask again.

A minute later, a long minute later, she sighed. "As the eldest of Edward's grandchildren, I think you should be included. Since Henry doesn't want to come, Milton will stand in for him as Betsy's grandchild. That way Graham's three children are represented."

Put that way… "I like the plan. Thank you." *I'll be watching you, Milton*. Jake straightened his shoulders. Forget about his cousin. "I have a lot to take care of before I can leave."

She placed a hand on his thigh then removed it as quickly as if she'd been burned. "Sorry. I didn't think of that. Will you have enough time?"

"Yeah, and I trust Greg and Ernie in my absence." He kicked against the rock. "And of course, Celia can cope with anything."

Leaning back with her hands behind her, Marlow glanced up at the sky. He did the same. The glorious swath of stars always confirmed his belief in the Creator. "This never gets old. Thanks for suggesting we come out here."

"I could stare at the Milky Way forever." But she didn't. Instead, she hopped off the rock, took a step and pivoted. "I have a problem."

"About the trip?" Her tone indicated she had something serious on her mind.

"Yes, no." She picked up a stone and flung it into the darkness where it landed with a thud. Tugging at a strand of hair, she rested her hip against the rock. "After we visit the lawyer and take care of whatever obligations Graham stipulated, we will have fulfilled his request, and I'll be free to return to Texas."

A hot knife sliced through Jake's heart. No, she couldn't leave Long Gully yet. He had to convince her to stay and scoured his brain for a reason. Uh-huh. Her grandparents. "What about the Finlays? What if they are family and want to meet?"

She hitched up on the rock again. "I have thought of that. While in Melbourne I can find their phone number and call. They live in Perth. I could visit them, and…and fly home from there. But if they—"

"Or, you could extend your stay at Long Gully." His gut muscles tensed as her waited for her response.

Facing him, she touched his arm. "That's what I was going to ask. If…if I need to, can I come back here?"

It took all his resolve to sit still and not wrap his arms around her. "You can stay until our next trip to Cunnamulla. Or longer." A lot could happen in two and a half weeks. "There's so much more I'd like to show you around the station." Instead of being relieved, she seemed to shrink. "What's wrong?"

"I would love to see what the life of a grazier is really about, but...I..." Her voiced wobbled.

He eased off the rock and stood close to her. "Tell me."

"It's true, I do want to see more of Long Gully, but what I really want is a safe place to return to if the Finlays are not my grandparents, or if they reject me." She swiped at her cheek.

Barclay, you missed her underlying plea for help. "No worries, Marlow." As much as it hurt him, he said, "When we leave on Tuesday, take all your belongings. If the Finlays want to meet, you'll be prepared. If not, then come back with me. We'll be your family." He wanted to add so much more, but changed his mind when she slid off the rock.

"It's been a long day. I'm going in. Goodnight, and thank you, Jake."

He turned on the torch and shone the light toward her. She hurried along, head down.

Let her go. Following a few steps behind, he kept the beam on her to illuminate her path.

****

Preparations for his absence from Long Gully filled the next day, and he didn't see Marlow again until dinner.

She and Bella chatted like old friends. "Dad, Marlow said when she's in Melbourne she'll buy me new brushes and acrylic paints. We checked the ones Mum used, but some of them are dried out and the brushes are losing their bristles. Oh, and more canvases. You can bring them all back with you."

Bella painting again. He never thought he'd see the day. She always balked whenever he mentioned the idea. "That's wonderful, Bella Bear. Mum would be so proud."

"I'm going to finish the picture I started with her, and then work on more. And when Marlow gets back to Texas, I'll send one to her."

"A grand idea." He glanced at Marlow and noticed the corners of her mouth turn up in a brief smile. She had told Bella about leaving Long Gully, and his daughter seemed to have accepted the decision with more maturity than he'd shown.

But Bella wasn't falling in love with Marlow. He gawked at the others around the table. No one reacted. They hadn't read his mind. "Thanks for a wonderful meal, Celia." He cleared his throat. "I still have things to do before our flight tomorrow. Excuse me, please. Goodnight, all."

Ignoring conversation from the table, he strode to his room, shut the door, and leaned against it. Was it possible to be in love with Marlow after only knowing her two, three weeks? Closing his eyes, he ran a hand through his hair. Did he think about her constantly, want her to be happy, and desire to share every little day-to-day event with her? Yes. Yes. Yes. And so much more. Watch her every move, seek her approval. Hold her close.

He stormed out of his verandah door, ran down the stairs, and jumped into the pool fully clothed. Wiping water from his face, he nodded. Yup, he was in love. The sweet but subtle scent of the eucalyptus trees surrounding the pool filled his senses. And in his haste, he'd snagged a small branch off a young tree. He crushed the wet leaves and inhaled. When he'd first met Marlow, he'd likened her presence to a flash of lightning which could herald refreshing showers or destructive storms. He might still encounter a storm or two, but at this point, he'd brave anything to accompany her in the rain.

At dawn, Jake dressed in a hurry, cut a couple of thick slices of bread in the kitchen, and fled the scene on his motorbike. He had one last item to discuss with Greg before the plane arrived, and he didn't want to face Marlow yet, in case she could see into his heart.

Jake met Greg in the W-2 paddock. The foreman provided updates on the state of the pasture and reported no new fence cutting incidents. "That's good news. One more task. Please, keep an eye on Paddy. I discovered he lied on his application, but I'm going to keep him on for now."

"Will do. The lad works hard, but he's impulsive." Greg, lanky and rawboned, rubbed his bald head. "We've been together a long time, mate. I'll keep order and watch out for Celia and young Bella." He shoved his hat on his head and extended his hand.

"Good on ya." Jake shook hands and then grabbed Greg's shoulder. "Appreciate all your help and support. We should be back on Friday at the latest. I'll send word if we're delayed."

Gunning the engine, Jake sped off. Now to pack and school

himself to sit with Marlow for hours and hours without displaying his true feelings. "Father God, please be with us as we travel to Melbourne and meet with the lawyer." He slowed to a stop and parked the bike beside the shed. "And please help me to be civil to Milton, and to allow Marlow to make choices that are beneficial to her, even if I don't like them." He slapped his hat against his thigh. "In Jesus's name. Amen."

When he entered the kitchen, Marlow sat at the table drinking a mug of tea and nibbling on a biscuit. He couldn't gauge her mood, except she appeared calm and serene.

"You're all packed up?"

"Yes. I said goodbye to Bella and Celia. They're in the office." She carried her mug to the sink. "I'm impressed with how Bella is coping with my leaving. She said she'll miss me, but there were no tears, like I expected."

"You're a blessing to her. She's always been a sweet kid, but she's matured so much and has turned into a young lady." He placed a hand on the small of Marlow's back. "Thank you. I'll be forever grateful."

Marlow acknowledged his words with a nod. "I'll get my things." She walked down the passage, and his heart thudded. He'd successfully kept his emotions hidden, or at least he hoped he had.

Ernie would drive them to the airstrip in about twenty minutes. Jake hurried to his room, showered, and changed into attire more suited to city life. Boots or shoes? Boots. He rummaged in his wardrobe for a newer pair, brushed off the dust, and put them on. Didn't want to arrive in Melbourne looking like a grazier. Except, he needed a hat. He did, however, choose one less stained and work-worn than his favorite. Then he threw a couple of shirts and pairs of strides into his duffle bag and added the rest of his gear.

Luggage loaded, they rode in silence to the airstrip. Even Ernie had nothing to say.

Quin, Milton's friend, landed right on time. He welcomed them aboard his four-seater, and once they buckled in, took off and flew over Long Gully.

Jake had seen the homestead from the air before, but he never tired of the sight. "Look, Marlow. You can get a good idea of the size of the place." He had to shout over the noise in the plane.

"It's magnificent. I see the paddocks."

A swell of pride covered his heart. He hoped his grandfather would be satisfied with his husbandry of the station. Placing a hand on his chest, he glanced at his companion.

Marlow stared out her window as if she, too, couldn't get enough of the scene. Turning, she smiled and gestured for him to move closer. "I'd love to explore more of Long Gully."

Before he could react, Marlow looked out the window again. He grinned and leaned back. Yes! Then he sobered. He'd welcome her return anytime, but hoped it wouldn't be because the Finlays rejected her.

Chapter 35

The bumpy, and at times, turbulent trip took six hours which included a refueling stop in Dubbo where they had a quick lunch and stretched their legs. Literally. The plane had little room for Marlow to move about, so it was no wonder Jake extracted himself as if he were a clown in a circus car.

Melbourne airport was a welcome sight. After they taxied toward the hangar, and the sound of the engine finally ceased, Quin turned and gave them a thumbs-up. "I contacted Milton. He'll meet you in a couple of minutes. Let him know when you want to fly back, but, uh, I'll have to charge you for that trip."

"No worries, mate. Will do." Jake set his hat on his head and made his way to the door.

"Thank you for a safe trip." Marlow slung her purse strap over her shoulder, squeezed between the seats, and followed Jake down the steps, glad for a second time that day she wore a pantsuit and not a dress.

On the ground, luggage at their feet, she and Jake waited for Milton. Fumes from nearby planes taking off or landing mixed with the hot air swirling around them.

Milton drove up in a sporty silver sedan, and stepped out dressed in a charcoal suit, white shirt, and purple tie.

Marlow wished she had her camera ready to capture the shocked expression on his face. He was *not* expecting Jake. Oops.

"Thank you for arranging the flight for us, Milton. We really appreciate your help." She hugged him, and adroitly avoided the kiss she was sure he aimed at her lips.

"My pleasure." He turned to Jake. "Haven't see you in a while."

Jake extended his hand. "I add my thanks. Marlow thought it best if one representative from each of Graham's kids be present."

The tight expression on Milton's face eased as he shook hands. "That makes sense."

Marlow couldn't help but compare the cousins. City versus country. Jake sure cleaned up well. His khaki slacks had an ironed crease down each leg, and the sleeves of his light blue shirt, rolled to the elbows, exposed his tanned, muscled forearms. She smiled to herself as she put her spin on an old saying: You can take the man out of the outback, but you can't take the outback out of the man. He exuded strength and determination. In contrast, Milton, slightly shorter than Jake, looked every inch the businessman. Handsome, well turned out. He probably wouldn't last a day mending fences or mustering sheep at Long Gully.

What an interesting thought. Marlow shook her head and grabbed her suitcase.

"I'll get that." Jake reached for the handle.

"No, I will." Milton attempted to take it from him.

For a moment, Jake glared at his cousin in a way that left no doubt he could pick up Milton as easily as he carried Marlow's luggage.

She headed toward the car. "How about you open the trunk, uh, boot, please, Milton?"

He complied. "I didn't know you were coming Jake, but you can bunk with me. I have a large flat, and Marlow, I arranged for you to stay with my parents."

"Or we could both go to a hotel. What do you think, Marlow?"

She knew what answer Jake wanted, but said, "I'll enjoy seeing your folks again." She climbed into the back seat before Jake could object.

The ride through the metropolis with honking car horns, the screech of tires, and the usual hustle and bustle, was a stark reminder they were no longer in the outback. And by the tense set of Jake's shoulders, he'd noticed the contrast, too. Or was he concerned about bunking with his cousin?

In a terse, business-like manner, Milton pointed out landmarks of interest as if Marlow and Jake hadn't seen them before.

An hour later, they arrived at the Harris's home in the suburbs. The large, two-story house stood on a manicured corner lot, surrounded by flowering shrubs. As soon as Milton parked in the driveway, the front door opened.

Liz and James greeted Marlow warmly. Excited to see Jake, they offered him a room for the night.

"Milton and I need to catch up, but thanks anyway." Jake hugged his aunt and uncle then slid a sideways glance at Marlow.

She gave him a nod, aware the decision came with some soul-searching on his part.

Liz hooked her arm through Jake's and pulled him toward the dining room. "We'll be ready to eat in five minutes. Milton, escort Marlow, please."

"My pleasure." He placed a hand on her arm. "I couldn't help but notice you brought a large suitcase. Does that mean you won't be returning to Long Gully?"

She explained her possible connection to the Finlays. "If we're related, and they want me to visit them in Perth, then I won't go back with Jake."

"How wonderful you located family. Call directory assistance and get their number. Mom and Dad won't mind the long-distance call."

Tempting, but she shook her head. "I must complete Graham's directive first."

****

Milton arrived promptly at eight the next morning. He and Jake seemed to be on better terms, so maybe the drive north to Bendigo wouldn't be as uncomfortable as the ride from the airport. Marlow hopped in the backseat, aware of Milton's disappointed expression.

"How long will the trip take?" Jake asked as Milton negotiated the neighborhood streets to the highway.

Milton checked his watch. "About two hours. We're good. I made an appointment for eleven o'clock."

Time passed quickly as they discussed a variety of topics, none of which touched on any sensitive issues. However, the nearer to their destination, the less they spoke.

With ten minutes to spare, Milton parked in front of the lawyers' office on View Street. Like so many of the wide streets they'd traversed in Bendigo, this one had a row of trees down the middle and was lined with two-storied buildings, all graced with upper verandahs and intricate wrought iron railings.

Jake opened the glass door for Marlow and Milton.

They approached the receptionist behind a huge mahogany desk.

205

Marlow gave her name. "I…we have an appointment with Mr. Floyd Windermere."

The young redhead produced a lopsided smile and picked up the phone. "Your eleven is here." She replaced the receiver. "Please, have a seat." Her smile lingered as she gestured to a group of padded, leather chairs.

Within a minute, a slim woman dressed in a smart navy suit entered the waiting room through a side door. Marlow glanced at her, then looked at the wall clock. Five minutes before eleven. It had never been her experience that lawyers were punctual.

The woman cleared her throat, and said, "Mrs. Barclay?"

Marlow turned. "Yes."

"I'm Floyd Windermere." She held out her hand.

Closing her gaping mouth, Marlow stood and shook hands. Now, she knew why the receptionist had smiled. "Pleased to meet you. I brought two of Graham Barclay's cousins, I mean, great-grandchildren with me." Tongue-tied with embarrassment, she ducked her head.

Jake and Milton stood and introduced themselves.

"Follow me." The silver-haired lawyer proceeded to her office, a large room, with paneled walls, a thick maroon carpet, and comfy-looking armchairs. But she directed them to a long conference table where a rectangular metal container, about ten inches square and six inches high occupied a spot at one end. "Before we go any further, please call me Floyd. I need to see your identification." She sat at the head of the table. Her short hair curled away from her face highlighting her dark eyes.

"Of course." Marlow extracted the necessary documents from her large purse and laid them down on the table, then sank into a chair close to Floyd. Jake, next to Marlow, and Milton across the table, produced their driver licenses.

Floyd examined the certificates, nodded, and pursed her lips. Marlow couldn't tell if she was satisfied with what she read until she stacked them all together and leaned back. "Everything is in order." Leaning forward, she pulled the box toward her. "I have no idea what is in here. My father and grandfather before him passed down the instructions. I'm honored to be the one to share the contents with you. Believe me, we've all wondered what Graham Barclay paid us a handsome retainer fee to keep for three generations." She withdrew a small key from her pocket. "Who wants to open it?"

"I think Marlow should. After all, she's the one who traveled all this way to arrange our meeting." Jake nudged Marlow's elbow.

"Agree. Without her perseverance, we wouldn't be here," Milton added.

Marlow drew in a breath and accepted the key. A heavy presence settled over her as if Steven watched the proceedings, but instead of feeling discomfort, she sensed his approval. "Here goes." She turned the key but nothing happened. After Marlow jiggled the key and gave it a hard twist, the lip popped open. An earthy, but not unpleasant odor escaped. She turned the box so Milton and Jake could see the contents.

"Another envelope. Oh, please dear God, not another code. And a bag of…" She picked up the small canvas sack. "It's heavy." She squeezed the pouch. "Feels like large marbles, or something."

"Dump them out." Jake pulled a handkerchief from his pocket. "Here, use this."

Marlow untied the drawstring and spilled the contents. Two dozen or more grape-sized rocks rolled out. "I don't understand. Why would Graham give stones to a lawyer for safekeeping?"

Fingering the rocks, Jake burst out laughing. "They're not just any stones. What we have here are raw opals. Probably worth a bundle, if I'm not mistaken."

"What are we supposed to do with them?" Milton took his turn touching the stones.

"The envelope may contain instructions." Floyd removed it from the box and handed it to Marlow.

"Silly me. Thank you." Hands trembling, she slit open the envelope and withdrew a letter. "I'll read it." She swallowed. "'Dear great-grandchildren. I hope you had no problems getting together to fulfill this obligation. When you read my letter, I will be long gone, but don't think harshly of me. I made a mistake, and now I want to make amends. I'm not proud to admit that in my youth I defrauded a business partner. I knew details of his shady past and threatened to expose him if he went to the authorities.'"

"No wonder he said there could be legal or financial implications." Jake tapped the table. "Go on."

"My, my. This is serious." Marlow shifted in her chair. "'The man's name was Zachariah Thomas. Please contact him or his family and give them these opals as a form of compensation. I waited for three generations to rectify my crime because I didn't want any family members to be held liable for my errors. Thank you.' It's signed and dated, Bendigo, 1924." Marlow blew out a breath and leaned back. "I don't know about you two, but I'm stunned at Graham's actions, but relieved. At least the task seems doable, that is, of course if we can locate Zachariah or his decedents."

Jake pushed back from the table and scratched his head. "I'm in shock, too. All my life I've heard stories about Graham Barclay, and they all portrayed him as a mighty businessman, a civic leader. And yet, he…he was a scoundrel."

"I feel the same way." Milton loosened his tie. "After great-grandmother Elizabeth died, Graham lived with Betsy and Bill, my grandparents. As kids, we visited frequently. Graham presided over all the activities like a general. I was in awe of him." He tsked. "I'm sad to hear about his shady dealings."

Marlow glanced at the men, then at Floyd. "Since I'm only a Barclay by marriage, I don't have a strong connection to Graham, nor do I know anything about him. He hid his unsavory deeds from his family, but I have the responsibility to carry out his wishes. How…how do we find the Thomases?" She wanted nothing more than to fulfill her commitment.

"I know of one prominent Thomas family in the area. I'll make a few inquiries. The questions need to come from me." Floyd raised her eyebrows. "Don't you agree?"

"Yes. Thank you." She slipped Graham's letter into her purse. "Can we wait here?" Although Marlow desperately wanted to locate the Finlay's phone number, she had to complete the task before her.

"Certainly. I'll have my receptionist bring you tea and light refreshments." Floyd exited the office.

"Whew." Jake stood and walked the length of the room. "This is not what I expected."

"Me neither." Shaking his head, Milton also stood and shoved his hands into his pockets. "Hope we don't find any more skeletons."

A slight tap sounded at the door. Jake opened it, and in walked the redheaded receptionist.

Milton stepped forward and took the tray from her, beaming a bright smile. "Thank you, young lady. Your hair is such a vibrant color. I love it."

She blushed, batted her eyelashes, and swung her shapely hips as she left the office.

Jake gave Marlow a what-did-I-tell-you look, and she smiled.

"I'm parched, and these sandwiches look delicious." She had no reason to scrutinize Milton any further and poured the tea.

Before they had a chance to drink or eat, Floyd returned. "That didn't take long. I located Zachariah's son. Owen Thomas lives south of Bendigo, in Heathcote."

Chapter 36

"I can't believe Owen's father never mentioned the fraud." Jake turned so he could see Marlow in the backseat.

"But Zachariah had told him to avoid the Barclays no matter what happened." She scowled as she toyed with the strap of her handbag.

"We know the reason, but to me, that would have been my cue to find out why. I suppose we'll never know what information Graham had on Zachariah." Milton switched lanes to pass a slow moving lorry. "At least, his family didn't suffer financially."

"Besides leaving town and starting over in Ballarat, their problems could have been so much worse." Marlow shook her head. "What if Zachariah's business venture failed? They could have been destitute. Might have turned to crime to survive. We need to thank God they weren't adversely affected by Graham's actions."

"True. I can't imagine what we'd do if that were the case. Of course, we don't know the value of the stones, but I, for one, would feel obligated to provide for, compensate, Zachariah's family." Jake kept his eye on Marlow. "I too, thank the Lord they didn't suffer because of our relative's actions. Owen can save the opals for his grandkids, or use the money to buy the boat he talked about."

Relaxed against the seat, Marlow stared out the window. She'd traveled so far to fulfill Graham's demands.

"How are you, Marlow?" Jake asked.

She looked at him, at first contented, then mournful. "I'm relieved. Graham's mysterious letter has been part of my life for nearly two years, and now that we've carried out his wishes, my obligation is over." She hung her head. "It's over, and I can go home."

Jake wanted to climb back there and hold her tight. She looked anything but relieved.

Milton glanced at Jake then in the rearview mirror. "Hey, Marlow, are you going to ring the Finlays tonight? Just remember Perth's time zone is three hours behind us."

She stared out the window again. "I know it's a big deal, but I'll wait until tomorrow. I've been through enough emotional turmoil today."

"What—?"

Jabbing Milton's leg, Jake whispered, "Don't go there."

"All right. No need to pulverize my thigh." His smile took the sting from his words.

Half an hour later, Milton stopped at his parents' home. "How about I take us all out for dinner? I'll see what Mum and Dad want to do." He climbed out of the car and ran up the steps to the verandah where his folks sat.

Jake turned to Marlow. "What do you want to do?"

"Right now, I just want to relax in the peaceful gardens for a bit."

He waved to his aunt and uncle, then followed Marlow to a vine-covered gazebo. She sat and watched him approach. He would have retreated if she hadn't patted the seat beside her. He joined her and waited for her to speak.

A minute crawled by, and then she cleared her throat. "I need time to get over this emotional hurdle. You understand?"

"Definitely. I can leave if you want me to."

"No. Please stay."

The words were music to his ears, and the sweet scent from the flowering vines a balm to his soul. "For as long as you need me." *One hour, or a lifetime.*

"This has been as strange day."

"Yup. First to discover Graham was a cheat, and then to find out Zachariah succeeded in spite of the fraud." Jake kicked at a pebble in the grass. "We narrowly avoided disaster."

"Uh-huh." Marlow clasped his hand. "Please give thanks for…"

"Nothing I'd like more." He bowed his head and held her hand as if she were a lifeline. "God our Father, thank You for a safe and productive day. We learned that people we hold in high esteem can disappoint us. Help us to always look to Your Son as our example. Be with us as we make decisions that will affect our futures. In

Jesus's name. Amen."

They sat in silence, Jake content to hold Marlow's hand and be as close as possible, forcing her words about going home far from his mind.

The Utopian interlude lasted a mere minute.

Marlow let go of his hand and plucked a leaf off the nearest vine. "I have a burden to share. Will you listen to my problem?"

"Of course."

Twisting the leaf, she lowered her head. "As you…this is so hard, but I trust you. I've shared a bit about my relationship with Steven, but I don't want to dwell on the past. Today, I fulfilled his dying wish. I brought the cousins together, we solved the puzzle, and now we've completed the demands Graham placed on Steven. I am relieved about that, but also—" She sprang off the bench. "I feel like such a hypocrite. I am relieved to be done with the whole mystery, because that means I'm done with…with Steven." She pivoted and glared at Jake. "Those are terrible words, but it's what I feel. I don't have to worry about him being disappointed anymore. I don't have to chastise myself for not standing up to him. I can…I can just be…me."

Jake opened his arms, and she fell into them as she sat, her head on his shoulder. She didn't cry, but he felt her sides expanding and contracting as she breathed hard. He rested his head on hers, stroked her hair, and murmured, "You'll be apples, Marlow. We all have events in our pasts that could overwhelm us if we let them, but you have memories of Eileen to hold close. Dwell on those positives. They will spur you on to do whatever you desire. Find your family in Perth, or not, return with me to Long Gully, or not." He couldn't bring himself to add Texas. "Your future is in your hands. Seek God's wisdom and direction, then ask His blessings on your decisions."

She released a huge sigh and straightened. "Thank you, Jake. I did not mention previously, but I had another compelling reason to fulfill Steven's demands. I hoped the task would bring closure to that part of my life." She tilted her head. "And I was right. I'm free."

Gazing deep into her eyes, he leaned closer, closer, but Milton rounded the corner.

"There you are. Who's in the mood for curry? There's a grand restaurant down the street."

"Sounds good." Marlow stood, but didn't break eye contact with Jake. She cocked an eyebrow and attempted to stifle a smile.

He grinned. Marlow had opened her heart to him. He had nothing to fear from Milton. Jake had seen no sparks fly between *them*.

Chapter 37

The piece of paper with the Finlay's number written in bright blue ink sat on the small table near the telephone. Marlow stared at the numerals. She regretted telling Jake she wanted to be alone to make the call. Too late to change her mind. He and Milton were on their way to the corner market to purchase ingredients Liz needed for a special teatime treat.

You can do it. Marlow swallowed hard and placed her hand on the receiver. She'd imagined this call ever since locating the phone number, but now doubt blanketed her mind. Would Ida Marie speak with her, let alone acknowledge any kinship?

Drawing in a deep breath, she picked up the receiver. With a shaking index finger, she dialed the number. Half a lifetime passed before someone answered.

"Hello." A calm, sweet-sounding voice.

Marlow gulped. "Ida Marie? I'm Marlow Barclay. I wrote to you—"

"Oh, oh, my dear. I must sit down. Hold on." A cushion whooshed. "Yes, I received your letter. You don't know how happy I am Gracie gave you our address. I have so many questions."

"So do I, but I don't know where to begin." Marlow twisted a strand of hair. "Is it possible, um…" She couldn't bring herself to ask right out if they were related. "I want to tell you about my mother."

"My dear, what you really want to know is if I'm your grandmother. Don't you?"

Marlow's throat tightened, and blood drained from her head. She latched onto the arm of the chair. "Yes."

"Tell me everything you can remember about your mother. Even if you wrote the details in your letter, tell me again."

She'd dreamed about this moment so often, now she couldn't think straight. "First of all, I want you to know she loved me and was a good mother. I wish I'd pressed her to talk about her Australian roots, but I didn't. Her name was Marie Kate Johnstone."

"Now that's interesting. Our daughter was Katie Marie. Did your mother use both names?"

"No. Just Marie."

"That makes me sad. Go on. I'll tell you why later."

"Mom told me she was born in Australia and moved to America in 1946. She was a brunette, average height, smart. For most of my life, she was a nurse."

"I hate to interrupt, but our Katie Marie loved to tend peoples' cuts and scratches and had a dozen dolls festooned with sticking plasters. Oh, my, carry on."

Marlow licked her lips. Coincidences were accumulating at an alarming rate. "She never talked about my father, in fact he's not named on my birth certificate. Mom died in 1964, when I was eighteen, a vicious bout of pneumonia." She drew in a big breath. "The only thing of value she had was the necklace, which your friend Gracie O'Bryan told me is unique."

"Yes. My Arthur has good taste when it comes to jewelry." Ida Marie muttered, then said, "I'm sorry about how she died. That must have been devastating for you."

"It was. But that's the past."

Ida Marie sobbed quietly. "I understand." She sniffled, then continued, "Let me tell you about our only child, Katie Marie. My dad named me Ida Marie and told me to never let people use only one name because I was special. I told our Katie Marie the same thing, and she loved the idea, so that's why I asked about her name. Anyway, she was a rambunctious, independent kid who fought against boundaries. Needless to say, she went off the rails and fell in with a wild bunch of teens." A door banged shut. "Sorry, my husband just arrived home. I'll have to be quick. We, um, he disowned her. She moved to Sydney, and I never saw her again. We did correspond for a few months." Another sniffle. "I sent her money often, and her necklace, because I hoped she'd remember the sentiment behind the gift. I'm so glad she kept it and passed it on. She did write about her marriage to Hamish Johnstone."

Marlow gasped. "My father?"

"Sorry, luv, I don't know. That was early in 1946, but he was killed in a diving accident, and she left for America soon after. That was my last communication from her." Ida Marie hesitated. "Uh, she said she could never forgive her father, and blamed me for not being able to change his mind."

Resentment and the lack of forgiveness had caused them all so much grief. Marlow took a moment to compose herself. "I noticed she kept Hamish's surname. No wonder I couldn't find her in the birth registry. I always thought Johnstone was her maiden name." Marlow's mind raced. "Do you know what month she left Australia?" There was a chance Hamish—

"I think it was soon after my birthday which is in late January."

"If your Katie Marie was my mother, then Hamish could be my dad. My birthday's in October." Marlow felt as if her spine turned to gelatin. She sank against the chair, and if she hadn't been holding the arm, would have spilled onto the floor. Her mother and father!

"That's possible." Ida Marie harrumphed. "But, luv, don't get your hopes up. I know nothing about this Hamish fella. But I suppose you could locate their marriage certificate."

"At least I have a name, and I'm not...illegitimate." Straightening, Marlow's eyes widened. Ida Marie had just acknowledged she was her grandmother.

"We're both learning so much today. But I have one more piece of information to give you. Do you have a map of Australia?"

"Sure. It's packed away in my luggage."

"When you can, turn to Victoria and look at the south coast. About three hundred and eighty Ks east of Melbourne is a small seaside town at the mouth of the Snowy River. We had a holiday cottage there and used to visit every summer. We sailed, swam. Built sandcastles by the score." Her voice cracked.

"And you made fresh pineapple sandwiches."

"She told you. I'm glad she shared those memories." Ida Marie cleared her throat. "The town is *M A R L O.* I know my Katie Marie spelled your name differently, but as soon as I read your letter, I knew you were our granddaughter. The name, the necklace."

Marlow blacked out for a second. Then excitement as fizzy as carbonated water churned in her insides. "I found my family."

"Yes, luv." Ida Marie murmured to someone in the background. "I have to hang up soon. Sorry, my dear, I hate to squelch our happiness. I want to meet, but Arthur doesn't agree. He accepts some of the evidence, but he's skeptical. He thinks, well, never mind what he thinks." She sniffed as if she cried again. "How…long will you be in Australia?"

Marlow's joy dissolved as quickly as snow in lava. "I not sure. I have five months left on my visa."

"That's good to know." Her sobs increased. "If Arthur changes his mind, maybe we can meet. But we must…keep in touch. Write often…my dear. I have to go. Arthur will get curious, and I don't want him to know I spoke with…you. Oh, Arthur, why, why?"

"I'll let you know my plans. Thank you, and I'm, uh, I'm glad to know who you are." Lame words, but that's all she could say.

"Cheerio, luv. Sorry."

A click ended the call and Marlow stared at the ceiling. From elation to desolation in twenty seconds flat.

Chapter 38

By the time Jake and Milton returned to the house, Marlow had regained her emotional footing. As least outwardly. Disappointment roiled in her stomach, and her heart ached as it had when Eileen died. Family connections were so close, yet she might as well be on another planet.

Marlow straightened her shoulders and entered the kitchen. Jake sat across from Milton at the table. Liz stood at the counter slicing a loaf of dark bread. "Can I help, Liz?"

"No, no, dear. Have a seat. We'll have lunch shortly. Now, tell us about your telephone call."

Marlow sank into a chair at the head of the small table and glanced at the men in turn. Each wore an expectant expression. "I'm still trying to comprehend the details, but I have two things to share. No, three. Ida Marie Finlay is my grandmother." A person she couldn't see or touch. She laced her fingers together and smiled in order to keep the tears at bay.

"That's great news." Jake placed his hand over hers. "But you don't seem too excited."

"I have mixed emotions. I am thankful I found family, but I'm disappointed because my grandfather is skeptical, and doesn't want Ida and me to meet." She shrugged. He'd disowned his own daughter and wouldn't acknowledge his granddaughter. "I don't want to dwell on that right now."

"Understandable." Milton reached out, then drew back. "What's the third thing?"

"My mother married Hamish Johnstone before she left Australia. The guy died soon after the wedding, but he could be my father."

"Oh, my dear. I can see why you're all messed up." Liz stirred a pot at the stove, releasing the tangy aroma of marinara sauce. "I'm so sorry you won't have the opportunity to meet your grandmother in person, but at least you have her name and address. Did she have any more information about your father?"

"No."

"I have an idea." Milton's eyebrows rose. "You can stop in Perth on your way back to America. Do you look like your mother? If so, surely Granddad will recognize you as being part of the family."

Marlow lowered her head. She didn't want to think along those lines. "I don't know. Right now, I won't make any rash decisions."

"Boys, leave her alone. Lunch is ready. Milton, set the table, and Jake, call your uncle, please."

The men stood. Milton left the room, but Jake hovered. "Marlow, will you come back to Long Gully or stay in Melbourne?"

The question hung in the air. Stay in Melbourne, travel to other places in Australia, maybe end up in Perth. Her heart squelched that idea. "I want to return with you, at least until your next trip to Cunnamulla." Being in the city set her nerves on edge, making her feel jittery and unbalanced. She'd come to appreciate the peace and quiet of life on the station, and she would have to be blind not to notice Jake's increasing attention.

****

Pleading a headache, Marlow excused herself after lunch and escaped to her room. She desperately needed time alone. To heal from the emotional strain of completing Graham's demands, and thus fulfilling Steven's dying wish, and locating her mother's family, the two goals of her Australian trip.

She collapsed into an armchair close to the window. A breeze ruffled the flimsy curtains, and chirps from birds in the shrubs soothed her ragged soul. Yes, discharging her obligations had lifted the weight off her shoulders and she had her closure. She could make decisions based solely on what she wanted.

Setting her elbows on the sill, Marlow stared into the lush gardens. For a moment, the old mantle of worthlessness that had haunted her for years surfaced, but she shook it off. She had accomplished her goals, and now there were so many avenues open to her. She had roots and could search for her mother's marriage certificate. Dig into Hamish's family background. Maybe locate more relatives. Even build a new life in Australia. She watched a small brown bird swoop onto a nearby branch and smiled. Or go back to Texas, finish her doctorate, and teach at the university.

An airplane soared overhead. They needed to arrange for their flight back to Long Gully. Marlow took one last look at the gardens, then stepped to the mirror. She pinched her cheeks to bring color to her pale face and headed to the door. Family research could wait. She wanted to go back to the station, help Bella through the last week of her school year, and revisit the child's concerns about attending high school in Cunnamulla.

Yup. After Marlow's agreed time in the outback was over, the possibilities were endless.

However, everything would change if romance blossomed.

Chapter 39

Unwilling to open up to Marlow and chat while in the car with Milton, Jake silently applauded when they arrived at the airport with time to spare. Quin would pick them up in thirty minutes.

Milton helped remove their luggage from the boot of his car. "Hey, Marlow, if you visit us again before you go back home, I'll take some days off and be your chauffeur and guide."

"I'll keep that in mind. Thanks for your help, Milton." She hugged him and stepped toward the hangar, carrying the package containing canvases, paints, and brushes for Bella, plus a few groceries, and her small case.

"Jake, I'm glad we had this time together."

"Me, too." Jake shook his cousin's hand, some of their old camaraderie still intact. "Let's not wait another ten years for a visit. Come to Long Gully. I'll show you my piece of the world."

"Maybe I will." Milton climbed into his car and slowly drove away, eyes straying from the road to Marlow seated on a bench near the hangar.

Jake grinned. Yeah, Milton had feelings for her, but seemed astute enough not to push his luck. Jake carried Marlow's large suitcase and his duffle bag to the bench. He was so pleased she decided to return with him he could have hollered from the rooftop. Instead, he sat beside her and stretched his legs. "I hope you noticed Milton and I resolved our differences."

She nodded. "Good for you."

"Yeah. It was time. He's still got an eye for the ladies, but he's not the Casanova I remember from our youth. He even apologized for misleading Laura, but I also had to swallow my pride. I attributed things to him that he didn't do. We came to a mutual agreement to keep the past in the past."

"I'm happy for you. Family is precious, and we must do all we can to keep those bonds secure."

"You know that firsthand." He turned to her. "Milton and I will never be best mates because of our differing lifestyles, but we won't be enemies, either." Jake was tempted to put his arm around her, but changed his mind. Not the time or place. "How are you today? Did you have a good rest last night?"

A jet taking off muffled her words. She stopped talking and waited for the noise to subside. "I was able to sleep and have put what I heard yesterday into perspective. Or at least, I think so. Yes, I found my grandparents, and although we probably won't meet, it's still reassuring to know who they are. Seems to give my existence more value. I'm not sure what I'm saying exactly, but after Mother died and I was an orphan, I always felt left out, alone. But now I have a foundation." She looked up at him. "Does that make sense?"

He did put his arm around her this time. "Yes. We all have a need to belong. When Steven and Eileen were alive, you had that, but after they passed, you were floating, anchorless, so to speak."

She rested her head on his shoulder.

He sighed and closed his eyes. *Hey, Quin, don't come yet. Please.* "I'm sorry your grandfather doesn't want to meet."

"But you know, the more I think about his response, the more I understand. Here I come out of the blue, claiming to be related. I could have stolen the necklace. Used the name Marie Kate for my mother because I knew of their daughter."

"Except, how would you have known about the town of Marlo? That to me, would be the clincher."

She sighed. "I always wondered where Mother got my name. I've never known anyone else called Marlow. Kids at school used to tease me and call me marshmallow."

"Well, they had one thing right. You are sweet."

She straightened and swatted his arm. "That's not funny." But she smiled and rolled her eyes.

"I think it is. See, I made you smile."

"There's Quin." She stood. "Time to squeeze into the tin can again. Are your knees prepared?"

"Yup. And I'm ready to get back to work."

The return flight to Long Gully took most of the day, and as before, Jake and Marlow couldn't converse much. Marlow slept part of the way, and Jake figured either she needed the rest, or she deliberately distanced herself from him. No doubt feeling the weight of not being able to meet the Finlays.

Circling Long Gully again brought a lump to his throat. Skyscrapers, miles and miles of tarred roads, and people by the scores had their appeal to some, but give him the outback any day. His heart swelled. Home. He glanced at Marlow across the narrow aisle. She stared out the window too. The slower pace of life on the station would help heal her wounds but he couldn't wait to show her more of the homestead, explain the shearing process, and take her out to his special glade. Let her experience more of the lifestyle required of his wife. Yup. Find out if there was a glimmer of hope for him before he asked her to marry him. She needed to know what she was signing up for first.

Ernie drove up as Jake and Marlow exited the plane. They waited for Quin to take off before heading to the homestead.

Marlow climbed into the backseat and closed her eyes.

Jaw set, Ernie loaded the luggage into the back of the cruiser.

"Everything good?" Jake asked.

"Nothing too serious. Young Paddy has gone. Took off early yesterday, as best we can tell."

"Does anyone know why he left?"

"Greg and I asked around, but no one knew. Oh, and there were two more fences cut. We found those the day you left."

Jake had his arm out of the window and pounded on the door. "I hate to say it, but the culprit has to be someone at Long Gully. A swaggie wouldn't stick around on a station this long to cause havoc."

"Too right. And we haven't hired any itinerant chaps since the shearing. What do you suggest we do?" Ernie slowed as he reached the yard close to the house.

"Greg and I will come up with a plan. Thanks for the ride, Ernie."

"How's Mary?" Marlow asked.

"A little better. She's resting a lot. Boss, we appreciate you letting her take time off."

"No worries." Jake climbed out of the vehicle and opened the passenger door for Marlow. "We're all in this together, mate." He picked up the large bags and waited for Marlow to collect her smaller items and the gift for Bella.

"Daddy." Bella charged out of the kitchen and flung her arms around his middle. "I'm so glad you're home."

"Bella Bear, what's the matter?" He dropped the luggage.

"It's Toffee. She's been missing for two days."

Chapter 40

The clock in the hall chimed twice. Unable to go back to sleep after her unsettling dream, Marlow climbed out of bed and sat on the verandah outside her bedroom. She draped the thin blanket over her legs and drew it up to cover her arms. Temperatures as hot as a brick oven during the day, but sometimes a cool breeze provided relief in the middle of the night.

In her dream, Marlow had fallen off a flying horse and plunged over a precipice toward a dark abyss. She'd woken with a sickening thump before hitting the ground. She shuddered at the memory and focused on recent events.

Toffee's sudden disappearance had dampened Jake's and Marlow's homecoming. Jake was faced with Paddy's departure and additional fence-cutting, and Marlow still struggled to accept the Finlay's decision not to meet. Solid Celia remained in control, commiserating with Marlow, showering sympathy over Bella, and reminding Jake he'd solved bigger issues than the fences before.

A dog barked in the distance, and Marlow stretched her legs onto another chair. Returning to Long Gully was the right decision. She had two more weeks to mull over her mother's family and to decide on choices for her future. Fourteen days. So many decisions her brain hurt. Would Jake mind if she stayed another month? Hmm. Christmas and New Year's at Long gully. Her heart fluttered and her skin tingled.

A squeaky door opened. Marlow sucked in a breath. She sensed Jake's presence and froze. Perhaps he wouldn't see her.

Flip-flop footsteps headed her direction.

"Couldn't sleep either?" he whispered.

"No." She tucked the blanket around her nightgown. "How'd

you know I was here?"

"I heard a door and knew it wouldn't be Bella. She's not a fan of the dark." He tucked his T-shirt into his shorts.

"Her room is so close, maybe we shouldn't be out here talking." But she didn't want to go inside to chat, either.

"Bella's a sound sleeper. We'll be fine if we whisper."

"What exactly do you want to whisper about?"

He moved a chair and sat facing her. "I've a lot on my mind. Greg and I discussed Paddy and the fence cutting. I think they're connected."

"Could Paddy be responsible?"

"Maybe. I don't know. The fence problem started before I hired him. Greg and I will increase the fence riders' responsibilities. Maybe add a chap or two. At a minimum, I'll have to hire another jackaroo to replace Paddy." He snickered. "You wouldn't by any chance want to patrol the fences."

She giggled. "Not likely. I love the outdoors, but I'd melt in the heat."

"I wouldn't want that." He tapped her arm. "Bella, poor mite, is really torn up about Toffee. It's not the first cat we've lost, and I had to remind her that life is harsh out here for small animals."

"She and I also had a talk. I'm glad I brought her the canvases. The gift cheered her, and she wants to paint again. I take that as a positive step in dealing with her grief."

"Definitely. She has changed so much since you've been in her life."

His compliment warmed her all over. "I've enjoyed our time together. She's a willing pupil and has taken to heart all the pointers I've given her."

"Like what, for example?"

"To read the cues her companions display. When she feels anxious or angry, to take a deep breath, relax her shoulders, and tell someone what's bothering her."

He folded his arms. "A lesson for all of us."

"Right."

"Bella mentioned a new girl she met at Maroola Downs last week. Did you see them together?"

"I did." Marlow was still embarrassed at how little attention she paid to anyone or anything other than her own problems that day.

"Why?"

"Bella was impressed with Lynn, and just by watching her and listening to her, realized Bella and her pals acted less grownup. Her words. To me, that's a big mark to her credit."

"Uh-huh. I must admit, I didn't focus on Bella much, but I did notice something about her new friend. Do you know how old she is?"

"Thirteen, according to Bella. She said her dad was recently hired on the station. Maybe that's why Lynn's not in boarding school yet."

"There could be another reason. From my brief observation, I believe Lynn might have a mental or physical impairment. I noticed her awkward gait, halting speech, and blank stares."

Jake slid down in this chair, his knees almost touching hers. "I didn't."

"I could be mistaken. But don't forget my life's work is with children who are…who have special needs."

"Would Bella have realized this?"

"Not necessarily."

"Interesting, nonetheless. Bella did say Lynn was different. Anyway, I'm glad my little girl was friendly toward her."

"Your Bella Bear has a kind heart." Marlow shifted away from Jake a bit. "She said something very sweet to me when I gave her the painting supplies. She said she'd prayed I'd return to Long Gully." Choking up, Marlow turned and stared toward the south. An orangey-red light flickered on the horizon.

"What—?"

"Smoke. I smell a grassfire." Jake jumped up and peered through the darkness. "Hurry. Wake Celia, please. Tell her to ring the gong and to ask one of the men to turn on the generator. I'll get dressed." He ran toward his room.

Marlow draped the blanket over her shoulders, hurried around the corner, and pounded on Celia's door. "Wake up. There's a grassfire." The aroma of ash hit her as she glanced at the horizon where the fire shimmered beneath an ebony umbrella.

A moan, thumping, a swath of light through the screen, and Celia appeared at the door, sliding her arms into her robe. "I know. The gong and the generator. I'll take care of it. Go to Bella. The fire will upset her."

Marlow entered the child's room prepared to wake her, but Bella switched on her flashlight. "Did…did I hear someone say 'fire'?"

"Yes, sweetheart."

"Where's my daddy?" She crawled out of bed and pulled yesterday's clothes over her pajamas. "Is he going out with the stockmen?"

"I don't know."

Jake called, "Bella, Marlow. Come outside, please."

Marlow threw on jeans, shirt, and sneakers, then joined Bella and Jake.

Gasping for air, Celia tromped along the verandah. "The men are coming. I told them to meet you here."

"Thanks."

Soon, bouncing rays from numerous flashlights and lanterns announced the arrival of the stockmen. Marlow had no idea so many men worked on the station.

"I hear the generator." Celia headed to the main door. "I'll turn on the lights." Within seconds, the verandah and the area beyond were bathed in harsh white.

The men extinguished their lights.

"How near is the fire, Dad?" Bella tugged at Jake's sleeve.

"It's not as close as it looks. The dark sky enhances the glow from the flames. But we can't take any chances." He silently counted the men. "Three men are missing."

"Two are sleeping out in the paddocks, and Eugene is wetting the burlap bags." Greg said.

"Right. Ernie, you stay and help Greg. I want four volunteers to ride out and determine if the fire is this side or the other side of the break. For those of you new to us, there are no homesteads in that direction. It won't be an easy ride, but you know the danger and uncertainty of living where bushfires rage out of control."

Mitch, Jarra, Pete, and Adam stepped forward.

"Good on ya, chaps. Jarra, you're in charge. Do you have your radio?"

"Yeah, boss." Jarra patted the radio clipped to his belt. "I'll call if we run into any problems."

"Now you lot, take canteens, shovels, soaked bags, and be careful. We'll leave the outside lights on to guide you home." Jake set his radio—a walkie-talkie-sized device—on the table. Hands on his hips, he watched the men depart in haste.

Marlow drew in a breath. Jake's leadership qualities shone. For some odd reason, she felt proud to be a Barclay.

The roar of dirt bikes blotted out any other sound, their red taillights disappearing into the night.

"The rest of you, stay close. If the fire is on this side of the break, I want you ready to defend the homestead and outbuildings. Greg, supervise the gathering of equipment. I checked the water level in the tank of our firetruck last week. It's good to go." Jake beckoned Ernie. "I want a word."

The men left with Greg.

"Why didn't you want me to ride out?" Ernie asked.

"Because your wife's pregnant." He held up his hand. "Don't argue. I really do need you here. Now, go help Greg, please."

Again, Marlow's heart swelled. Jake didn't broadcast the pregnancy in case Ernie and Mary hadn't shared the news, and yet, he made Ernie still feel valued.

"I'll put on the kettle." Celia's answer to all life's problems.

Marlow's mouth watered just thinking about a cup of hot tea. And maybe a biscuit.

Bella slipped her arm through Jake's. "Daddy, I'm scared."

"Oh, Bella Bear, I know this is a concern for everyone. But we have never been wiped out by fire. One came pretty close years ago. So, praise God, we've been spared." He patted her head. "Remember, we understand fire is master out here and we respect its power, but we know what to do, so let's relax, keep watch, and pray."

"Okay." Her voice sounded confident, but she clung to him.

"Help me arrange the chairs, luv." Jake and Bella set three chairs in a row. "Sit here with the ladies." He took the tray from Celia when she emerged and set it on the small table then picked up his radio. "I'll be with Greg if you need me. Celia, do you have your radio?"

"In my pocket." She poured the tea after he entered the house.

While they drank, the pulsating red glow seemed to mesmerize them. No one spoke or moved, until the emergency alert on the transmitter in Jake's office had Celia on her feet in a second.

"It's probably neighbors calling to check on us." She hurried inside.

Bella moved her chair closer to Marlow. "I hate fires."

"Because of what happened to Trish?"

"Yeah." She grasped Marlow's hand. "Her scars still hurt sometimes."

Marlow had no quick response, so said nothing.

"Grassfires can be terrible. Do you know that earlier this year there was one in Victoria and South Australia? Over seventy people died and lots more were left homeless."

"That must have been dreadful." Marlow squeezed her hand. "But like your dad said, all the men here are prepared."

"I know, but I don't have to like it."

Before Marlow replied, Celia returned. "That was Kevin O'Bryan from Maroola Downs. He was concerned about our safety. He said from their place the fire looks like it's on our doorstep." She paced to the wall and stared out at the flame-lit sky. "I'll let him know how far out the fire is when the chaps come back and report."

To ease the tense atmosphere, Marlow changed the subject. "Hey, Bella, I just remembered. You gave your Thanksgiving presentation while I was gone. How'd it go?"

She shrugged.

"Now, young lady. You know Miss York raved about your talk. She's going to keep it to use for her other classes." Celia turned and picked up the tray. "Anyone for more tea? No? Then I'll make sandwiches for the men when they return. Come help me, Bella."

"All right." She moved as slowly as a tired snail and followed her aunt.

Marlow stared at the fire spread across the horizon. Such devastation. Footsteps trod up the stairs, and Jake opened the screen door.

"What's the matter?"

"I'm not sure. Since the men aren't back yet, I suppose the fire is farther out than I thought. Which is positive, but I can't shake the feeling something's wrong, so I'm going after them."

Before long, the buzz of Jake's bike and the rays of his headlight announced his departure.

Bella dashed outside. "Who was that?"

"Your daddy has gone out."

"No! Why did he leave me?" She sat and covered her face.

"He'll be fine." Marlow slipped her arm around Bella and pondered her words. Aha. "Was Trish's daddy away when the fire started?"

Bella nodded.

Without another thought, Marlow bowed her head. "Father, God, please protect all the men who are out there tonight and bring them safely home to us." The first prayer she'd voiced for anyone else to hear in a long time. She wiped at a stray tear and buried her face in Bella's hair. Best not let the child know she was worried too, or that her concern increased the moment Jake set out.

A few minutes later Celia joined them. "Jake went out, didn't he?"

"Yes."

"Just like him. Put someone in charge, then take over." She harrumphed. "Is it my imagination or is the fire dying down?"

Marlow looked again. "I think you're right. That's good news. Jake should be back anytime now." She squeezed Bella's shoulders. "See, sweetheart. The flames seem less intense."

Barely raising her head, Bella glanced out then cuddled next to Marlow's shoulder again.

Ears straining to hear motorbikes, eyes scanning the dawn-kissed horizon, Marlow comforted Bella, which in turn, put her mind at ease. The air was heavy with the acrid smell of Mother Nature's pyrotechnics. Flecks of black ash floated by, landing with a delicate touch on the furniture and floor. Marlow brushed some off the table and examined her black-streaked fingers.

Celia straightened. "Listen. Do you hear the bikes?"

Bella sat up, and Marlow walked to the wall. "Yes." She ran down the front steps to the illuminated driveway, joined by Bella and Celia. Jake was not one of the riders, and her heart plummeted.

Jarra stopped his bike in front of them while Mitch rode to the yard.

"Where's my dad?" Bella latched onto Marlow's arm.

"Well, it's like this. That young hothead, Adam, tried to race in front of us, and he hit a rock. Landed on his head. Jake sent us to ask Miss Celia to be prepared."

"What's Adam's condition?" All business, Celia adjusted the clasp holding her knot of hair in place.

"Jake and Pete waited with him. He only lost consciousness for a few seconds. But they're riding slowly beside him." He turned. "That's them now." The faint whine of motors confirmed the arrival of the dirt bikes.

"I'll get an examination area prepared in the kitchen." Celia turned toward the steps. "Bella, luv, come help me, please."

"What about the fire?" Marlow kept her eyes on the approaching men.

"It hit the break and is burning itself out. We can be thankful the wind died down, and Long Gully is out of danger." Darra doffed his hat and drove off.

The three remaining men and bikes bumped over the terrain beyond the garden, Jake and Pete alongside Adam. Marlow blew out a breath and stepped forward. "Celia is set up in the kitchen." To her untrained eyes, Adam looked all right.

"Thanks." Jake led the others around the back.

Marlow hurried inside to the kitchen. "Do you need any help?"

Celia shook her head and opened the door as Jake and Pete ushered in Adam. "Sit here, young man." She pulled out a chair and immediately began a physical exam of his head and face. "Pete, take that platter of sangers out to the men, with our thanks."

"Will do. See you later, boss." He picked up the food and backed out of the door.

Standing off to the side, Jake acknowledged Pete's words with a nod.

Although covered in dust with black ash smears streaked over his face and clothes, and his lips pressed into a thin line, he'd never looked more appealing. Marlow couldn't take her eyes off him and stepped closer, almost overcome by the reeking smoke.

"Ooh, I don't feel good." Bella covered her mouth.

Marlow reluctantly shifted her gaze and noticed Bella's ashen face. "Run to the bathroom, quickly. I'll come with you."

The child leaned over the basin, and her stomach heaved, but she didn't throw up. She ran the water and rinsed off her face.

Marlow handed her a towel. "Feel better?"

Nodding, Bella slid down the wall and sat on the tiled floor, her arms around her bent knees. Marlow joined her and stared at the tub. What a night. Threat of the fire's destruction and possible danger for the men. For Jake. She placed her arm across Bella's shoulders. "It's all right, now. Your daddy is home, safe and sound."

The grandfather clock in the hall announced the hour. Six chimes. Marlow giggled, imagining the pendulum swaying back and forth. She saw herself sitting on it, swinging to Texas, then back to Long Gully. Texas, Long Gully.

Cuddling Bella close, Marlow knew what she wanted. To jump off the pendulum and trust God for a safe landing with Jake at her side. A life at Long Gully with Bella and Celia and Jake…if he'd have her.

Mantra. What mantra? She was falling in love with the boss.

Chapter 41

The whole household was off kilter. According to Celia, this was the latest Bella had slept since her mother's passing. Marlow drained another mug of coffee and slouched at the kitchen table while eyeing Jake. He'd showered and changed clothes. "What are your plans for today?"

He stabbed his last piece of bacon and chewed, then took a swig of coffee. "I'll check on Adam, put the word out over the radio I'm looking to hire a couple of jackaroos and, I don't know. The trip to Melbourne and then the fire, I'm not sure if I'm coming or going."

"You're staying put." Celia added more coffee to his mug. "You need to rest, and, well, just be with your daughter. She missed you while you were gone, and then Toffee disappeared, and the fire. She might have grown up some as you say, but inside she's still a little girl."

"Strewth. I forgot about the cat." He stirred milk into his coffee. "You're right. Did you tell any of the men about Toffee?"

"I did, but obviously don't have any news. Bella was very good about not searching beyond the last shed."

"Then, I have an idea. I haven't been to the single quarters in a long time, so I'll go down there, check on Paddy's place, and call for Toffee."

Marlow stood and stretched. "Bella will appreciate that."

"Why don't you come with me?" Jake picked up the stacked plates. "We'll let Bella sleep, and you can reassure her I did look for her cat."

After Marlow's self-revelation earlier that morning, being alone with Jake would make it difficult to hide her love for him, but she'd be able to explore more of the station. "I'd like that. When do you want to go?"

"Now."

"I'll get my hat and sunnies." Ha. Picking up the slang already. Marlow hurried from the kitchen. She tiptoed past Bella's door and collected her items. At the last minute, she grabbed her camera and slung the strap around her neck.

Jake waited at the kitchen door. "It's a long walk down there. Mitch is working on my motorbike, so we'll take the cruiser."

Whew. Seated behind Jake, holding onto him would test her resolve.

Marlow ran down the stairs before anyone noticed her flushed cheeks.

They drove slowly along the track Bella had taken on Marlow's tour, and then veered left after they passed the shearing shed.

"One day, I want to take you in there to show you the lifeblood of our existence. Wool and everything connected to it."

"I'll enjoy that."

They passed a row of houses, some with gardens. All were shaded by tall gum trees. "These cottages are for the married hands, and that bunkhouse is where the shearers stay." Jake pointed to a long, stone barn-like building. He stopped in front of a house with a patch of green lawn and several shrubs. "This is Nellie's home. After Celia examined Adam and declared he had a mild concussion and scrapes and bruises, we brought him here so she could take care of him."

Nellie opened her screen door and called, "Hey, Jake, Marlow. Come in. Want some tea?"

"No, thanks. I've come to check on Adam." He waited for Marlow then followed her into the house.

"You'll find him in the kitchen, peeling potatoes. I'm doing all the cooking for the single hands now that Mary's dealing with morning sickness." Nellie cocked her head toward the sitting room. "Come have a chinwag with me, Marlow."

Nellie entered the room and settled on the sofa, while Jake strode down the hall, presumably to the kitchen.

Marlow dropped into the armchair. "This is a nice place."

"Yeah. I'm grateful Jake lets me have a house all to myself. After my husband died, I had nowhere to go, and I certainly didn't want to be a burden to Ernie and Mary. This suits me fine, and I earn my keep." She crossed her legs, smoothed her skirt over her knees, and pursed her lips.

Obviously, she had more on her mind than the house. Marlow searched her memory for something that might be bothering the woman. Aha. "How's Mary?"

Nellie's face brightened. "I'd like to talk to you about her. Celia said you work with special needs kids. Although Mary talked to her doctor, she's still worried about this pregnancy, and, you know, the possibilities."

"Celia did mention Mary's concerns."

"I've also tried to discuss the matter, but I was wondering if you could have a word."

"Of course. When would be a good time?"

Jake's deep voice drifted in from the kitchen.

"Come for tea tomorrow afternoon, about three. I'll make a fresh batch of Lamingtons. Mary knows about your profession, and I'll tell her you're coming. I don't want to spring anything on her."

Marlow glanced up as Jake entered the room. "See you tomorrow." She stood and walked out the door with him.

"What's happening tomorrow?"

She climbed into the cruiser. "Girl talk, is all." His raised eyebrows and quirky smile made her giggle.

"So, none of my business."

"Right. Please stop here so I can get a photo of the houses. This is a good spot." She leaned out the window and took the shot. The trees above the roof lines were a perfect backdrop. "Drive, on, please sir."

"Certainly, madam."

"How's Adam?"

"Fine. His cuts and bruises will heal in no time. But his ego might take longer. He can go back to work on Monday."

"That's good. These accommodations are far from the homestead. No wonder you don't let Bella come here by herself."

"Although she's been around the perils of living in the bush all her life, she sometimes lacks common sense. I can't protect her forever, but I will while I can."

He pulled up outside an *L*-shaped building with six doors on one leg, and seven on the other including an open area at the end. Again, tall gum trees hovered over the site, providing shade not only for the quarters, but for the parked vehicles and motorbikes.

"The single blokes' quarters. They each have a bedroom, but there are communal bathrooms in the middle and an outdoor kitchen. These utes and bikes belong to them. I've found that they take better care of the transportation when they use their own."

Holding onto her camera strap, Marlow climbed out of the vehicle. "No gardens here."

Jake snorted and walked toward the first door. "Nope. These chaps might appreciate green grass and flowers, but most of them are too focused on work, salary, and, um, booze to do any gardening."

To be expected. Marlow aimed her camera at the building, catching the sunlight at a unique angle.

"This was Paddy's room." Jake yanked on the screen door and pushed open the wooden door. "What a mess."

Marlow entered the stifling hot area, about twelve by twelve feet. A bare mattress on the bed, dresser drawers hanging open, trash strewn over the floor, and a cardboard box filled with stumpy brown bottles sat under the open window on the other wall. "Typical for a young guy, I suppose."

"Yeah. The amount of stubbies surprises me." Jake pointed to the bottles. "I didn't know Paddy drank that much. He never seemed hungover and was a good worker." He pivoted and examined the closet.

"No sheets or pillows. Did he take them?" Marlow approached the window.

"We don't supply bedding. The stockmen bring their own swag."

"Hey, look at this screen. It looks like someone has been scratching at it."

Jake peered over her shoulder. "Yeah. Why would he do that?"

Marlow shrugged and switched her gaze to a heap of dirty rags near the box. Wait. Not all rags. Black fur. "Oh, my dear Lord." She knelt and touched the pile. "It's Toffee. She must be dead." Scooping her up, Marlow stood. "No, she's breathing."

Jake reached her side in an instant. "Quick, let's go to the kitchen for water." He escorted Marlow outside, and they ran to the far end of the building. "Come here to the sink." He turned on the faucet.

Marlow cradled the cat while Jake dribbled water over her head. He tried to get some into her mouth, but she didn't cooperate.

"Try again and wet her body."

"To lower her temperature. Good idea." Jake continued his ministrations, to no avail.

Shirt dripping, wet cat cradled in her arms, Marlow sank to the ground. "It's no good. Toffee's too far gone." She sniffed. "Did Paddy lock her in his room deliberately?"

"I don't know." Jake gritted his teeth. "If I ever see that kid again, I'll…" He joined Marlow on the ground and held her.

Tears formed, and she let them fall. Head against Jake's shoulder, she closed her eyes. "How are we going to tell Bella?"

Chapter 42

Sitting on the floor, backs to the wall, Jake rubbed Marlow's shoulder. She had cried herself out and sat listless, nestling Toffee in her arms.

He leaned his head against the concrete. If Paddy locked up the cat on purpose, then Jake had better brush up on how to judge character. He had no idea the lad could be so heartless. It wouldn't have taken long for a small animal to be overcome in this heat.

Marlow tensed. "She's moving."

"Huh?"

"Look." Marlow stroked Toffee's head. "She's trying to open her eyes."

Jake stood, took one long step to the sink and splashed water into a chipped enamel bowl then squatted beside Marlow. "Here, see if she'll drink some."

Laying the cat on her outstretched legs, Marlow dabbed water around Toffee's mouth. The cat moved her head side to side, and finally her little pink tongue poked out. Marlow dribbled drops on her tongue, and Toffee attempted to right herself.

"Let me take her." Jake moved the cat onto her side on the ground and held the plate close to her. She raised her head and lapped a couple of times, then closed her eyes again. "Good girl. She's dehydrated and weak. Let's see if she'll drink a little more, then get her home to Bella."

Marlow coaxed the cat, and she lapped for a few seconds, then a feeble meow escaped. "She's still burning up. I'll wet her fur again before we leave." She scooped water from the bowl and soaked the cat's chest and abdomen. "That should be enough for now."

Jake straightened, offered Marlow his hand, then she picked up Toffee.

"I'm glad I brought the car."

The jostling ride roused Toffee, and by the time they reached the house, the cat was more alert. "Let's get her inside." He ran up the kitchen steps carrying Marlow's camera and hollered, "Bella, luv, we found Toffee."

A squeal, and Bella barreled down the hall in her pajamas. "Where is she?"

Marlow entered at that moment. "Here, but she's weak. Take her carefully."

As gently as if handling delicate crystal, Bella cuddled her pet and snuggled into the damp fur. "Thank you, thank you. Toffee, you silly thing. Where have you been?"

"We found her trapped in a vacant room of the single quarters." Jake gave Marlow a look he hoped cautioned her not to mention Paddy.

"I heard the good news." Celia appeared from the dining room. "Poor kitty-cat. Heat exhaustion no doubt. Bella luv, put her in the bath. It's the coolest place we have. Make sure she has plenty of water but don't give her any food yet."

Bella started down the hall with Celia on her heels. "And keep her fur dampened."

Jake sank into a chair and set the camera on the table. "Bella doesn't need to know the details."

Nodding, Marlow touched her camera. "Thanks for bringing it in."

"When will you get your film developed?"

Her eyes narrowed, and her brow furrowed. She rubbed her temple. "It depends on…how long I stay in Australia."

"Of course." She'd hesitated? "Have you thought any more about visiting Perth, even though your grandfather doesn't want to meet?"

"Yes. But not yet. I'm still coming to terms with the fact I have family, even some who might not want to see me. But I long to talk to my grandparents, show them photos of Eileen."

"I understand. The business with Graham's letter made me realize I've lost touch with too many relatives. I need to do more than send Christmas cards once a year."

Celia returned to the kitchen, a frown creasing her brow. "Bella's staying with Toffee. I told her she can feed the cat bread soaked in milk after a while. Now, I'll get lunch ready, then I must have a lie down. I'm too old to deal with palavers so early in the morning."

Marlow chuckled. "I agree. After lunch I'll take a nap, too."

"Since Paddy's gone, I'll pitch in more on the station over the weekends. No rest for me." He stood and clipped his radio onto his belt then collected a couple of Celia's extra meat pies from the fridge.

She tapped his shoulder. "Where did you find Toffee?"

Jake whispered, "In Paddy's room."

"The scoundrel."

"But we don't know if it was deliberate, and Bella mustn't find out." He reached for his hat, then stopped. "Hey, ladies, let's pray." Celia and Marlow gathered close. "Father God, thank You for keeping us safe last night and for us finding Toffee in time. Please comfort Bella and help Marlow in her quest for family. In Jesus's name. Amen."

"Thank you, Jake." Celia patted him on the shoulder. "You're a good lad."

He snagged his hat from the rack and gave Marlow one last look before exiting and running down the stairs.

"Hey, boss, your bike's fixed." Mitch pushed Jake's motorbike into the yard. "I changed out the sparkplugs."

"Ta. How are you on spare parts?"

"Good for now."

With tucker and a large canteen, Jake set off to the W-2 paddock. He spent the rest of the day checking fences, pastures, and waterholes. Between tasks, Marlow occupied his thoughts. He had to find time to take her into the bush to experience the outback beyond the comfortable house, to see all aspects of life on the station. Reality before romance.

****

Sunday lunch after their simple service consisted of leftovers, and although tasty, the meal was not up to Celia's usual excellence. She looked tired. Maybe the daily chores around the house were getting too much for her. Time to see if one of the stockmen's wives would like the job, and Bella could do more, too.

"Go have a lie down, Aunty Celia. I'll clean up." He gathered the plates and gave her a look he hoped begged no argument.

"I'll wash, and you dry." Marlow picked up two serving dishes and headed to the kitchen.

His aunt, who usually never acknowledged she needed help, nodded and sighed. "Thanks. I'm still knackered from yesterday." She groaned as she stood.

"Sleep as long as you want." He waited until he heard her bedroom door close then he finished clearing the table.

Marlow piled clean dishes in the drying rack. "I hope there's nothing wrong with Celia."

"Tired, is all. She's such a workhorse that I sometimes forget she'll be sixty-two next birthday." He grabbed a dishtowel and a platter.

"I'll help as much as I can while I'm here. And Bella can pick up the slack."

"I thought about asking Nellie or Darri. Of course, I'll have to override Celia's wishes." He chuckled. "Talk about stubborn."

"Ask Celia to teach Bella to cook. That way she can still be in charge."

Jake opened a cupboard and found a place for the mugs. "That's a great idea. You read her right. In case you haven't realized it, this is Celia's domain."

"I noticed." She drained the sink and wiped down the counter. "How's Toffee?"

"Sleeping a lot, but eating. Bella won't let the cat out of her sight. I don't blame her, poor mite."

Marlow hung the dishrag over the tap and dried her hands. "It's almost time for me to visit Nellie. Would you like me to ask her about helping Celia?"

"Thanks, but not yet. All joking aside, that's a decision I need to make with Celia's input."

"Good point. May I drive your cruiser?"

"Of course. I'll get the keys." He draped his dishtowel over his shoulder and headed to his room. Although curious about Marlow's upcoming visit, he hesitated to ask too many questions. Especially after she said yesterday that it concerned 'girl talk'. He returned to the kitchen and handed her his keyring.

"Thank you. I won't be too long."

Before he could censure his tongue, the words spilled out. "Girl talk, hey? Does Nellie want to share her recipes? Or—"

Marlow pivoted at the door and stared at him. "Not exactly." Her voice was coated in sarcasm. "We're going to address Mary's concerns about her pregnancy."

"Right. I didn't mean…"

She strode out, and the screen door slammed behind her.

Why on earth had he sunk to using old clichés about women's roles? No wonder Marlow hurried out.

He dried the rest of the dishes and put them away. How was he ever going to tell Marlow how he felt if he couldn't read her well enough to know when to hold his tongue?

****

Standing in the passage, Celia leaned against the wall. She waited for Jake to leave the kitchen before entering. Unable to sleep, she'd come for a glass of lemonade and overheard the tail end of the conversation. Marlow's tone seemed a bit extreme, but she had been acting differently since their visit to Melbourne.

Celia accepted Marlow's disappointment with the Finlays not wanting to meet her, but she also seemed distant, especially with Jake.

With a sigh, Celia opened the cupboard to get a glass, shook her head and smiled. Jake had misplaced everything. Cups were with bowls, plates alongside glasses, and when she opened the fridge, she found a stack of little plates next to the butter. *What a state he must be in*. Her heart melted a little.

She sat at the table sipping her drink, thoughts of Jake and Marlow filling her mind. Since the morning after the fire certainly, and maybe before, Celia had caught Marlow looking at Jake with something akin to admiration, even tenderness in her eyes. But if she planned on leaving Long Gully, she might be trying to distance herself from the pain of unfulfilled love.

And what about that rascal, Jake? He had stars in his eyes when he watched Marlow. How could she intervene and get them together?

Chapter 43

Still embarrassed at her unwarranted sarcastic tone with Jake earlier, Marlow waylaid him on his way to the dining room. "Before we go in, please let me apologize for how I answered you this afternoon. I don't know what came over me."

"You were probably labeling me a male chauvinist, which I assure you, I am not. I also spoke without thinking." He held out his hand.

She clasped it and raised her gaze to his face. Doubting her ability to keep from declaring her love, she released his hand and hurried into the dining room.

During the meal, her mind drifted back to the moments before she'd left the kitchen to visit Nellie. She'd been dwelling on the tenderness Jake had shown toward Toffee, his concern for Celia, his willingness to help in the kitchen. And in Marlow's eyes, nothing made a man look more masculine than drying a delicate crystal bowl.

She nibbled on a chunk of bread. Her comment was her attempt to hide her true feelings.

The next morning, Marlow traipsed down the hall toward the kitchen. No sound of any other human stirring. Good. The longer she had without facing Jake the better. Before she opened her heart, she had to know whether or not he was interested in developing a romantic relationship with her.

At the arched doorway, Marlow stopped and surveyed the kitchen. No Celia, no coffee on blue stove, and no breakfast preparations. "Celia?" Marlow called.

No reply. She walked to Celia's bedroom and gently knocked on the door.

A faint, "Come in."

Celia lay in bed, the covers in disarray, her red hair spread over the pillow, and dark circles under her eyes.

"Good morning. How are you?"

"What's the time?" Celia tried to sit up and fell back among the pillows. "Ooh, my head hurts."

"Then you're not going anywhere. Can I get you anything?"

"Yeah." Celia pointed to her wardrobe. "Top shelf, pills in the blue bottle. And some cold water, please."

Marlow produced the medication then hurried to the kitchen.

Jake stood beside the stove, brow furrowed. "Where's Celia?"

"She has a headache, and I told her to stay in bed." Marlow managed the sentence without looking at Jake.

"Good idea. I'll make the coffee before I go to see her."

Carrying a glass of water, Marlow entered Celia's room and then felt her forehead. "I don't think you have a fever."

Pills and drink in hand, Celia scowled at Jake as he stood in her doorway. "Now, don't worry about me. I'll be as right as a trivet in no time."

"Maybe so, but you'll also let us wait on you for a change. Bella and I will do breakfast, and—"

"I'll take care of lunch and dinner." Marlow set her hands on her hips. "In fact, this will give me the opportunity to use some of the special ingredients I purchased in Melbourne."

"What will you make?" Jake asked.

"A surprise."

After swallowing the pills, Celia pulled the sheet up to her chin. "Thanks, you lot. I just need some peace and quiet. And leave the curtains closed. The sun will be too bright on these old eyes."

Marlow and Jake left the room, and he closed the door. "She's never been sick as long as she's been here, but I'll rely on her medical knowledge and try not to worry."

"I'll keep a close watch on her."

"Ta. I need to spend the whole day out again. Will you still be able to help Bella with her schoolwork and painting, and do the meals?"

"Absolutely. There's room in the kitchen for the easel. That way I can take care of two things at once."

"I didn't mean you couldn't manage. I just didn't want to burden you."

"No worries. I appreciate your concern." She knew he didn't doubt her abilities.

Jake produced a breakfast of baked beans on toast with rashers of crispy bacon. Marlow had seen the item on Australian restaurant menus, but this was her first taste. Unusual, but not her favorite. No one at the table offered much conversation, which, for Marlow, was ideal.

Bella's school session went off without a hitch, and Marlow made frequent trips to Celia's room. The patient requested nothing more than tea. However, on her third visit, Marlow noticed a few magazines on the floor beside the bed. Hmm. Celia could still read the fine print even though she had a headache.

For lunch Marlow made a spinach quiche served with fresh tomatoes. Celia ate a sizable portion, but remained in her room. Later in the afternoon after Bella completed her assignments, she set up the easel in a corner of the kitchen. Marlow had offered to help Bella finish the painting she'd begun before her mother passed away. A bittersweet experience, no doubt.

This was the first time Marlow had seen Bella's painting. The eighteen by twenty-four-inch canvas depicted a billabong surrounded by gum trees, vaguely familiar. They had already reviewed how to arrange her palette, which brushes to use for different effects, and how to mix paint colors. Wearing an old shirt of Jake's, Bella looked the true artist.

"Do you recognize the place?" She set the box containing her tubes of paint on the table.

"Sort of."

"It's where we stopped for lunch on our way from Cunnamulla."

"Where I met the snake."

"I need to add the logs and finish the trees. I think I'll include some galahs."

Marlow placed her hand on Bella's shoulder. "You okay?"

The child nodded. "Since visiting the cemetery, I can remember Mum without being sad. Completing this painting will be a way I can honor her memory."

Well said, young lady.

Keeping an eye on Bella's progress and offering advice when asked, Marlow gathered items she'd purchased at a specialty shop in Melbourne, and staples from Celia's monstrous pantry, then prepared the ingredients for her fajita dinner. Spanish rice, dough for the tortillas, chicken strips and sliced onions sprinkled with fajita seasoning, Pico de Gallo, although she had no jalapeños. None of her offerings might look right to a Texan, but they would taste great.

While the chicken and onions sizzled in the pan and the rice simmered, Marlow rolled out another tortilla and set it on the griddle. Commotion at the backyard sink caught her attention, then footsteps announced Jake's arrival. No one else had his firm tread. His figure filled the doorway, and she became aware of her disheveled appearance. Messy apron, hair escaping the ponytail, perspiration covering her face. Well, there was nothing she could do.

She pushed a strand of hair out of her eyes. "Why are you home so early?"

Jake set his thumbs in his belt loop. "How's that for a welcome."

"Dad, look at my painting," Bella cooed.

He moved closer to the table. "It's marvelous, luv. I'm so proud of you. This is—"

"I forgot, I have something to show you." She set her brush in the jar of water, dashed down the hall, hollering over her shoulder, "I'll be back in a jiffy."

He turned toward Marlow and touched her forehead. "A new kind of makeup? It's not really your color."

His proximity turned Marlow's legs to jelly and her mind to a blank canvas. "Huh?"

"Flour all over your forehead."

"Oh." She couldn't concentrate on anything but the broad expanse of chest that seemed to surround her. An attempt to raise her hands failed as they were tangled in her apron. When she looked down to free them, she felt the warmth of Jake's hand on her shoulder.

"Marlow…"

She raised her head slowly, eyes focused on his shirt buttons, sunburned throat, stubble-studded chin, sensitive mouth forming the syllables of her name, eyes, warm blue pools murky with—

"What's that awful smell, Marlow?" Bella bounded into the kitchen, a magazine in hand.

"No! The tortilla is burning." Marlow turned and flipped the charred remnants off the griddle.

"I hope dinners not ruined." Seated at the table, Bella thumbed through the pages.

"I made plenty." Marlow fanned away the smoke with her apron which also helped cool her heated cheeks.

Jake sat, and she sensed his eyes on her. To distract him from her reaction, she repeated her question. "Why are you home so early?"

"If I'm not welcome, then I'll go back to my sheep."

"No, Daddy. We're having fajitas for dinner."

"Fa…what?"

Marlow turned off the burners on the stove. "Fajitas, a meal adapted from Mexican cuisine that is very popular in Texas."

Jake pursed his lips.

"Don't look so doubtful. I'll explain how to assemble them when we're seated."

"Some assembly required. In that case, I'd better shower. The food smells delicious." He attempted to stand but Bella grabbed his hand.

"Wait, Dad. Look what I found in this magazine." She pointed to an opened page. "It's a competition for amateur artists. They have lots of categories, and one is for outback landscapes."

He perused the information. "Paintings must be sent in by the end of December. Do you want to enter? We can take your canvas on our next visit to Cunnamulla."

"Of course, but the fee is high."

"Thirty dollars." He ruffled her hair and stood. "I think we can scrounge up that much. After all, your painting is wonderful."

"Thanks, Dad." Beaming, she watched him walk down the hall. "Is it time for me to cleanup?"

"Yes, sweetheart, and please set the table."

While Marlow spooned the food into serving dishes, Celia appeared in the doorway.

"I'm feeling so much better. Thought I'd bath and dress. The food smells divine. Can I help?"

Marlow gave her a once-over. Color back in her face, eyes bright. All positive. "Glad you're up and about. This place is not the same without you. We're almost ready to eat, so have a seat in the dining room." She hurried to her room, removed the apron, brushed her hair, and made sure she had no more flour on her face.

Remembering the sensation of Jake's hand on her shoulder while standing less than six inches apart sent a wave of heat over her. She took a deep breath and headed to the dining room.

When everyone was seated and Jake had offered the blessing, the local residents looked expectantly at Marlow.

She uncovered the dishes, served a spoonful of rice onto her plate, then grabbed a warm tortilla from the tinfoil wrap. "This is how you assemble a fajita. First, take a tortilla, then place the chicken along the middle, and add whatever other ingredients you want. Grilled onions, grated cheese, shredded spinach which should be lettuce, and top it with Pico de Gallo."

"What's that?" Tortilla in hand, Jake raised his eyebrows.

"It translates to rooster's beak, a fresh accompaniment to many Mexican dishes." Marlow added a little of each item to her tortilla and topped it off with a tablespoon of Pico de Gallo. "Roll it up, like so, and carefully take a bite, and hopefully, all the fillings won't land in your lap."

She waited until the others had assembled their fajitas and watched as first Jake then Bella took bites. Marlow began to eat. "Dearie me. I'm making more mess than anyone else."

Celia tsked and stared at the tortilla slowly unraveling on her plate. "I can't eat this with my fingers."

"Give it a try, Aunty Celia. It's fun." Bella licked her lips. "Mmm. Super."

"Fun for you maybe. I have to stick to my tried and true method." She ate the fajita with her knife and fork, cutting each ingredient into dainty pieces.

"That's a first for me. I've never seen anyone eat a fajita with utensils before."

Empty dishes attested to the success of the meal. Even Celia had seconds.

While Bella washed the dishes, Jake and Celia retreated to the verandah. Marlow set up the tea tray, satisfied her meal had been enjoyed. She poured boiling water into the teapot. Why did she derive such satisfaction from her successful preparation? Because Steven never had anything good to—

"Stop." She slapped the cozy onto the teapot.

"What did you say, Marlow?"

She picked up the tray and turned. "Nothing, sweetheart. See you outside in a minute." As she neared the screen door to the verandah, Marlow heard Celia mention her name. She stopped.

"And she has adapted to our way of life so easily. Anyone would think she was born to it."

"I noticed, too. One of these days I want to take her out to the paddocks, to experience the lifeblood of the place."

"Good idea, but go soon, luv."

Jake coughed. "Um, Aunt Celia, I'm glad to see you up and about with a healthy appetite, but tell me straight. Were you feeling ill today?"

Marlow frowned. A strange question.

"Jakey, my boy, what do you think? I've never let a little old headache keep me in bed before."

The tray shaking in her hands, Marlow bumped open the door with her hip. What was Celia up to?

Chapter 44

As the sun eased over the horizon, Jake knocked on Marlow's door.

Seconds passed then she opened it a crack and blinked at him.

"How would you like to join me on horseback for another tour of my place?" Anxiety-fueled knots roiled in his gut. "I assume you ride since you said you worked on a cattle ranch in Texas."

"I do." She rubbed her eyes. "When?"

Whew. She agreed. "As soon as we've eaten a quick bite."

"Give me ten minutes."

"I'll be in the kitchen." Heart thumping, he retreated and packed a saddle bag with meat pies, two apples, and bottles of lemonade. *Thank you, Lord. Please give me the right words to say to keep me from chasing Marlow away.* He ran outside and secured the bag to his saddle. If Greg hadn't been watching, he might have cheered on his way back to the kitchen.

Mugs of coffee, and bacon-and-egg sandwiches on the table, Jake paced the small room. Then he sat, and his knees bounced to an unheard rhythm.

Dressed in jeans, boots, and a long-sleeved pink shirt, with a pink bandana around her neck, Marlow walked down the hall.

He stood and tried not to stare, but he couldn't help himself.

Camera strap around her neck. Hair in a ponytail. The coconut aroma of her sunscreen. Hat and sunnies. He smiled. She'd used the slang word the other day. Good on her.

They ate in silence. He, for one, didn't want to say anything to make her change her mind, and she, probably because she wasn't quite awake yet.

Roosters crowed as Jake and Marlow made their way to the

stables where the saddled horses waited. "I'll ride Sully, and Ziggy is ready for you."

She checked the girth, then talked softly to the horse while stroking his neck. "Good-looking animals."

"Yeah. They're Australian stock horses. Bred for our needs and conditions. Even-tempered, with agility and stamina. Most are bays."

"They sure have muscular shoulders and hindquarters. I'm eager to give Ziggy a test run."

"Um, we—"

"Wrong choice of words. I meant, test ride. No one but a sadist would expect these gorgeous creatures to run in this heat."

Jake grinned. A woman after his own heart. He cleared his throat. *In more ways than one, I hope.*

Marlow used the mounting block he'd set in place. Once settled in the saddle, she said, "Thanks for the extra boost."

"No worries. Bella doesn't ride often, but she needs the block, too."

They cantered down the driveway and veered to the east past the shearing shed, static from his radio and the clip-clop of the horses the only sound. There was so much he wanted to say, but to gauge her receptiveness, he'd stick with mundane details. "I'll describe things as we ride along, but anytime you've had enough, just say so."

"I'm curious about it all." She pointed to her left. "If I'm not mistaken, that uneven horizon indicates hills."

"Correct. The Grey Range. Nothing too impressive."

"A change from the flatness, nonetheless. And this vegetation. I haven't seen these little trees before. They look like strangers in an unwelcome place. How do they survive out here?"

"They're dwarf acacias, locally known as mulga scrub. The trees are drought resistant, and you'll see later how the sheep enjoy the scant shade they provide." So far, so good. "If you'd arrived a couple of months earlier, you would have seen the land covered in wildflowers."

"Wildflowers?"

"Yeah, spring rains. They're like magic, they bring out the flowers, but neither last very long, the rain nor the flowers."

"The trees look deformed, almost as if they lost the battle with the elements."

There was no sign of boredom or distaste in her expression or words. "You got that right. Only the strong and persistent survive." He slowed as they approached a gate. He opened it for her, then followed through and secured the latch. "We're in C-2 paddock now." Before he could provide more information, his radio crackled. "Sorry. I must respond." He pulled it from his belt. "Jake, over."

"Adam here, boss, where are you? We have a problem. Over."

"Just entered C-2. What's wrong? Over."

"I'll be there in a tick. Over."

Minutes later, a dust trail and the buzz of a bike announced Adam's arrival. Jake reined in. "What's up? No more fence problems I hope."

"No." Adam doffed his hat to Marlow. "Morning, miss. It's one of the boreholes in this paddock. The water has stopped flowing, the tank is empty, and the troughs are almost dry."

"But it worked fine a few days ago."

"Right. I'm by myself, so I radioed Greg, and he said you might be here. I'm off to pick up some tools." Adam turned and rubbed the kelpie's head. Old Scratch was a pro at sitting behind a stockman on a motorbike.

Jake patted Sully's neck to calm his restlessness. They'd never had this many problems on the station over the course of one month. "Get the tools and see what you can do at the borehole. I'll join you after I show Marlow—"

"Should I go back to the house?" She removed her bandana and wiped her forehead.

"Definitely not." He turned to Adam. "I'll see you in a couple of hours."

After the lad sped away, Jake prodded Sully. "I've been looking forward to our ride for too long to abandon it now." How had she reacted to his decision? He wasn't about to look back, but when she caught up with him, her smile was all he needed.

"That dog seems right at home. Do all the kelpies ride on the bikes?"

"Yeah. Or in the bed of a ute, even in front across the saddle." He gestured. "We train them as pups. They are very intelligent and love human approval."

Jake led the way through the scattered acacia trees, some no taller than the horses. "I want to show you a mob of sheep in this paddock."

"I've been on a sheep station over three weeks and have yet to see any. I'm beginning to doubt they exist."

He chuckled. "At last count we had close to 20,000."

Her jaw dropped. "Wow."

"I have over 1,000 square kilometers—"

"Square kilometers, square miles, whatever measure you use, it's a huge, incomprehensible size."

"Yeah. If you are going to raise sheep in these arid conditions, you'll need about ten acres per head. I don't think I've been to every corner of the land myself. I have to trust my station hands. We've been fortunate in our choice of people—Paddy notwithstanding. We're blessed with a good water supply and adequate wool prices."

"A hard life, but you obviously find it rewarding."

"I do. This place is in my blood. Some people find our land appalling, ugly even. Others love it instantly." He glanced at Marlow. Dare he ask? "Which group are you in?"

Her delayed response curdled his stomach. He almost broached another topic when she turned to him.

"The latter. Ever since I've been in Australia, I've had a strange notion I'd been here before. Not in the reincarnation sense, but in a deep-down longing fulfilled. I take it as a challenge, as if the land is daring me to live in it and succeed. Of course, my mother was Australian, but being here and connecting with my grandmother has only intensified the feeling."

Her answer pleased and disappointed him. She loved Australia, but that was very different than saying she loved the outback. Far from it. But the day was young.

The horses walked through the changing vegetation. "This clumpy stuff is Mitchell grass."

"It shimmers in the heat and look how it spreads out as if it's on a russet sea." She jutted her chin toward the horizon. "Do the sheep eat Mitchell grass?"

"Only as a last resort. They'll devour forbs, bluegrass, and saltbush first."

Marlow pointed to a dust cloud in the distance. "Another rider?"

"No. Sheep gathering by the water troughs."

Five minutes later, Jake and Marlow neared the water tank and windmill. Sheep milled around, but scattered as they approached. Jake jumped off Sully and offered a hand to Marlow, but she dismounted without his help. They led the horses to the water. The sheep gathered under the shade provided by a grove of mulgas. Baaing incessantly, they wouldn't return to the troughs until the horses moved.

"You *do* have sheep. Lots of the critters. Some are much bigger than I expected. I can see their skin through the small tufts of new wool growth." Marlow removed her hat and fanned her face, chasing away the flies.

"We had eight shearers here in August. Now that's a busy and exciting time. Celia and Nellie spend hours cooking and baking for the crew. But getting wool ready for market is what station life is all about." As much as he wanted to share more, he'd keep the rest of the explanation until they were inside the shearing shed. "Obviously the lambs haven't been sheared yet. Most of them were born back in March."

Marlow removed her sunnies and took photos while chatting. "The pregnant heifers on the Texas ranch were kept close to the barns. How do you deal with the ewes?"

"We have a special paddock near the silo where we keep the pregnant ewes. They need extra nutrition, and we can provide help during birth if necessary."

"What breed are they?" Marlow squatted to take eye-level pictures.

"Merinos. They have the best quality wool, but their meat is not that good. We raise a crossbreed we use for mutton in the south paddock."

She tried to pat an ewe, but it scooted forward, pushing though the mob.

"They're not exactly friendly." Nothing had deterred Marlow yet. Jake tipped his hat off his forehead and rubbed his chin.

Standing with her hands on her hips, she studied the milling sheep. "Are they always this vocal? They haven't stopped bleating."

Jake chuckled. "Sheep are not the smartest animals, but they don't like being separated from their young. Each lamb and ewe pair have a unique cry. The mother calls, the baby responds, over and over, until they are together again."

"Ahh, that is so sweet. Endearing."

More photos. Jake noted Marlow aimed her camera at him a couple of times.

"When do you use the kelpies?"

"Stockmen take dogs with them on most runs in case they're needed. Always when we muster the sheep, that is, we gather them to move them from one waterhole to another, or from one paddock to another."

"I'd like to see that."

"I'll make it happen."

Marlow wiped her upper lip. "Whew, it's hot. I'd say mid-nineties."

"Yeah. Only eight o'clock and already thirty-five Celsius at least. Dip your bandana in the water and wrap it around your neck. You'll be surprised how that will cool you."

She did as he suggested, and he followed suit.

"That feels good."

He studied her face. No sign of boredom, or worse, taking offence at the tang of sheep manure or the swarming flies. A surge of excitement invaded his being. The trip was succeeding beyond his expectations.

She redid her ponytail, returned her hat to her head, and looked up at the windmill. "Let me see if I have this straight. The windmill pumps up the water, it's stored in the tank, then it's delivered to the troughs."

"Exactly. There's a fill valve in the tank that shuts off the motor in the shaft to keep the water level optimal. We also have fill valves in the troughs to they never overflow. We use troughs here because the soil is prone to making cloying mud, which is not good."

"That's interesting. How many waterholes do you have?"

The sheep ignored their conversation and nudged each other to get to the troughs.

"Let me see, there are three in each paddock, and one close to the house, that makes ten manmade. There are also several natural billabongs scattered about. Sheep need water at least every two to three days. More frequently as the summer progresses."

She tugged at her bandana. "I don't understand how they can survive with their thick wool coats."

"Merinos have to be sheared every year because they've lost the natural ability to shed. If not, they would either die from the heat, or their wool would get so heavy when wet at a waterhole, they'd get stuck in the mud and starve." Marlow's eyes hadn't glazed over yet. Jake wiped his face then tied his handkerchief around his neck. "Along with other jobs such as vaccinating and crutching, stockmen patrol each waterhole and drag out the waterlogged sheep. It doesn't matter if they're shorn or not, some of them wander too far in and get stuck."

"I did notice skeletons during the ride."

Marlow had asked a load of questions. All positive as far as he was concerned. She wouldn't have bothered if she wasn't curios.

With a whinny, Sully moved away from the trough and a dozen sheep took his place. Jake grabbed the reins. "I hate to leave the shade, but I must see what's wrong with the other waterhole. Ride due south and follow the fence to get back to the homestead. It's a straight shot, and Ziggy knows the way."

Marlow used the side of a trough to help her mount Ziggy, adjusted her sunnies, then directed the horse away from the sheep. "May I come with you instead?"

"Of course." He beamed. She wanted more. Bonza.

The ride took them in a north-east direction. A few kangaroo skeletons littered the way. "Life is harsh out here. Lack of grazing, disease. During the drought a couple of years ago, we had to haul in feed for the sheep. The roos and emus didn't fare too well."

"That's sad." She rode in silence, her mouth in a grim line.

There wasn't a whole lot he could add. He didn't control the elements.

They continued to trek for half an hour, without another word. Although concern over the nonfunctioning waterhole crowded his mind, Jake's desire to show off his land and assess Marlow's response to outback life was ever-present.

He pointed to the outline of trees and the water tank shimmering in the distance. "That's our destination."

"Is it the same system as the waterhole we just visited?"

"No. Here the pressure is sufficient that we don't need a windmill to pump up the water. We call it a natural bore, free-flowing. My dad drilled through the rock and installed piping to channel the water and concentrate the flow. The pipe leads into the tank, which supplies the troughs. It does have a switch-off valve, but the pressure is never strong enough to cause the tank or troughs to overflow. If the water wasn't controlled, it would gush up, a lake would form and evaporate, wasting the precious resource."

The clanking of metal-on-metal greeted them as they neared the site where Adam worked. "Have you located the problem?" Jake handed his reins to Marlow and climbed down.

"Yeah. The tank, pipes, and the troughs are all okay, but the valve is closed, and I can't open it."

Scratch sniffed Jake's boots, and he bent to pet the dog. "I'll see what I can do." He felt the pipe from the dishpan sized valve handle along the rounded *L*-shape to where it entered the ground. "The pipe's vibrating a bit." He glanced at Marlow who now stood beside the horses in the shade. "That means there is water in it." Straightening, he extended his hand. "Give me a crowbar, Adam. Let's see if we can open this thing together."

Jake shoved the crowbar through an opening in the handle, and Adam grabbed the other end. One pushed while the other pulled the crowbar, but the handle didn't budge. "Try again." Jake gritted his teeth, and Adam grunted, but no luck.

"I think someone glued it shut." Adam wiped sweat off his forehead.

"You could be right, lad. Fences cut, now this. Water flowed here recently, so I know the valve worked then. I think it's deliberate."

Marlow had tied the horses to a tree branch and handed Jake his canteen. "The same person?"

He took a long swig then swiped his sleeve across his mouth. "Yeah. Messing with a waterhole out here is tantamount to treason."

"What are you going to do?" Adam grabbed his canteen and squatted in the shade.

"Replace the valve. Go home and tell Mitch. He might have to order one. Of course, tell Greg because he'll have to get the stockmen to muster the sheep to another waterhole."

"Righto." Adam gathered the tools and dumped them into a bag on his bike. "Anything else?"

"Tell Greg I'll be back after lunch."

Adam whistled and sat on his bike. Scratch jumped up behind him, and he drove away.

"Although Adam came a cropper trying to show off the other night, he's a good station hand." Jake watched him disappear in a cloud of dust, then turned to Marlow. "I'm sorry our ride was interrupted. I wanted to take you to a billabong similar to the one Bella is painting. But, with this detour, it's too far away."

Marlow took a sip from her canteen. "I'd love to go. Will you have time next week?"

Her words tickled his heart. "I'll make time." He glanced at the horizon to hide his grin. He must look like the proverbial cat who swallowed the cream. "I packed lunch, but it's too early to eat and this is not the ideal setting."

"Agree. Too many flies, and besides, I'm not hungry yet."

"Let's go home." He loosened the horses and gave Marlow her reins.

His boot missed the stirrup twice as he watched her stand on a stump and mount Ziggy with ease.

They ambled back toward the station following the dividing fence. She'd been genuinely attentive to his descriptions and asked clarifying questions, not just being polite. That was not her style. If she wasn't interested, she'd have gone back to the homestead at his earlier suggestion.

Jake squared his shoulders to loosen the damp shirt from his back. Grime from working with Adam streaked his sleeves, and his hands were dirty. Marlow was probably hot and sweaty, too, but she appeared to be content. And looked like a million dollars. He couldn't ask for more.

Chapter 45

In the distance, the shimmering air blurred the hills which resembled giant rust-colored domes dancing on the horizon. Marlow shifted in the saddle. Tomorrow, she'd ache in places she'd rather not mention, but the ride was so worth the inconvenience.

What a country! The outback assaulted man, beast, and vegetation with equal strength. She'd seen nothing to compare in her travels in America or other parts of Australia. The horseback ride was up close and personal, very different to viewing the land from a vehicle. The combination of open spaces, the immense expanse of clear sky, and strange aromas and sights at every turn were unique.

She glanced at Jake, his back as straight as a fence post, one hand holding the reins, the other on his hip. In his element.

He returned the glance and smiled. "Are you all right?"

"Yes. I'm just trying to digest all I've seen and learned today."

"I have plenty more to share. But I'll leave it for our next ride."

Content with his response and apparent mutual desire to ride in silence, she revisited her earlier words to him, *a deep-down longing fulfilled.* Yes, she loved this country. The heat could not detract from the beauty of the vast, dry, dusty land. But the tug on her soul was much more. It was the people, and the yearning to belong. Nascent at first when Steven found his great-grandfather's letter, the longing blossomed the more they discussed a trip to Australia to address Graham's demands. Although she'd desperately wanted to share her growing interest in tracing her family with Steven, he always pooh-poohed her desire. But she'd succeeded, and now love of her mother's birthplace filled her soul.

Marlow took a drink from her canteen, and since the horses were walking at their own pace, she was able to wet her bandana again. She wiped her face then wrapped the cloth around her neck. "Do you guys ever get used to the heat?"

He harrumphed. "Sort of. We tolerate it and respect its strength. Stay hydrated, never go anywhere without a canteen or a radio, don't overexert yourself, your horse, or the dogs. Wear sensible clothing such as a hat and long-sleeved cotton shirts. People have lived with the high temps for eons."

"I'll take your word for it. I love the evenings when the heat finally releases its hold. What's the hottest temperature you've experienced?"

"Oh, that would be…probably forty-four or five." He rubbed his chin. "One hundred and ten, or there about. It's not just the heat, you have to be wary of the high UV rays."

"Yeah, and the skin cancer that might—"

"Strewth, I don't believe it." Jake prodded Sully to the right. "More problems."

Marlow followed him. Instead of cut wires, three posts in a cross fence in the neighboring paddock had been snapped at ground level.

"This is a new form of destruction." Jake dismounted and climbed over the fence. "Sabotage, as far as I'm concerned. There's no way an animal could have done this."

"Not unless you have an elephant on the loose."

Shaking his head, he grimaced. "I'd rather deal with a runaway jumbo than a person we can't identify." He pointed to Sully. "Look in my saddle bag, please, and give me the coil of rope."

She made Ziggy sidestep close to Sully then grabbed his reins before locating the rope.

Ready with his pocketknife, Jake took the rope, cut off a length, and latched the end post to the dividing fence. "That'll do for now. I must contact Greg."

While Jake radioed his foremen, Marlow surveyed the now familiar landscape. The undamaged fence sputtered away in a straight line through the red earth, pointing to the cobalt sky. Cobalt blue, her new favorite color.

Jake swung his legs over the fence then mounted his horse. "Let's get moving. This trip hasn't gone according to plan. I wanted to show you all aspects of station life." He raised his face to the sky and sighed. "Well, I suppose I have. Life here is unpredictable. We're always at the mercy of the elements, but right now we're also at the mercy of someone who means me, us, harm."

"Since Paddy's gone, it can't be him."

Jake hesitated a moment. "I don't think it's Paddy, but I could be mistaken."

"What else can you do to catch the miscreant?"

Jaw set, he looked straight ahead. "The only way we'll nab this guy is to keep more stockmen out in the paddocks. I've already increased the fence riders' responsibilities. Now I'll have to warn the bore runners to keep extra watch for problems, too. I asked fellow graziers to spread the word I'm looking to hire. When next in town, I hope there'll be several blokes interested."

And perhaps family men. The train of Marlow's thoughts heated her cheeks more than the hot atmosphere had done. If she declared her feelings for Jake and he reciprocated, and that led to…marriage. Whew. She wiped the bandana across her face. Then she'd use her experience to facilitate School of the Air for all the kids on the station. Even those who didn't want to go to boarding school. Surely, knowing their children's needs were considered would encourage qualified men to work for Jake.

Marlow glanced at him. Good thing he couldn't read her mind. At some point she needed to tell Jake she loved him, but waiting until they were ready for the trip to Cunnamulla seemed prudent. That way, if she was mistaken in his attraction to her, she could pack up and leave Long Gully. However, today's ride seemed to be his desire to show her more of the lifestyle on the station away from the comfortable house, which could hint at a romantic interest in her.

In the meantime, her curiosity spurred plenty more questions. "The valve contraption you need to replace, if Mitch doesn't have one, do you have to wait until you visit town?"

"No. I can order parts, and the mail plane will deliver them."

"That's handy. Why can't the plane deliver everything you need? Why do you have to shop once a month?"

"Some stations can have everything delivered. But we're not considered remote enough to warrant regular service."

Marlow burst out laughing. "Not remote enough."

"No. There are stations a long day's drive away from a town or settlement."

"I can't imagine being any more remote than Long Gully."

"Not only are they far from town, they also don't have close neighbors. At least there are several stations within a few hours' drive from us. We interact socially and can call on them in emergencies.”

A hint of uncertainty touched his sentences. Marlow didn’t know how to react, but Jake’s next words provided clarity.

“While you’ve been at Long Gully, have you missed city life? Phones, radios, TV. Electricity whenever you want it. Shopping centers and crowds of people.”

His concern for how she accepted life on the station added to her belief he cared. She contemplated his question and answered with wholehearted truth. “Not much. I never was what you’d call a social butterfly. It would be nice to call my friends and chat occasionally, but I never spent hours on the phone, even as a teenager. Some TV shows are enjoyable, but I haven’t once wished we had reception out here. However, an all-encompassing bubble of insect repellant when outside would be helpful.” She swatted at the flies and giggled. “Seriously, I haven’t missed city life. I enjoy the peace, the freedom, the slower pace.”

“Good.”

She barely heard his reply over the clip-clop of the horses, but it warmed her heart. The outline of the homestead and outbuildings broke the horizon. The horses seemed to sense they were close to home and increased their speed.

“The house is a welcome sight.”

“We’ll be home soon. I’ll take Ziggy and Sully to the stables.” Jake cleared his throat. “I hope you enjoyed your ride.”

“Yes, thank you. I can now write to my friends and say I’ve seen some of your sheep.”

“If no more catastrophes occur, I will take you to that special place next week.”

“I look forward to the day.” And she’d take her tube of lip balm. Never had her lips been so dry and cracked.

The horses cantered toward the house where several people gathered in the yard.

“I wonder what’s going on?” Jake rode ahead.

Marlow reined in beside him, and they both dismounted.

One of the men took charge of the horses.

“Nellie, what happened? Is it Bella?” Jake asked.

“No, luv. It’s Celia.”

Darri took Jake’s hand. “She fell and sprained her ankle. Come, see for yourself. She's fine, but complaining about all the commotion."

Nellie and Darri followed Jake inside.

Celia sat in an armchair in the living room, her bandaged ankle resting on an ottoman, Toffee curled up in her lap.

"Now, don't fuss." Celia patted the armrest. "Come, Jakey, sit."

He perched on the armrest and kissed her forehead. "Don't scare me like that. Tell me all about it."

"I will, Dad." Bella approached him, hands behind her back.

Very subdued, or calm. Marlow couldn't tell which.

"Out with it, Bella Bear. What happened?"

"Well, I was working in my room on the sample exam questions Miss York sent. I heard a thump and a cry. Aunty Celia had tripped over the mat in the bathroom. She felt the bones in her foot and said nothing was broken, so I ran outside and rang the gong."

Not subdued. Definitely calm.

Bella took a breath. "Jarra arrived first, and I asked him to get Nellie and Darri. I explained what happened. They came inside and carried Aunty Celia in here. She told them what to do and where to find bandages."

"Well done, young lady." Jake held out his arms and embraced her.

"Yes, luv. You did everything right. No panicking and not a tear in sight." Celia ruffled Bella's hair.

Taking Nellie's arm, Darri edged toward the door and said, "Remember, we're just a yell away."

"Thank you for taking good care of her." Jake stood and shook hands with the ladies before they left the room.

"It's been quite a day." He removed his hat. "I'll wash up and get some tucker. Then I must talk to Greg."

"No worries. Lunch is in the fridge." Resting against the chair, Celia closed her eyes.

"Hey, are you all right?" Marlow hesitated to put her grimy hand on Celia's forehead, but Jake had no such compunction.

Two seconds later, he said, "No fever."

Marlow sank onto the sofa, glad the dark blue-and-tan stripe wouldn't show any dust she might deposit. "Good. Can we get you anything, Celia?"

"Yes, please. A cup of strong, sweet tea. I think I'm suffering from shock. And Jake, my boy, a sprain won't result in a fever."

"It doesn't hurt to check." He hovered over his aunt, worry lines mixed with the dirt on his face.

Heading toward the door, Bella said, "I'll make tea and set out the food." She halted at the archway and turned. "Dad, guess how you treat a sprained ankle?"

"I don't know. How?"

"With rice." Bella chuckled.

"Rice?"

"Yeah. Let me see if I get it right. Rest. Ice. Compression. Elevation. *R I C E.*"

"That's it. And I've taken anti-inflammatory pills, too." Celia gave Bella a thumbs-up.

"I think I'm suffering from something, too." Marlow removed her hat and fanned her face. "Your words seem to be bouncing off the walls."

"You'll feel better after you cool down a bit." Jake squatted by the ottoman and touched Celia's toes poking out of the bandage, then looked at Marlow. "Well, I wanted you to see and experience life on the station to its fullest and—"

"What if Celia had broken her leg?" Marlow stared at him. She'd been truthful when she said she didn't miss the city, but she hadn't taken medical needs into consideration.

"We have an extensive first aid kit, and crutches, splints, slings. Several workers are trained in CPR. At Long Gully we're also fortunate that we can rely on Celia's nursing experience. For serious medical issues, however, we call the Flying Doctor Service."

"Of course I've heard of that organization. I forgot for the moment." Marlow rubbed her temple and eased off the sofa. "I'll shower before lunch. That should help me feel better."

"It will, luv." Celia gestured a shooing motion. "Go on, now."

As Marlow trudged down the hall, Celia's next words stopped her in her tracks.

"Jake, I didn't plan this. I did sprain my ankle. Not like my spell yesterday, this is real."

Aha. Celia's headache had been a sham. To what end?

Chapter 46

By Friday, the aches in Marlow's body had eased enough for her to get out of bed without groaning. She'd availed herself of the liniment in Celia's first aid closet for two days, but disliked the strong herbal smell and decided not to use any more. Maybe before Jake's next tour she should take Ziggy out for a couple of short rides.

Not today. She had a special meal planned for dinner to celebrate the last day of school. Bella squealed with delight when Marlow mentioned pizza.

All in all, preparing meals while Celia rested and worked on her tatting hadn't been the chore Marlow envisioned. A well-stocked pantry, vegetables from the garden, and any amount of beef, chicken, or mutton she needed made the job relatively easy. To top it off, everyone liked her food. Marlow was pleased by their compliments, and her confidence grew with each word of praise.

As Marlow covered the dough with a cloth, Bella entered the kitchen, carrying the canvas mail bag and whistling. "Thanks for supervising my exams yesterday and today. I think I did all right. Well, that's another school year over with and I'm freeee." She set the bag on the counter and twirled.

"What will you do with all this freedom?"

"Paint and paint some more. And swim."

Marlow placed the bowl of dough on the counter. "Who will meet the mail plane now that Paddy's gone?"

"I don't know. Dad will sort it." She peeked at the dough. "How many pizzas will you make?"

"Three, with different toppings. I'm limited in what I can use, but they'll taste great."

"Yummy. Can't wait." Bella cocked her head. "Do you mind if I set up my easel so I can begin a new painting?"

"Let's go to the verandah instead. I'm finished here for the time being, and I'm hot."

"Good idea. I'll see if Aunty Celia wants to come too."

Celia had mastered the use of crutches and joined Marlow and Bella on the verandah. "I'll be glad when my ankle is healed, two to three weeks, in my estimation. I feel so useless." She sat and propped her foot on a cushioned chair Marlow set in place.

"You'll be fit in no time. You have to be. We're running out of fresh bread, and that's one item I'm afraid to try."

"There's nothing to it. I'll sit in the kitchen and demonstrate. Besides, I'm tired of tatting."

"Your work is so intricate and beautiful."

"Ta. It does keep me busy, but I'd prefer to be in the kitchen." Celia shifted her legs and winced. "How about we have a go tomorrow?"

"If it won't be too much for you."

"I'm tough." She folded her arms and eyed Marlow. "I have to say, I'm impressed with how you've filled my shoes."

"Oh, Celia, don't say that. There's no way I can—"

"Well, you have. Preparing all the meals, supervising Bella's school, even making sure Darri used the special furniture polish today." She nodded. "Admirable job."

The glint in Celia's eyes worried Marlow. What was she implying?

Celia cleared her throat. "I never got around to asking you about your ride with Jake the other day. Did anything unusual or special happen?"

Frowning, Marlow stared at the woman. "I'm sure he told you about the borehole and the fence. But other than that, nothing of any consequence."

"Oh. I'd hoped…never mind" She sighed. "Is he taking you out again?"

"We had planned on next week, but not with your—"

"Don't worry about me. Nellie or Darri can always help if necessary."

Bella stepped away from her easel and tapped Celia on the shoulder. "Excuse me, Aunt Celia. The plane has come and gone. Do you want me to bring the mail bag out here?"

"No, luv. Will you sort it, Marlow? There's a dear."

"Certainly." Marlow hurried inside. She might have a letter today. The bag contained fewer items this week, so she found three addressed to her in no time. Two air letters from Texas, and a large envelope from Perth. Carolyn's and Fran's correspondence could wait. Marlow tore open Ida Marie Finlay's envelope. Out spilled a dozen or more photographs.

Marlow sank into a chair. Heart thumping and hand shaking, she picked up the first picture of an infant propped up by pillows. She turned it over. *Katie Marie, seven months.* "Mama." Tears formed, and she let them fall. More photos of her young mother at different ages, and one of Ida Marie and Arthur, taken ten years ago. She ran a finger over their faces. "Hello, grandmother and grandfather." Ida reminded Marlow of her mom, same oval face, sandy hair, sweet smile. But Arthur was a surprise. He could have been a star in an old-time movie. Bushy, graying hair with matching beard and mustache. Even a monocle. "I bet you're a character."

The tears turned to sobs. Her chore to sort the mail forgotten, Marlow gathered her letters and ran to her room where she collapsed onto the bed and buried her face in the pillow.

Nothing or no one could fill the void left by Eileen's and Steven's passing, but the photos wedged their way into her heart and found a welcome corner to reside. Marlow wiped away her tears. "Father God, thank You for family and…" She had no more words and closed her eyes.

****

Dinner that evening was a festive affair. Who knew pizza and salad would qualify to help the family celebrate? Marlow shared her photographs and snippets of news from her Texas friends. She did not, however, relay Carolyn's question about snagging the good-looking grazier. Bella's friend, Trish, had written to say her mother was pregnant, and Jake's correspondence revealed workers in the opal mine had hit a rich seam. Celia claimed her ankle was healing faster than expected. Cheers all around.

The pleasant evening passed quickly, and after Marlow prepared for bed, she stood in her dark room and stared out the window into the black void. Too bad she didn't have the courage to walk to Jake's room and ask him to accompany her to the rocky outcrop where she could declare her love. But common sense prevailed. Better follow her original plan and speak to him before the trip to town, which would be…in one week. Seven days. She could wait that long.

Marlow's bread making event with Celia the next day was interrupted by a squawk from the transmitter in Jake's office.

Minutes later, he entered the kitchen. "That was Kevin O'Bryan. They want to attend our service tomorrow, and I said it would be all right. He apologized for such short notice."

Marlow's heart sank. Preparing food for the family was one thing, but for guests, especially Bridgette, was something else completely. Her dismay must have been blazoned across her face.

Patting her hand, Celia said, "You'll be apples, luv. We won't have to prepare all the food because Gracie always brings a variety."

"At least we'll have bread." She pointed to the pans ready for the oven, but the knots in her stomach tightened.

"Kevin said they're bringing the Smiths, their new hire and his family, Marlow. The bloke with the daughter Bella likes." Jake looked at Marlow, and his brow furrowed. "Sorry. I shouldn't have agreed without asking you. I know Celia will help as much as she can, and you could ask Nellie—"

"No worries." Sure, with Celia's guidance the food would be great, but who would help her face Bridgette? For Jake's benefit, she smiled as he left the kitchen.

Under Celia's tutelage, Marlow made shortbread, Anzac biscuits, and a lemon sponge cake. Other than pecan pie, her dessert skills were almost nonexistent.

"Jake will prepare meat for the barbie. If we do potato salad tomorrow morning, that should be enough." Celia wiped her face with her apron and eased her bandaged foot off the low stool. "Hand me the crutches, luv. I'm off for a lie down."

The rest of the day passed in a blur, and as tired as Marlow was, she fell asleep within seconds of closing her eyes.

Busy in the kitchen the next morning, Marlow was unaware the visitors had arrived until Bella dashed into the room. "They're here. I'm so excited to see Lynn again."

Marlow followed her down the hall and onto the verandah. She patted the wide pink band holding her hair back, content in the knowledge the color set off the blonde highlights and coordinated with her pastel striped sundress. No matter what she wore, though, she couldn't complete with Bridgette's curves and sophistication.

Shoulders back, Marlow stood at the opened screen door and

welcomed the guests as if she were the mistress of the house. Heat shot up her neck. Well, with Celia conspicuously absent, someone had to fill the role.

Wearing an orange top and black slacks, and carrying a large basket, Bridgett bounded up the stairs. "Hey, Marlow. Show me where to put the food, please."

"Sure." Marlow led the way to the kitchen. "Leave the items that need refrigeration here and take the rest out to the ping-pong table."

"Will do." Bridgette set down the basket and began removing covered bowls. "I must apologize before Mum gets in. I'm sincerely sorry for saying Jake and I are engaged. Of course, we're not. I don't know what came over me, and, uh, I hope I didn't cause any trouble."

Marlow stared at her wide-eyed for a couple of seconds. Certainly not what she'd expected. "No problem." She'd rehearsed a spiel which was now useless. "Jake—"

"There you are, Marlow, my dear friend's granddaughter." Gracie entered and deposited a container on the table. "Ida Marie wrote to me, luv. I'm so glad you connected, but too bad about Arthur."

"Mum, I think they're ready for us outside." Toting the basket, Bridgette slipped her other arm around her mother's shoulders. "Marlow, I'd like to discuss something with you later." With that, they headed down the hall.

Marlow exhaled a massive sigh. So much for the confrontation she'd imagined, but bearing grudges was unhealthy for the soul. She stared out the door. Jake stood at the grill under the carport and poked at the burning wood. Little wisps of smoke drifted into the kitchen. The area's most eligible bachelor, according to Lion, and he wasn't interested in gorgeous Bridgette. Grinning, Marlow set a few items in the fridge, then joined the group seated on the verandah, ready to worship.

The brief but uplifting service led by Jake added another layer to Marlow's respect and admiration for him. He wasn't ashamed to discuss Graham Barclay's misdeeds, and to reiterate the need to put their faith and trust in Jesus Christ alone.

Jake scored a dozen more points when he suggested the men clean up and wash the dishes after lunch. Seated on the verandah with the other women, Marlow basked in the warmth of being with family and friends. Even Bridgette proved to be more pleasant than she'd imagined. But that impression could be due to Marlow's changed attitude.

After the men joined them and they'd indulged in tea, cake, and biscuits, Bridgette caught Marlow's eye and cocked her head.

Marlow took the hint. "Hey, Bridgette, I have something in my bedroom I'd like to show you."

She followed Marlow down the verandah to her door. They passed Bella's room where she and Lynn seemed to be having a grand ol' time singing pop tunes.

"I'm glad little Lynn has found a friend." Bridgette stepped across the threshold and stopped, hands clasped in front as if ready to be chastised.

"Have a seat at the desk." Marlow sank onto the bed, not sure what to expect.

"Thanks." The brunette sat and stared at her feet. "I have a couple of things to address. First, I need to add to my apology. I was jealous of Jake's interest in you. That Sunday, he couldn't stop talking about you, and well, after the fiasco with Gail, I thought I had a chance, but then you entered the picture." She lifted her head, her face ruddy. "I'm sorry again. Of course, he'd deny an engagement when you asked him, but you might have left Long Gully anyway, and then…"

Bridgette's words *he couldn't stop talking about you* rang in Marlow's heart. That had to bode well for her upcoming declaration. "Thank you, I guess. I don't know what else to add."

"Nothing. I wish you two well. But I have another serious matter on my mind." Bridgette leaned forward. "Jake told me about your career working with special children. Lynn's parents, Howard and Muriel, informed Dad about her needs before they accepted the job. She's such a sweet kid, but she struggles with the schoolwork."

"You mean the School of the Air?"

"Yes. You see, she fell off a horse last year and suffered a severe head injury. Not only does she have brain damage, she is now epileptic. She missed a lot of school and is repeating Year six. With those underlying issues, Lynn can't go to boarding school next year, and the reason her dad accepted the job is I told him I would help her mom with the schooling. After all, I participated in the School of the Air, as did my brothers." The expression on Bridgette's face seemed to indicate she really cared.

Marlow's attitude softened even more. "How can I help?"

"I'm not sure. The Smiths previously worked on a station close to Cloncurry, and Lynn went to the local school. But Muriel and I had a difficult time with our curriculum and how best to teach Lynn. She is eligible for support lessons, which we'll take advantage of next year." Bridgette pursed her lips. "I was wondering if you could help us, give us some tips. Things we can do during the holidays to help her catch up."

Excitement bubbled in Marlow's veins and her thoughts collided with each other. Had Bridgette secretly tapped into her mind and discovered her desire to provide an alternative to sending kids away to boarding school? Naturally, all depended on Jake's response. "I'll be honored to assist any way I can."

"Good." Bridgette let out a sigh. "That's a relief. I'll arrange for you to spend time at our place. Read Lynn's school records and talk with her and Muriel."

"Excellent. We—"

"Bridgette, luv. Time to go." Gracie's voice floated into the bedroom.

Marlow stood and smoothed her skirt. The day certainly had not gone the way she anticipated. "I'll wait to hear from you."

"Jake said you might be leaving Long Gully soon. I'd set up a meeting before everyone travels to Cunnamulla next Friday. Will that be all right?"

"Yes." To hide the smug expression she was sure covered her face, Marlow glanced at her dresser. Aha. Her camera. She'd taken photos of Celia, Bella, and Jake individually. Now would be the perfect time to have someone take a shot of them all together. In case her plans backfired. She picked up the camera and opened her screen door. "Bridgette, would you mind taking a photo of the family and me? I might not have another opportunity."

Taking the camera, she cleared her throat. "Get them to gather on the stairs."

Marlow found Celia seated on the verandah and handed her the crutches. "Can you walk to the steps so we can take a family photo in the sunlight?"

"Yes, my dear. Help me up. I'll stand by the post on the top step."

With Celia leaning safely against the post, Marlow rounded up Jake and Bella. "Bridgette's waiting to take a photo of us. Come quickly, let's gather around Celia."

"Yay." Bella ran up the stairs and posed next to her aunt.

"No, child. Stand in front of me to hide my bandaged foot."

Bella complied. "Marlow, can you take one of Lynn and me, too?"

"Of course." She hesitated. Where to stand? With Bella or next to Celia? She needn't have worried.

Jake slipped one arm around Celia's shoulders and held out his other arm. "Come here, Marlow." He leaned down and whispered, "This is where you belong." He drew her close.

Aiming the camera, Bridgette called, "Say cheese."

Marlow needed no encouragement to smile as the pressure of Jake's fingers on her waist increased, and she reciprocated by placing her arm around him.

Chapter 47

Jake sat on the chair in his bedroom ready to remove his boots. Why prepare for bed when he knew he wouldn't be able to sleep? He extinguished his lamp, stepped outside, and tip-toed across the verandah and down the steps to the pool area.

The faint aroma of eucalyptus assailed his nostrils and sent his senses reeling. Although the smell was familiar, this time it brought back memories which knotted his stomach muscles. The night he admitted he loved Marlow and wanted her to stay at Long Gully forever. The night he jumped into the pool fully clothed.

He squatted and swished his hand in the water. Taking Marlow to Galah Glade couldn't come soon enough, but he was not sure how to broach the subject of marriage since he didn't know for certain how she felt about him. He stood, then ambled along the path to the bench, light from the half moon barely enough to guide his way. Marlow chose not to stay in Melbourne, so that was in his favor, but women could be so intricate and deep.

Toffee jumped onto the bench and brushed against his arm. He whispered, "I'm glad you recovered, silly cat." She nudged his hand as if asking for attention. Jake obliged and stroked her back. "You'll have to be my sounding board. How should I proceed?" The cat climbed onto his lap and set her front paws on his shoulder. "Whoa, Toffee. You've never done this before. Are you trying to tell me something? I should stop dilly-dallying and get to the point. Explain how I feel. And ask Marlow outright."

If loud purring was a sign of approval, then Jake had his answer. He picked up Toffee and set her on the ground.

To be perfectly frank, Jake was scared to death and still uncertain of his way forward. He bowed his head. "Father God, please show me the right time to talk to Marlow and give me the words to say. I place my future in Your hands, but help me to accept Marlow's answer, whatever it may be. In Jesus's name. Amen."

Early the next morning, Jake entered the kitchen to find Celia seated at the table, the aroma of fresh coffee nipping at his taste buds. "What are you doing in here?"

"I'm not an invalid. I wanted coffee, and so I made it. Here." She pushed her empty mug toward him. "Refill, please."

"You're getting bossy again. Must be feeling better." Jake grinned as he poured.

"I am, but I also want to talk to you before the others get up."

"And I have a question for you." He sat opposite Celia. "Your headache the other day. What were you playing at?"

Celia glanced down the passage, then whispered, "I'm not blind. I see how you and Marlow look at each other when you think no one's watching. I was trying to give you two time alone together."

"You're a busybody." He drained his mug and set it on the table.

"If you don't do something quickly, she'll be gone. To Melbourne, or Perth, or Texas."

"Why did you say Melbourne? Has Marlow said something about Milton?"

"Aha. You automatically thought about him, but I don't think she's romantically interested. However," she glared at Jake, "if you don't act now, you'll lose her." Celia sipped her coffee. "And there's Bridgette hovering in the wings."

"You don't have to worry about Bridgette." Jake leaned back and balanced the chair on two legs. "I want to take Marlow to Galah Glade."

"Then do it. Now."

"Greg and I have work to do today. I'll take her tomorrow."

"Take who where?" Bella entered the kitchen, yawning.

Jake held out his arm. "Come here. Bella Bear. I have some questions for you." He settled his arm around her waist. "Do you like Marlow?"

"Dad." She pushed away. "Of course, I do. Why ask such an inane question?"

"Inane?"

"On the vocabulary list Miss York provided. Well?"

"A few more questions first. Would you like her, that is Marlow, to stay at Long Gully?"

"You mean for another month, or longer?"

"Longer."

Bella paced around the table, biting her lip, a frown wrinkling her young brow. "What do you mean?"

At that moment, Marlow shuffled down the passage. "Everyone's up. Sorry, I overslept." She adjusted the belt of her denim skirt and sat next to Celia. "Ooh, someone please pour me some coffee."

Jake stood, filled a mug and handed it to her along with the milk. Her appearance almost robbed him of speech.

Celia stared at him while Bella frowned.

"What have I missed?" Marlow asked.

"I'll, um, talk to you later." Jake grabbed Bella's hand. "Come with me, please." He exited the kitchen via the back door and wiped beads of sweat off his upper lip. That was close. Too close. "Let's finish our conversation away from the house."

"I understand. You don't want Marlow to hear us." She let go of his hand and ran to the vegetable garden fence. "Is this far enough?" She set her hands on her hips and tilted her head.

"Yes. Do you know what I'm going to say?"

"I think so."

"I love Marlow and want to marry her, that is if she'll have me. But I need your blessing. And Rick's."

Bella took a deep breath. "Believe it or not, I've thought about Marlow being my step mum, only once or twice. After all, you kept reminding me she was just staying a few days."

"That's—"

"Please wait. I have more to say. I do love her, but I won't be hurt again, won't get my hopes up. What if Marlow accepts, I get all excited, and then she breaks it off, like Gail did? I can't have my heart shattered again." Bella marched toward him. "I'll pretend this conversation never happened."

"But I broke off the engagement."

She glared at him, then ran to the steps and entered the kitchen.

Jake hung his head. He had a lot of explaining to do, but Bella needed time to think about their conversation. Especially after his last statement.

He spent the day with Greg and two stockmen mustering sheep from W-1 paddock to C-1, and arrived home dirty, tired, and worried. Good thing the station hands needed no guidance from him. He'd been locked up with his guilt and doubt, and barely said a word to anyone.

After showering, he knocked on Bella's door. "We need to talk, luv. Can I come in, or do you want to go to the verandah?"

She set her book on the bed and pointed to her door. "Outside, please." Standing by the screen, she scowled at him.

He felt like holding up a shield to ward off the darts from her eyes. "Bella, I'm sorry—"

"Why did you let me think Gail broke the engagement? Don't you know how that made me feel? She professed to love me, and then, poof," Bella snapped her fingers, "she was gone. I always wondered what I'd done wrong." She folded her arms and tapped one foot. Any minute he expected to see steam shoot from her ears.

"Come here, luv." Jake sat and beckoned her. Two, three seconds, then she dropped her arms and approached him. "Oh, my dear little girl. I failed you again." He tried to embrace her, but she resisted.

"Why, Daddy?" She plopped into the chair beside him.

"There's an unwritten rule in society that the woman gets to break an engagement. To save face, or whatever. That's what Gail wanted, and she got her way. I never gave any thought to how the decision would affect you. I didn't know you blamed yourself. Saying I'm sorry doesn't seem adequate." He held out his hand. "Please, forgive me."

A minute dripped by in slow motion, and then Bella grasped his hand. "Don't keep things from me again. I'm stronger than you think, and I would rather be told the truth than nothing or a lie that's supposed to protect me."

Twelve going on twenty. Where had his little girl gone? But she was right. "From now on, I promise to tell you the truth. Deal?" He squeezed her hand.

She responded by kissing him on the cheek. "I expect you to keep your word." She stood and faced him. "You can propose to Marlow."

His heart almost burst out of his chest. "I'm taking her riding tomorrow and will ask her then."

"All right." Bella's shoulders dropped.

"What now?"

"Nothing. See you at dinner." She stepped into her room and closed the door.

Still dancing on a cloud, Jake retreated to his office to review accounts, then had a positive conversation with his son. All on board. Now to convince the main player.

When Marlow called everyone for dinner, Jake entered the dining room, stepped behind her, and touched her shoulder. "Do you have any pressing plans for tomorrow?"

She turned, her face flushed. From the heat of the kitchen or his proximity? "Other than meal prep, not really. Do you have something in mind?"

"I do." He grinned. "I want to take you to my spot of heaven on earth. We need to leave early, and this time we'll take the bikes. Do you want to ride your own, or sit behind me?"

"I can't handle this rough terrain." Her cheeks flushed a deeper crimson. "I'll go with you."

Which was exactly what he wanted to hear. "Good choice."

"What about Celia?"

"Don't tell her because she'll pitch a fit, but I asked Nellie to come over and help out."

Marlow swiped her hand across her face, offered him a brief smile, and left the dining room.

Plan in motion, Jake almost jumped and clicked his heels together. Good thing he didn't try. His flip-flops wouldn't have made any noise, and he might have come a cropper and landed on his rear.

Head down, Bella entered the room and went straight to Jake's side.

"What's the matter, luv?" He put his arm around her. "I just radioed your brother and he's good with the plan."

She didn't react as he expected. In fact, she didn't do anything except cling to him.

"Talk to me, child. I can't help if you don't tell me what's wrong."

By this time Marlow and Celia had entered.

"We'll be back in a moment. Carry on without us, please." Jake ushered his daughter out to the verandah again. "Tell, me Bella Bear. Are you still concerned about me proposing to Marlow?"

They sat in the same chairs they'd occupied not an hour earlier, and Bella leaned her head against him. "I'm happy and sad. Isn't that silly. How can I be both at the same time?

Was she regretting her approval of Marlow? "The emotions are closely linked, luv. Are you happy about Marlow?"

She nodded.

"Are you sure?"

Nodding again, she looked at him.

"What makes you sad?" He figured he knew the answer, but Bella needed to voice her concern. If he'd learned anything from Marlow's counseling, it was the necessity to put emotions into words.

"Mummy. I still love her, but am I being a traitor by loving Marlow?"

"No, no, sweet. Mum will always be in our hearts, and we'll never forget her. But she'd want us to be happy, and I think Marlow will complete our family." He embraced Bella and rocked her gently. She had to process his words.

They sat in silence a minute or two, then Bella raised her head. "If Marlow says yes, Dad, you have to buy her a diamond and sapphire ring."

"Diamond, sure, but why sapphires? Did she tell you she liked them?"

"I have a magazine that lists birthstones for each month. Her Eileen was born in September, and—"

"And sapphire is the stone for that month." He gazed at her upturned face. "I think a diamond and sapphire ring will be perfect, Bella Bear. What a wonderful idea." He kissed her forehead. "I love you and your kind, thoughtful heart."

She rose, stepped to the door then turned, hands on hips. "And Dad, when you want to buy me a present, can I have a ring or necklace with Mum's and my birthstones?"

He chuckled. "Yup. A special present for my girl."

Chapter 48

The shrill five o'clock buzz jolted Jake from a sound sleep. He didn't normally set an alarm, but he wanted to have everything ready for the ride before he woke Marlow. Dressed in the clothes he laid out the previous night, he prepared enough bacon and eggs for everyone—so Celia wouldn't have to cook—then made four sandwiches. He'd informed her of the trip. She was ecstatic, but scolded him for asking Nellie to help.

Coffee ready to pour into the flask, paper wrapped sandwiches, apples, filled canteens, and bottles of lemonade. Radio clipped to his belt. All set. He turned to head down the passage, but Marlow stood in the doorway dressed similarly to their last ride. Except this time, she wore a blue checked shirt. "Morning. You're up." Tongue-tied already.

"I set my alarm." She placed her hat, sunnies, and camera on the counter. "Are we going to eat breakfast first?"

"I'd like to get an early start. We can have coffee now, or take it with us. I packed our food to eat later. Is that all right?"

"Sure. I'd like my coffee now, though."

He poured two mugs and sat at the table.

Marlow blew on her drink before taking a sip. "You've been busy this morning."

"Yup. I'm eager to get started." As much as he wanted to take her to the shearing shed and explain the process, their destination was of paramount importance. If all went according to plan, Marlow would have a lifetime to learn about shearing sheep.

They drank in silence.

She drained her mug, grabbed her hat and camera, and tilted her head toward the door. "What are you waiting for?"

He didn't even try to hide his grin while he packed their picnic into a canvas bag then opened the screen door. "Our adventure awaits."

After filling the petrol tank earlier, he'd parked his bike under the carport. Once he stowed the food in the saddle bag, he started the motor and invited Marlow to climb aboard.

"You'll have to hold on to me."

She tentatively placed her hands on his sides.

"You can do better than that. This is going to be a rough ride because there's no marked track." He grabbed her hands and drew them around his middle. "That's better. We'll ride about twenty-five miles this morning."

"I'm ready."

He drove slowly so as not to wake Celia and Bella, but once past the sheds, he opened the throttle and headed northeast. The sun peeking over the horizon promised another scorcher. For the next forty-five minutes the noise of the bike made conversation impossible while they rode east across the rolling dunes and undulating patches of stubby grassland. An hour later, he stopped to allow a spooked mob of kangaroos to pass. When the dust settled, he turned and said, "We have another thirty minutes. Do you need anything to drink?"

"Nope. Ride on, Captain."

He chuckled and saluted. "At your service, madam."

When the landmark group of boulders became clearer through the shimmering haze, Jake slowed again and pointed. "That's our destination."

"Good. Because I think my bones are becoming disconnected."

"No worries. I added a special glue to our canteens."

Her turn to chuckle.

Eager to put the last phase of his plan into action, he drove as fast as possible. He wanted Marlow to accept the land in all its harsh beauty, and so far in the weeks she'd been at Long Gully, nothing she'd said or done hinted at her rejection of what she saw.

Bike parked in the shade of a gum tree, Jake removed their picnic items, and handed Marlow a canteen.

"Thanks. I need lots of sticky water."

They both gulped down a good amount, then Jake held out his hand. "This way." She grasped his hand, which sent a charge up his arm. He led her around the boulders, through a group of acacias toward the swaying gum trees that lined the large billabong. Watching her reaction did not disappoint.

She stopped dead in her tracks and removed her sunnies. Mouth agape, eyes shining. "Oh, my. What a magnificent sight."

Jake bowed his head. *Lord God, please may Marlow's heart be as open to my words as it is to Your creation.*

He gave her time to appreciate the scene while inhaling the invigorating eucalyptus scent and listening to the parrots and cockatoos squawking. "Although I've been here several times, I'm always amazed."

She nodded and beamed. "This is a landscape I'd like to paint. I've been tempted since Bella started painting again, but this…" she gestured, "this is worthy. I must take dozens of pictures." Camera aimed, she shot one view after another. "I love how the clear blue sky is reflected in the water. I haven't seen one cloud since being at Long Gully."

"Nothing unusual. We can go months without clouds. But when they gather, they're spectacular."

Two more shots. "The gray-green branches trailing over the water's edge make it look so peaceful and calm." Walking closer to the water, she pointed. "Aha. A shady, grassy spot, just waiting for us and our picnic." More photos.

Caught up in her excitement, Jake followed and set the bag of food on a small rock in the area she identified. His original choice, but he was thrilled she noticed it. "Give me your bandana and I'll wet it for you."

She handed it to him before taking several more pictures.

While wetting her scarf and his handkerchief, he washed his hands, then stomped on the grass to chase away unwanted guests. "We can eat when you're ready." He removed his hat, ran his fingers through his damp hair, and wiped his face and neck. The slight breeze added a welcome cooling effect.

Marlow washed her hands, then joined him on the grass. She also removed her hat, undid her disheveled ponytail, and wiped her flushed face. "Why are you staring at me?"

"Enjoying the sight."

Her blush intensified. Was this the right moment?

But she reached for the bag of food and said, "I'm hungry. How about you?"

Breakfast first, then a declaration of love. He opened the bag and handed her a sandwich and bottle of lemonade. "An interesting menu, but it's the best I could do."

"I'm disappointed."

His stomach muscles clenched. "Why?"

She hiked a shoulder and sighed. "No billy tea. I've been in the outback a month, and no one has offered to make me a cuppa."

"I didn't have room to bring the equipment…"

A crooked smile broke her deadpan expression.

"I promise. Next time."

"No problem. Bacon and eggs on Celia's bread. Always a good combination."

Which will taste like caviar and ambrosia with you. Mouth full, he nodded and kept his gaze on her. He couldn't help himself. She had proven to be steadfast, honest. Rekindled her faith, loved his Bella, filled the gap left by Celia's accident. And, he grinned, she was oh, so easy on the eyes. Heat rose up his neck.

"What's so funny?"

To give himself time to come up with an answer that wouldn't embarrass him, he wiped his face and neck again. "I'm going to be brutally honest." He dusted crumbs off his shirt. Shooed away flies. Set down his empty bottle. But the words wouldn't come. "Strewth. I can't believe how hard this is."

"Jake, I don't expect a philosophical answer." Marlow placed the bottles and wrappers in the bag and removed the camera strap from around her neck. "I know you have something on your mind, so talk to me."

Something on my mind. You bet. He stood and offered her his hand. "Come. My words need to be said face to face."

She accepted his help and rose. "That serious?"

"Yes." He kept a hold of her hand and looked deep into her eyes. He couldn't deal with the unexpected range of emotion displayed and let go, stepping back. "Um, maybe not." He scratched his head. "You already said you like Australia, but do you like the outback?"

"Yes."

"How about living on the homestead?"

"Yes."

She wasn't making this easy.

"You're doing a good job coping while Celia's recuperating.

Has that…? I don't know where I'm going with this."

Hands on her hips, she smiled. "You're the poster child for beating around the bush. Say what's on your heart."

This time he knew how to interpret what he saw in her eyes. "Marlow, please don't leave Long Gully. You can't leave me. I love you." Don't stop there. "Will you marry me?" His heart pounded, and his stomach knotted while he waited for a sign, an answer.

Taking tiny steps, she slowly closed the gap between them. His fingertips itched to touch her face, her hair. One meter apart. She seemed to float toward him, as if her heart was attached to his. Her hands on his chest burned through his shirt. He gulped. She tilted her head, her fingers climbed up, up and around his neck. Her lips parted. "Kiss me, Jake Barclay."

He'd take that sign any day. "My pleasure." His words were barely above a whisper. He drew her close. The first kiss was soft and comforting. They pulled apart, each drawing in shallow breaths. Then he covered her mouth with his as her body melted against his.

Chapter 49

Breathing hard, Marlow backed away from Jake. How bold of her to ask for a kiss, but how satisfying. Her senses on overload and her knees wobbly, she lowered herself onto one of the boulders. His masculine smell, the feel of his hand on her back, her neck, his smoothly shaven chin. The passion of his kiss. A shiver of pleasure crossed her shoulders.

Faced with the urgency to respond to Jake's declaration, she questioned her choice. Leave her friends and career behind in Texas? She'd survived a month living on the station, but could she call it home for the rest of her life?

Marlow gazed at the cobalt sky, the blue-green trees, the violet hills shimmering beyond acres of sunburnt earth, her eyes feasting on the sight. Seconds of uncertainty over, she turned to the man standing beside her.

Their gazes locked, and he joined her on the boulder. The raw passion in his frost-free eyes shook her to the depths of her soul. He loved her, and he waited for her answer.

She couldn't escape the intensity of the moment as he drew closer and closer, but she had to slow down. "Jake." Teetering on the edge of the precipice from her dream, she latched onto his hand. Would he save her? "I love you, too."

He gathered her in his arms as if he knew she needed rescuing. "I want to take care of you for the rest of our lives."

Resisting the desire to kiss him again took all of her resolve. She laid her head on his chest, and muttered, "Believe it or not, I have thought about being married to you."

He pulled away and looked at her. "You did? When?"

"The night, or rather, the morning after the fire." Her cheeks tingled. Talking about who fell in love with whom first was juvenile, but so intimate.

"Aha. I beat you to it. I realized I loved you the night before we flew to Melbourne."

Snuggling next to him, she chuckled. "And it's taken you this long to tell me." She tsked. "Jake, Jake. I thought you were a man of action."

"I am, but I didn't want to scare you off, and I waited for the right time and place." His hold tightened. "By your, uh, willing participation in our kisses, I'd say you haven't been deterred. However, I still want an answer."

Her turn to pull away. She placed her hands on his chest, then wound them around his neck. "This certainly is the right time and place. Yes, Jake, I will marry you." Their next kiss lasted way too long for her sanity. Scooting a few inches away, she gulped in air. "Whew." She swiped a hand across her face. No more breathtaking kisses. Not yet. "So much to discuss and plan. Where do we begin?"

"Australian law requires us to complete a NOIM, Notice of Intended Marriage, at least thirty days before the date."

Thirty days. Long enough to get her brain around the idea of marrying an Australian, gaining a son, a daughter, an aunt, giving up her life in Texas, which until now had all been a theoretical pipe dream. Daughter? "What about Bella? We must be careful how we tell her."

"No worries. I have her blessing. Rick's, too." Jake's grin lit up his face.

"You sneak." She swatted his shoulder. "No wonder Bella gave me a strange look when I bade her goodnight. And I suppose Celia is in on the deal."

"Naturally."

Slipping her hand through his arm, she inched closer. "It's nice to know your family approves."

He rested his head on hers. "They're your family, too."

She sighed and allowed her jumbled thoughts to come to order. Texas. After the wedding, she'd have to return to sell her home, and say goodbye to her friends. Maybe Jake could accompany her, and she could show off her handsome grazier. Sort out her immigration status. But that was down the road. Immediate plans. "Can we take care of the form when we go to Cunnamulla on Friday?"

"Yup. And we must arrange for a minister from one of the

churches in town to perform the ceremony."

"Billy McIntosh can't do it?"

"No. He's not licensed. But I know one of the pastors well. He'll help us out."

"You're talking about a wedding in front of people, not just a quiet affair."

"I thought we could use Lion's all-purpose room at the hotel. Is that all right?"

"Perfect. What else?" She straightened. "I must write to Ida Marie. Wouldn't it be wonderful if she and my grandfather came to the wedding?"

"How about your Texas friends? I'll pay their way."

She stared at him. "That would be lovely, but they'd need visas and…and." She did a quick calculation. "Texas schools will be back in session by the second weekend of January. So, thanks, but no. I'll be more than satisfied with the Barclays and any Cunnamulla folks you invite."

"Whatever you desire, my sweet."

Glued to his side, Marlow gestured toward the water. "I appreciate you bringing me here. I'm honored you shared this enchanting place with me."

"I found it about a year ago. When I visit, I always leave rejuvenated, at peace, and ready to carry on with life." He squeezed her side. "A life with you."

She slid her arms around him and allowed his words to fill her soul. "Thank you for restoring my faith."

"No, no, luv. You returned to God. Your faith wasn't buried. I only helped you remove a layer of disappointment."

Nodding, she bowed her head. "Well, God used you. Will you pray with me, Jake?"

"Nothing I'd like better."

"Thank You God for sending me an honorable, worthy man. Bless our union…" Her voice cracked.

Jake picked up where she left off. "And thank You for sending me a virtuous woman. May we live our lives to bring glory to Your name. Amen."

Wrapped in his arms, Marlow remained still for at least a minute until a commotion in the branches above caught her attention. She cleared her throat as a vestige of tightness lingered. "Those birds are so colorful and noisy. What are they?"

He looked up. "Cockatoos, mulga parrots, and those bright ones are lorikeets, and of course galahs. This is, after all, Galah Glade."

"I remember them on our trip from Cunnamulla. Their pink feathers are unique."

"You got that right." He checked his watch. "It's almost time to leave, but I have a few more things to discuss."

"About us?" A tinge of apprehension colored Marlow's joy. She shifted on the boulder and picked up her camera. Something to keep her hands busy.

"Yeah. Don't worry." He must have sensed her changed attitude. "It's nothing drastic."

She smiled, but twisted the strap anyway.

"There are a couple of things you need to know about Celia." He kicked at the dirt. "I offered her a home at Long Gully for as long as she wants. She loves to be in charge of the kitchen."

"Which is fine by me."

"She's the boss, all right. And you're okay for her to continue?"

"Why not? I might soon be your wife, but I won't take Celia's place as long as she is willing and able. Maybe we can share some of the chores."

"That's a good idea. Later on if necessary, we can hire a stockman's wife to help out."

Speaking of how life should continue, now seemed the perfect time to air her plan. "I have a proposal I'd like to throw your way." Marlow set down the camera. "You mentioned once you have a hard time hiring qualified workers because some parents are concerned about sending their children to boarding school. What if I offered to supervise not just the School of the Air program for the young kids, but also the correspondence courses for the older ones? Especially for those who are only thirteen or fourteen."

"You'd do that?"

"Sure. Nothing I'd like more." Remote and long distance learning were a greater challenge than teaching at the University of Texas any day. "Remember Lynn Smith, Bella's friend from Maroola? Well, last Sunday Bridgette and I discussed her schooling. Due to the child's medical issues, she can't attend boarding school. Bridgette asked for my help." Marlow shrugged. "Problem solved."

Jake nodded. "I can see that all panning out. However," he

prodded her knee, "don't let Bella persuade you to teach her all the way through high school."

"How about just next year? Give her time to mature and get used to having me in her life permanently. I would never want her to think I sent her away."

"That's an agreeable plan." Jake set his elbows on his knees. "I've been thinking about Bella and her painting. I'd like to check out an art school for her down the road."

"Excellent idea."

"I'll chat with her about it." He turned toward Marlow. "A couple more things. I think it's admirable that you want to help the children, but you must know that I won't hold you back on anything you want to do. Paint to your heart's content. I'll buy you all the equipment you need. Even turn one of the rooms into a studio for you. And Bella. As long as you spend time with me, you have *carte blanche*."

Whatever I want? Might as well go for gold. "I could write the book that's been on my mind for a long time."

"Book?"

"Yup. I want to write about my experiences working with children with special needs."

"Wonderful. I'm sure it will be a bestseller." His chuckled. "I'll buy you a typewriter for a wedding present."

"Ahh. How sweet." She snuggled next to him again. Marlow needn't have worried about what he had to discuss. How long would it take her to come to grips with the fact that in spite of his Barclay blue eyes, Jake was nothing like Steven? She sighed, sure the sound could be heard all the way to the homestead.

"It's time to go." Jake handed her a canteen. "Want a drink before we leave? I'll take a different way home. We should be there in about forty-five minutes."

"Thanks." She took a long swig then wiped her mouth on her sleeve. "As wonderful as it is to ride on a bike with you, I'll be very glad to get home." Camera and canteen in hand, she took one last look at the oasis while Jake gathered the bag that had held their picnic. Hand in hand, they returned to the bike. His quip about a wedding present in mind, she patted him on the shoulder. "I have one caveat to this marriage deal."

"And that is?" He shoved on his hat then stowed their canteens.

"Do I have to change my last name, or should I hyphenate it?"

Brow furrowed, he rubbed his chin. "Well, you don't have to change it if you don't want to." Then his brow cleared. "Oh, you goose. Marlow Barclay-Barclay. Very funny." Towering over her, he slid his hand behind her neck and kissed her.

In that moment, her last name didn't matter at all.

Chapter 50

January 15, 1984

The month had zoomed past. Sometimes Jake had to hold on to a solid object to keep his feet on the ground. Now, standing in front of family and friends in Lion's crowded all-purpose room, he couldn't believe the day had arrived. Their wedding day.

He tugged at his shirt collar. Why had he let Rick tie a Windsor knot? Too late to change. Jake had decided to wear his navy-blue suit because all the women in his life had new outfits. Why did they call them outfits? Anyway, Celia sat in the front row in her splashy emerald green 'outfit'. She did look smart. Even Rick, his best man, wore a suit. Jake had not been allowed to see Bella's dress or Marlow's outfit. *Patience, Barclay.*

He elbowed Rick and whispered, "You have the ring?"

His son nodded and rolled his eyes.

He'd already asked that question. Twice. Jake dabbed his handkerchief to his upper lip and brow for the third time. He should have asked Lion to place a fan aimed right at his face. The ring, a diamond surrounded by sapphires, was perfect. While in Cunnamulla last month, Jake had called a jeweler friend in Brisbane, described what he wanted, gave him Marlow's size, and made arrangements for the ring to be sent via special delivery. He'd also commissioned a necklace of amethysts and opals for Bella, Laura's and her birthstones. He patted his shirt pocket. A gift for after the ceremony.

Earlier, Rosie had informed the group that Marlow would be delayed a few minutes. Guests chatted quietly while Lion played a variety of show tunes on the old piano brought in for the occasion.

Jake wanted to run to Marlow's room to find out what happened, but she hadn't asked for his help. Shifting his weight from foot to foot, he checked his watch. Only five minutes late. Well, he'd already waited a month. They'd had a bonza Christmas with Rick, all the hands, and many of their teenaged children. Marlow helped Celia prepared a feast they were still talking about. Jake smiled then pursed his lips. Yeah, a grand day, but the following Friday Marlow received the sad news her grandfather had passed away the week before Christmas. Marlow's sorrow was eased when Ida Marie accepted their wedding invitation. In fact, she was with his bride right now.

Marlow, the love of his life. Jake bowed his head. *Thank You, God, for this second time around for me. I've been blessed to have two women to love.* He glanced at the wall clock. Ten past the hour.

Jake caught Rosie's eyes, but she shrugged.

No telling what Ida Marie and Marlow were doing, but surely… Jake took a deep breath. What was five more minutes when he had a lifetime to look forward to?

Rick leaned close and whispered, "Bella told me she won a prize for her artwork."

"Yeah. She received the news yesterday. Third place in the outback landscape category. And an offer to paint more to sell. She's chuffed." Jake dabbed at his face again. "She also made good marks on her school report."

"She's a smart little ankle biter." Rick harrumphed. "I suppose I'll have to stop calling her that. My sister is getting taller."

Jake checked his watch again. Three minutes had crawled by.

Lion stopped playing and turned. "Hey, Jake, have you scared her off?" Other guests joined in the chuckling.

Vince, the local copper, added, "Yeah, mate. When is this shindig getting started?"

Even Charlie added his dig. "Hey, Jake, has Marlow run off with the family silver?"

More laughs and a few coughs.

Rosie stormed down the aisle and parked herself in the middle. "You heard what I said. Marlow is…altering her dress. So, unless you want to deal with me, you lot better keep your opinions to yourselves."

Silence reigned. No one messed with Rosie.

Why make alterations this late? "Give Marlow a few more

minutes." Jake smiled and inwardly scoffed at a tinge of doubt. Surely Marlow hadn't reneged. If she changed her mind, she'd send Bella or Ida to tell him. Not leave him at the altar.

"In that case, I have to sit." Portly Pastor Ross Young waddled to the front row and plopped down.

"Do you want me to check on her?" Celia asked.

Shaking his head, Jake tugged at his collar again. "Ida Marie would let us know if Marlow needed a lot more time. I'm sure nothing's wrong." But he didn't believe his own words. A cold prickle skittered across his shoulders.

Movement outside the window caught his eye. Paddy, or someone who looked like him, skulked past.

Jake motioned for Greg, seated on the second row, to come forward. "I think I just saw Paddy outside. I know he used to work at the Carson's place north of here, so he might have a legit reason for being in town, but please check."

"Will do, boss." Greg strolled down the aisle.

"Hey, Lion, mate, play "Get Me to the Church on Time". That might spur on my bride." Jake resumed his place next to Rick and attempted to smile.

Lion grinned. "Here goes."

He banged out the lively tune, and with each pounding note, Jake's heart sank a little lower.

Chapter 51

"Bella, sweetheart, please tell Rosie we'll be a few more minutes. The repairs to my suit are taking longer than expected." Marlow stitched up another rip in the skirt while Ida Marie reattached buttons to the jacket.

"Righto." Halfway to the hotel room door, Bella stopped and turned. "Are you sure it's okay with you that I don't call you Mum?" She gnawed the inside of her cheek and frowned.

"Come here, sweetie." Marlow set the skirt on the bed and held out her arm.

Bella sat next to her, hands clasped tightly in her lap, her floral dress billowing around her.

"We've addressed this before, but it bears repeating. You had a loving Mum, and I will never try to take her place. Just like I don't expect you to take over Eileen's corner of my heart. Our loved ones who are no longer here will always be a part of our hearts, our memories, and our lives."

"I just wanted to make sure." Picking up her colorful bouquet, Bella headed to the door again. "I'll deliver the message then wait for you in the lobby."

"See you soon."

Seated at the dresser, Ida Marie threaded her needle. "I'm sorry your granddad couldn't join us today."

"I grateful you are here, though." Marlow smiled at Gran. "Thank you for coming."

"I wouldn't have missed your wedding." She brushed a strand of snow-white hair out of her eyes. "He was coming around, you know, to accepting you." Her voice wavered.

Marlow's throat tightened, and she coughed. "I wish I could have met him."

They worked without talking, the whirl of the fan the only noise.

After locating the last rip, Marlow began to sew dainty stitches. When she'd returned to her room after lunch, she noticed the damage to her suit. She'd set it out on the bed, and someone had ripped off the buttons and stabbed through the skirt, even cutting slits in the bedspread. Ida Marie had reported to Lion who notified Vince, the off-duty cop, and he conducted a preliminary investigation. The window screen had been removed, and a trio of teens had been seen loitering in the vicinity, but they were long gone.

"If it wasn't those kids who tried to ruin my outfit, I'd think someone wants to sabotage this marriage. Won't they be surprised? Another stitch or two and I'll walk down the aisle."

"What is this world coming to?"

Marlow ran a hand over the linen fabric. "Cobalt blue is my perfect color. I have to wear this outfit because I didn't bring another one." She cut her thread, then stuck the needle back in the travel-size sewing kit. "Done. I'm so glad Rosie had a kit stashed away in her purse. We need to hurry."

"I'm on the last button. Jake loves you, and he'll wait." She chuckled. "Besides, I'm glad you don't have another suit. This color suits you."

Marlow slipped her legs into the skirt and closed the zipper, then put on her heeled cream-colored sandals. She eyed Gran as she held out the jacket. Ida Marie certainly didn't look her age. At seventy-eight she was spry and thin, hair in a short bob, and dressed in a soft pink suit which highlighted her Finlay necklace to perfection.

After she buttoned the peplum jacket, Marlow examined her reflection. Some of the areas she'd stitched were noticeable. She smoothed the skirt as best she could. "That will have to do."

Ida Marie handed Marlow her necklace. "I'd like to think that this brings Arthur and our dear Katie Marie here with us today."

"That's a lovely sentiment." Marlow fingered her pendant and blinked in an effort to keep the tears at bay. On top of being late, she didn't want raccoon eyes. She heaved a sigh. If only she had a physical reminder of her precious Eileen to wear today.

"I have a present you might like to wear seeing as you don't have a veil or a hat." Ida Marie opened her purse and withdrew a silver headband studded with opals similar to the Finlay necklace.

"Oh, how gorgeous." Marlow gingerly held the band.

"I know you've already had your hair done, but maybe we can insert the band somehow."

"Yes, yes." She faced the mirror. Her coiffure was different to her everyday style—ponytail turned into a pretty knot of curls, sprayed in place. "Instead of wearing it like a band, let's slide it around the curls." Feat accomplished, Marlow patted her hair. "That's great, and it seems secure."

"You look lovely, my dear. Are you ready to get married?" Ida Marie stood at Marlow's side. They were the same height, had similar facial structure and smiles.

Marlow straightened her shoulders. "I am."

A knock sounded.

"That must be Rosie coming to check on us." Marlow turned and called, "Come in."

But Rosie did not enter. A tall blonde dressed in a sleeveless black pantsuit and carrying a small cushion slammed the door behind her. "Oh, I see you repaired your outfit."

Marlow's smile turned to a scowl. Her heart pounded and her stomach quivered. "What's going on?" Her voice rose. "Who are you?"

Slipping her hand into her pocket, the woman remained in front of the door. "At this point, my name's not important. I want you—"

"I'm not interested in what you want, lady." Marlow grabbed Ida Marie's arm. "Come, Gran, we're leaving."

"Not so fast. I have a gun." She moved her hand in her pocket.

"It that right? I don't believe you. Let's go."

The woman smirked and pulled out a small revolver. "I don't want to use it, but I will if you mess up. I even brought my own silencer." She held the cushion in front of the weapon and aimed it at Ida Marie. "You wouldn't want to see your grandmother hurt, would you?"

"No." Marlow let go of Gran's arm and cast a quick glance around the room, searching for something she could use as a weapon. A book. The telephone. A slender but stout vase. The dresser chair, if nothing else.

Anger etched deep lines on the intruder's brow and around her grim mouth.

Stay calm. Don't fuel her rage. Marlow softened her tone.

"Please leave Gran out of this. What do you want from me?"

"Be careful, luv," Ida Marie murmured.

"Now we're talking." The woman gestured with the gun for Marlow and Ida to sit on the bed, which they did. "I'm Gail Carson. You might have heard of me."

Gail, as in Jake's former fiancée. "I know who you are. But why did you damage my clothes, and why are you here now?"

"Isn't it obvious?" Gail dragged the chair over to the door and sat. "I don't want you to marry Jake. I know it's trite, but if I can't have him, then no one can."

"Someone's bound to come looking for me, for us, soon. I sent Bella out a few minutes ago. She'll tell Rosie we're almost ready."

Gail chuckled, but the sound held a menacing note. "Dear little Bella won't get far. I gave her a little task to do for—"

"You what?" Marlow rose and stepped toward the door.

In a flash, Gail stood and waved the revolver. "Back. Get back."

Deliberately standing in front of Ida Marie, Marlow spread her arms. "You will not hurt anyone in this family. If you harm a hair on Bella's head, do you think Jake would ever have you in his life again? And to stop me from marrying him, you'll have to kill me." Marlow inched toward the side table and the vase.

"Well, yeah, but he won't be happy, and…and that's good enough for me."

Marlow slowly reached for the vase, but Gail caught the movement and aimed the gun at Marlow's head.

"Get back on the bed. Now. Don't even think about calling for help. I *will* shoot you or your grandmother. Or both."

Marlow didn't trust the volatile woman and complied.

Chapter 52

Although Greg reported no one had seen Paddy, Jake's internal caution meter spun at full tilt. His hands fisted and he leaned closer to Rick, raising his voice over the singing guests. "I want to check on Marlow myself."

"I can go."

"No, no. You stay and keep the restless hoard in line." He forced a smile and addressed the crowd. "I promise there will be a wedding today. I'll be right back." To his surprise, no one harassed him as he made his way to the lobby.

Jake stopped at the desk manned by Alex, one of Lion's twin grandsons. The lad, about fifteen, munched on a bag of crisps. "Hey, have you seen anything suspicious this afternoon? I mean, anyone hanging around who wasn't a guest."

Crunch. Crunch. He shrugged and swallowed. "I haven't been here long. Grandad told me to come at half past one but I was late."

"Since you've been here?"

Another crisp, another shrug. "Yup, I suppose."

"Well, who, what?"

"One second." Alex licked his fingers. "There was a good-looking sheila with a man. Or could have been a kid. I dunno how old he was."

Jake almost reached over the counter and grabbed the youth by his shirt. "And?"

"And, oh, you want details." He scrunched up the empty bag and tossed it over his shoulder. "They came into the lobby, looked around. Pointed. Whispered to each other. Then they went down the south wing."

Not Marlow's wing. "Did they return?"

"Nope. Might have gone out the back."

"When did you see them? How long ago?"

"I dunno. Ten, Fifteen minutes."

The timing fit with the possible sighting of Paddy, but would he be involved in anything sinister? Jake shrugged. "Describe this couple, please."

"Sure. The sheila was blonde, had a hot figure." Alex tilted his head and winked. "And the bloke kinda looked like Paddy something or other. But he never took off his hat so I can't be sure."

Jake tapped the counter. "If you see either of those people again, please notify Officer Vince Kendall. He's a guest at my wedding. Thanks a bundle." Jake ran down the south wing and out the back door.

Breath coming in gasps, he searched the parking lot. Ten or so vehicles, dust bins, a shed. And…a trail of colorful bits of paper. He picked up a couple. Fresh flower petals. From a bouquet? Way too coincidental. A wedding. His daughter the only member of the bridal party to carry a bouquet. Marlow had declined one. But why was Bella out here?

Grinding his teeth, he followed the trail right up to the closed door of the shed and listened. A clang. No one in their right mind would work with the door closed in this heat. Hand on the latch, Jake set his feet shoulder-width apart, ready to face any foe.

The door opened. He jerked back as if he'd touched a hot stove.

Paddy stepped out and his eyes bugged. "You?"

Jake grabbed the lad's arm, twisted it behind his back. Removed his tie and looped it around Paddy's wrists, making it as tight as possible. "Now, kid, where's my daughter?" For good measure, he yanked on the tie.

"I…don't know what you're talking about."

Jake barked, "Where's Bella? I know you took her." He glanced in the shed. Garden equipment, broken boxes, a bed frame. And Bella's denuded bouquet.

"She's not here."

"I can see that. But she was." Jaw clenched so tight his teeth ached, he bowed his head. *Lord, please give me a calming spirit.* He waited a couple of seconds. "Paddy, I'm so angry I could break you in half, but I won't. Where is Bella?"

Paddy huffed and struggled, but Jake held him firmly. "What are you going to do with me?"

"Turn you over to Vince Kendall. But not until I find Bella." Jake marched toward the door and then stopped and glared at the lad. "Why, Paddy? What have we done to deserve this?"

He kicked at gravel and didn't raise his head. "Um, nothing. I...I'm sorry. I enjoyed working for you, boss, really I did. But—"

"But what?" He towered over the lad.

"All right, you win." Paddy shrugged. "I didn't want to, but she made me"

"Who?"

"Miss Carson threatened to fire Mum, spread rumors about her if I didn't...I'm embarrassed to say."

Jake tugged at the tie again. "You'll be more than a little humiliated when the day is done. Let me guess. She told you to cut the fences, clog up the windmill, tamper with the boreholes, kill Toffee. Right?"

"Yes. No. Hang on. The cat's dead?"

"Don't act surprised."

"I took her to my room, but I let her out before I left."

"We found her in there, barely alive." Jake glared at the lad. "Did Gail tell you why she wanted you to vandalize my station?"

"She was mad at you for breaking off the engagement. She wanted to cause mischief and make life difficult for you." Paddy rolled his eyes. "I'm sorry."

"Where's Bella?"

Shoulders stooped, he jutted his chin toward the door. "I...I didn't do everything Miss Carson told me to. She wanted me to leave Bella in the shed, but I couldn't. Too hot, so I took her to room eight. Tied up, but I didn't hurt her. I like her."

The words were barely out of Paddy's mouth before Jake yanked open the door and propelled his captive to room eight. The door was locked. "Key?"

"Back pocket."

Hand shaking, Jake unlocked the door, shoved Paddy onto the bed and scanned the small room. The wardrobe, the only place. He slid open the accordion door. His blood boiled. Bella sat in the corner, legs outstretched, gagged, hands tied in front. And unconscious. "Bella Bear, my baby." He scooped her up and turned. "What have you done to my child?"

"Nothing. I swear. She was fine when I closed the door." All color had drained from Paddy's face.

"You call this fine?"

Bella stirred.

Chapter 53

The standoff, or rather seated showdown, lasted at least ten minutes. Marlow tried every counseling trick she knew to convince Gail she played a losing hand. Nothing worked. Even Ida Marie's questions or advice were met with disdain. But Marlow paid close attention to Gail's responses, and came up with a possible explanation. "Gail, I know why you're procrastinating. You want Jake to come looking for me, don't you?"

Gail set her elbows atop the cushion on her knees, the revolver held loosely in both hands. "You think you're so smart."

"Am I right?"

"Yeah. Sooner or later, he'll come because he won't send anyone else."

"And then what will you do?"

A flicker of indecision crossed Gail's face, and she licked her lips. "I'll deal with him then. No worries."

So, she didn't have a plan. "Do you want to physically hurt me? Hurt him?"

Shrugging, Gail crossed her legs. "At the moment, I imagine he has his hands full. I saw Bella leave your room and set up a minor distraction for Jake."

"Is Bella in danger? Surely, you wouldn't harm a child." But Gail had threatened Bella with boarding school far from home. An ache formed in Marlow's throat, and she rubbed her neck. What could she do? She glanced at Gran sitting calmly beside her.

The woman winked at her then turned to Gail. "I must go to the, uh, ladies room, please." Ida Marie eased off the bed. "I take pills that make me…"

At first, Gail's countenance didn't change, but then the lines around her mouth softened. She hesitated, glanced at Marlow, at Ida

Marie. "All right, but we'll all go."

Meanwhile, Ida Marie had inched closer to Gail. Gran turned, and before Marlow could standup, clutched her chest then collapsed in a heap.

She gasped and yelled, "Gran," and in the same instant, bolted toward Gail.

The woman had no time to aim her weapon. Marlow pounced, jostled the gun out of her hand and threw the weapon across the room. Gail lunged at Marlow. They fell onto the carpet and rolled toward the bed with Marlow pinned.

"Gran, go get—" Gail's elbow slammed into Marlow's chest cutting off her words. Out of the corner of her eye, Marlow saw Ida Marie use the chair to help her stand. Thank the Lord she didn't hurt herself when she dropped to the floor.

Outweighed, Marlow struggled to move Gail off her. One final push freed her left arm. She grabbed Gail's blonde locks, only to have a wig come off in her hand. She tried again and pulled her hair, but Gail reciprocated. Marlow's precious band went flying, hair flopped in her eyes, and she heard a rip. *Mess with my perfect outfit again?* She raised her knee and kicked out, catching Gail in the stomach, winding her. Marlow wriggled free, got on her knees, and grasped the stout vase. But Gail leaned back, out of range.

Gran came to the rescue. She drew a can of hairspray from Marlow's cosmetic bag on the dresser and sprayed it in Gail's face. The woman squealed, rubbed her eyes.

Marlow stood, vase in hand. "I've waited too long for a worthy man, and you will not stop me from marrying Jake." She raised the vase and hit Gail over the head.

She crumpled to the carpet, moaned, then lay still.

Drawing in a ragged breath, Marlow stared at Gail, at Gran. "I only meant to incapacitate her long enough for us to get out. Is she…"

Ida Marie felt Gail's pulse. "She's alive, breathing. Let's leave quickly."

All Marlow could do was nod. She'd never been more afraid. Ida Marie helped straighten her hair into something presentable and replaced the band. "Gail tore your jacket lapel."

"I don't care. I have to make sure Bella is all right."

Ida Marie deposited the discarded gun in her purse, then led

Marlow toward the door. "What shall we do with Gail? Lock her in?"

"No. She can get out the window." Marlow turned. "Get the belt from my robe. I'll tie her to the bed post."

"Grand idea."

With Gail secured in the room, Ida Marie closed the door, then arm in arm, she and Marlow hurried down the hall. "Listen, the guests are singing."

"I wouldn't have thought Lion knew show tunes." She patted Gran's hand and smiled. "He has hidden talents. Now, we must find Bella. Gail could have lied, but I need to be sure."

A commotion from the south wing caught Marlow's attention, and she stopped in the lobby.

Jake strode down the hall holding Bella's hand on one side and his other hand on the shoulder of a vocal, young man. As they neared, Marlow recognized Paddy.

"There you are, Bella. What happened?" Marlow rushed forward and hugged her.

"We'll tell you in a minute." Keeping a hand on Paddy, Jake called, "Hey, Alex, go get Vince for me, please."

"It was horrible, Marlow. Paddy took me outside and put me in a shed. I ruined my bouquet dropping petals along the way. Daddy said that's how he found me."

Gail's accomplice. "Quick thinking, my sweetheart. Are you okay?"

Bella nodded. "I fell asleep tied up in a wardrobe."

"No need to tell you I was worried sick." Jake thumped Paddy on the back. "At least he didn't leave her in the shed as Gail instructed."

"Speaking of… Ida Marie and I had just repaired my outfit— that Gail had cut up—when she barged in, armed, and kept us—"

"Gail? Are you two all right?" Jake threw a glance at Gran, then embraced Marlow in a hold so comforting, she never wanted to be released.

"Hey, Jake." A burly man approached them. "I'll take Paddy off your hands."

"Thanks, Vince." He shoved the lad forward. "While you're at it… Wait, where's Gail?"

"Unconscious in my room."

Ida Marie handed Vince the revolver. "She threatened us with this."

Jake's arms tightened around Marlow. "I'm so sorry you had to endure Gail's jealousy. I'm assuming that's why she came."

"Yes, but I bashed her over the head and told her no one was going to keep me from marrying you."

"That's my girl."

By now Lion, Rick, Greg, Rosie and a few guests had joined them in the lobby.

"Right, you lot. Get back inside." Jake shooed them away then bowed his head. "Thank You, God, that we are all safe. Please bless our union and our lives together." He raised his head. "Let's get married, Marlow."

"But I look a mess. My hair, my outfit."

"You look perfect. Do you mind that I don't have a tie?"

"No worries."

Jake kissed Marlow's forehead. "I like how you're picking up the lingo." He then motioned for Bella to come close and kissed her, too. "Are you ready, Bella Bear?"

"Yeah, but how can I be flower girl if I don't have any flowers?"

"Hold on." Rosie hurried into Lion's office, returned with a bunch of pink, plastic roses and thrust them into Bella's hand. "Will these do?"

"Thanks." Bella smiled at Marlow. "I'm ready, if you are?"

Her throat tight and her heart full, Marlow nodded.

After Jake escorted Bella down the aisle, Lion played the Wedding March.

Marlow slipped her hand through Ida Marie's arm and entered the room. The guests stood and turned to look at her, but she only had eyes for the ruggedly handsome, dependable, trustworthy, Spirit-filled man up front. Jake. Her Jake. As she drew closer, she focused on his eyes. No ice in his Barclay blues today.

THE END

American Christian Fiction Writers Genesis Award winner Valerie Massey Goree resides with her husband on the beautiful Olympic Peninsula of Washington State.

After serving as missionaries in her home country of Zimbabwe and raising two children, Glenn and Valerie moved to Texas. She worked in the public school system for many years, focusing on students with special needs. Now retired in Washington, Valerie spends her time writing, and spoiling her grandchildren.

Valerie loves to hear from her readers.

Social Media:
Facebook: https://www.facebook.com/ValerieMasseyGoree/Author

Website: www.valeriegoreeauthor.com

Goodreads: https://www.goodreads.com/user/show/8318966-valerie